PRAISE FOR FIONA O'BRIEN

We hope you enjoy this book. Please return or renew it by the due date. *06/22*

You can renew it at www.norfolk.gov.uk/libraries or by using our free library app.

Otherwise you can phone 0344 800 8020 - please have your library card and PIN ready.

You can sign up for email reminders too.

D1513717

LIB NORFOLK COUNTY COUNCIL CE

NORFOLK ITEM

30129 087 396 173

Fiona O'Brien left an award-winning career in advertising to write full time. *None of My Affair, No Reservations, Without Him, The Love Book* and *The Summer Visitors* have all been bestselling novels. She lives in Sandymount, Dublin.

 f fionaobrien

 fionaobrienbooks

 @fionaobrienbks

Fiona O'Brien

the
summer
we were
friends

HACHETTE
BOOKS
IRELAND

Copyright © 2021 Fiona O'Brien

The right of Fiona O'Brien to be identified as the author of
the work has been asserted by her in accordance with the
Copyright, Designs and Patents Act 1988.

First published in Ireland in 2021 by HACHETTE BOOKS IRELAND
First published in paperback in 2022

1

All rights reserved. No part of this publication may be reproduced,
stored in a retrieval system, or transmitted, in any form or by any
means without the prior written permission of publisher, nor be
otherwise circulated in any form of binding or cover other than
that in which it is published and without a similar condition being
imposed on the subsequent purchaser.

All characters in this publication are fictitious and any resemblance to
real persons, living or dead, is purely coincidental.

Cataloguing in Publication Data is available from the British Library

ISBN 9781529354171

Typeset in Adobe Caslon Pro by Bookends Publishing Services, Dublin
Printed and bound in Great Britain by Clays, Elcograf S.p.A

Hachette Books Ireland policy is to use papers that are
natural, renewable and recyclable products and made
from wood grown in sustainable forests. The logging and
manufacturing processes are expected to conform to the
environmental regulations of the country of origin.

Hachette Books Ireland
8 Castlecourt Centre
Castleknock
Dublin 15, Ireland

A division of Hachette UK Ltd
Carmelite House, 50 Victoria Embankment, EC4Y 0DZ

www.hachettebooksireland.ie

In memory of my brother Dermot,
who died on 20 April 2020, leaving us far too soon.
Remembered always with love.

Prologue

Afterwards, when locals reflected on the whole affair, no one had had the slightest indication that this summer would be different from any previous ones. After all, life in a small seaside town tends to follow a fairly predictable rhythm. Slow and quiet in the winter months, people hunkering down to shorter days, longer nights, darker skies and more turbulent seas. Then, with the promise of spring, rousing themselves to undertake the cleaning, painting and repairs necessary to be ready for the coming season. In this respect, Derrybeggs was no different from countless other seaside towns whose inhabitants depend on the whims of tourists and day-trippers to visit and stay awhile. Like other remote corners of the world, they are a tightly knit community – hardy, loyal, and fiercely protective of one another.

It's true that many of the young people leave, lured by the promise of modern, faster, more lucrative lifestyles, only to return in years to come as sentimental tourists, but those who stay reap other rewards.

Although living cheek and jowl with this level of

neighbourly intimacy can sometimes feel irritatingly claustrophobic, the people of Derrybeggs tolerate it with reasonable good humour. For how else can a small community protect itself?

So, it would be reasonable to assume that an unfamiliar character turning up and lingering for a while would not go unnoticed ... and this indeed was the case when Charlie first made his appearance on that memorable June day last summer. Charlie couldn't remember his name, or anything much else about who he was before he turned up in Derrybeggs – but that was how the whole thing began ...

Mac

Mac woke early, prompted by the mild adrenalin rush that accompanies the departure day for a long-anticipated vacation. Leaping out of bed, he felt energised, despite his seventy-two years – and, glancing in the mirror, reminded himself, with a small sense of triumph, that he was younger than three of the four remaining Rolling Stones. The thought always made him grin. Twenty of those years had accumulated without his beloved Linda by his side. Life without her passed more slowly, he found to his cost – he tried to fill the time as best he could. As a retired teacher, this was a relatively easy task to accomplish. He had a regular pension, he tutored from time to time, and there was always something new he wanted to learn. To relax, he played the piano. He had almost taken the musical route full time, but his love of learning and the desire to pass it on to a younger generation eclipsed the lure of a composing career – although he had composed a few pieces he was quite proud of. He could still knock out a good tune if he put his mind to it.

But after Linda died he was lonely. She was a victim of 9/11 – they both were – but Mac had survived unscathed … on the outside anyway. The trauma took longer – he still didn't react well to loud noises. That trip to New York was to celebrate her birthday – little did they know it would be her last. They were not blessed with a family, and had never felt the need to adopt. So now Mac was on his own. A former student of his had recently suggested that Mac look for company online. At first the idea didn't appeal. But then he thought, Why not? And that had led to the happy coincidence he could never have anticipated. By complete chance he came across his childhood sweetheart from high school – Jessie. She, too, had been up close and personal with bereavement, having lost her husband. Her daughters had persuaded her to go online to make some new friends – and that was how Mac and she had found each other. They had been corresponding and talking for about three months now.

He clicked on the email he sent her after they first spoke on the phone and read it one more time before logging out.

My dear Jessie,
I can't tell you how good it was to talk with you yesterday on the phone. For all the time it's been since we've seen each other, the years fell away as soon as I heard your familiar voice and we talked and laughed like youngsters ...

It was a blessing, Mac felt, to have found an old friend to connect with – someone he didn't have to introduce himself to. For all that it had been fifty-odd years since they'd seen each other, those same years fell away as he and Jessie chatted and laughed like it was yesterday. He had booked his vacation prior to connecting with her – a couple of weeks in Ireland to research a project he was interested in – influences of early Celtic music on American country. Jessie was of the shared opinion the trip would do him good. She had a family wedding to organise so they'd agreed to meet up when Mac came back. The thought cheered him. There was something soul-destroying about returning home to a house filled with nothing but memories. Now he had something to look forward to. He checked the house one last time, straightened the framed photograph of him and Linda on the hall table, and left for Logan International. Next stop Shannon airport.

Derrybeggs, Ireland,

twenty-four hours later …

One

One of the many ironies of old age, Peggy O'Sullivan observed, as she groped to turn off her phone alarm before it went off, was that, although she needed less sleep and could wake up ready to spring out of bed at a totter, if not a leap, there was far less for her to do. That meant the additional hours gained, especially now in summertime, could stretch ominously ahead if she didn't plan her days with precision. Routine was everything – and she had hers down to a fine art. It was said you could set your clock by her. Looking out of her window, another beautiful June day seemed poised to unfold in Derrybeggs.

At this time of year Peggy would normally have been tying up details for the local annual film festival she had been involved with for many years, but younger people had taken over now and Peggy had deduced that her services were no longer required. This had not been articulated, of course – she was still on the committee, such as it was – but some of the younger women, particularly that blow-in from Dublin, Kate Carmichael, and her crowd had muscled in on the event, declaring it needed a cultural makeover to drag it into the twenty-first century. The makeover, as far as Peggy could determine, seemed to consist of vast amounts of energy being spent on finding a suitable celebrity to be guest of honour at the two-day event and very little else – even though the festival was due to open in three weeks' time. Many other important details, Peggy knew, had been overlooked. There had been little advertising for starters, hardly surprising, Peggy thought, since they didn't have a venue. The community hall where they used to show the films was unavailable due to fire damage, and the committee was now searching frantically for a suitable substitute. The shabby old golf club had disappeared, replaced by a new posh version complete with spa, but when they had relayed the request to the American headquarters of the property mogul who now owned it, the cost of renting it was ridiculously prohibitive. That was the problem, Peggy had pointed out, when transatlantic billionaires were in charge of a major part of Derrybeggs's facilities. Oh, well, it wasn't her place to interfere – no one was interested in her opinion any more.

But a distinct sense of panic was making itself felt in the village now. Local business depended on the economic boost of the annual festival, not least the Seashell café, which benefited from the catering contract. At least a celebrity had been nailed down as guest of honour. She hadn't been the committee's first choice (the American movie star filming in Dublin had politely declined) but Peggy was looking forward to meeting Molly Cusack. She remembered her as a child when she and her parents used to holiday in Derrybeggs, and Molly had gone on to become extremely successful on the British small screen, starring in several much-loved TV sitcoms over the years.

Peggy was heading out on her Rollator for her morning coffee when she saw him …

She could get about in her small flat with her walking stick, but she needed the security of something more substantial to make her way to the village and back. The Rollator was marvellous – a walking frame on wheels, Dr Rob had explained to her, with a bag for some light shopping, and if she got tired she could put on the brakes, pull down the small seat, sit on it and have a little rest. She did this quite often, not because she needed to but because she liked taking a little breather to pass the time and look about her – it made her feel more connected to things. It also meant she missed very little. It was amazing what you saw and heard if you were old and quietly observant – almost as if you were invisible.

That morning Peggy took her usual route, turning right out of her front gate with Muppet, her beloved poodle/ Yorkie mix trotting beside her. To her left, a low haze hung over the lake – it would burn off later – and a quartet of swans glided over the calm silver water. Along either side, ancient dry-stone walls were drenched with a scarlet trail of fuchsia. The village – when she reached it – seemed quieter than usual at this time of the morning. It greeted her cheerfully, vibrant in its new summer best, brightly painted houses and shops seeming to jostle for attention. Lovingly tended flower baskets hung from awnings and lamp posts, and cascaded from newly purposed beer barrels. The place was a profusion of colour.

She had been looking forward to her first cup of coffee when she saw the café wasn't open. For a moment she wondered if something was amiss – never in living memory had the Seashell not opened on time – then checked her watch. She was an hour early. How on earth had that happened? She never got the time wrong. For one horribly long second she wondered if she was losing her marbles – was this how it started? It gave her such a jolt she had to pull up on the pavement and sit down. She took out and lit a cigarette with trembling fingers.

That was when she noticed him. A younger man – in his seventies, maybe. And handsome, a distinguished profile, but he looked down on his luck. He was peering into the café window, trying to work out if it was open, she assumed. She hadn't seen him before – he definitely wasn't local.

'It's not open,' she said, pointing to her watch. 'Doesn't open till eight. I don't know how I'm this early – I must have got the time wrong.' She shook her head, blowing a plume of smoke from the side of her mouth.

He strolled over to her, smiling. 'Are you all right there? Can I give you any assistance?' He seemed concerned.

'I'm fine, thank you. Or, at least, I would be if I hadn't somehow muddled the time – and now I'm an hour early, which knocks my whole day out. I can't think how I managed that. No wonder Muppet was surprised to be going out.' She reached down to ruffle the dog's head.

'That's a cute dog you've got there,' he said. 'Not open till eight, huh? That's pretty strange. What kind of a one-horse town won't serve a guy a cup of joe before work?'

'You're not from around here, are you?' Peggy smiled up at him.

'It's a pretty place … nice to be by the ocean again.' He gestured towards the sea.

But Peggy noted he hadn't answered her question. 'I've lived here all my life.' She tilted her head. 'And every day there's a different view. Are you visiting?'

He smiled again, rather absently, as if he was lost in thought. Then he collected himself. 'Say, can I help you at all?'

She thanked him, but said no, explaining that she sometimes liked to stop and sit for a while before continuing on her journey – or, in this case, that she would sit outside until the café opened. 'No point going back now. Muppet and I will just enjoy the view.'

'I understand.' He nodded. 'Good call.'

He was very nice, Peggy thought. Very gentlemanly. 'I'm Peggy,' she said. 'What's your name?'

'Good to meet you, Peggy.' He smiled. 'I think I'll be getting along now. You have a good day!'

She thought that a little odd. But then Americans *could* be odd.

Two

Being fourteen sucked, Franny Relish decided, kicking a clump of pebbles out of the way as she settled under her favourite sand dune on the headland. So did having a surname like Relish but her mam should have thought of that before marrying an English guy with a silly name. But if she hadn't, Franny wouldn't have had Dad in her life – and that didn't bear thinking about. Mam and Dad were the only good things in her world right now – although they had their faults, of course, like all parents.

It was early morning, and Franny had an hour before her shift started at the Seashell café where she was working for the summer. That meant she could cut through the golf course on her way to work and sit for a while in her favourite spot, looking out over the ocean.

Franny wasn't an ideal name either, her friend Sheena had advised her. Sheena was very well up on these things and advised Franny to change it to something more on trend – like Chesca or Frey, which would sound way better on social media – but Franny had been christened Frances because her mam had promised to call at least one of her children after St Francis, and since her elder sister was Clare, and they had been hoping for a boy next, Franny had been saddled with Frances. When she had floated the idea of changing it, though, her mam had been uncharacteristically annoyed – although lately anything that Franny mentioned to do with Sheena seemed to set her mam off. Franny suspected that this was because Sheena and her family were from Dublin and had only come to live in Derrybeggs because her dad had been posted here for work. Sheena's dad, Don, was something to do with broadband facilities – but he'd liked Derrybeggs so much he'd built a second home here.

Sheena's mum, Kate, was finding it hard to adjust to living in a small village – but Franny's mam said that Kate's habit of airing her opinion about everything that was wrong or needed improving wouldn't endear her to anyone anywhere. Either way, Franny had more important matters on her mind – changing her name was the least of her worries. She chewed her thumbnail. What did your social-media profile matter when the world was ending before your very eyes and no one in charge was doing anything about it? If it wasn't for Greta Thunberg and their generation, the world would probably have ended already.

This was the only subject she and Dad disagreed over. Dad said not to be worrying her head about it, that the world would be around long after everyone was gone, which didn't make Franny feel any better. But it was all coming to pass. Even her favourite spot here in the sand dunes might be taken from her. The local golf course had been bought and redesigned by its new American owners and was almost ready to open. Everyone was very excited about it, except Franny. The clubhouse was finished, apart from the snag list, and had been transformed into a cutting-edge example of modern architecture, all wood and glass and sweeping curves that blended cleverly into the brooding hills and mountains behind. Franny's dad, Mike, was one of the electricians working on the clubhouse contract. And some American was coming in to sign off on it all.

Franny was concerned. Her mother Sheila was on the film festival committee and when they had tried to get the new luxury golf club as a venue, the American owner had quoted an impossible price. Rich Americans didn't care about small village life outside their business interests, Franny's mam said. Franny had been more worried about the rabbits and the *Vertigo angustior* snail, whose habitat might be under threat, but the ecological laws had all been strictly complied with from the outset – so her snails were safe. All the same, Franny's mind was not at rest. What if they decided to expand the golf course even further?

She was so lost in thought that it was a moment before she realised someone was speaking to her. 'Excuse me,' the old guy was saying. 'Could you direct me back to Main Street? I seem to have lost my bearings.'

He was an American – she could tell by his accent. She pointed the way. 'Are you someone to do with the golf course?'

'Excuse me?' The question seemed to take him by surprise.

'You're American – I was wondering if you've something to do with the golf course?'

'Oh, uh, I'm just passing through.' He scratched his head, looking into the distance.

Franny frowned. The stranger was being evasive. Franny preferred clarity.

'That's a good spot you've got here.' He smiled. 'Pretty part of the country.'

'Not for much longer.' Franny said darkly. 'They've redesigned the golf club into a fancy resort.'

'Is that so?'

'Not that it matters now – everything's ruined for people our age.'

'How'd you work that out?'

Franny looked at him to see if he was making fun of her, but he seemed genuinely interested. 'We've nothing to look forward to except climate change – extreme weather and mass extinction.'

'That's a pretty sweeping statement.'

'It's true,' Franny said. 'Previous generations have ruined it for us.' She didn't say, *you people*, although she wanted to.

At least he didn't contradict her, Franny conceded, watching his reaction. He was nodding to himself, looking out to sea.

'Guess you're pretty concerned about this?' He turned to her.

'Wouldn't you be? If you were my age?'

'Probably.' He rubbed his chin. 'How old are you?'

'Fourteen.'

'Thing is, most things you worry about don't actually happen. That's a fact. Ever heard the expression *Cometh the hour, cometh the man?* Or, indeed, woman?'

Franny hadn't. 'What's it mean?'

'It means that throughout history, just when things seem worst, when everything seems hopeless, someone always comes up with a plan to fix things – to save the day – just at the right moment.'

'Do you really believe that?' Franny frowned.

'Sure. Human beings have been around for an awfully long time, young lady, and that's what we're good at. We might make some pretty stupid mistakes along the way, but we've always figured things out sooner or later.'

'So you think we can fix this?'

'Sure we can. Someone will – might even be you.' He smiled. 'I'd better be getting along now. Thank you for pointing me in the right direction – I hope I didn't disturb you.'

She watched him stroll off towards the village, hands in his pockets, whistling a tune. There was something reassuring about him, Franny thought. Maybe he was right. He was way old, older than Dad, and seemed very wise. Maybe things *could* get better. Anything was possible – even Sheena was always saying that.

Three

Molly checked her appearance in the hall mirror before heading out to the waiting taxi to take her to Heathrow airport. She didn't bother with dark glasses – the feeblest disguise employed by people who really *did* want to attract attention to themselves: the curled dark grey wig would be more than effective, particularly when coupled with a light raincoat and sensible shoes. For now, she took a last look at her shoulder-length layered blonde bob, before it disappeared under the wig, then hid her slim figure under the dowdy coat. Her normally dewy complexion was concealed under a heavy dusting of face powder. Usually Molly employed makeup to help her look younger. Ageing herself made a change but it was also alarmingly easy. The forecast was good – she had checked before leaving – but June was always unreliable, especially in Ireland. In London they were having a particularly warm spell, and underneath the wig her scalp prickled uncomfortably.

It wasn't that she was terribly famous, more irritatingly familiar. Over the years she had featured in enough weekly TV dramas and sitcoms for people to feel compelled to stop her in public and ask the inevitable

questions – 'Don't I know you? Aren't you that actress
who …?' Mostly she was more than happy to stop and
chat. After all, if you were going to invade people's living
rooms on a regular basis, she felt, the least you could do
was say hello to them in real life.

In the back of the taxi, on her way to Heathrow,
Molly scrolled through the email from her agent on
her phone and felt another dart of panic. It was just
under three months since Larry had suggested she
write a memoir and at the time it had seemed like a
good idea. Now he was cheerily asking about the word
count. There was a time, Molly reflected, as she hastily
clicked out of the email, when the notion of writing a
memoir would have brought her out in a nasty rash. The
very thought of it had made her insides curl. Memoirs,
she reckoned, meant life as you knew it was behind you,
along with your career. Your shelf life was over and all
that remained was to record the luminous moments,
deflect or sensationalise the less than pleasant episodes,
slap it between two covers and hope that it would bring
in a few bob.

But then, so stealthily that she had hardly noticed
it – not unlike some unwelcome hormonal upheaval –
acting work had begun to dry up. That, and the horrible
coincidence of Molly losing her two best friends in
quick succession, had led to Larry suggesting the
memoir as a possible stopgap while she considered her
career options. Molly could still hardly take in that
her dear friend and contemporary Julia Hepworth had
had a stroke and was confined to a nursing home for

the foreseeable future. Beautiful Julia, darling of stage and screen, with an accent that could cut steel and an attitude that could level cities, was now without speech and paralysed. Julia and Molly had attended RADA together in the seventies, and embarked on a lifelong friendship. Just a month later, Molly's other cherished friend, darling Nigel, who had been her on-screen husband for the run of a hugely popular TV series, and a lifetime friend and ally, had been found dead at the foot of his stairs. It was too cruel, too unreal. Molly had counted on marching irreverently into old age with Julia and Nigel.

Finally, to cap it all, a role she had been assured of, one she had been prepared to throw herself into – relied on to get her through this awful time of grief and loss – had gone to another actress. A forty-seven-year-old actress. That the role in question was to portray a sixty-five-year-old business maverick (Molly was a well-maintained sixty-three) was apparently inconsequential. The woman in question, her usurper, was a good actress – Molly was an admirer of her work – but she looked and acted like a teenager off screen, and was (Larry reliably informed her) on her third face lift. 'Seriously, Moll, this came from totally out of left field. Alex swore the part was yours.' Larry had been furious. 'The contract was—'

'Oh, never mind,' Molly said, when she got her wind back. 'It's not as if someone's died.'

'Well, no, but—'

'I'll take it as a sign.'

'A sign of what?'

'That I need another career.' She was only half joking.

'Don't be silly.' Larry smiled. 'This is just a tricky patch.' He looked at her over his glasses. 'You're too old for leading lady and too young for old dame. Although I have been thinking.' He leaned back in his chair, wearing his *I'll just try floating this idea out there* expression.

'What?'

'How would you feel about a writing a memoir?'

'What – now?'

'You've led a very interesting life, Moll, got legions of devoted fans – they'd lap it up – and I know just who to pitch it to. It'll be nicely lucrative too.'

'I'm not sure I could do it.' Molly was reticent. She allowed the suggestion to linger.

'Of course you can. You'd be a lovely writer – I know you would. No one tells a story like you do when you're in full flight. Writing's the same as talking – it's all about the voice.'

'Do you really think so?'

'Definitely. In fact, the more I think about, it the more certain I am. And' – he held his best card till last – 'you'd be able to tell all those wonderful anecdotes about Julia and Nigel and the scrapes you got into over the years. People would adore to read about them.'

'That's true – it's a shame to keep them to myself.' She chewed her lip. 'All right – I'll do it!'

'Marvellous!' Larry's intake of breath followed by a rush of relieved enthusiasm told Molly everything she needed to know. That for a while, six months at least, her acting career, or lack of it, wouldn't be Larry's problem.

'Any thoughts on a title?' Larry was clearly keen to get down to business.

Molly hadn't, but one came to her now. '*Acting Out?*'

'See? You're a natural! I love it!' said Larry. 'Hurry up and write it and send me your first draft – I can hardly wait.'

In the event, she hadn't had to write a first draft – just a sample chapter and a vague outline had been enough for Larry to secure her a deal – but now she needed to get down to work.

Buoyed up by Larry's enthusiasm and her own impulsivity, Molly had happily thrown herself into her new project. She'd exchanged her rather dated old laptop for a razor-thin shiny new one, downloaded some snazzy software – she wasn't quite sure what it was for, but people on forums seemed to rate it – and spent quite a lot of time flicking through on-line writing courses, often getting lost for hours in distracting links. She'd had no idea writing could be such fun. She even ordered some gorgeous new cashmere loungewear so she could look the part – pyjamas, although handier, would have been a step too far, and not quite as glamorous.

When she signed the contract, Larry took her to lunch in their favourite Soho haunt and they celebrated with champagne. Now it was real. She had a new career, starting right now. The trouble was, when all the excitement was over and she was back in her flat, with a deadline to work to, Molly found the blank page very uncooperative. She had made notes, lots of them, scribbled in various notebooks and journals over the years – but as soon as she began to write a piece in earnest she decided before she reached the end of the page she didn't like it. The problem, she felt, was that writing a memoir about her life when it didn't seem quite over was proving tricky: it was getting in the way – blocking her.

Then the days began to slip by, sneakily, gathering momentum just when she wanted them to slacken to their previous interminable rhythm. She began to panic. It occurred to her that perhaps all she needed was a change of scene. Then – as if to facilitate such – the invitation had arrived. Molly opened the envelope. These days her post seemed to consist of either bills or obscure theatre promotions, neither of which she felt inclined to study. But this, forwarded from Larry, turned out to be a strangely formal invitation asking her to be guest of honour at the annual film festival in Derrybeggs.

Molly was so surprised she had to sit down. Derrybeggs! Her eyes filled as she looked at the invitation in her hand and the memories came flooding back. A trip to Derrybeggs would be like going home. Molly's late parents had hailed from Dublin, but every year the family had holidayed in Derrybeggs, staying in the old family hotel on the lake. Molly had spent many happy summers there and, since the invitation's arrival, she had been counting the days until she was back in the little village just a stone's throw from the Atlantic Ocean.

In under a week Molly had organised a house-sitter for her London flat, and found what looked like an idyllic writer's cottage in Derrybeggs. She booked it for a month – that way, she figured, she could have some time to herself, get a feel for the place again, and begin work on her memoir before the opening night of the film festival, which was in three weeks' time. It would be a relief to be somewhere different, somewhere she could reflect with unbiased perspective, somewhere that the absence of her two dearest friends wouldn't be waiting for her around every corner, in every favourite haunt.

Ireland was far enough away, yet close enough to get home in a couple of hours if she was needed. This was unlikely, though, as the two people who had needed her most were now unreachable. That was what happened when you were a single woman of *a certain age*: beloved friends – her 'team', as she liked to think of them – began to be picked off, one by one ... It wasn't that her age made her feel invisible to others, as so many women complained, more as if lately she had been feeling like a ghost in her *own* life. Of all the many and varied roles she had played on screen she was least prepared for this one, the final act, on her own. There was no rehearsal and no script to follow. She would have to make it up as she went along.

At Passport Control she got a quizzical look from the bloke behind the screen, as he glanced at her passport and back up at her altered appearance. But he simply raised his eyebrows and waved her through.

On the plane with the rest of the Dublin-bound passengers, she claimed her window seat and took out her iPad. She was joined by a rather overweight man in the middle seat and a young girl in the aisle seat, who immediately began to type furiously on her laptop. The man shifted in his seat and smiled at her apologetically. She felt his gaze linger on her and made the mistake of looking back at him.

'You're very familiar,' he said. 'Do I know you?'

In reply she smiled, shook her head, and put on her headphones.

'I could swear...' were the last words she heard.

Four

Dot was checking her Airbnb page when she flicked over to Facebook and smiled at the latest post from her daughter, Laura, with her three little girls, all perched at various heights up a climbing wall, their faces turned to the camera gleeful with triumph. They were due for a visit home this Christmas from Perth, and she couldn't wait to see them. Technology was wonderful, but nothing beat the warm embrace of the all-encompassing hug she longed to give her granddaughters.

Scrolling down the page, her balloon of pleasure was rudely deflated when she saw Kate Carmichael's latest post. She and her sidekick Ellen Markey were at a table in the Seashell, raising glasses of wine to the camera and grinning aggressively. The post was tagged 'more great ideas for the #filmfestival'. Dot let out a long breath, if only it were true – but she knew it was more fake news. She was tempted to comment beneath the post 'It'd be nice if you let the rest of the committee know' but thought better of it. There was no point in stooping to Kate's level – but, and not for the first time recently, Dot was beginning to wonder if she had made a mistake in moving to Derrybeggs.

She had thought joining the committee for the film festival would be a good way to meet people and make some new friends but it had very quickly become clear that Kate Carmichael was an arrogant, ignorant woman who, with her pal Ellen Markey, clearly wanted as little to do with Dot as possible. She had felt quite hurt by their attitude until Peggy O'Sullivan had told her not to let it upset her. 'That Kate one's a blow-in – and so are you but you're a better class of one!' Peggy cackled. 'She knows you have real taste – you're showing her up for what she is, a jumped-up Celtic Tiger wan whose poor husband has more money than sense. Sure look at that awful McMansion of a house they built compared with what you've done here.' Peggy indicated Dot's beautifully restored home. 'She knows you see through her – like I do – and that you'd be bound to come up with better ideas. That's why she's keeping you at arm's length. Take it as a compliment – I would.'

Dot had tried to be friendly to Kate and Ellen – and had been left in no doubt that her overtures were not appreciated. Thankfully, the rest of the committee and the other locals she was slowly getting to know were extremely welcoming, although she understood you had to be patient to be accepted into any new community.

The news hadn't been received well when she had informed her adult children she would be selling the family home in Dublin. The objections and laments came thick and fast across various oceans and time zones.

'You can't, Mum!' Laura gasped, then wailed, from her beachfront house in Perth.

'You're not serious?' Patrick said, in clipped tones, from Boston. Then, collecting himself, he followed up with 'Are you sure that's wise?'

Only her younger boy, Mark, had expressed any faith in her or understanding of her situation. 'Ah, no, Ma,' he'd said from somewhere in Thailand. Then, 'Hey, it's your life, Ma – you gotta do whatever works for you.' That simple acknowledgement from the other side of the world had almost brought her to tears.

In the event, the house, a lovely family home in an affluent suburb, had sold quickly, snapped up by returning ex-pats and their soon to be five children (the woman was expecting twins). Dot was delighted a young family had bought it and that children would be tearing around the place again. She had worried some builder might buy it and turn it into an apartment block or cram several townhouses onto the lovingly tended garden. But the new owners had no such plans. Having just sold their tech start-up company for a great deal of money, they could afford their dream house back home and, apart from 'updating the kitchen and maybe doing a little decorating work', they planned to leave it pretty much as it was.

Dot wished them well. It was their home now, not hers, and although it had been a beautiful family house, it had not always been the happy home for her that others might have assumed.

Three years had gone by now since Martin had died of his inevitable heart attack – brought on by cigarettes, fine wine, and nightly whiskey – leaving Dot, for the first time in her life, financially independent. Although Martin had been a successful barrister, throughout their marriage he had made her account for every penny she spent. She had grown to loathe the humiliation of having to list every item purchased – even down to a teapot that had to be replaced. The one time she had broached the subject of going back to work, after the children had started school, to earn her own money, she had been met with a look of incredulity and a flat no. As Martin had reminded her, she had everything she needed, didn't she? Everything a woman could want. And, to the outside world, she did.

Now she regarded her *old life*, as she called it, with a kind of benign pity for the woman she had been and the sometimes arid marriage she had endured. Now she was free to make her own decisions, to handle her own money, create her own life. And selling the family home had been just the beginning. She hadn't rushed into anything, hadn't been impetuous, but about eighteen months after Martin had died, she had gone away for a weekend break with her cousin Felicity, back to the spot where she had holidayed as a child with her late parents. On a drive around some old haunts after a lovely lunch at their hotel, she had discovered, to her delight, that the romantic Old Rectory on the cliff was for sale and she hadn't hesitated. That it needed a complete renovation had not put her off – on the contrary, she embraced it as a welcome project. This was what she wanted, what she needed. A home of her own and a new life she could create. That it was in a faraway corner of Ireland, a stone's throw from a small village on the Wild Atlantic Way, had only increased its desirability.

Explaining to her children why she was suddenly moving to a remote part of the country was never going to be easy. That none of the three actually lived in Ireland at present hadn't lessened their collective disapproval. How would she survive on her own in a big old house? What about hospitals and decent shops? Hours away! But Dot had given up living her life for other people and their rules. Life was simply too short. She had done her duty, been a good wife, a good mother (she hoped: one never knew on that front, really). Now her children were reared and had independent lives. It was time for her to reclaim hers.

It hadn't been easy, renovating the old house, but she had done it, and now had a beautiful home with two converted cottages to the rear. It was after the project was finished, when she had time to settle and reflect, that another realisation had dawned on her. She was lonely. Not terribly, not in any isolated way – at least, no more than any outsider arriving into a new community – but while initially she had loved the solitude, having the house to herself and Honey, her yellow Labrador, she missed the sounds and even irritating debris of normal life, such as doors slamming, or laundry left on the bathroom floor. That was how the upmarket guesthouse idea had taken root.

The website had followed. Then she had linked it to her Airbnb account and Rob, the new locum doctor, had arrived ten days ago and settled in so easily that he hardly seemed like a guest at all. Rob had grown up in Derrybeggs but had spent most of his working life in the UK. He was staying at Dot's now while the new apartment that came with the surgery was finished for him. An attractive man, he was a similar age to her and great company. He reminded her of Tristan, one of the vets in the TV series *All Creatures Great and Small*, which she had loved. Already she felt as if she had known him for years.

Now, somewhat apprehensively, she was expecting two guests arriving today. A well-known English actress, Molly Cusack, was taking the one-bedroom cottage and was due to arrive this evening sometime. She was staying for a month – which Dot assumed meant she must want a quiet holiday before assuming her role as guest of honour for the film festival. Although seeing as they didn't have a proper venue for opening night there might not be any festival this year – so perhaps Molly might not turn up. Well, she'd soon find out. Which reminded her that another committee meeting was looming – and since she had offered her reading room as the venue, she had to make sure everything was shipshape.

An American, Ryan Shindler, an executive with the American property company that had taken over the golf course, was also arriving today. He was in the larger cottage – the original booking had been for him and his girlfriend, but he had emailed earlier to say something had come up and she couldn't make it. Dot hoped they hadn't had a row, or a break-up – it was such a romantic little cottage, ideal for a lovers' getaway. Ryan had requested a dozen red roses and champagne to be waiting on their arrival. Luckily, once he had updated his booking, Dot had had time to cancel the order.

She was having a well-earned cup of tea and a scone at the kitchen table with Honey at her feet when she remembered she needed to pick up the dessert she had ordered for her guests' first dinner together. Although the cottages were self-catering, dining in the main house was always an option. Everything else was under control, and a trusty chicken casserole ready to go into the oven, but after setting up rooms, and making sure everything was perfect, Dot had been unable to face any more cooking and had ordered dessert from the Seashell – it would be made with local produce so she didn't feel she was cheating. But if she didn't get a move on she'd be late.

Five

Behind the counter at the Seashell Merry was scrolling through the latest research postings from her former workplace at Florida State University's Coastal and Marine Laboratory. Suddenly her attention was drawn to a news headline: *Four youths have been given a suspended sentence for the manslaughter of Douglas Jeffrey Fairfax*. She sucked in her breath. Her lawyer had already been in touch about it but seeing it in print took her unawares – as did the accompanying jolt. For a moment Merry was transfixed as the memory assaulted her. She logged out of the site quickly and closed her laptop – thankful that no one had witnessed her reaction.

The Seashell was almost empty now, Kate Carmichael, Ellen Markey and one man remaining. Merry wished they'd get a move on. This seemed unlikely, though, as Kate had – after pointedly glancing at her watch – ordered another two glasses of wine. She was doing it deliberately, of course. The woman knew full well that Merry was longing to close up. She'd been staring at them, willing them to go for the last hour, while they sat on and on, their languid posture and droning conversation daring her to rush them. They reminded Merry of the sort of rich, entitled women who used to hog all the beach loungers and umbrellas in Florida, sipping cocktails, while she and Doug were off surfing in those happier days before the accident. Merry would have liked to tell Kate and Ellen to get lost, to sling their hook – but she didn't know which would be worse: giving them the satisfaction of letting them see how pissed off she was or biting her tongue and cheerfully depositing their order with a smile. Yet there they were drinking her wine and eating her food while discussing hiring out-of-town caterers instead of the Seashell café for the film festival contract. Merry's mother Eva – notoriously difficult to provoke – was threatening to resign from the committee as a result.

The festival was turning into a shambles just when local businesses, B&Bs and pubs were most depending on it. Derrybeggs was small and finding a new venue for the opening night was unlikely. The community hall was out of action, the nearest hotel banqueting facilities were already taken and somehow, under the new committee, the whole thing had ground to a halt. The locals would not be happy if the festival was a write-off. The two days at the end of June were a much-needed economic injection to the small community, and the Seashell had always done the catering.

Finally, after what seemed an eternity, the two women left. Now there was only the old guy, sitting in the corner, staring out of the window. He'd been there since she'd started her shift. Hopefully a bit of noise would hurry him and she could close up early.

She went to work quickly, clearing cups and plates,

polishing tables, loading glasses into the dishwasher. Her mum would come by later and finish off, leaving things ready for the morning. Merry just had to complete her shift, and then she was out of there. Escape was her motivation, these days. Since the accident, she could be around people for only so long.

Setting out some fresh napkins, Merry studied the man at the corner table surreptitiously. Looking out over the peninsula and the inlet beyond, he was very still, lost in thought as the sun sank slowly towards the water. Perhaps he was meditating – something else Merry had never gotten the hang of. She had always been a doing person, and now more than ever she couldn't bear being still.

As if on cue, her mother materialised, but instead of waving Merry out of the door as she usually did, Eva was giving her conspiratorial glances and, once behind the counter, beckoned her over with a tilt of her head.

'What's going on?' Merry leaned on the new zinc countertop and blew a strand of hair out of her eyes.

'Him.' Eva nodded in the old guy's direction.

'He's been here since I started this afternoon,' Merry said. 'Only had one coffee, said he had to meet someone here, but he wasn't sure what time.'

'That's just it.' Eva looked worried. 'There's been talk in the village about him. I think he might be lost, or wandering maybe.'

'I'll have a word with him …'

'Don't upset him, Merry – although your hair …' Eva shook her head.

'Don't start.' Merry shot her a warning glance before

making for the guy's table. Her shoulder-length hair was colourful at the moment – black at the roots, then pink, graduating to bleached blonde, a sort of horizontal three-tiered effect. When she'd seen it for the first time Eva had cried. 'You are intent on destroying everything nice about yourself.' She sniffed.

'Hi,' Merry said, reaching his table. 'Mind if I sit down for a minute?'

He looked around and, without missing a beat, said, 'Please do. I'd be delighted.' He had an American accent.

Up close, he wasn't as old as Merry had thought he was. Maybe not that much older than her mum, actually. He was a bit dishevelled, or perhaps rumpled was a better word. His hair was shaggy and mostly grey, but you could tell it had once been blond. His eyes were deep blue and hooded. When he smiled, she could see he might have been a heart-breaker in his day.

'And to what do I owe this unexpected pleasure?' He seemed genuinely pleased and, coming from him, the comment was charming, not cheesy.

'My mum is concerned about you.' Merry decided not to beat about the bush. 'That's her over there.' She pointed to Eva behind the counter. 'She's the boss.'

He waved at Eva, and Merry smiled, watching her mother's face pink as he called, 'Hey, Mom!'

'Why is she concerned?' He was worried. 'I haven't done anything wrong, have I?'

'Not so far as we know.' Merry smiled. 'It's just that you've been here since I started my shift, and we're going to be closing soon.'

'What time is it now?'

'After six.'

'Six. I think I'm supposed to meet someone here, you see, but I can't remember what time we arranged. Time kinda slips away from me, these days.' He was apologetic.

'Well, never mind, tell me who it is and perhaps we can call them.'

'Call who?'

'Whoever it is you're supposed to be meeting?' She raised her eyebrows.

'Oh, you can't do that.'

'Why not?' Merry probed.

'I wouldn't want to disturb her. She's probably at work.'

Now Merry wasn't sure what to say. 'What's her name, your friend?'

He looked evasive. 'Oh, you wouldn't know her.'

Merry tried another tack. 'And you?' she said gently. 'What's your name?'

He looked away, apparently concentrating intently. Then his eyes, clouded with uncertainty, swivelled back to hers. 'That's the thing. I can't seem to remember,' he said sheepishly. 'Believe me, I know how stupid that sounds.'

Merry took a deep breath. 'It's not stupid at all, just a bit inconvenient, but we won't worry about that just now, right?'

'You're not mad with me, then?' He looked vulnerable.

'Of course not!'

He seemed relieved.

'I know,' she said. 'Let's give you a temporary name, just for the moment.'

His face relaxed. 'That's an idea!'

She looked at his outfit of jeans and *Je suis Charlie* T-shirt.

'Charlie.' She pointed to his T-shirt. 'Let's call you Charlie for now.'

'Charlie!' He glanced down at himself. 'That's a good name. I like it!'

'I'm going to bring you some more coffee, Charlie – you stay right there.' Then Merry went back behind the counter to bring Eva up to speed. 'We need to call the doctor, Mum.'

The Seashell was still open when Dot hurried towards the entrance at ten past six, which was fortuitous. As she pushed open the door, though, and the rope of intertwined bells and shells announced her arrival, she could tell at once something was up. Rob was there, with a man she didn't know, while Merry and her mother Eva were talking quietly to each other behind the counter. They seemed concerned. It took a moment for anyone to notice Dot.

'Sorry I'm late. I almost forgot to pick up the dessert I ordered, Merry. My other guests are arriving this evening,' she explained. 'Have I come at a bad time?'

'No, of course not,' Merry said, heading into the kitchen. 'I'll get it for you now.'

'I'd have brought it over, if you'd forgotten.' Eva said, smiling. 'I could have done with a chat to take my mind off that last committee meeting and those insufferable women. We had Kate and Ellen in here earlier – Merry had to serve them. I wouldn't have trusted myself. But …' Eva lowered her voice '… we've got a bit of a situation here.' She nodded in the direction of Rob and the stranger. 'He doesn't seem to know where he is. Probably Alzheimer's or something like that.'

Merry reappeared from the kitchen with Dot's dessert in a box, and recounted the incident. 'He's been sitting here all afternoon, said he was supposed to meet someone but couldn't remember who or what time … so we called Dr Rob.'

'Poor man,' Dot said. 'Is he from around here?'

'That's what we're trying to find out. Rob's been phoning around the nursing homes and hospitals, but no one's claimed him yet. He's American – at least, his accent is – but he doesn't even know his name, poor guy. We've called him Charlie because of his T-shirt'

'Well, that's one way of remembering it, I suppose.'

'Hello, Dot.' Rob came over to her and Merry. 'Keep an eye on him, would you? I need to take this call outside – it's breaking up.'

'Come and meet him,' Merry said. 'He's a sweetheart.' She went across to his table, Dot following her.

'How're you doing, Charlie?' Merry sat down beside him, indicating for Dot to join them. 'Can I get you anything else?'

'No, thank you, I'm good. Your Dr Rob is being very helpful. He's making some calls, I believe.'

'This is Dorothy, though everyone calls her Dot. She runs a guesthouse near here.'

'Hello, Charlie.' She shook the hand he extended. 'Pleased to meet you.'

'Good to meet you, Dorothy. That's a pretty name.'

'Thank you.'

'Gift from God.' He smiled at her.

'What?' Merry frowned.

'That's the meaning of the name Dorothy, *gift from God*.'

'You're right.' Dot smiled. 'Though it's a long time since I've heard that said.'

'You girls both have pretty names here – Dorothy and Merry.' He paused. 'Merry's an unusual name – is it local?'

'It's short for Merope,' said Merry. 'After a star.'

'Ah, of course. The Pleiades, right?' Charlie smiled. 'Merope – the lost sister.'

Merry was startled. Her name, pronounced Meh-ro-pay, was usually too much of a struggle to explain to people. 'You're right – but experience has taught me Merry's easier for general introduction purposes.'

'I can appreciate that,' Charlie said. 'Say, what's the name of this place, again?'

'You're in Derrybeggs, Charlie,' Merry said. 'And this is our local café, the Seashell …'

'Right, right.'

Just then Rob came back. 'No luck, I'm afraid. And the social worker can't get here till tomorrow.'

'Could I use your restroom, please?' Charlie said.

'Of course.' Merry got up. 'Let me show you where it is.'

Rob sat down opposite Dot and rubbed his face. He

looked tired. 'Well, this is some turn-up for the books. They've filled you in?'

'Yes, poor man. He seems remarkably unperturbed.'

'One of the few perks of his condition, I'm guessing.'

'Is it Alzheimer's, do you think?'

'It's possible.' Rob was circumspect. 'Hard to be sure – there could be several explanations.'

Dot gave an involuntary shudder. 'And he has no idea where he's from, or where he should be?'

'If he does, he's not saying – and I don't want to press him. He might get upset.'

'Of course. He seems perfectly lucid, though, apart from that.'

'Yes, he does.' Rob was thoughtful.

'So, what happens now?'

'Good question. The guards don't have any missing person on their books of his description. None of the hospitals or retirement homes in the district have reported anyone missing – more to the point, they're all full. A hospital wouldn't take him anyway – and the social worker can't get here till tomorrow. Which leaves us with a Charlie-shaped problem on our hands.' Rob smiled as Charlie and Merry returned.

'You know,' Charlie began, 'you good people don't need to wait with me. I'm sure you've got lives of your own to be getting on with – I'm quite happy to sit here.' He was optimistic.

'That's just it, Charlie.' Rob exchanged a concerned glance with Merry and Dot. 'I'm afraid Merry needs to close now so you can't stay here.'

'Oh, Lordy, I've been holding you all up?' Charlie was clearly appalled. 'That's just terrible. I didn't realise. I'm so sorry. I'll be on my way now. Say, have I paid you for that coffee?' He patted his pockets for the wallet he didn't have.

'Yes, of course,' Merry said. She looked upset. 'Don't worry about that, Charlie.'

Dot never knew what made her say it. Perhaps it was the helplessness in Charlie's expression, or perhaps because Martin, if he had been alive, or was watching proceedings from above, would have self-combusted with outrage at the idea. But very calmly she heard herself say, 'Charlie can stay with me – for a night or two anyway. Wouldn't that be a solution? I have the space, and another American guest is arriving this evening. That might make him feel more at home.'

'Really?' Rob said.

'Why not? It makes sense. I've got the rooms, and there'll be other people to chat to – I've organised dinner for eight o'clock.'

'Well, if you're sure, that would be wonderful, Dot,' said Rob.

Only Charlie seemed unaware of the collective relief.

Six

She was hopeless. No, scratch that, she was a lunatic. Her children were right. She had no idea what she was doing. That much, at least, was clear now. What in the name of God had she been thinking? In the space of one ill-considered conversation, she had invited a complete stranger, who was clearly not in control of his mental faculties, into her home to stay with her on the day her latest paying guests were due to arrive.

Although, as Dot considered her spur-of-the-moment invitation to Charlie, she was pretty sure she had taken him in because he was as lost as she sometimes felt – far from her old home and friends.

She was relieved that at least Rob would be there. Apart from being a doctor and able to keep an eye on Charlie, his suggestion that he could spare some clothes for him (they seemed more or less the same size) solved a practical problem. Rob would be good company at dinner too, and he could tell people far more about Derrybeggs than Dot could.

'So, the way I look at it,' Charlie was saying, when she realised she had been walking the five minutes or so to her house absorbed in her own thoughts as he was chatting companionably, 'the way I look at it is that these things usually resolve themselves.'

'Yes, absolutely!' she agreed. 'You're quite right.' She hadn't the slightest clue what he had been talking about. She had to snap out of it and pay attention. Speaking of which, her attention was now drawn to a figure, who appeared to be sitting on the wrought-iron garden bench just beside her front door, making a fuss of Honey. It was a woman, who looked up then. Dot almost stopped in her tracks, but remembered herself and her manners enough to keep putting one foot in front of the other, to hold out her hand and fix a friendly smile on her face, although truth be told, she felt like turning tail and running inside. It was *her*! Molly Cusack was talking now and Dot forced herself to be calm and act as if finding celebrities sitting outside waiting to be let into her home was second nature to her.

'Is this your dog?' Molly asked. 'I'm in love with her already!'

'Yes, this is Honey. I'm so sorry,' Dot said. 'Have you been waiting long? I just nipped out for a few minutes and got delayed, I'm afraid.'

'Not long at all, don't worry. It's nice to get a bit of air – I've been on the go all day, or it certainly feels that way.' She smiled her famous smile and got to her feet. 'You must be Dorothy?'

'Yes, that's me – but call me Dot, please. Everybody does. Now, follow me and I'll show you to your cottage.'

'Hello.' Molly was looking at Charlie with interest. 'I'm Molly.'

Dot remembered she hadn't introduced them. Oh, Lord ... 'This – this is Charlie,' she managed.

'Like the shirt says.' Charlie smiled and pointed to his T-shirt. 'Hello, Molly.'

'Ah,' Molly replied. 'You're American.'

'It would appear so – yes, indeed.'

Molly laughed, and Dot realised she thought Charlie was being witty. Perhaps he was for all she knew.

Whatever his situation, Charlie certainly had an air of quiet confidence about him, a gentility that seemed to disguise his wounded memory. It was almost as if he were too well-mannered to allow people to become embarrassed or discomfited on his behalf. As a result, he was relentlessly charming – which must have been so hard for him. Dot found it unaccountably touching.

'What a gorgeous house!' Molly looked around her as they passed through the small outer hall leading into a larger one, admiring the beautiful mirror and graceful staircase. While Dot had maintained the integrity of the interior, restoring the Old Rectory's impressive cornicing and other period features, she had been persuaded to be adventurous with contemporary paint shades, textures and tones, and the finished result was spectacular – like a very cool Scandinavian hunting lodge, one designer friend had commented – which was exactly the result she had hoped to achieve.

'Thank you, it's been a real labour of love to get it to this stage, but I've enjoyed every minute of it,' she said. 'Now, you're in Fuchsia Cottage. Can you manage your bags? I can help you— Oh, Honey!' Dot gasped as the dog pushed ahead of her, almost tripping her. 'You'll have to watch out for her. She has a habit of getting under your feet if she likes you – just shove her out if she's ever bothering you.'

'I love dogs. She can hang out with me any time.'

'Allow me,' Charlie said, picking up Molly's bags.

They followed Dot across the kitchen and dining area, through French windows and into the garden. They walked along a gravel path, which turned quite abruptly to the left, behind a thick hedge, leading into a secluded area where two beautiful cottages faced each other across a small courtyard. 'Oh, these are so lovely!' Molly said. 'And I can smell the sea.' She stretched out her arms and inhaled deeply.

'Well, it's only a stone's throw away from us.' Dot unlocked the door to Fuchsia Cottage. 'Honey and I usually manage at least one walk on the beach every day.' She smiled. 'I'll leave you to settle in. You must be tired after your drive. Just shout if you need anything. Dinner's at eight.'

Seven

Merry grabbed her hoodie, put on her trainers, and pulled the door to her mother's small white house behind her, a sudden gust of wind blasting her hair. Eva had stayed behind to lock up the café after Charlie, Dot and Rob had left, but Eva would be hurrying home up the steep cliff road soon and Merry wasn't in the mood for talking. She wasn't in the mood for thinking either, but she had less control over that. Running helped clear her head, and she could rely on Beth not to ask constantly how she was feeling. The small beach was pretty much empty now as she made her way to Pirate's Cove, looking down from the cliff road. A few late stragglers were collecting their belongings, working up the energy to climb up the winding steps and head back to the village to enjoy a summer evening. A gentle breeze was coming in from the bay. She knew her way blindfolded to this place, which was just as well as she was pretty much on autopilot these days.

It was coming up to two years since Doug had been killed and sometimes she found herself so lost in thought or memories she had trouble remembering which life she was inhabiting – her previous one in Florida with Doug and her research at the Coastal and Marine Laboratory or here and now in Derrybeggs, where she had grown up, and had returned to hide and heal.

She wondered briefly how Dot was getting on with Charlie. It had been really nice of her to take him in – no one had been expecting that. At least Charlie would be safe there. She wondered if anyone was looking for him, desperately searching, or was he simply just another poor soul who'd wandered off from his residential care home or hospital trolley? What happens when you matter so little that people stop looking for you or don't even notice you've gone? Well, Charlie wasn't her problem. Merry had enough problems of her own and she didn't want to think about them right now.

Beth was waiting for her at the bottom of the steps, doing some stretches against a wall of rock. 'Hey,' she said, looking pleased as she straightened up. 'I thought maybe you weren't going to make it.'

'Had a situation at the café.' Merry filled Beth in on the stranger as they began their run.

'What a nightmare,' Beth said. 'Here we both are, trying to escape our respective homes for an hour or so, and this poor guy can't find his way back to his. Ain't life strange?' Beth, who'd had her first baby, was vocal about the need for adult company and getting out of the house – particularly as she worked from home as an artist in her studio.

Merry knew Beth understood that she was just trying to survive the only way she could. Living with her parents at the age of thirty-three had never been part of the plan – but here she was. She could have stayed on in Florida, of course, continued her term as a marine field researcher – the faculty had told her to take as much time as she needed – but Merry would forever associate Florida with Doug, and she couldn't bear to remain there without him. So, she had come home and gone back to doing something that required nothing of her except mechanical repetition – working in her parents' café, where she had grown up. It was meant to be temporary – just until she recovered enough to face the world again – but eighteen months later Merry wasn't any closer to moving on.

'I know I give out about the place.' Beth puffed. 'But I really do feel lucky to live here. I mean, look at that!' She flung out her arm to indicate the view as they ran beneath the cliffs. It was a perfect summer evening: the sun lowering into the west, the tranquil sea bleeding into the horizon, and the cloudless sky meant it would be a good night for the star watchers who frequented the area.

'I don't think I could live anywhere that wasn't near the sea,' Merry said. 'It's too big a part of me.'

'Well, I don't see why you'd ever have to.' Beth snuck a glance at her friend but Merry didn't respond. She knew Beth wanted to know if she was considering staying on for good in Derrybeggs now she was back, but Merry wasn't ready or able to make that kind of commitment.

It had always been the ocean for Merry. Ever since she could remember she'd wanted to be around water. Her mum said she roared blue murder every time she took her out of the bath, and that was before she could talk. Some kids were rocked, some given soothers or toys, but when Merry was inconsolable, the only thing that calmed her was putting her into water. She relaxed instantly. If only it still worked. Easy therapy.

Growing up in Derrybeggs she had learned to cook and wait tables in the Seashell. Her Dutch parents, Jan and Eva, had bought the ramshackle café in the eighties when they had met and fallen in love on a cycling tour of the Ring of Kerry. The originally drab exterior had been painstakingly covered with thousands of seashells, in swirling, intricate designs, making it so eye-catching it had become a local landmark. Eva's glorious baking and proper coffee (introduced long before the café revolution made its way to rural Ireland) had become a firm favourite in the town. Merry's dad, Jan, grew all their own vegetables and ran a brisk sideline in supplying the organic produce that was so much in demand. Off season, life at the café slowed to a gentle rhythm, but now, facing into the summer, the place would be packed with tourists eager to experience its quirky individuality and excellent food.

Merry knew her parents kind of hoped she might make a career of it, expand the family business, but the lure of the ocean had been too strong. Marine biology was her thing, and although she spent summer holidays working in the café, serving her apprenticeship, once she had enough cash she was out of there, chasing water.

Through her twenties she'd travelled on rice boats with sails made of old sheets and jeans with a drunken skipper to research reefs in Madagascar. She'd educated impoverished fishing communities to rebuild local octopus reserves. She'd measured fish off the Maldives in dugout canoes about as stable as floating bathtubs, and worked on reef conservation in Mauritius. While her girlfriends were sunning themselves on exotic beaches with cocktails, Merry was up to her gills in fish and statistics. But she wouldn't have had it any other way. She had been living her dream. But then there had been the accident and Merry had come home, barely able to function.

She knew she was taking out her anger on those who loved her most – her parents, and Beth, not to mention clients at the Seashell – but she couldn't seem to help herself. And she hated herself for that too.

'Can we stop for a minute?' Beth wasn't as fit as she had been pre-pregnancy.

'Sure.' They slowed to a jog, and paused at the large rock shaped like an armchair at the far end of the cove. While Beth caught her breath, Merry sat on the rock gazing out over the sea, outwardly calm and serene.

'Okay, I'm good now,' Beth said. 'Let's head back. You okay?'

'Sure.' Merry blinked hard and rubbed her eyes.

'It'll get easier,' Beth said softly, putting a hand on her shoulder. 'One day at a time, yeah?'

Eight

It was almost seven o'clock when, after a spectacular cliff drive and views of the ocean that stretched all the way back home, Ryan Shindler finally drove through the pretty village of brightly coloured houses. Following directions, he turned right after a ruined castle and spotted the sign that pointed to the Old Rectory. After touching down in Shannon from JFK airport, he had visited a business associate of his boss Frank's for a meeting that had gone way over schedule. Even though he was tired and wired from travelling, Ryan always found driving relaxing, and with every mile he had felt himself unwinding. It was a beautiful evening, and the scenery was so different from New York, he might have been on another planet. *Relax, kiddo*, Frank always said to him, when Ryan would dash from one meeting to another. *You ain't got nothing to run from, no more* ... and for a while Ryan almost believed him. His life had got better, *much* better, since he'd been working for Frank – unbelievably better – but that didn't stop him looking back over his shoulder every now and again, which made him want to keep up the pace, just in case.

Pulling into a garage to refuel, Ryan checked his phone, full of the usual urgent emails but no message from his girlfriend, Joni, which made him feel equal parts relieved and disappointed. It had been two days now, and Joni had obviously meant what she'd said. Clearly she was giving it time to sink in. Joni needed to communicate like other people needed to breathe – her million-plus followers on Instagram were testament to that – so her silence spoke volumes. He couldn't say he was altogether surprised – after all, he'd been through a version of the Talk with every girlfriend he'd ever had, and there'd been a few. But this one had taken him by surprise, both by its brevity and its businesslike presentation. It had been well thought through on Joni's part – which was exactly what he would have expected from her. 'Attention to detail' should have been her middle name. There had been no warning, no wheedling, and crucially she hadn't uttered the fatal words – *Honey, we need to talk* – which struck fear into the hearts of better men than him.

Instead, she had seemed her usual cheerful self, giving no clue to the bombshell she was about to drop until they had eaten their appetisers in their favourite restaurant and were toying with their wine. 'Ryan,' she'd said briskly, 'I need you to listen to me for a minute.' Something in her tone made his head snap up. 'We've been together for a year and a half now – you know I love you, and you've led me to believe you love me too.' Her expression was unapologetically frank.

He had felt the prickle of dread, then, on his skin. 'You know I do.'

'Good. That makes this easier. I want to get married, Ryan.' She'd held up her hand to stop him interjecting. 'I had, I will admit, hoped you might propose to me before now – but when you bought me diamond earrings and not a diamond ring for my birthday last week – very beautiful and generous diamond earrings – I knew we were in trouble. And before you say otherwise, I realise you have acquired somewhat of a reputation in this respect.'

'Reputation?' Despite his horror at the turn the conversation had taken, Ryan was intrigued.

'As a commitment-phobe,' she'd said matter-of-factly. 'I understand – believe me, I do. I used to be one myself until I met you. And that's how I know that when you meet the right person any reservations you might harbour towards marriage simply fall away.'

This was news to Ryan. 'They do?'

'I'm not going to continue like this, Ryan, so here's the deal. I'm prepared to give us eight more weeks.' Here she paused to make a mental calculation. 'That's around eleven per cent of the time we've been seeing each other, which I think is fair. During this interim,' she went on, 'you may propose to me at any time or, indeed, I may propose to you. After all, we live in an equal society. I have to warn you that either way I intend to post about your reaction. After all, my one million followers on @houseofgirls are almost as much invested in this relationship as I am, and whatever the outcome, it will provide a much-needed platform for initiating a discussion about this whole subject, which is so fraught for women these days. Guys can string you along for ever – and no matter how much work you have done, or however many of your eggs you freeze – we only have a limited shelf life. This is a fact, however much we might dress it up or try to avoid it. I did a graph on the subject – it was very interesting. Every year a new crop of girls is coming up behind us.' She frowned.

'What are you talking about, Joni?' Ryan was incredulous. 'Every year a new crop of guys are coming up behind me, too! What's that got to do with anything?'

'Precisely – but the graph works in men's favour. I am not interested in younger men. I want a man from my own peer group, my own generation. In short, Ryan, I want you. This may not sound romantic, but I can't afford to let romance, or indeed chance, dictate my life. So there it is. We have eight more weeks together – or maybe a lifetime. The choice is yours.' Then Joni smiled at the waitress who had brought their main course and cut into her *filet mignon*, while Ryan contemplated the seafood platter in front of him, which he now felt unable to eat.

After dinner, Joni had declined to come back to his apartment as she usually would. Instead she'd kissed him lightly on the lips. 'Think about what I've said, Ryan. Surprise me!' Then she hailed a passing cab and disappeared into the night.

That had been two days ago, and he had heard nothing from her since. *Nada.* And he hadn't felt compelled to reach out to her, either. He was still in shock – maybe. And now here he was in Ireland without her, which was ironic, as he had planned this business trip to double up as a perfect romantic getaway for him and Joni. Sure, he'd have to work for three weeks or so, and sign off on the new golf resort Frank's company had developed in Derrybeggs, which would mean making sure every detail of the club was finished to perfection, but they could have combined it with a really nice vacation. And Joni could have used the material for her social-media feed. That was why Ryan had gone to such trouble to book the romantic cottage for two and rent the upmarket car Joni had wanted.

But things happen for a reason, right? That was what Frank always said. Who was he to know? But then Joni had told him she wouldn't be going with him to Ireland as things stood. That had been the other bombshell she dropped.

Either way, he supposed, he could relax now, take a moment to breathe, because the axe had been lifted, albeit temporarily. All he needed was a few weeks – he could work it out. He could work anything out, given a bit of time to think. But even so a small voice niggled in his head. What if Joni was right? Was there something missing in him, something that made him unable to commit? What was love, anyway? Joni was everything he'd ever wanted in a woman. Maybe if she proposed he should just say yes. Ryan needed and wanted a family of his own – even though his own experience of family had been far from ideal.

Back on the road, Ryan realised his satnav was telling him to turn right, through wrought-iron gates, flanked by crumbling pillars covered with ivy, and up the curved driveway that ended in front of a large house. He was tired after the long day of travelling and the light glowing from behind the windows was welcoming. Getting out of the car, he stretched, surprised by the heavy sweetness of the air. The front door was ajar, and he pushed it open with his shoulder, lugging his bag into the hallway and dropping it, where he guessed someone would come by to pick it up and take him to his cottage. There was no reception desk, no bell to ring. It was just a house, a pretty spectacular one, with a real turf fire burning in the hall – and a delicious smell floated to him from the direction of what he assumed must be the kitchen. He was about to try to call or text someone, when a yellow Labrador hurtled into the hall to greet him, wagging its whole body, followed by a tall, elegant woman with a smile and a smudge of flour on her nose. 'You must be Mr Shindler,' she said. 'I'm Dorothy, but everyone calls me Dot, and this is Honey.' She indicated the dog, which was sniffing him thoroughly.

'That's me! But call me Ryan, please.' He shook the hand she held out.

'Let me show you to your cottage, Ryan. We'll go through the kitchen, if you don't mind – you don't have to, of course, generally speaking, but it's quicker than walking around the outside. Follow me.' Dot was friendly, but brisk.

'Oh, sure.' Ryan grabbed his bag.

Whatever was cooking reminded him of how ravenous he was. He hadn't thought to stock up on groceries, figuring he'd do that later, or the next day, and hoped he was right when he thought he remembered something about dinner being included – only he couldn't remember if he'd reserved a place. The kitchen was cool, with a natural slate floor, elegant dark blue cabinets and stark white walls. Three different cookers (he counted them), a gas range, an electric and a steam oven, were installed along an industrial-looking exposed brick wall.

'I'm a pretty keen cook.' Dot smiled at him, following his gaze.

He followed Dot along a gravel path, taking in the landscaped gardens to his right, until she turned abruptly left into an area sectioned off by a thick laurel hedge, where two immaculately restored cottages were separated by a small courtyard. His was the larger one.

'Here we are,' she said, opening the door and handing him the key. 'Sundew Cottage. I'm sure you're tired after your journey, but if you need anything let me know.'

'Thanks. Say, are there any good restaurants around here you can recommend?'

'If you're prepared to drive further afield you'll find a few. Otherwise there's just our local café, the Seashell. But dinner here is in about fifteen minutes – I've included you, unless you'd rather make your own arrangements?'

'No, ma'am! That's music to a hungry man's ears. I meant to stop for something to eat along the way, but I've been running on coffee all day.'

'Well, I'm pretty sure we can do a little better than that.' She smiled. 'You'll find some basics in the fridge, Ryan, and some fruit. See you for dinner later.'

After a quick shower, Ryan unpacked his stuff and had a look around. The cottage didn't disappoint, and although the romantic vibe was pretty lost on him, it was a welcome change from his usual hotel rooms. He wondered what Joni was doing now. Probably covering a fashion shoot for her website, or working on the thousands of emails she received. One of the things that had attracted him to her was her work ethic – it helped that she understood the demands of his own career on his time – but sometimes he worried that she was too relentless about building her brand.

Joni had been right when she'd said he had a reputation – but she didn't know the reasons behind it. Ryan kept that part of his past to himself. When thoughts of the trailer park that had passed for a home surfaced – and the mother who had run out on him, his dad, and his little brother Jimmy – Ryan banished them swiftly before they led to the question that really gutted him. *How can kids be so unlovable that even their mother walks out on them?*

Small wonder Ryan was cautious – but with Joni he thought maybe he was getting past that, maybe things could be different, that maybe they really did have a future. Ryan had even been considering asking Joni to marry him before she had sprung the ultimatum. His friends and Frank thought she was terrific – she was smart, sharp and beautiful. There was no downside. But something was bothering him – he just couldn't put his finger on what it was. Ryan didn't know how love was supposed to feel. Maybe that was the problem. Maybe he should just bite the bullet: if it was a business proposition he wouldn't be sitting on the fence. Why should committing to your choice of life partner be any different?

Nine

The cottage was perfect, Molly thought, as she walked around her small home for the next month and admired the cosy stove. Although it was June, the evenings could still be chilly, and Dot had told her she wanted to make sure the place was warm when she arrived.

Dinner was in ten minutes. It seemed to be an opt-in-or-out arrangement, and Molly was glad she had asked to be included for this first night as she hadn't had the energy to do a food shop. That could wait until the morning. She was also pleased she had picked up two bottles of wine in Duty Free that she could bring to dinner. For now she would just get the rest of her things from her car and have a quick freshen-up.

She had unpacked quickly, always eager to get settled as soon as she could in a new place, probably a habit acquired from decades of working on different sets – the sooner you learned your way about the better! She would do a recce of the location tomorrow morning. It seemed to her, as she walked around the cottage arranging her few things, almost as if Dot had read her mind as to what she needed. One pretty bedroom with a very comfortable (she had tried it out) brass bed, a small bathroom with a lovely rolltop slipper bath, a tiny kitchen with chalk-blue-painted wooden cupboards, and a sitting room with – she could hardly believe it – a small old-fashioned writing desk in front of a window that looked out onto a pretty cottage garden, now bathed in evening sunlight: perfect for her to work at. Hopefully the change of scene would make her writing routine click into place.

Julia and Nigel would have loved hearing about her trip to Ireland – they'd probably have joined her at the first opportunity. What fun they would have had! Molly wondered if she would find more such good friends. It seemed unlikely that she would ever forge such meaningful bonds at this stage in her life. But she wouldn't dwell on that now: plenty of time to think about the past when she began her work tomorrow.

On her way out, Molly made sure to lock the quaint front door, and had a quick look at the slightly larger cottage across the way from her, which earlier had seemed uninhabited, but now showed signs of life. The lights were on, and the door was ajar. She knocked on it, had a little peep around and floated a 'Hello' across the threshold, but no one appeared. She hoped they were nice, whoever they were – it would be good to have a friendly face or two around. Dot seemed lovely, and charmingly chatty, Molly thought, but then any host has to be friendly to their guests. It didn't mean there was any possibility of real or lasting friendship there – and it would be silly of her to assume there was. Pity, she could have done with someone her own age for company.

'Evening.'

The deep southern drawl that came from behind her made her jump back, as if she'd been caught snooping, and Molly felt her face pink. 'Oh, hello! I wasn't – that is, I was just wondering if there was anyone—'

'Guess if we're going to be neighbours we should introduce ourselves.' The owner of the drawl slung a computer bag over his other shoulder and extended his hand to her. 'Ryan Shindler.'

'I'm Molly – I arrived about an hour ago.' She was babbling, like a young girl, which was ridiculous. But the tanned young man was extremely good-looking, and was sizing her up. Not in *that* way – good heavens, she was old enough to be his mother – but more likely wondering if he'd be saddled with a nosy neighbour!

'Good to meet you, Molly.' He was looking at her curiously now. 'Don't I know you from somewhere?' His eyes narrowed, then creased in amusement. 'That's it – you're the actress from *Hornetsville*!' The title of the hideous series she had starred in about five years ago at a particularly lean period in her career took Molly by surprise. How would he know that? She didn't think it had sold in America. Just remembering the ghastly series (shot for a Japanese network) of a town overrun by giant hornets and the extremely unlikely lengths the locals of said town employed to defend themselves – led by Molly as a sort of futuristic sheriff with insect DNA – made her cringe. The only comfort was that the cash had come in very handy at the time and the series was unlikely to be shown outside Japan. She must ask Larry about that …

'I just got here too,' Ryan was saying now. 'Well' – he tilted his head towards the open door of his cottage – 'I gotta get set up in here. Guess I'll be seeing you around.' He didn't look thrilled at the prospect, Molly felt, but then he smiled at her. A gorgeous, lopsided grin, which made him look terribly appealing.

'Yes, of course. See you later!' She gave a little wave as she made for the garden path. 'Cheerio!' she called. *Cheerio?* She sounded like someone out of a 1950s sitcom! Who said 'cheerio' any more?

Ten

Dot checked on her casserole, which was coming along nicely – another five minutes or so would do the trick. Rob was putting together some clothes for Charlie, and was upstairs with him. Dot had put Charlie on the second floor, in a particularly nice room at the back of the house (although she thought all her rooms were lovely in their own way). She was setting out her favourite white linen napkins when Molly appeared from the garden with two bottles of wine under her arm.

She proffered one now. 'I picked these up in Duty Free – thought we could use them as an icebreaker.' She grinned.

'Oh, that's so kind of you!' Dot found a corkscrew and handed it to her. 'I could do with a glass now, if I'm honest. My nerves are getting the better of me.'

'I can understand that,' Molly said. 'But don't worry – the table looks perfect, and I can talk for England. I've just met my neighbour too – the lovely American chap.'

For a wild moment Dot thought she was talking about Charlie, who was upstairs, then remembered Ryan. 'Yes, he seems very nice.' She took the glass Molly handed her gratefully. 'His girlfriend was supposed to be coming too, but she had to cancel, apparently. I think he's here to sign off on everything at the new golf club. The grand opening isn't until next month – the golfers among us have been talking of little else.'

'What shall we drink to?' Molly asked, raising her glass. 'The film festival?'

'How about to meeting new friends?' said Dot.

'Perfect!'

'Speaking of which' – Rob came down the three steps into the kitchen, looking pleased – 'the clothes are a near perfect fit. Charlie's just having a quick shower.' He noticed Molly for the first time. 'Hello! Oh, you're … um … aren't you?' Rob wasn't usually lost for words, and Dot suppressed a smile at his astonishment in finding himself face to face in her kitchen with the well-known actress.

'This is Molly,' she said.

'Of course you are!' He shook hands with her. 'I didn't think you'd be arriving yet for the festival.'

'And this is Rob, our resident locum GP. Molly's come over early to get out of London.'

'It was a spur-of-the-moment thing, really,' Molly said. 'But I'm hoping to get some work done on my memoir, and I needed a change of scene.'

'Well, Derrybeggs is about as far from London as you can get – metaphorically speaking.' Rob lifted his glass to both women. 'Here's hoping you enjoy your stay.'

'Something smells really good.' Charlie made his way

into the kitchen, startling them. 'I hope I'm not intruding. I just followed my nose.'

'Of course you're not!' Dot recovered herself quickly. 'Please – come and join us. Dinner's almost ready.'

Dressed in his new clothes, and with his hair freshly washed and brushed back, she would hardly have recognised Charlie as the man they had been discussing in the café. He looked fresh and rested, and was disarmingly relaxed and cheerful.

'Molly, you remember Charlie. You, er, met earlier.'

'Of course I do.' Molly was clearly curious about him.

Dot cut in quickly to distract her: 'Rob and Charlie were just sorting something out for me upstairs.' How could she explain about Charlie now?

'Dr Rob and I are old friends now – right, Dr Rob?' Charlie said, grinning.

'Indeed we are, Charlie.' Rob smiled, but he was having a hard time dragging his gaze away from Molly, who was now offering to help Dot dish up.

Luckily, Ryan chose just that moment to join them. 'Uh, have I come to the right place for dinner?' He closed the door behind him, and Honey jumped out of her basket to give him a special welcome.

'Yes, and your timing is perfect!' said Dot. 'Now, please, do sit down, everyone.'

'Can I lend a hand? It looks like you could use some help.' Ryan gave her his lopsided smile.

'Thank you. Would you look after everyone's glasses, Ryan? The wine's there.' She indicated the bottles on the countertop. 'Everyone, this is Ryan.' She retrieved the plates from the oven. 'Charlie, what would you like to drink?'

'Just water for me, thank you.'

Dot worried that she hadn't had a chance to explain to either Molly or Ryan how Charlie had turned up and was now regretting it. But she hadn't planned on everyone sitting down to dinner together so easily, and they were chatting away to each other. As long as Rob was here everything would be fine, she thought.

'So,' Rob said, 'what *is* the story with the festival?'

'There's a festival?' Ryan asked. 'I didn't notice any billboards on the way into town.'

'Our annual film festival – and lack of advertising is just part of the problem, I'm afraid,' Dot said. 'I'm relatively new in town myself so I didn't like to throw my weight around, but I wanted to join the committee. I'm quite good at organising things and I thought it would be a great way to meet people, and make some new friends. The thing is, I didn't know what I was letting myself in for. The new management on the committee are doing things very differently from previous years, so I'm told, and they've lost the run of themselves. They started off with very grandiose ideas and forgot about the bread and butter stuff.' She shrugged. 'Now no one seems to know what's going on. The most pressing problem is lack of a first-night venue. There was a fire at the community hall where we used to hold it and everywhere else seems to be booked up.'

'It's no skin off my nose,' said Molly. 'I mean, I don't mind if it doesn't go ahead – I just wanted a change of scene and a nice place to try to do some writing. The film festival was just a lovely excuse to come back to Derrybeggs.'

'You've been here before then?' Rob said.

'Yes.' Molly smiled. 'A long time ago – I used to holiday here with my family at the old Lake Hotel. It must be forty years since I was here.'

'So did I,' Dot said. 'We used to rent a house on Harbour Terrace every year. I fell in love with the Old Rectory when I was ten years old and vowed I'd live here one day. It's only taken me fifty years to manage it! I wonder if we ever crossed paths.' She had been amazed to discover when she had looked up Molly's online bio that the actress was three years older than her, although even on close inspection Molly could have passed for a late forty-something. Dot averted her gaze quickly, but it was hard not to stare – and she noticed she was not the only one gazing admiringly at Molly. Rob was hanging eagerly on her every word.

'Well, I was born and bred in Derrybeggs,' he was saying now, 'but I ended up living in the UK, thanks to a very pretty and persuasive nurse called April. Sadly, April died five years ago and since my kids went off travelling … Well, I was finding life a bit lonely and looking for a change of scene. When I saw the vacancy for a locum here in Derrybeggs, I jumped at the chance. It's good to be back home for a while – I know old Dr Walshe from way back so it helps that his patients feel they're not talking to a complete stranger.'

'And you live here with Dot?' Molly was clearly curious.

'Oh, Rob's just staying here as a lodger until the new apartment attached to the surgery is ready.' Dot felt suddenly self-conscious. 'All the same,' she said, bringing the conversation back to safer territory, 'it'll be a shame if the festival has to be cancelled – it's a much-needed boost for the town, and I know Eva and Jan at the Seashell rely on it hugely – they generally do the catering every year.'

'Well,' said Molly, 'it sounds like you could do with a bit of help. And I'd be happy to lend a hand. I've got lots of experience, obviously – there must be something I can do. Why don't you set up a proper meeting with your committee members and we'll put our collective heads together, see what needs doing?'

'Really? That would be amazing!' Although, knowing Kate Carmichael and how dismissive she had been last time, Dot wasn't sure any outside offers of help would be well received. But Molly was a celebrity, their chosen guest of honour: they could hardly refuse to hear any suggestions she might have – and a cancelled festival wouldn't bode well for anyone on the committee.

'I don't know a whole lot about the movie business,' Ryan said, 'but back home it seems to be all about reality TV – I guess it's the same here? My girlfriend is pretty involved in that sort of thing.'

Dot looked blank, but Molly agreed with Ryan. 'Reality TV is terribly popular.' Charlie nodded amiably to most of the conversation.

'I think,' Dot said, 'one of the problems this year is that the community feels cold-shouldered. There's nothing that really involves them in the festival.'

'Your point about reality TV is a good observation.' Molly was thoughtful. 'What about having a competition? That would encourage people to get involved.'

'What kind of competition? We don't have time for anything much,' Dot worried. 'I mean, writing a screenplay or something would require a judging panel and submission rules ...'

'Oh, no. I was thinking of something much simpler. Something like a five-minute documentary made on your smartphone. After all, people seem to be constantly filming on their phones, these days, and pretty much anyone can make a five-minute film. I could get a friend of mine' – she named a well-known documentary producer – 'to judge them. I'm sure he'd love to come over for the day. That could be fun.'

'Great idea!' said Dot.

'Well, that sounds like a plan,' said Rob, tucking in to a second helping. 'This casserole is delicious, Dot. I always say good food promotes good thinking!'

Dot was delighted that the subject of the film festival seemed to be catching people's imaginations. It was proving such a distraction that perhaps no awkward questions would be asked until dinner was over and she had a moment to explain to Molly and Ryan who Charlie was, and how he had arrived there, realising that neither she nor anyone else knew the answers. Nonetheless, she needed to put them in the picture.

'That was delicious, thank you,' Charlie said now, as Dot collected the plates and took them away. He cleared his throat and, looking around the table, began, 'I realise this might sound a little strange …' – he paused, leaning his elbows on the table and steepled his fingers – '… but can someone please tell me where I am? And what the heck I'm doing here?'

Dot was glad she had put down the plates or she might have dropped them. A frozen pause descended on the table as all eyes swivelled towards Charlie. It was ironic, she thought, but if one didn't know his situation, at this very moment Charlie could have passed for any number of professional men who sat around boardroom tables asking for important facts and figures and evaluating the responses. He looked expectant but his tone was grave.

Ryan frowned, and glanced around the table. Molly was aghast. Dot sat down and began as gently as she could, while sticking to the facts. 'You're in Ireland, Charlie,' she began. 'In a village called Derrybeggs. You're in my house …' Here she paused. 'You're in my house because you were found wandering.'

'Wandering? In Ireland?' He looked at her intently.

'Yes, in a manner of speaking. The people who found you were concerned because you didn't seem to be aware of where you were, or why you were there – in the café. You also didn't seem to know your name or where you were from. So we decided to call you Charlie until we learned what your correct name is.'

'Don't I have ID on me?' Charlie frowned.

'None that anyone could find,' Dot said. 'But please try not to worry. There are people trying to find your family, or relatives – or your wife, if you're married.'

'Wife … family …' He tested the words. 'I'm not sure …'

An expression of deep sadness crossed his face as he fell silent.

Dot carried on: 'The police are on the case. I'm sure it will only be a very short time before they track and make contact with your people and find out where you live.'

'The police, huh?'

'So in the meantime, just for a few days, it was decided you should stay here. I have the rooms and, well, it seemed the sensible solution.' Dot chewed her lip.

Charlie digested the information thoughtfully, nodding occasionally. 'Well, it's the damnedest thing – but there's no denying I don't have any memory right now of where I should be. None whatsoever.'

'Please don't worry about it if you can help it.' She looked anxiously at Rob.

'You see, Charlie,' he said. 'You may have been in an accident – or be suffering from some kind of shock, or trauma.' He didn't mention Alzheimer's or dementia, in case it upset him. 'But, as Dot said, the police are handling things now, so really, I'm sure someone will have reported you missing, and they'll be getting in touch very soon with news.'

'Man,' Charlie said, shaking his head, 'I don't know what to say.' He looked around the table. 'Except, of course, how grateful I am to you – to you all – and to everyone who is helping me. And I must apologise for the disruption I'm surely causing you.' He sounded strangely formal.

'Oh, please don't apologise!' Dot said. 'We're happy to have you here, aren't we?'

Molly, Ryan and Rob nodded enthusiastically.

'What a fascinating story.' Molly was hanging on every word.

'Well, that's one way of looking at it.' He returned her gaze. 'Pretty inconvenient, though, I'd say.'

'You seem, if you don't mind me saying so, very calm about the whole thing,' Molly said.

'I'm pretty sure that's my first attempted response in a threatening situation. And believe me, I feel threatened.' He let out a long breath that was close to a whistle.

'We're not threatening people, Charlie,' Rob said. 'You can consider yourself safe here, wherever you hail from. You're among friends.' Rob's tone was light, but he was observing Charlie carefully.

'Oh, don't get me wrong!' Charlie held up his hands. 'I can tell you're good people. I didn't mean I was threatened by you guys. But it's a pretty threatening situation to find yourself in – I mean, no one wants to wake up one day and have to ask, *Who am I?* Do they?'

'No, indeed,' Molly said. 'You poor man! I wish there was something I could do.'

'Well, you've all been kind enough to tolerate this pretty disruptive intrusion on my part. That's very generous of you. I won't forget it.'

Molly rushed to fill the rather embarrassed silence that followed the innocent remark. 'Well, I certainly hope if I were ever in that situation someone would do the same for me.'

'So, you're guests of Dot too?' Charlie looked around the table.

'Yes,' Dot said quickly. 'In a manner of speaking. Molly and Ryan arrived today. Ryan beside you is also American.'

'A fellow countryman? Well, I guess my accent's a bit of a giveaway – or let's hope it is. That narrows the field somewhat, at least,' Charlie responded. 'Although the US is a pretty big place – even I can remember that!' This lightened the somewhat sombre tone that had descended. 'Well, never mind about me. How about you, Ryan, do you have family? Are you married?'

'I was born and bred in Kentucky – got out of the trailer park and got myself a life. I ended up in New York working for a real-estate mogul.'

'Sounds like quite a story there.'

'I won't lie, it wasn't easy.'

'I'll bet. I'd like to hear it,' Charlie said.

'There's not a lot to tell.' Ryan shrugged. 'We were poor and my mom left. Dad didn't handle it well so my little brother went to live with an aunt. I stayed as long as I could, then got the hell out.'

'What happened with your mom?'

'Don't know. Dad wouldn't talk about it. Just said she'd run out on us. I don't remember much about her. Her parents were Irish – I remember that – but we never met them. She'd cut ties with them before we came along. Seems like that was a pattern in her life.'

'That's tough.' Ryan felt Charlie's gaze on him.

'You do what you have to do.' Ryan poured himself some water. 'I have a girlfriend, though – we're thinking about getting married.' He smiled.

'Well, that's great. Did you meet at work?'

'Uh, no. She's an influencer – a very successful one. She's got, like, over a million followers.'

'Influencer? What's that?'

'Well.' Ryan tried to explain. 'They're individuals who have built up a big social-media following. They collaborate with brands and help them to achieve their marketing objectives. They can make a lot of money – but it's hard work.'

'I've heard of these people.' Molly nodded, although the rest of the table seemed bemused.

'Well, it's been a long day.' Ryan stood up. 'I'm ready for bed.'

'Of course. You must be exhausted after all your travelling. Good night,' said Dot.

'See y'all tomorrow.' Ryan waved as he disappeared out of the back door.

'If nobody objects' – Charlie got to his feet – 'I'd like to get some air for a few minutes before turning in. I'm feeling tired and, well, it's been a lot to take in.'

'Of course it has.' Dot got to her feet too. 'Rob, will you take Charlie for a ….'

'I'll be fine on my own, believe it or not,' Charlie said. 'Right now, I'd just like to take a few minutes, a quick stroll, stretch my legs, but if you'd feel better with someone accompanying me …'

'Under the circumstances' – Dot felt uncomfortable – 'I think it would be best.'

'Of course,' Rob said, getting up.

'Great. Let's go.'

'Well ...' Molly said, blowing out a breath when she and Dot were alone. 'That was an interesting start to my stay.'

'I'm so sorry.' Dot put her face into her hands. 'I meant to tell you and Ryan about Charlie, to explain the situation, but I wasn't expecting him to come down when he did, and then I didn't get the chance. I hope you're not upset?' She put some coffee on.

'Upset? Why on earth would I be upset?' Molly grinned. 'Fascinated, maybe, intrigued, but upset? No way!'

'Oh, good. I was worried you might think it was irresponsible of me, having him here when we know nothing about him, but I thought Rob could keep an eye on him. He's booked Charlie in for tests at the hospital tomorrow.'

The coffee was ready and Dot poured for them both.

'Poor Charlie.' Molly took her cup and sat down.

'Rob looked him over earlier and said it seemed to be some sort of cognitive impairment, bless him, but he seems calm, if confused about where he is, or how he got here. But otherwise he appears to be ...' Dot shrugged and sipped her coffee.

'Quite the gentleman, I'd say.' Molly was thoughtful. 'You found him in the café, you said?'

'Yes, it was Eva, who owns it, and her daughter, Merry, who raised the alarm, so to speak. They called Rob and the police.'

'I think it's wonderful what you're doing, letting him stay here.'

'Do you?'

'Yes, I do. Imagine if it were us, or a son or daughter or brother of ours, who was in trouble. Wouldn't you want someone to take them in and look after them until you could find them? You're being a veritable Good Samaritan. I think it's incredibly Christian of you.'

'I don't know about that.' Dot shook her head. 'But there's something about him, isn't there? Something that makes you feel, I don't know …'

'Interested?'

'I was going to say protective.'

'He's very good-looking,' Molly observed.

'I hadn't thought about that.' Dot smiled. 'He certainly looks a lot better than he did when we found him this morning.' She drank some more of her coffee. 'But, yes, he is an attractive man.'

'Presence.' Molly nodded. 'That's what he has. His voice too,' Molly went on. 'I'm very sensitive to voices, and he has a nice one, a lovely pitch, and a great turn of phrase.'

'You have been paying attention, haven't you?'

'Hard not to – I was riveted! Not often a tall, lost, attractive stranger turns up on someone's doorstep, quite literally. Besides, it's part of my job description to pay attention to things like that,' Molly pointed out. 'All that voice coaching and working on accents I've had to do over the years. Old habits die hard.'

'I hadn't thought of it like that.'

'In fact,' Molly said, 'it might be an idea to take an audio recording of Charlie – I could send it to my voice coach and she could have it analysed, pinpoint what part of America he comes from.'

'Can they do that?'

'Don't see why not – I'm sure there's software for that sort of thing. My coach has a pretty good ear anyway – it's worth a try.'

Just then Charlie and Rob arrived back.

'There's an incredibly clear sky tonight,' Charlie said. 'The stars are out, thousands of them. It's been a long time since I've had such a clear view – you could almost reach up and touch them.' He sounded wistful.

'We're in a dark sky reserve zone here. That's why it's so clear – I sometimes forget that.' Dot smiled. 'Would you like some coffee?'

'Not for me, thank you. I'm going to call it a night. Sleep well, ladies, and thank you again for your kindness and hospitality, Dot.'

'Not at all, Charlie. Good night.'

'So far so good,' Rob said, sitting down at the table and reclaiming the remnants of his wine. 'He's a lovely fellow. I had a word with him when we were walking – told him if he was worried or anxious in the night that I'd left a mild sedative by the bed.'

'How did he take that?'

'Said he didn't think he'd need it, but he was grateful to have it.' Rob paused.

Dot sighed. 'What a day. I'll understand if you decide to flee tomorrow,' she told Molly. 'No one would blame you.'

'Are you kidding? But I might have a nightcap and then I'll go to bed.'

'I'll join you, if I may,' Rob said. 'It's been a very strange day.'

'There's plenty of wine left, and there's a bottle of port in the guest lounge. Help yourselves!' Dot said. 'I'll leave you to it, if you don't mind.' She suddenly felt a bit awkward. 'It's been a long day, as well as an odd one, and I'm tired. See you in the morning – and thank you, Rob. I couldn't have managed without you.'

'My pleasure, Dot – the least I can do. And thank you for that lovely dinner. Good Night.'

'Sleep tight,' said Molly.

Upstairs, in her spacious bedroom looking out over the sea, Dot undressed, feeling not a little unsettled. Thank goodness they had all got through their first dinner anyway. Everyone had been so nice, so understanding, when it might have been very awkward. Molly seemed lovely, but she was a famous actress, Dot reminded herself. She was probably wary of people trying to make friends with her. In any case, she was just passing through. All the same, it was like a breath of fresh air having her around. She was so glamorous and free-spirited. Dot wished she could be more like that – but she had been businesslike and conservatively dressed all her married life: she would hardly know how to change at this stage.

Yes, it had been an extraordinary day, and she had behaved in a manner most unlike her. What would her children say if they knew she had a strange man living under her roof? Well, he'd be gone before she'd have to tell them. But it was the other man, sitting downstairs having a nightcap with Molly, who was on her mind. She knew it was ridiculous but she couldn't help feeling a bit left out. Maybe that was because it had just been her and Rob for the last ten days, until the others had arrived, and she had grown used to his company. She could have stayed chatting with them both, of course, but something had made her feel a little superfluous to the situation, perhaps that Rob had seemed so taken with Molly – which was why she had claimed she was tired. And she was weary – but it took longer than usual for her to fall asleep.

Eleven

Back in his cottage Ryan made a few work calls while the time difference still allowed. The internet connection didn't seem as reliable as he had hoped: he'd check that out with Dot tomorrow. But right now he was bone tired. Come to think of it, Dot had seemed pretty wiped out herself by the end of dinner. He couldn't say he blamed her. *Man!* When Charlie had seriously asked if someone would mind telling him where he was and what he was doing there he had almost choked on his wine. He sure hadn't seen that coming! Neither had Molly, if the look on her face was anything to go by.

Dot had handled the situation like a real pro, he thought. It must have been super-awkward for her. Not as awkward as it was for Charlie, though. Ryan couldn't begin to imagine not knowing who you or even your family were – it didn't bear thinking about. Because then he had to ask himself, Do I even know who I am? And he wasn't at all sure of the answer. He wondered why he'd been so open about his family history at dinner. Usually it was a subject he avoided like root-canal treatment. But Charlie had asked so simply, and was in such a lonesome position, it hadn't seemed right to be evasive. He really hoped for Charlie's sake his folks would show up soon, but either way – Ryan yawned – he wasn't planning on getting involved in any local dramas. He had enough going on in his own life. He was here to do a job – that was all.

Thinking of family brought him back to Joni. Everything about her was different from his own family. Looking ruefully at the big empty bed in the cottage, he couldn't help thinking how much more inviting it would be if she were there to share it – how silly it was they weren't together. He took out his phone and pressed her number, then lay back on the bed crossing his feet.

'Hey, sweetheart.' Ryan's voice was warm with equal parts affection and wine.

'Hey, yourself!' She sounded surprised and pleased to hear him. 'How are you doing?'

'I'd be doing better if you were here. There's an awfully nice big empty bed.'

Joni laughed softly.

'Actually, I'm dead beat and just about to turn in … I wanted to hear your voice.'

'What's the cottage like?' He heard the smile in her voice.

'It's cute – you'd love it.' For just a beat Ryan wondered, Should he ask her to marry him right now? Her voice was warm, he was missing her, and—

'Well, I did choose it!' She was teasing.

'Joni?'

'Mmm?'

'What are you doing now?'

He listened as she reeled off a list of items and places on her to-do list that made him feel even more tired than he already was. And, somehow, the tender moment slipped away.

'Listen,' Joni said, 'I have to go now, honey. You get some sleep and call me tomorrow. Love you!'

'Love you too.' Ryan was thoughtful as he hung up and put his phone on the table. Maybe it was just as well. He pulled off his shirt. Maybe he *should* let Joni propose. It had been her suggestion, after all. But there was nothing to stop him buying a ring. That way he'd be prepared even if she did catch him off guard. Then he'd be covered either way, which felt like a good strategy. Minutes later he was flat out on the bed.

The lyrics of a country tune floated by somewhere in the distance, reminding him briefly how long it had been since he'd picked up his guitar. That had been the other thing that had got him through the tough times. But then he had met Frank Levi and his life had taken a very different turn, leaving his guitar and song-writing far behind.

Merry couldn't sleep and had given up trying. She sat now on the back-door step of her childhood home letting the gentle night wash over her. A full moon was high, lighting Jan's polytunnels and the fields beyond. In the bushes to the right something rustled and moved, and in the distance an owl called. Above her, a thick river of stars twisted through the night sky. It was too early in the year to see the Pleiades, or the Seven Sisters, as they were often called: they would become visible in the autumn.

When Merry was little, the story of them had entranced her, made her feel special. Her parents would take her – all three bundled up in winter woollies – to their special spot on the beach where they would drink hot chocolate and tell Merry the story.

> *In the constellation of Taurus a group of stars is known as the Pleiades,*
> *often referred to as the Seven Sisters. Of this cluster, Merope is the faintest.*
> *She is often called the Lost Sister, because at first she was not seen by astronomers,*
> *or charted like her sisters. According to legend, this was because she hid her face in shame*
> *after falling in love with a mortal man ...*

Little did Merry know back then how relevant the legend would become to her.

I am cursed, she thought. It didn't matter what she did – she had been named after a star in a stupid legend and the legend had come true. She'd fallen in love with Doug, held out for him, married him. A wonderful man, worth any wait, because she'd believed that one day he would show up in her life and he had. But wonderful though he was, Doug had still been mortal – all too mortal. And he'd made a very mortal mistake, which they had been trying to work out. And now she had to carry the guilt of the argument they'd had before he was killed – and wrestle with her struggle to forgive the man who had died to save her life.

Twelve

Joni was thoughtful after Ryan's call ended and was having difficulty focusing on work. She was relieved he had sounded so warm when they were talking despite the ultimatum she had given him – but he had made no mention of it, either.

'Uh, hello! Earth to Joni,' Imran, her long-time friend and stylist, quipped.

'Sorry!' Joni returned her attention to the particularly beautiful, soft as butter, leather satchel on the table in front of her and plucked at the strap mindlessly. She and Imran had been discussing a brand collaboration with its young duo of designers.

'I think it would be a good alignment,' Imran said. 'They're young, cutting edge, and their autumn line is to die for. We need to move quickly or someone else will – but I know they like what you're doing.'

'Okay, let's talk to them – set it up.' Joni trusted Imran's judgement implicitly, and relied on it more than she liked to admit. It wasn't just because he was her dear friend – or like the brother she'd never had – but, more importantly, he was the talented retail and fashion mind she valued most. He was one of New York's top stylists and they'd known each other since high school. She couldn't have imagined setting up her hugely successful lifestyle brand without his help and input. Now, run from the top floor of her grandmothers' house in Brooklyn, she was ever-mindful of her brand @houseofgirls and its million followers. Whatever happened with her and Ryan, she couldn't afford to let herself get distracted. Her followers had to come first. They were invested in this ultimatum, waiting for an answer too. So were her two grandmothers: their not so subtle hints about settling down had been landing all too regularly. At least her mom didn't press her on the subject. But it wouldn't have mattered what they said: Joni loved her mom, sister and grandmothers to the moon and back.

For as long as she could remember Joni had lived in a house full of women. She had vague, incoherent memories of a deep male voice at home in her very young years, as a toddler maybe, a person who'd picked her up and swung her high till she felt giddy, then handed her back to her mommy. A person whose presence was not always reassuring. A person who shouted, so she would run away and hide, a person who made her mommy cry.

Joni tried not to think about her father because he had left when she was almost three years old. She didn't remember the dingy apartment she and her older sister Meggy had lived in back then in Willets Point. *Lucky for you*, her mom would say to that. Because after Dad had left they'd moved back to her mom's old house in Brooklyn where *she* had grown up with *her* mom and dad. Grandpa and Grandma Burke. Grandpa had died shortly after, so Joni didn't remember him either, but Grandma Millie was still very much alive at eighty, reinvigorated by the acquisition of two new hips and a heart bypass. Joni's mom, Maria, said Grandma Millie would outlive them all. *She'll never die – we'll have to shoot her*, which made Grandma Millie cackle with laughter.

Grandma Millie blamed all difficulties that came their way on her daughter's unsuitable choice of husband and the inevitable demise of that ill-fated marriage. Despite her vilification of the entire Italian-American community of New York, Grandma Millie had executed an unexpected about-turn when least expected. When Joni's Grandma Romi was left widowed and penniless by her restaurant-owner husband, abandoned by her only son and forced to throw herself on the mercy of the welfare system, Grandma Millie had announced that she should come to live with them.

'You're kidding, right?' Joni's mom had said.

'Where else is she gonna live?' Grandma Millie looked up from her knitting. 'I never liked the woman, God knows, and the less said about her son, the better. But she worked hard, same as I did. She kept her marriage together and raised her son as best she could. She deserves a roof over her head and family around her in her old age. We all do.'

Joni was too young to be party to the conversation although she'd heard about it often over the years. In the event, the offer had been extended to Grandma Romi, who had accepted it gratefully, although not without reservation. *Would she have her own bathroom? Would Millie be mean to her? They had never seen eye to eye, so how would she manage to live in the house of a woman who disliked her and detested her only son?* No one but the two women had been party to the finer details of the arrangement. But a trial period had been agreed upon, and Grandma Romi had moved into the basement and never left. That had been twenty-one years ago, and Joni couldn't have imagined life without her two grandmothers.

So Joni and Meggy had grown up enveloped by a blend of Irish and Italian femininity. Grandma Millie went to Pilates, but she also knitted, baked Irish soda bread and backed horses. Grandma Romi only had to be shown an image of a dress online or in a magazine before she determinedly brought it to life on her sewing-machine. She also had a lifelong collection of zealously guarded movie magazines. Weekends were spent baking and watching movies accompanied by cookies and ice cream. The grandmothers ran a tight ship, resulting in an immaculately kept house and a kitchen that Maria, who worked as a nurse in the ER, was hardly allowed into. 'She works too hard as it is. Let her rest when she comes home.'

That no men intruded upon their cosy household hadn't occurred to Joni. It had been one of her girlfriends who casually asked her, 'How come your mom never remarried? She's cute, and not *that* old …'

Joni had asked her mom later that evening. 'Oh, honey, bless your heart!' She laughed and hugged Joni as she made for the refrigerator. 'What an idea! I don't have time to get married again. Anyhow, why would I want to when I have my two beautiful girls to keep me company?'

That had elicited glances of doting approval from the grandmothers and a sense of deep reassurance in Joni's own little heart.

'Who needs men?' Grandma Millie would say. 'They're nothing but trouble, right?' *Right!* confirmed the chorus. But somehow Joni got the feeling that the women weren't telling the whole truth, that something in her life was missing. In all the TV spots and magazines, pictures of happy families looked out at her, and they all had a dad somewhere. She found herself watching families in the park and her own friends' parents – even the ones who were divorced – and they all seemed to have a dad they could spend weekends and holidays with, sometimes even a new dad when their moms remarried.

When they were older, and Meggy was studying nursing, like their mom, she told Joni to get over it. 'Dad didn't want us, so why let him live rent free in your head? He has a whole other life now in Florida – he doesn't care about us. He doesn't even care about his *own* mother, Grandma Romi!' All of this was true, but none of it made Joni feel any better. So Joni worked hard at school, like her mom told her to. Her fifteenth birthday came and went quietly by most standards, although on that very day, 6 October 2010, another new venture was also having its birthday. Social media – which Joni loved with a passion – gained a new platform in the shape of Instagram, although Joni was blithely unaware back then of how intimately acquainted with it she would become.

Eventually, of course, there were boys. Joni was rather afraid of them so she had never courted their attention.

She kept to herself, apart from her two best friends, Becca, a tall, blonde, studious girl, and Imran, a Syrian boy. But Joni was pretty, strikingly so, and boys mistook her reticence for aloofness, which made them all the keener. It wasn't long before number 1227 Brooklyn Heights became known not just for the pretty Irish-Italian sisters it housed, but also for the astonishingly warm welcome any boy lucky enough to make it through the front door would receive. For all their derision, and constant assertions that no woman needed a man, Grandma Millie and Grandma Romi adored having them in the house. This was a revelation to Joni, who had watched open-mouthed as boys were fussed over, seated in comfy chairs and fed a succession of delicious pastas, cakes and, later, beers and wines. Her grandmas turned into altogether unrecognisable versions of themselves when young men were in the house. Even her mother, exhausted from a day or night shift at the ER, would sit down to join them for a drink. 'Just the one!' Before Joni's eyes Maria relaxed, laughed and lost the tense frown she usually wore along with her scrubs.

Unlike Meggy, who had had a steady boyfriend since she was sixteen, Joni dispensed with one boy after another – six months was the longest one had lasted – and the grandmas would sigh, saying, 'We'll miss Joe/Danny/Lenny, but if he's not the one ...' They would exchange sentimental smiles and winks. Joni knew they worried about her, although they didn't need to. She wasn't going to let any man mess up her life, no matter how much her grandmas fawned over them. She majored from New

York University in sociology and digital marketing, then did her internship in the media department of a hot new advertising agency. But all the while she was working towards her real goal. She made friends with the creatives, watched fashion stylists on the sets of TV spots and learned tricks of the trade from photographers.

At home in Brooklyn Heights, she'd had the top floor of the old house to herself since Meggy had moved out to live with Josh, her boyfriend. After work and at weekends, she'd transformed it into her studio and office. The grandmas watched goggle-eyed as willing friends hauled up clothes, props and other paraphernalia until Joni was satisfied her enterprise could begin. The website and its accompanying social-media feeds were launched, and @houseofgirls became hugely successful. Joni commented on fashion and style, shared her grandmas' baking, knitting and life-experience tips, had a health blog for women that was run by her mom, and a weekly tip for the horses, courtesy of Grandma Millie, called @Milliesfillies, which proved particularly popular.

When @houseofgirls celebrated its first year in business, Joni had more than two hundred thousand devoted followers and a ticket to every hot opening in town. She was on her way to achieving the financial independence and success she had craved. The hours were long and unsociable – influencers didn't get days off. Everything was fodder for the 'gram. Joni worked with brands and products she felt she could promote, and mostly deflected the increasing trail of hopeful young men who approached her. She dated more out of a concern for keeping her brand current and visible, and since she had to be seen in the city's hot new restaurants and bars, she figured she might as well do it in the company of an entertaining, preferably hot guy, although mostly she preferred hanging with her old gang, Imran, now a successful stylist, and Becca, diligently climbing the finance ladder.

'Mr Perfect doesn't exist,' Imran told her regularly. 'You do realise that, don't you?'

'I'm just picky.' Joni scrolled through her DMs as Imran put the finishing touches to an Urban Cowgirl look he was styling for a shoot. 'I just haven't met the right guy yet.'

'Good luck with *thaaat*.' Imran was sceptical.

'He's out there – I know he is.' Joni sounded surer than she was.

But then eight months ago, while she was casually swiping right on a potential Tinder match, Ryan Shindler came into her life.

Joni didn't like to dwell too much on whom she would choose if it came down to her followers or Ryan. In the world in which she'd grown up, women who relied on men hadn't done too well out of the exchange. But she was prepared to commit her life to Ryan – or at least some of it. There was always divorce if it didn't work out, right? So she must love him a lot. Ryan was successful, handsome and good for her career – even if he did think Instagram was a crazy game. But that was before he realised how much money she was making from it.

Thirteen

Molly blinked awake and looked at her watch in disbelief. It was half past eight! She'd slept right through the night! She'd even managed without her sleeping pill, which sat on the bedside table beside the untouched glass of water. And she still felt deliciously sleepy. For a moment she thought about drifting back – she couldn't remember the last time she'd slept so soundly – but sunlight was streaming through the little paned window prompting her to begin her adventure and investigate her surroundings.

After a quick shower and a cup of tea, she was ready. She didn't rush to scan the news on her phone or listen to a favourite podcast, as she usually did. There was something about the silence here that was different – calming, reassuring. It didn't feel empty or ominous, as it had in London. She pulled on her wax jacket and opened the front door of her cottage to find Honey sitting outside, thumping her tail in greeting. 'Well, hello to you too!' Molly said. There was no sign of life from her neighbour across the way, although the curtains were open, so perhaps he was already about his day. Either way, Honey seemed to think Molly a better bet for some company, as she gazed expectantly up at her.

Molly didn't feel like going through Dot's house just yet, so she followed the path around to the right, Honey at her heels. This led to a little lane, and a gate, and another lane, which led out onto the road, then around a curve, where Molly stopped to take in the breathtakingly beautiful bay that stretched out its arms before her. Dot hadn't been exaggerating when she'd said they were minutes from the beach, and Molly longed to walk there, but for now she wanted to get her bearings, which meant turning the other way, and heading into the village.

It didn't take long. There was Main Street, of course, with a small supermarket, O'Hagan's pub, and some dear little shops. Off to the left, along another little street, she found the bank, and the library, and in the other direction a sweet little Church of Ireland church that seemed to be closed, but advertised a gathering and a show for a local artist in a week's time. She followed the road on, which led to a pretty harbour, where a few small fishing boats were being worked on and a series of gulls cried and wheeled overhead.

Honey went to investigate some nearby baskets while Molly sat down to take some photos of the restful scene, when she felt someone observing her.

When she turned, the girl – young, sturdy build and wild dark hair – looked away, embarrassed to be caught, but then sneaked another glance. Honey ran up to her, and the girl bent down to make a fuss of her.

Molly walked over to her. 'Hello.'

'I know you, don't I? From the telly.' The words rushed out as the girl straightened.

'Probably.' Molly smiled. 'I'm Molly. I'm staying at Dot's place for a while.'

'I guessed.' The girl pointed to the dog. 'Everyone knows Honey.' She shoved her hands into her pockets. 'I'm Franny. You're here for the festival, aren't you? We didn't think you'd be here so soon. My friend Sheena's going to be psyched! I can't wait to tell her I met you.'

'I've just come away early for a bit of a break – some quiet time – before the festival.'

'Then you're staying where Charlie is.'

'Yes. Well, not exactly. Charlie's in the main house. I've got one of the cottages.'

'But you've met him? Talked to him?'

'Oh, yes. He's very nice.'

'I know. I've met him too – he asked me for directions yesterday. It must be horrible not knowing where you are, or who you are – I can't imagine. I didn't know that then, obviously.'

'He's being really brave about it. Hopefully we'll find out where he's from soon – lots of people are working on it.'

'That's what they said about climate change – and no one's done anything about that except someone my age. Adults just talk. They never do anything unless there's loads of money in it.' Franny sounded cross.

'You might have a point there.' Molly was careful not to smile, although Franny's face had set in a spectacular scowl.

'And now some mega-rich Americans have bought our golf course. They'll probably end up wrecking the environment. It shouldn't be allowed. Ecological experts had to get involved to make sure they didn't upset the environment of the *Vertigo angustior*.' Apparently registering Molly's blank response, Franny elaborated. 'That's a snail.'

'Oh, I see.' Molly thought of Ryan, and remembered him saying he was involved in a new golf resort. She supposed he was well used to disgruntled locals and knew how to handle them, but she thought Franny might not be so easily won over. 'Are you very interested in the environment?'

'Oh, yes. I'm thinking of being something to do with marine conservation when I'm older. Like Merry used to do. Do you know Merry? Her parents own the café. I work there on Saturdays and holidays. I'm on my way there now. Merry's a good friend of mine.'

'I look forward to having coffee in the Seashell – and meeting Merry.'

'She's really nice, but she's been different since she came home from America.' Franny seemed disappointed. 'There was a horrible accident and her husband was killed – it's changed her.'

'That's so sad.' Molly brushed away a strand of hair that had blown across her face. 'How old is she?'

'Thirty-three. Our birthdays are a month apart, and she's always been like an older sister to me.'

'Well, she's certainly young enough to meet someone else she can fall in love with one day. Although that's not something to say to a grieving widow.'

Franny nodded. 'My mam warned me not to say that to her, ever.'

'Very good advice.'

'Have you ever been in love?'

'Yes, I have, several times. But it didn't work out very well for me. After a while I decided to forget about men and concentrate on my career.' Molly smiled.

'What's it like being a famous actress?' She fixed Molly with a quizzical gaze.

'I'm not that famous. It can be a lot of fun if you're cut out for it – and not everyone who wants to act *is* cut out for it. But it's jolly hard work. There's a lot of luck involved too. You don't want to be depending on it totally to earn a living – not until you get going anyway. Why do you ask? Was it another career you were considering?'

'Me? No way!' Franny was clearly under no illusions. 'I'm not thin enough, or pretty enough – but Sheena's thinking about it. You'll meet her if you're here for a bit.'

'Franny, acting isn't about how thin or pretty you are.' Molly was patient and tried to keep exasperation from her voice. She couldn't bear to think of the pressure young girls were under these days, not to mention the misconceptions. 'It's about the ability to express and inhabit another character believably. You have a wonderfully expressive face.'

Franny gave a tight little smile and blushed. But Molly could tell she was pleased – that she had said the right thing.

'Mam's always telling me I'm too nosy, but you have to have an enquiring nature. But then people keep telling you *not* to ask questions either – so how are you supposed to find anything out?'

'I think you're right,' Molly said. 'You would need an enquiring nature, but there's a difference between being enquiring and being *intrusive*. Does that make sense?'

'I'd hate to think I was being intrusive – especially when people were upset.'

'I'm sure you'd never be intrusive.' Molly felt a rush of affection for this young local girl, who seemed to carry the worries of the world on her shoulders – she was so unlike other teenagers Molly was familiar with, who all seemed sophisticated beyond their years. Then an idea struck her. 'But if you want to put your enquiring nature to good use, and take your mind off climate change and golf courses for a bit, why don't you see if you can dig anything up about Charlie? I'm sure you're much better on the computer than any of us oldies.'

'I might. Anyhow, I'd better get going. I can't wait to tell Sheena you're here.' Franny waved as she walked away.

Molly sat for a little longer, taking in the sights and sounds of the harbour as a gentle breeze lifted her hair. She wondered how Charlie was feeling today – and, while she thought of it, she emailed her old voice coach to ask if she would look into tracking down Charlie's accent if she sent her a recording. It was a long shot, but every little detail would help.

After a while she whistled for Honey and, on a whim, went over to look at her childhood friend Sally Doherty's old family house. It was still there on Harbour Terrace, where the houses seemed far more groomed and prosperous than they had when she was last here. But this house seemed empty – possibly it was a holiday home now. Anyway, what had she expected to find? She peered through the windows for old times' sake, then turned around to make her way back.

'You won't find anyone at home in number three.' An elderly woman on a Rollator parked outside smiled at her. 'You won't remember me but I'm Peggy O'Sullivan. I'd know you anywhere! Welcome back to Derrybeggs, Molly Cusack.'

It took a minute, but Molly *did* remember Peggy – although she was frail now the voice was unmistakable. 'Of course I remember you, Peggy!' Molly hugged her. 'It's been a long time.' Peggy used to run the funny little shop that sold sweets and seaside trinkets when Molly was a child. She remembered eagerly getting a new bucket and spade and inflatable swimming ring there every year as a little girl.

'It certainly has,' Peggy said. 'You're over for the festival, of course?'

'I am. I wanted a bit of a break before it – although I hear on the grapevine things haven't been running according to plan.'

'You can say that again.' Peggy gave a bark of a laugh. 'I'm on the committee, in a manner of speaking, but all of us seniors were left in no doubt that our opinions were very last-century so we left them to it. At the time it seemed sensible.'

'Dot was talking about it at dinner. She's going to call a meeting, and I'm going to help if I can – all hands on deck sort of thing. She's speaking to your chairperson today, as far as I remember. You'll come to the meeting, won't you, Peggy? It'll be fun.'

'I'm not sure that's how Kate Carmichael will see it.' Peggy grinned. 'But I'll be there – if only to see Kate and the Culture Club put through their paces.'

'Good. I'll let Dot know you're coming.'

'I'll look forward to it.' Peggy set off. 'You haven't changed a bit, you know!' she called over her shoulder.

It was funny, Molly thought, as she strolled back to the harbour with Honey, how easily the years fell away now she was back in Derrybeggs. It was almost possible to imagine she had never spent all those years in England desperately building her career. It had seemed hard back then when she had been going to endless auditions looking for a break, but now they seemed easy compared with the other task that lay ahead of her of meeting Larry's deadline – thinking of which, she should do some writing this afternoon. And yet it was so hard, making an effort with her memoir. The constant looking back at what had gone before made Molly feel as if her life were already over.

Fourteen

Sitting at the breakfast table, Dot stared grimly at her iPad. She had left the most challenging call until last, although now she knew she should have spoken to Kate Carmichael first and got it over with, since the woman was in the chair. But for one thing she couldn't face her cold, so to speak, and for another she wanted to sound out a few of the others to see how they felt about calling this impromptu meeting: that way she could bolster her confidence. So far the reaction was positive – particularly when it was announced that Molly Cusack would be in attendance. Now Dot pressed Kate's number on her iPad while she sat at the kitchen table and glanced at the newspaper beside her.

'Hello? Yes? What is it, Dot?' Kate's exasperated voice made her head whip up. To her horror she realised she had somehow pressed the FaceTime option and not a normal call. Blast these wretched contraptions! Now Kate, who appeared to be juggling golfing paraphernalia and exiting her truck of a car was peering crossly into her phone and would see that Dot, whose rapidly pinking face was makeup free, had flour on her hands and now her nose. The realisation made her promptly lose what little air of authority she had hoped to inject into the call. She tried hurriedly to explain she was calling because there was a need for an extraordinary meeting of the committee and that she was ready to hold it at her house.

'What? I'm running late already, Dot. I can't discuss this now – it'll have to wait.'

'I'm afraid it can't, Kate,' Dot said, standing her ground and running a hand through her now floury hair.

As if to distract her further, Charlie and Molly chose that very moment to wander into the kitchen, Charlie ambling down the three steps leading from the hall at one end, looking well rested and cheerful, and Molly coming through the back door from the garden. They met in the middle of the room by the table where Dot was sitting and were now exchanging morning greetings, swapping details of how well they had slept. It was becoming like Grand Central Station.

'Oops, sorry.' Molly clamped a hand over her mouth and reached across the table for the jug of milk. 'Didn't realise you were on a call.' She backed away quickly.

But not before Kate Carmichael had caught sight of the famous actress on her phone screen. Kate's tone changed accordingly, immediately becoming both conciliatory and condescending. 'Of course, Dot, yes, I understand. Ellen and I will be there.' There was a brief pause. 'Is that who I think it is in the background with you?' Kate adopted a conspiratorial manner.

'Yes, it is, Kate.' Dot maximised the effect of the happy coincidence. 'And I'm happy to say Molly Cusack has been kind enough to agree to join us at this meeting to offer her unparalleled experience. Haven't you, Molly?' Dot motioned for Molly to look into the camera and Molly obligingly waved on cue.

'Well! *Well*!' Kate was momentarily stymied but recovered herself in time to say, 'Please tell Molly how *very* much I'm looking forward to meeting her. Now I really must dash.' And the screen cut to black.

'Thank you for that,' Dot said to Molly, who was pouring tea from the pot.

'Any time.' Molly grinned. 'Is she the one? There's always one on every committee.'

'Yes, Kate Carmichael is the one. But at least we've got a meeting nailed down in a week.'

'Great. You can fill me in later.'

'I was thinking' – Charlie sat down between them – 'I'd like to go into the village this morning, take a stroll, go back to that nice café, the Seashell. Dr Rob is taking me for some tests this afternoon, so I may not get the chance if I don't go now.'

'I'd like that too,' said Molly. 'I'd be happy to go with you?'

'You've got yourself a deal,' said Charlie, smiling as he took the coffee Dot had poured for him.

'Speaking of deals,' Molly went on, 'I had an idea last night after you'd gone to bed, Charlie. I was just saying to Dot that it might be an idea to record you speaking for a few moments and send it to my voice coach. She might be able to narrow down your accent to a particular area – it's a long shot but every little helps. What do you think? Would you be willing to do that?'

'I think that's a really great idea. I'd be happy to do it.'

'Great stuff!' Molly whipped out her phone. 'Let's do it now.'

'That reminds me,' said Dot to Charlie. 'We'll need to get you a phone so you can be contactable. We can put all the relevant numbers into it so we're at the touch of a button if you need us. I'm going into town today – I'll pick one up.'

'Good thinking,' said Molly.

'Could I read something to record?' Charlie asked. 'I'd feel kinda self-conscious just talking 'bout nothing in particular.'

'Of course you can,' Molly agreed. 'Whatever you feel most comfortable with.'

'There's shelves stacked with books in the reading room.' Dot pointed. 'I'm sure you'll find something there – it'll be quieter too.'

The reading room lived up to expectations with restful dove-grey walls, a large bay window and two comfy couches either side of the fireplace. Along the length of one wall were floor to ceiling book shelves. In an alcove at the other end of the room an old upright piano stood – almost hidden. Charlie wandered over to the shelves and perused a few titles before settling on and taking down a large volume of poetry.

'Ready?' asked Molly, as she primed her phone to record. 'Just a minute or two will do.'

Charlie scanned the contents, found the page he was looking for, and began to read.

Listening to him, Molly thought how right she had

been last night when she'd observed to Dot that he had a lovely voice.

'"The mind is its own place and in itself, can make a Heaven of Hell, a Hell of Heaven."' Charlie closed the book. 'Will that do?'

'That was lovely.' Molly saved the recording and sent it to her voice coach as an attachment. '*Paradise Lost*.'

'Thought Milton would be kind of appropriate under the circumstances.' Charlie was rueful. 'Reminds me I'm not alone in forgetting who I am or where I'm from – folks have been losing sight of things since time immemorial.'

'Don't you worry.' Molly took his arm. 'You're going to find out who you are very soon – I just know it. You know your poetry for starters – that's a clue! Now, let's take that stroll into the village.'

Fifteen

The sun was blazing through the café window, and Merry was opening the morning's post when she caught sight of an American stamp halfway down the pile on an official-looking envelope. She hesitated, then took a deep breath and opened it – it was the court-appointed lawyer. He was flying over and wanted to meet her in person because apparently there were important matters to discuss regarding insurance. She shivered. Did he mean money? As if money could ever compensate for Doug's death. The doorbell tinkled and she shoved the letter under the counter as if it were a guilty secret.

'Good morning, Charlie.' Merry showed him to a discreet table with a view over the bay.

'Hello again, Merry! Molly is coming back to get me so I won't be here the entire day again.' He smiled.

'That's fine, Charlie.' She gave a half-smile. 'What can I get you?'

'Coffee, just black, please.'

*

As Merry left to get his order, Charlie looked around the place, taking note of details he had failed to notice yesterday. The location was beautiful: the building looked out from a peninsula across an inlet and then to the Atlantic beyond. The café itself was painted in varying shades of blue and some seriously good seascapes were artfully arranged on the walls. A rope twisted with seashells and small bells served to announce when anyone came in or went out of the door. Everywhere he saw shells of varying shapes and sizes displayed on any available nook or cranny. The place wasn't to everyone's taste, he guessed, but it had a definite charm all its own. At any rate Charlie thanked his lucky stars he had wound up there – however arbitrarily. Thanks to the good people of this place, he felt protected and cared for at a time when he was acutely vulnerable.

Who am I? The question reverberated around his head till it made him nauseous. Yesterday, when they'd found him, he was still reeling from confusion – but today the seriousness of his situation stood out in sharp relief. At least he hadn't lost his marbles – not as far as he could tell anyway. His mind was still functioning – he could reason, remember the people and place since he had shown up here. But what had happened to him? His stomach lurched when he considered the possibilities. Thank God people were looking into the case. Dr Rob had organised cognitive tests for later today, while Dot and her guests couldn't have made him feel more welcome or been more concerned for him. Everyone was being so kind. So, he would just have to struggle through this terrible episode – whatever it was – just continue to be as pleasant as he knew how, and hope desperately that some missing part of the jigsaw would come together, that some clue would surface to indicate who he was and who his people were. Until then he had to act as normally as he felt able to. Show his gratitude to these good people. *Just be yourself*, the instruction echoed in his mind. If only, he thought, he knew who that was. How could he be himself? he wondered miserably, when his entire life had just been wrenched away from him.

*

'That's him, isn't it?' Franny whispered, when Merry came back behind the counter. 'I met him yesterday. He was lost and asked me for directions.'

'Charlie's staying at Dot's until they can find out where he's from.'

'It's so horrible that he can't remember. He seemed so nice.'

'He *is* nice. He just can't remember stuff.'

'I was telling him how I'm worried about climate change and stuff and he was really nice to me – said most things people worry about never actually happen.'

'He's right.' Merry smiled. 'Most things don't.' She turned away quickly.

'Oh, God, I'm so thick!' Franny clamped her hand to her mouth. 'I didn't mean—'

'It's all right, Franny. Look, I've had to get used to the way things are now and I'd much rather people didn't keep walking on eggshells around me. Honestly! This is how my life is now and I've accepted it. You keep calling things just the way they are – that's what the world needs more of.'

But as Merry turned away from Franny, she was transported back to Santa Barbara and that awful day again. She saw the imposing exterior of Our Lady of Sorrows Church bathed in mid-morning sunlight as clearly as if it was yesterday and not almost two years ago. The serenity of the day was marred by the flock of heartbroken mourners in head-to-toe black emerging from funeral cars, like a cloud of blackbirds. She had felt, rather than seen, the visceral hatred of Doug's mother and sisters, who thought of her as the woman who'd stolen their beautiful boy – not once, but twice, this time finally.

They must have thought she'd cast an evil spell over him. And it had been like magic. Doug had been engaged to Kristy when Merry had walked into his store to buy diving gear. Two weeks later, he had broken off his engagement, and he and Merry were together.

They would hate her even more when she was the beneficiary of the insurance payment.

They'd been married quietly, early one Saturday morning, in a tiny quaint church in the Latino quarter, just the two of them. Shortly afterwards, they'd gone to Derrybeggs for a belated and distinctly crowded honeymoon. Little had they known then how short-lived their life as newly-weds would be.

The funeral had been painstakingly put together, with hushed collaborations over which Merry had been consulted and had as quickly dismissed. Merry could still barely remember the sequence of that hideous day. But she would always remember her mother-in-law's parting words to her outside the church when Merry had tried to offer her condolences. Betty had looked at her with raw hatred and said, in a voice as cold as ice, 'Please don't! My son is dead because of you.'

'She doesn't mean it,' Eva whispered afterwards, as she and Jan ushered her away, gaunt with shock and grief themselves. But Merry had known Betty meant every word. What Betty couldn't have known, though, was that her shattered daughter-in-law concurred wholeheartedly with her sentiments.

Pulling herself together, Merry took Charlie's coffee over to him, swerving just in time as the doorbell jangled and the opening door almost caught her.

'Nice save,' said Charlie, as she placed the coffee in front of him.

'Occupational hazard.' Merry smiled thinly.

'Oh, hey, Charlie,' said Ryan. 'I didn't see you there, how're you doing?'

'I'm good, thank you!' Charlie smiled. 'Would you care to join me?'

'Uh, thanks, Charlie, I appreciate the offer, but I need to send some emails – work stuff. The connection at Dot's isn't good. She said it was better here.' He turned to Merry. 'Could I get an espresso please, and your internet password?'

'Sure, the password's Seashell. I'll bring your coffee over.'

'May I?' He gestured to a corner table.

'Be my guest.'

'Just passing through?' Merry asked, when she came back with his coffee.

'Thank you. No – I have some business at the golf course.' Merry was halfway towards the counter when he called her back. 'Excuse me?' He was pleasant but Merry sensed the flicker of irritation. 'This is an Americano. I asked for an espresso.' He smiled.

Damn! She hadn't been paying attention. 'No worries. My bad. I'll be right back.'

She should have guessed, Merry thought, heading back behind the counter. She'd heard talk of some whizz-kid guy being sent over to sign off on the golf club. She knew his type – rich, good-looking, and entitled – and driving as ostentatious a car as it was possible to find with an eco-friendly badge on it. Merry knew exactly what those people were like. Same as the kids who'd mowed Doug down in the water, and kept driving right on.

Sixteen

Kate Carmichael had driven a considerable distance to do part of her weekly shop at the lovely smart deli supermarket in another town. This was partly because she needed a fix of what she called 'decent, contemporary brand choice', but also because she preferred to shop and browse anonymously. In Derrybeggs, everyone knew who she was, and she felt the contents of her trolley were simply one of a long list of things that were discussed about her in detail among the locals. Not that she cared, of course, but shopping was something she found soothing. She liked to lose herself in the process and she couldn't do that when she felt people were peering at her and making mental notes of her choice of groceries. Derrybeggs was far too incestuous. Everyone knew everybody else and their business – which seemed to take place for the most part in that dreadfully twee café, the Seashell. The walls had ears in that place – but the coffee was good and Jan's organic vegetables that Kate had delivered couldn't be bettered. Restaurants for miles around swore by them.

This train of thought brought Merry to Kate's mind. Merry was a rather odd girl, in Kate's opinion. She'd heard all about what had happened – how her husband had been killed in a boating accident and how Merry had come home from America. Kate had been in Derrybeggs only a short while when she'd heard the story – and had conjured up a rather sympathetic image of a grieving young widow and was prepared to act accordingly, offering Merry her deepest condolences when she eventually met her. Her illusions had been rudely shaken, if not shattered, when she had approached Merry in the café one day. And her name was odd – Kate had called her Mary for ages before someone told her it was Merry. Her parents were Dutch so presumably that was it.

But when Kate had offered Merry her condolences and assured her in a very confidential manner that she was available for coffee or lunch to talk, if Merry ever needed a sympathetic shoulder, Merry had been polite but unforthcoming. Not at all as grateful or enthusiastic as Kate would have liked. In fact, Kate had felt quite rebuffed, although she couldn't quite explain how, in so many words. It was more the girl's manner. The thing was – and Kate had discussed this with Ellen – that Merry didn't appear to be grieving. In fact only the other day, when Kate had been on her way back from a talk by a visiting health expert and had stopped to pick up a coffee to go in a trendy new restaurant, she had seen Merry having lunch with a very attractive guy. Merry was listening intently to whatever he was saying. They had the look of a couple deeply interested in one another – not related, although of course it was possible. At any rate Merry wasn't behaving like a woman stunned by grief – for all everybody talked about how sad it was.

Kate hadn't been happy with the way the last committee meeting for the film festival had gone. It was hardly *her* fault that the community hall had been damaged in a fire. It was high summer so of course everywhere else was already booked up – what did the committee expect? She had been downright magnanimous, she felt, in offering to host the opening night in her own house – but that idea had gone down like a lead balloon. Just as well, really: when she'd mentioned the idea to her husband Don afterwards, thinking she might still be able to swing it with the committee, he'd said, 'No way, absolutely not,' with such vehemence Kate was taken aback. It wasn't often he put his foot down about something but when he did, he was as stubborn as a mule. At least she didn't have to renege on the offer to the committee – that would have been even more awkward – but the fact that they had turned it down without considering it was irritating enough in itself.

But what else could they expect? Ellen had said afterwards. The locals were bound to resent someone like Kate, who had such flair and was from Dublin, trying to drag their pathetic little film festival into the twenty-first century. 'Let them at it!' had been Ellen's advice. But Kate did not want to leave things as they were.

Then this morning Kate had been interrupted on her way to meet some friends for a quick nine holes in a neighbouring course by that blow-in Dot – whom everyone had taken under their wing since she had bought and renovated the Old Rectory. Kate didn't get it. The woman was older than her by at least a decade and was hardly stylish – in fact her entire wardrobe, as far as Kate could make out, seemed to consist of wax jackets, quilted jerkins, jeans and wellies. Her house was nice, if you liked that sort of thing, but not a patch on Kate's own modern mansion. She had picked up the call from Dot accidentally, hitting Accept instead of Decline as she juggled her clubs, to be informed that an extraordinary meeting of the committee was called – and not only that but that Molly Cusack, whom Kate and Ellen had actually approached to open the festival in the first place, would now be joining their meeting to help. It was totally out of order. She, Kate, was chairperson – she should be calling the shots. Well, they could go ahead and make their silly plans. She had a plan herself that would make them sit up and take notice – and also make her look good.

She reminded herself of her current favourite motto from Michelle Obama: *When they go low – we go high.*

Seventeen

It was just an email, like the other emails Ryan had sent her. The last time they had spoken was when he had called her the night he arrived in Ireland. Joni was back in her office at the top of her house, after an early start at a photo shoot in Central Park with Imran for some new looks for her website. Now Imran had gone to get some coffee so she could study Ryan's emails in peace. The latest one had pinged on her phone when they were shooting – but when she saw it was from Ryan, she was too frightened of being distracted or upset to open it. It had been a wise move on Joni's part: if she'd read the email during the photo shoot, the whole park and its environs might have heard her scream in frustration. Also she didn't want to give Imran, who had been cautioning her more and more about Ryan recently, the information or the satisfaction. She had waited until she was home, away from prying eyes, although she'd had to sneak upstairs quietly to avoid Grandma Millie, who had been busy in the kitchen with her first batch of soda bread.

Now, at her desk, Joni read the email again, practising her special slow yoga breathing technique. *Hey, sweetheart* – well, nothing new there: Ryan's preferred term of endearment had always been 'sweetheart'. Then there was a bit about the place, how cute the cottage was, how much he thought she would have liked it, how work was keeping him super busy. Something about a film festival in the local town and an actress called Molly Cusack, who was staying there – Joni thought the name rang a bell, but didn't know her. And then … Joni's gaze sharpened as she reread the information. Then Ryan went into this bizarre account of some dinner in the main house and some guy called Charlie, who wasn't really Charlie but they had called him that because he couldn't remember his real name or who he was or where he came from. He had been found wandering in the area and the woman who owned the guesthouse and cottages seemed to have just *taken him in*. I mean, what the hell was that about? Was it some kind of halfway house, or something? Joni had read about places like that where people went from prison or rehab to a kind of semi-normal house or sheltered development so they could readjust to life outside an institution before being let out to fully integrate into normal life.

She clicked on the website again of the idyllic country house by the sea and the two adorable cottages on its land, but there was no mention of sheltering ex-cons or addicts. She couldn't figure it out. But that wasn't what was worrying her: Ryan did not appear to be reflecting on their situation as he should have been. Joni got up from her laptop and began to pace the room. This wasn't how it was supposed to go. She had listened to people, her friends, her followers, and all of them had been in agreement that she should give Ryan an ultimatum: if he wasn't prepared to commit to a future with her, he wasn't worth it and she was wasting her time.

Joni found herself chewing a nail as she paced, a habit she hadn't indulged in for at least twenty years. What if – it didn't bear thinking about, but she had to consider the possibility – they were all wrong? What if she was on course not to a happy proposal but to losing Ryan? She felt a cold hand clutch at her heart. Either way, she had to reply to the stupid email and she had to strike the right note. She must not show any weakness, or betray any nerves, but she had to feign interest and compassion towards the situation 'Charlie' found himself in. So she sent back an email saying how pleased she was that he was enjoying the place and how busy she was with her website. She looked forward to hearing more about Ireland. Then she signed it with her two usual kisses, and hoped against hope that when she pressed the send button, he would be as disappointed with her email as she had been with his.

The sound of her grandmothers laughing floated up from downstairs as the door opened and Imran appeared with their coffee. 'You're looking anxious. What's up?' He gave her a knowing look.

'Nothing,' Joni lied, taking the coffee gratefully. 'At least, nothing a good dose of caffeine won't fix.' She smiled up at him.

'It's no use bluffing. I know that look – it's the same one you used to get when you thought you hadn't studied hard enough for a test. You're worried about something. Can I help?' He was sympathetic. 'You know my mission is to make your life easier. Speaking of which,' he waved an envelope at her as he sat down at his desk, 'I got us front-row seats to the Harper's gig.'

Joni's face lit up. 'Get outta here!'

'You're welcome!'

'What would I do without you?'

'Let's hope you don't ever have to find out.'

Eighteen

Rob was concerned. He had thought this would be an open-and-shut case. But now, five days into the bizarre chain of events, no one was any closer to knowing who Charlie was, or where he was from. Since Dot's house had become the hub of all things Charlie-related, Rob had swung by on his way back from visiting a patient to bring her up to speed with the latest developments, which happily coincided with afternoon tea.

He was also hoping he might catch Ryan if he happened to be around. Rob was dying to get in a round or two on the spectacular new links when it opened, which would certainly put Derrybeggs on the map – as far as golf courses were concerned, at any rate. Rob doubted he could afford to fork out the outrageously expensive joining fee he had heard rumours of – anyway, he wouldn't be around long enough to justify a year's membership – but Ryan might be able to arrange for him to have a three-month temporary membership, or something like that. He liked Ryan: he had talked to him at length at that dinner at Dot's house and found him to be an entertaining and level-headed young man.

It had been quite a night, what with Charlie suddenly

wondering where he was, and meeting Molly Cusack, the famous actress. Dot had handled the whole evening really well – he had to hand it to her: he would never have thought for a moment she would offer to take Charlie into her home, but her kind act had earned her a new place of respect in the heart of the community. Derrybeggs, like most villages, tended to be wary of newcomers, especially the second-home brigade. But Dot had sold up in Dublin and moved lock, stock and barrel to Derrybeggs, which must have taken a certain amount of courage, especially as a widow, Rob felt. He admired her for it, but not as much as he admired her for taking Charlie in – way beyond the call of duty. It showed you could never tell what people were capable of when the chips were down.

'It's very peculiar,' Rob said now, as he munched an apple turnover in Dot's kitchen. 'No one seems to have lost a relative from their home. No retirement homes or hospitals have reported anyone missing.' He and Dot had been making constant phone calls since Charlie had arrived in the village and neither they nor the police had had any report of anyone missing.

'The social worker came yesterday to see how he was doing and brought more clothes, but she didn't say much,' Dot said. 'Just wanted to know if it was all right for him to continue staying here – they're covering his costs, at least.'

'And is it all right for him to stay?' Rob was concerned. 'It's a big imposition.'

'Oh, I don't mind. He's such a nice man – he's no trouble.'

'But he can't stay indefinitely.' Rob frowned.

'Well, no, but they'll find out where he belongs any day now, surely.'

'I'm not so sure,' Rob said. 'Detective Foley called about an hour ago to say Interpol were involved – that means this may not be as simple as it would seem.'

'How d'you mean?' Dot was perplexed.

'Well, it wouldn't be the first time something like this has happened. I've been doing a bit of research myself. There was a chap a few years ago found wandering on a beach – no memory, no ID. One of the theories was he'd jumped ship – I think he turned out to be with the Norwegian Navy in the end. In another case a chap was found wandering outside a Tesco in the UK – but he clearly had Alzheimer's. He had an American accent, and could only tell people his name was Joe. Took them seven months to track down his people. It turned out he'd been flown over by his son and dumped in the UK – the guy had paid an accomplice to lead poor Joe out of town and leave him somewhere he wouldn't be traced to. Very sad.'

'How cruel!' Dot was horrified. 'What happened to him?'

'There was a happy ending, of sorts. Once he was identified, he was repatriated to the US and, last I read, was happy in a state care home. While he was in the UK they had to put him in a residential care home too.' Rob was thoughtful. 'That's what will probably happen with Charlie, too – if no one claims him.'

'But he doesn't have Alzheimer's, does he?'

'I'm pretty sure it's not that, although there's always a chance – the final tests come back later this week but the cognitive specialist I spoke with doesn't think it's impairment of that nature.'

'What could it be, then?'

'The specialist offered another possibility – one that had crossed my mind too. He may be suffering from dissociative fugue state.'

'What on earth is that?'

'A sudden and complete memory wipe, basically.' Rob reached for a scone. 'And it can happen to anyone – at any time.'

'Really?' Dot looked alarmed.

'Yes. I could be sitting here right now one minute talking to you – and the next I might have no idea where I am or who I am.'

'Just like Charlie.'

'Yes. But obviously if you're in familiar surroundings with family or friends when fugue strikes, they can get you help and explain the situation. It can also sometimes be triggered by trauma – but not necessarily. Funnily enough, it can happen if you're swimming in cold water – but that seems to affect men more than women and it wears off faster, usually within twenty-four hours. There's another name for that – can't think of it just now. Basically' – Rob tapped the side of his head – 'the mind is a wonderfully unpredictable instrument. But I promise you, Dot, whatever happens to me, I will never forget how delicious these scones are.'

'Just who made them for you!' Dot laughed. 'But don't worry, I'll remind you.'

'On the bright side,' Rob went on, 'the positive aspect of fugue – although it's terribly frightening for the person undergoing it obviously – is that the memory almost always returns, sooner rather than later. But here's the thing. When the memory *does* return, the person often forgets entirely whatever happened to them while they were in the fugue state.'

'Sort of like a blackout?'

'Exactly. So our Charlie could come to, suddenly or gradually, and when he does he'll have no idea of who we are or what he's doing with us but will be entirely clear about his "real life", his previous existence.'

'How extraordinary.' Dot shook her head.

'What's extraordinary?' Molly came in and sat down at the table. 'Oh, tea and cakes – just what I fancy!'

'I can recommend the scones,' Rob said, 'and the lemon drizzle cake and the apple turnovers.' He looked down and patted his waist. 'So long, pal, it was nice seeing you again.'

'Don't be silly!' Dot laughed. 'Rob's been bringing me up to speed with things – tell Molly.' She got up to make more tea while Rob filled Molly in.

'Well,' Molly said, 'I've got my own contribution to make to the general update.'

'Oh?' Dot put a fresh teapot on the table, then began to pour. 'What's that?'

'My voice coach has come back with some interesting results on Charlie's accent.' She lifted her eyebrows.

'According to her, and some nifty software, Charlie speaks with a forty per cent Boston accent with sixty per cent undertones of North Carolina. They can probably identify it even further but that would cost money.'

'They can be that specific?'

'Apparently so, yes.'

'How interesting.'

'That's excellent!' Rob was impressed. 'I'll tell Detective Foley – if you'll give me the details, Molly?' he said.

'So what do we do now?'

'Perhaps in the meantime we can try to prod his memory from time to time? Gently, of course,' Molly suggested.

'No harm in trying – as long as we don't distress him,' Rob warned.

'Of course not.' Molly looked hurt.

'Well, I'd better get back to the surgery.' Rob was regretful. 'I'll leave you two sleuths to it. And thank you again, Dot, for that wonderful afternoon tea. I'll see you guys later.'

Rob was thoughtful as he walked back to the surgery. He saw a lot of difficult cases in his line of work as a general practitioner, but something about Charlie had tugged at his heartstrings since he had met and got to know him. How could someone so nice and mild-mannered not belong to anyone? Rob couldn't work it out. Charlie hadn't been living rough – that much was clear – and hadn't mentioned any family, so far. It was too bad. Rob wondered what his own late wife, April, would have thought about the whole business. He still talked to her – not out loud, of course – still consulted her as he always had on anything that was bothering him.

Since losing her to cancer almost five years previously, Rob had eventually grown used to the gargantuan gap she'd left in his life, which he'd had the good sense not to rush to fill. He was more fortunate than many: he had his work, his children, young grandchildren, and he was really enjoying this locum position in his old hometown of Derrybeggs, which had a wonderful community of people he was getting to know more each day. Living in Dot's house, he was slipping into enjoying home comforts again – and it was so nice not to have to worry about what to cook for himself. Rob had never been very good in the kitchen.

He was also pretty taken with Dot, if he was honest. She was exactly the kind of person he admired, a lovely personality, engaging company, and a very attractive woman, which she clearly didn't realise. But he was only here for six weeks, Rob reminded himself. There was no point in trying to initiate a relationship. Anyway, he had his life and friends back in England – although they were really April's friends. Rob knew exactly what April would have said about Charlie's situation. *Just be kind. Whatever we do we must be kind to the poor man.*

Nineteen

The girl with the crazy-coloured hair didn't like him. That much was obvious, Ryan thought, folding himself into a booth in the Seashell and opening his laptop. He had watched her surreptitiously for the last couple of days when he stopped by for his caffeine fix. She was pretty – no question – but the multicoloured hair distracted from her looks. He had driven to the Seashell that first time because he needed to go on somewhere else afterwards – but parking the Porsche Cayenne E-Hybrid in full view outside the café had clearly been a mistake. It hadn't taken long for locals to notice it, and a regular parade of admiring teenage petrol heads had been patrolling it ever since. He had noticed her then, with a knowing expression on her face as she had looked out of the window, clocked his car, and returned behind the counter with a set of readymade assumptions about him. Well, what about it? That was *her* problem. He had enough to preoccupy him right now.

The most immediate matter was Joni's email right in front of him. He ordered his espresso and skimmed the brief note again. Joni was annoyed with him – he could tell by the breezy but disinterested tone of the email –

and he knew why. He couldn't say he blamed her: she had laid her cards on the table with the ultimatum and he hadn't referred to it since, either when they'd spoken on the phone or in any of his emails or texts. But on the other hand Joni should have been here with him: she was the one who had backed out of this trip. He was wondering about the ring issue too. He was thinking about buying one – but although he wanted to be spontaneous and would have liked to surprise her, Joni had very definite views on jewellery. She would almost certainly want to choose her ring – and film the purchase. Out of interest he googled diamond engagement rings, just to get an idea of what he would be expected to spend, and scrolled up to the more expensive models. Then he leaned in to have a closer look.

The low appreciative whistle startled him. Merry had arrived with his coffee and glanced at his open screen. 'Those are some serious knuckledusters!'

Ryan was tempted to tell her to mind her own business – her raised eyebrows told him the remark wasn't intended to be flattering and, perversely, this annoyed him. But he wasn't going to let her see that. What did he care what she thought? Instead he looked as if he was seriously studying the selection. 'Which one would you choose?'

She shrugged. 'They're not really my thing – way too ostentatious.' Now she was definitely having a pop at him.

'Maybe.' Ryan was deliberately noncommittal. 'Guess everyone feels the need to express themselves differently.' He allowed his eyes linger on her hair for a beat.

'Guess so.' She grinned as she turned to go. But not before he'd seen the flare of annoyance in her eyes.

She could dish it out, Ryan thought. But she didn't like being on the receiving end. People rarely did. Normally he wouldn't have bothered with the retort, but he didn't feel the need to be sucker-punched while paying for a quiet cup of coffee in the only café around here. Whatever was bothering the girl, her customers were not the people she should be taking it out on.

Back at the club Ryan made his rounds. Everything was almost finished, and they were bang on schedule for their grand opening night in August. A few issues had still to be resolved. An enormous glass sheet was due to arrive from Germany and would provide a spectacular wall looking onto the fourth hole but was holding up laying of the floor in that section. A few electrical snags had to be ironed out too, but overall things were looking pretty good. The locals were excited about it, and everyone he had met so far was very positive and supportive.

It was while he was on his rounds, signing off on various projects, that the idea came to Ryan. The conference-centre auditorium would make a perfect venue for the film festival opening night. It could be scaled to size with partitions and came equipped with every cutting-edge technology necessary. Since meeting Dot and Molly and hearing all about the problems the committee were facing, it seemed like an obvious thing to suggest. He'd have to run it by Frank, of course, but he'd sell it as a good opportunity to have a trial run for their own grand opening ceremony, which would happen the month after the festival. Frank would be there for that while Ryan would be trouble-shooting Frank's *next* project, whatever and wherever that turned out to be – there was always another.

Right now he had to sort out his personal situation. He and Joni needed to talk. This whole thing was weird, what was going on between them, but he wasn't up to any emotional wrangling today. He'd call her tomorrow. In the meantime, he'd have a word with Dot and suggest the golf club as a venue for their opening night – it was never any harm to get on the right side of the locals.

It had been Dot's suggestion that they hold the committee meeting in her large sitting room, which made a welcome change from the draughty old corner of the community centre where they had gathered before the fire damage. This had the added advantage that neither she nor Molly had to go out, which was a relief – there had been other work for Dot to do. Although she was nervous, particularly at the short notice at which the meeting had been called, and Kate Carmichael's lack of enthusiasm before she'd realised Molly Cusack would be at the meeting, Dot was excited.

Ryan had suggested and offered the golf club conference centre to her as a venue to solve the problem of the festival's opening night and Dot was thrilled. She had pointed out to Ryan that Kate Carmichael had tried that path and failed. But Ryan assured her he would sort it. He had to run it by his boss, Frank Levi, but that would be a formality: Dot should feel free to tell the committee at the meeting. Between that, and Molly's idea of the competition for locals to make a five-minute film on their phones, Dot felt a much-needed injection of good fortune had finally come their way.

Dot had set up the large table and chairs and a bowl of artfully arranged white hydrangeas sat happily on a nearby side table, close enough to lend a touch of fragrance and colour but without cluttering the space.

By seven thirty everyone but Kate and Ellen was seated. Dot had arranged the places so no one was at the head of the table. Peggy O'Sullivan was beside Molly. Sheila Relish, Franny's mother, was on Dot's left, and hadn't stopped talking since she'd arrived. Eva and Jan, from the Seashell, were opposite Sheila and chatting to Beth, who, as the local artist, was in charge of all things visual. It was now a quarter to eight, and although Dot had poured coffee and encouraged everyone to tuck into the selection of cakes and pastries, people were keen to get started. 'No offence,' said Sheila, pointedly. 'But we haven't got all night – if people want to be late that's their problem.'

'I agree,' said Molly. 'Let's get started.'

Just then the doorbell and a volley of barking from Honey announced the latecomers.

Kate Carmichael and Ellen Markey looked as if they had come straight from the hairdresser via the makeup studio.

'Welcome!' said Dot, ushering them in. 'You've met

everyone here except Molly.' She made the necessary introductions.

Although there were two obviously empty seats on either side of the table. Kate lingered – unnecessarily, Dot thought – to talk to Molly in a rather over-effusive manner. Then she managed to appear pained and bewildered at the same time. 'So sorry I'm late,' she said, deliberately placing her iPad at the head of the table, beside Molly. She smiled graciously. 'Oops! I seem to be missing a chair.'

'You're here – or over there.' Sheila Relish indicated the two vacant chairs. 'There's no one at the head – is there, Dot? First come first served. Once a teacher ...' She grinned. 'I'm used to organising classrooms,' she explained, to no one in particular, as Kate slunk resentfully into the appointed place at the table.

'I've taken the liberty of drawing up a quick agenda,' said Dot. 'You should have one in front of you. Now, apparently there are no minutes from the last meeting.' She looked to Kate for confirmation.

'Ah ...' Kate scrolled down her screen, and frowned. 'I don't think we'd actually settled on appointing a secretary, had we? She looked at Ellen. So ...' She gave a little toss of her hair.

'I managed to jot down a few notes from last time,' Dot volunteered, passing them around.

'Excellent,' Molly said. 'Let's have a look.'

'Now,' Dot said, after they had run through some minor items. 'As you know, there was an undercurrent circulating in the village that the locals were feeling uninvolved this year, so Molly has come up with a wonderful idea for a simple competition pretty much anyone can enter. The idea is to make a five-minute documentary on any subject of your choice, filmed on your smartphone.' Everyone thought this was a great idea – even Kate, although as Molly had pitched it she could hardly have found fault with it.

'We just need a name for it now,' Molly said.

'Film-on-fone?' Sheila suggested.

'I think that's very catchy,' said Molly. And everyone agreed.

'There is something else.' Dot couldn't help smiling. 'A very recent development – and one I'm very happy to be able to share with you.' Everyone looked at her expectantly, except Kate, who seemed bored, and Ellen who was making a point of studying her nails.

Dot went on: 'As some of you know, Ryan Shindler, chief operations officer of Levi International, is staying in one of my cottages. Ryan is here to sign off on the golf club and, as things are going according to schedule on his plan and he's aware of our lack of a venue, he has very kindly offered the conference centre to us for our opening night, which, I'm sure you'll all agree, will solve a very important problem we've been wrestling with.'

Molly, who already knew of the offer, smiled at the expressions of relief and delight around the table as the news registered – until Kate Carmichael interjected.

'Sorry to burst your balloon, Dot. But that's a non-runner.' Kate was dismissive. 'I approached Levi International *months* ago to request the golf club as a venue. It was the obvious choice, after all. But they were asking for an insane amount of money – weren't they, Ellen?'

Ellen nodded vigorously. 'Yeah, what was it? Ten grand for the night.'

'Exactly. So I told them where to shove it – not in so many words, obviously.'

'Yes, I'm aware of that, Kate,' Dot said, trying to keep her voice even. 'But Ryan has assured me he will sort the matter out – and I have every faith in him.'

'Good luck with that,' Kate smirked. 'Ryan's just a minion. If you want to take him at his word, that's your prerogative, I suppose.'

After that, the mood was subdued as they chatted about the lack of other venues. Eventually Dot called the meeting to a close. 'Any other business?'

'Actually, yes.' Kate sat up straighter. 'I've been thinking.' She paused for effect. 'I think it would be a lovely gesture if the committee were to erect a memorial to Doug, dear Merry's late husband.' Kate laid a consoling hand on Eva's arm. 'I was thinking of a tasteful stone bench somewhere prominent in the village, but if anyone else has any other suggestions?' Kate glanced at Molly to see if her suggestion had suitably impressed the visitor.

There was a rather surprised silence around the table – which Kate interpreted as awe.

Beth, Merry's best friend, chewed her lip and studied her notes. Jan seemed to shrink into himself. It was Eva who spoke first. 'Thank you, Kate,' she said slowly. 'I'm sure we all appreciate such a thoughtful idea on behalf of our daughter – but Merry is still very ... delicate about what happened. I think it would be best if I ran your very kind idea by her to see what she thinks about it.' Eva's face had paled and she looked uncomfortable.

'Of course.' Kate was gracious. 'Take as much time as you need.'

'I think that's everything, then,' said Dot.

Much as she would have loved to discuss the matter further, Sheila Relish had to rush and dashed off straight after the meeting. Eva, Jan and Beth strolled home with Peggy, who was leaning on her Rollator, keeping her company as they made their way through the village.

Peggy thought the idea of a memorial bench for Merry's late husband was very nice. She was a fan of random opportunities to sit down, she said, which was something you only came to understand and appreciate as you got older. Would there be a plaque on it? And what would it say? She wasn't sure it should be right smack-bang in the middle of the village, though. Wouldn't it be nicer to have it somewhere quiet and reflective where people could contemplate nature and the ongoing cycle of things?

Eva and Jan were quiet, but Beth spoke for them both when she voiced her thoughts. 'I'm not sure it's such a great idea, to be honest. I know it's a nice thing to suggest and all, but I'm not sure Merry would see it like that.'

'That's what I'm afraid of,' Eva agreed. 'I couldn't bear to upset her any further.'

'I know if I had lost someone I loved so young' – Jan's grip on his wife's hand tightened – 'I would not wish to pass by a reminder every day.' Usually so quiet, he spoke firmly.

'I'll talk to her about it, if you like,' Beth said. 'I'm meeting her tomorrow anyway.'

'That would be ideal, Beth, thank you.' Eva sighed with relief.

＊

In the kitchen after the others had left, Dot and Molly were having a post-mortem on the meeting, and in particular Kate's suggestion. Charlie joined them for a cup of tea and some leftover cake.

'I must say,' Molly mused, 'I thought it was a very odd thing to bring up at a committee meeting for the local film festival. Wouldn't it be a matter for the town council?'

'That's exactly what I thought.' Dot filled Charlie in on what had transpired. 'I suspect, knowing Kate Carmichael, the suggestion was intended to make a favourable impression,' she added, lifting her eyebrows.

'It was suggested for Merry's late husband, you say?' Charlie frowned. 'I didn't realise she was a widow. How sad.'

'Yes,' Dot said. 'It's coming up to two years since he was killed in a boating accident.'

'Merry's a young woman.' Charlie was thoughtful. 'A memorial to her young husband is going to be there for an awfully long time.' He spoke slowly. 'I'm not sure everyone would be happy having to confront a constant reminder of a lost love every day. It may be something she feels she *should* seem grateful for but is at least ambivalent about – and perhaps later regrets.'

'Wise words,' said Molly.

'Oh dear,' said Dot. 'That's what I was afraid of. It's very delicate, isn't it?'

Twenty

The following day was Merry's afternoon off – and Beth had suggested they grab some sandwiches, maybe a bottle of wine, too, and share a picnic lunch at one of their favourite childhood haunts by the ruins of the old Norman castle outside the village. They sat in the shade of an old oak tree, where the only sounds to be heard were an enthusiastic blackbird overhead and the intermittent drone of diligent bees.

Beth thought it might be as good a time as any to sound Merry out about Kate Carmichael's suggestion of a bench dedicated to Doug's memory.

'She what?' Merry's sandwich paused in mid-air.

'She wants to set up some kind of memorial to Doug in the village. A sort of tribute thing, I guess.' Beth was hesitant. 'She brought it up in the meeting just as we were wrapping things up. Naturally we wanted to run it by you to see what you think.'

'What I think is' – Merry put down her sandwich – 'that Kate Carmichael is an interfering busybody.'

'Right. Is that a no, then? It doesn't have to be a bench.'

'I don't care if it's a flying saucer, Beth.' Merry's

voice rose. 'I don't want or need a *memorial* to Doug just because Kate bloody Carmichael wants to attention-seek. I have my own memories, thank you very much. I don't need to walk past some ghastly reminder every day just in case I, like, might *forget* about Doug.' She exhaled. 'This is absolutely nothing to do with Kate Carmichael! She should mind her own bloody business – and, frankly, I'm surprised Dot or anyone else on the committee didn't tell her as much. I mean, what the hell has that to do with the film festival anyway? Is she thinking of writing a screenplay about Doug, too, maybe?'

'Okay, okay.' Beth held her hands up. 'I just said I'd run it by you – no need to shoot the messenger.' She kept her tone light. 'I'll tell Dot. Don't worry, there'll be no more said about the matter.'

'I'm sorry.' Merry rubbed her face and sighed. 'I don't mean to have a go at you. But there are things you don't know about. Doug wasn't exactly a saint.'

'If you find any man who is, let me know what planet you visited!' Beth was making light of it. 'They all have their drawbacks, but we can't live without them, can we?'

'It's not quite as simple as that.' Merry was serious. 'Not in this case.'

'What do you mean?'

'Mum and Dad know but I haven't shared it with anyone else. I just wasn't ready to.' Merry bit her lip. 'Doug's ex-fiancée, Kristy, had just found out she was pregnant when Doug broke up with her. She never told him. He only found out about it when the baby – his son – was almost six months old.'

Merry paused as Beth took in the startling news. 'He told me about it. He never tried to hide it but … it was difficult. Doug's family adored Kristy – they had always treated her like a third daughter. She was best friends with Doug's sisters … She told them about the baby first – after she'd gotten over the shock of Doug breaking up with her. Doug's family supported her wholeheartedly, of course.'

'Oh, Merry. I'm sorry – that must have been so hard.'

Merry made a wry face. 'It wasn't easy. We were working things out, just trying to come to terms with the bombshell and how it would affect our marriage when – when …'

'That's awful!' Beth chewed her lip. 'But, Merry, I know it must have been difficult discovering Doug was a father, for both of you, but he chose *you*. He loved *you*. I can understand you being angry and upset about it – but knowing Doug chose you must bring you some comfort.' Beth put a hand on Merry's arm.

'Yes.' Merry nodded, although her expression was hard to read. 'You're right, of course it does.' She smiled, and shrugged. 'Do you mind if we don't talk about it any more, just now?'

'Hey.' Ryan ran into Charlie as he was going around the front of Dot's house to get his car. One of the architects at the golf club wanted to show him some new specialist light switches and had suggested she meet him at a showroom in the next town about an hour's drive away. 'Whatcha up to?'

'Oh, nothin' much.' Charlie grinned. 'Just working out what to prioritise in my busy schedule.'

'You fancy a ride? I'm heading into Clanad 'bout fifty miles away. Got a little business to take care of – it'll wile away an hour or so?'

'Sure! I'd like that. I'll just let Dot know in case anyone gets worried about me.'

'How's it going up at the club?' Charlie asked, when they were on the road.

'We're getting there – it'll be real nice when it's all done.' Ryan glanced at him. 'How are you doing?'

'Well, Molly took a voice recording and had it analysed by her voice coach. Apparently, I'm sounding like Boston with an undertow of North Carolina.'

'I was pretty sure I picked up a southern twang all right,' Ryan said. 'Not that I'd want to venture a professional opinion or anything.'

'Thing is, I could have lived in lots of places for all I know, right now.'

'Man – it's a bummer.' Ryan shook his head.

'Tell me about it.'

Just then, out of nowhere, a sheep appeared in the middle of the road, and Ryan swerved to avoid it – almost colliding with a pickup truck that came around the bend right at him. 'Shit,' he muttered, as he swerved hard to get back to the right side of the road, narrowly avoiding the truck. 'What in the hell?'

'Whoa!' Charlie laughed nervously as he grasped the overhead handle. 'Nice swerve. You have good reflexes!'

'Phew! That was way too close for comfort.' Ryan pulled over to catch his breath. 'Man!'

'Looks like the other driver feels the same way!' Charlie indicated the truck, which had pulled up on the opposite side of the road from them.

'Are you okay?' Ryan turned to Charlie.

'I'm fine. But I'm not so sure she feels the same way.' He grinned, pointing to the lithe figure striding towards them, radiating fury.

'Oh, no, not her.' Ryan got out of the car.

The baseball cap that had hidden her hair in the truck was now being waved in outrage in one hand while the other ran through the multicoloured hair blowing around her face.

'What the hell did you think you were doing?' she yelled. 'You almost killed me!'

Ryan held up his hands. 'It was the sheep – it just appeared right in front of me!' He was more shaken than he sounded.

'What sheep?' She looked around disbelievingly. It was nowhere to be seen.

'Look, I'm sorry – but I swerved to avoid a sheep. Believe me I don't drive like that for thrills. There was a sheep in the middle of the road! I swerved to avoid it. I'm sorry – really I am, but it was a close thing for me too.'

'You were on the wrong side of the road!' She shouted. 'In your stupid flash car!'

'I said I'm sorry!' Ryan ran his hands through his hair. 'It was an accident.'

'Of course it was! That's always the excuse.'

'Look, lady!'

'Save it! I don't want to hear it! Just keep to your own goddamn side of the road!' And she ran back, leaped into her truck and pulled on to the road, her pink ponytail swinging angrily behind her.

Back in his car, Ryan sat for a moment, shaking his head.

'That was one angry lady.' Charlie chuckled.

'I can't say I blame her.' Ryan let out a breath. 'What kind of place has sheep wandering all over the highway anyway?' He drove onto the road again, checking his mirrors carefully.

'You like her, don't you?' Charlie grinned.

'Are you kidding? She's crazy,' Ryan protested. 'Not my type, at all.'

'She's real pretty, though. The hair's unusual, I'll grant you – but it's kind of cute. She's feisty! If I were forty years younger ...'

'So how old are you, anyway?' Ryan smiled, despite himself.

'No idea! One of the perks of my condition. But the face that looks out at me from the mirror is way older than I feel. Think that's the same for all of us over a certain age.' He smiled. 'Don't worry about Merry. She'll get over it.'

'That's her name? Mary?'

But Charlie wasn't listening. He was gazing out of the window, smiling, lost in thought.

Twenty-one

'So did she look as if she'd had work done?' Franny was in Sheena's bedroom where Sheena was simultaneously scrolling through Molly's acting-career history online and applying a generous helping of contouring powder under her cheekbone. She hadn't been altogether happy that Franny had met the famous Molly Cusack before she had. After all, it was Sheena's mother, Kate, who was heading up the film festival committee. But she was willing to appear gracious in return for verifiable information.

'I don't know. I didn't know who she was at first.' Franny searched for the right response. 'I just thought she looked familiar – you know, normal – but then I realised I'd seen her on the telly.'

'She's sixty-three, it says here.' Sheena extended a slim arm to inspect her newly painted nails. 'That's, like, nearly as old as Gran.'

'I don't think she's *that* old.' An image of Sheena's peevish grandmother rose in Franny's mind. 'She was really nice.'

'She's probably had at least one facelift – you'd have to at that age – and she doesn't even live in Hollywood. In LA they're having facelifts at thirty.' Sheena was a big fan of plastic-surgery programmes, which she watched avidly. 'That gives us fifteen years.'

'Speak for yourself! I'm not having any surgery. Anyway, I'm not trying to be an actress, like you are. I want to be a marine biologist, like Merry – although sometimes I think I might like to be a reporter.'

'You'll still probably need to have work done.' Sheena paused in her makeup ritual to glance at Franny speculatively. 'Everything's on TV, especially reporting, and that means high definition. Have you seen the girls on Sky? They're all *stunning*. They all look, like, perfect.'

'I just want to find out about people and write about them.' Franny was getting the twisty feeling in her tummy that happened quite a lot when she talked to Sheena, these days. 'Or maybe I could be a vet. Animals don't care what you look like.'

'Eeeew.' Sheena screwed up her nose. 'Imagine having to put your arm up a cow's—'

'Stop!' Franny covered her ears. 'Or maybe I'll just work in the café for ever.'

Sheena shook her head. 'No. You're brainy, Franny,' she said, in a rare display of solidarity – although she managed to make the compliment sound like a drawback. 'You'll probably be reporting back from mad places all over the world.'

The prospect didn't fill Franny with cheer. She wanted to stay in Derrybeggs and live near her parents and sister, after going to university somewhere else, for a while, maybe. 'I'm not sure I'd want to travel that much.'

'Never mind,' said Sheena. 'I'll give you my first exclusive interview when I'm famous and you can come and stay with me in LA.'

Franny wished she could be as certain as Sheena always was about everything. It must be wonderful to know exactly what you wanted to do instead of lying awake at night worrying. Mam kept telling her that everything would work out fine and not to be listening to Sheena, who was only putting ridiculous ideas into her head. 'I was thinking ...' she said.

'Mmm?' Sheena's head was tilted back as she mascaraed her already densely boosted eyelashes.

'... of setting up a GoFundMe page for Charlie.'

'But you're not really into social media, Franny, are you?' Sheena pointed out. This was a grave oversight on Franny's part, Sheena felt, as she paused to admire her handiwork.

'You don't have to be for a GoFundMe page, but I'd already thought of that. I was going to ask Molly Cusack if she would support it. She really likes Charlie and she must have loads of fans.'

This got Sheena's attention. She blinked rapidly. 'That's not a bad idea. D'you think she'd agree to it?'

'Dunno.' Franny shrugged. 'But there's only one way to find out.'

Twenty-two

When Dot tapped on Molly's door that afternoon to find out if she wanted dinner, the door swung open – and there was Molly, sitting at the desk, sobbing over her computer. For a minute Dot was so taken aback she didn't know what to do. Then Molly looked up and saw her.

'I'm sorry,' Dot said quickly. 'The door was open. I didn't mean to intrude—'

'Come in!' Molly blew her nose. 'You're not intruding.' She stood up. 'I could do with a cup of tea. Would you join me?'

At the small table in the kitchen Molly held her mug in both hands and decided to be honest. 'I'm in a bit of a crisis. Oh, nothing drastic,' she added hurriedly, seeing the concern on Dot's face. 'This memoir's so hard to do. And life in general, really. My career has pretty much come to a standstill, and while one always tries to prepare for that in this business, it's still rather demoralising when it happens. Then,' she took a deep breath, 'what really distressed me was losing my two best friends in the world quite suddenly within three months of each other. One, Nigel Garfield, died.'

'Yes, of course,' said Dot. 'I remember reading that somewhere – he was your on-screen husband for years, wasn't he? In that wonderful sitcom.'

'Yes, and the other friend, Julia Hepworth – very few people know this, but it's bound to make the news one of these days – she's had a horrible stroke.' Molly's voice began to catch. 'I'm sorry, I still can't believe it. She's paralysed and without speech, I'm not sure if she even recognises anyone. I went to visit her with her daughter and it was ghastly – I had to leave I was so upset.'

'That's so cruel.' Dot shook her head. 'Of course I know her as an actress, such a beautiful woman. I always loved her in everything she did. I'm so sorry to hear what's happened to her.'

'And she was – is, I mean,' Molly corrected herself, 'just as lovely in real life. Everybody loves her – it's impossible not to.' Molly swiped at the tears that had suddenly run down her face. 'This is just so – so horribly cruel, as you say. It would have been better if she had died. I know that sounds bad – but she didn't deserve this hideous thing.'

'That's terrible,' Dot said, patting her hand. 'I can't imagine how hard that must be for you.'

Molly looked up suddenly from the tissue she was sniffing into. 'Oh, bless you! That's so kind. I didn't mean to go on about myself. I hate self-pity.' Molly didn't want to impose on Dot, who was probably feeling obliged to be nice to her guest.

'But to lose your two dearest friends and within such a short space, that's huge.' Dot was serious. 'Are you – forgive me, I don't mean to pry – married at present, or do you have a partner?' Dot was worried about sounding too inquisitive – after all, Molly was famous and would have millions of friends and wannabe friends.

'No, actually, I'm not, and you're not prying. I'm quite happy to chat about it – in fact, it's a relief to talk to someone.' She blew her nose. 'I was married once, when I was much younger.'

Dot nodded. She'd thought Molly had been married – she was sure she had seen a photo in a magazine years ago.

'It didn't work out – didn't last long at all. We made each other terribly miserable, so we divorced. After that, I had one or two relationships, but I never found the right person. I threw myself into my work, and the rest, as they say, is history. As a strategy it worked quite well.' Molly was rueful. 'Until the last six months or so at any rate – and then, well, life suddenly became a bit much.' She gave a watery smile. 'The most important relationships in my life turned out to be with my friends.' She shrugged. 'It was my agent who came up with the idea of writing a memoir – and I agreed. And then I got invited to open your festival. I thought I could take a sort of sabbatical, and get stuck into my book. I've always liked the idea of writing, but it remains to be seen whether or not I'm any good at it. I'm beginning to doubt it. I haven't been able to get going at all with it. I'm worried I might have writer's block. Imagine if I can't do it – I'd have to give the money back.'

'I'm sure it won't come to that.' Dot laughed. 'Look on the bright side – at least if it's a memoir, you don't have to make it up!'

'It's funny you say that,' Molly said. 'I used to hate the idea of writing a memoir, always thought it meant you were finished, that your life was over – but after all that's happened recently, with Nigel and Julia especially, I just feel this obligation to record at least some of my memories before it's too late … but now that I have to do it, it's like pulling teeth.'

'I can understand that.' Dot nodded. 'And I'm sure you've led a fascinating life compared with most of us.' She smiled. 'I love reading about other people's lives – biographies are far more interesting than fiction, I always think. Except the ones that are written by twenty-something celebrities on a fairly regular basis, updating us every decade or so.' She laughed.

'I know!' Molly groaned. 'What about you? Would writing ever appeal?'

'No, I don't think it would ever cross my mind – I don't think I'd have the patience for it. Don't get me wrong, I love to be creative, but I prefer the sort of creativity you can see quicker results with, like baking or – renovating an old house, indeed!' She gestured at the walls around them.

'What a wonderful project to take on,' Molly said. 'Was it all in a very bad state?'

'Hadn't been touched since the 1950s, at a guess.' Dot smiled. 'And that was just the linoleum. We had to gut it and renovate, rewire, replumb, add a few bathrooms and practically rebuild the cottages. It was hard work, but very rewarding.'

'Well, you've certainly done a fabulous job, the bits of it I've seen anyway.'

'Thank you. It's kind of you to say so. In many ways that was the easier part of the move. Settling in here has been harder than I'd hoped.' Dot found it a relief to be able to confide in someone who wasn't local or, indeed, a relative or friend who might have said, *We warned you*.

'It's bound to be a huge change.' Molly was sympathetic. 'It's very brave of you – I'm not sure I could do it.'

'Most people have been very kind and welcoming – I mean, there's no reason why anyone *should* go out of their way to be particularly nice to me, another blow-in.' She paused. 'It's just that one or two have been ... unnecessarily unpleasant. It's just made it harder – that's all.'

'I bet I can guess who that is – and I don't even live here! But the others seem nice – and Rob's lovely!'

'Yes, he *is* a sweetheart. He's been wonderful with Charlie.' Dot was alarmed to feel her face pinking at the mention of Rob's name and quickly pretended to blow her nose.

'I thought you were a couple when I first arrived,' Molly said, with a twinkle in her eye.

'Oh, no! He's just—'

'I know all that now.' Molly smiled. 'But I think he really likes you! You'd make a really sweet couple!'

Dot blew her nose again. 'You and I have both discovered life can be a lot simpler without men in it.' When Dot put her tissue up her sleeve she brought the conversation back to the house, much safer ground. 'I'll give you the guided tour sometime, if you'd like.'

'I'd love that,' Molly said. 'It must have cost a pretty penny.' She looked around her.

'Let me put it this way. There was quite a lot of money accruing to me by the time my husband died.' Dot was enigmatic. 'And I wanted a completely new start. I've always loved this old house – ever since I was a child.'

'What do you mean' – Molly looked at her with interest – 'there was money accruing to you? That's an odd thing to say, if I'm not being too nosy. Was it a divorce?'

'No, not a divorce. But seeing as you've told me a bit about your life, I'll tell you a bit about mine, as long as we can keep it just between us?'

'Of course!' Molly was eager to listen.

'Marriage isn't always all it's cracked up to be – as you discovered.'

'Tell me about it!'

'I was married to a very controlling man. I had to note down every penny I spent. I had to go through the household accounts with him meticulously every month.'

'No! Really?'

An hour later the two women were still deep in conversation when there was a ring at the doorbell. After a minute Molly returned with Franny, who was quite red in the face and carried a laptop under her arm.

'Franny's had an idea!' Molly cleared a space at the table where Franny sat down and prepared to make her pitch.

'You know you told me to see if I could help find out about Charlie and everything?' she said to Molly.

'Yes, I do. Franny and I got chatting at the harbour,' Molly explained to Dot.

'Well, I've had an idea.'

'Go on,' Dot and Molly said together.

'I thought we could set up a GoFundMe page, telling people about Charlie's situation and asking for help,' Franny said. 'Once we have an online presence, there's no telling how many people it could reach all over the world.'

'I think that's a very good idea,' said Dot, who hadn't a clue as to what a GoFundMe page was, but was eager to sound enthusiastic. 'Rob was pointing out that Charlie may have to go into some sort of residential home – hopefully it won't come to that – so it would be great to raise some money to put towards whatever he might need.'

'Or he could stay here, rent a flat and maybe have a carer.'

'Do you think people would really respond?' Molly wondered.

'They would if you were willing to help out.' Franny held her breath. 'I could do all the setting up and everything – and be the page admin – but you're famous! Millions of people must know you. Then everyone will want to help find out where Charlie's from. We could use the donations to help him.' Franny chewed her lip, looking hopefully from one to the other.

'It sounds like a very interesting approach, I must say,' said Dot. 'What do you think, Molly?'

So much for escaping to her quiet bolthole in the

countryside, Molly was thinking, before the festival PR machine went into action. Once the media got hold of this she would be inundated with queries, requests and probably interviews – but then, she supposed, that was the whole point of it, and if it helped find Charlie's people or home, then what could be too much trouble? She couldn't possibly refuse. 'I think it's a great idea too, Franny, and I'd be honoured to host the page.'

'Brilliant!' Franny sat down and opened her laptop. 'Let's do it now!'

Twenty-three

Charlie's GoFundMe page was up and running. It had been live for two days and had already got some traction – but it was when Ryan came into the kitchen at lunchtime that things really moved up a gear. He found Dot and Rob attempting to note down the more promising leads or suggestions in response to the post. When they explained to him what they were doing, Ryan was enthusiastic. 'It's a cool idea. I could ask Joni to put a link to it on her social-media platforms.'

'Your influencer friend? You think she might help us?' Dot asked.

'I don't see why not. It's not exactly her area, finding people, but it would be a good way of getting the page out there, particularly in the US. Since it looks like that's where Charlie hails from, hopefully someone will recognise him. It's worth a try anyhow. I'll be talking to her later so I'll run it by her then.'

'Wonderful!' said Rob.

Back in the office at the golf club, Ryan was delighted he had something interesting to talk to Joni about. Up to now he'd been sending emails full of small-town talk, and he could tell from her replies that she was genuinely confused about what was happening in his head. But finding Charlie's people was a real challenge – and Ryan knew Joni loved a challenge. He began to write her another email, then realised he should probably call her. He wasn't even sure why he was hesitant to do so. He'd never had any problem talking to her before. Maybe it was the physical distance between them. After all, this was the longest time they'd been apart since they'd become a couple. 'Hey, sweetheart,' Ryan said warmly, as Joni picked up on the third ring. 'How're you doin'?'

Happily, Joni sounded just like her old self, and chatted away as if she were in the next room and the Talk had never happened. Ryan felt relief and affection well in him and was particularly pleased she seemed happy to hear from him. He let her chat for a couple of minutes until there was a natural pause and she asked him how he was doing.

'I'm missing you, darlin'. Matter of fact …' – he paused – '… there's something I want to ask you. It's kind of a proposition you might be interested in. You'd really be helping me out … In fact, I can't think of anyone who'd do a better job …'

'Sure, shoot!' Joni sounded interested, just as he'd guessed she'd be. So he filled her in on the situation.

'And that's really it.' He'd explained about Charlie and his predicament and the GoFundMe page. 'We just need to get the word out there – if you would share the story with your followers.' He said he'd email her all the relevant links and that he'd talk to her tomorrow. 'I don't have to tell you how much I appreciate this, sweetheart – I know how busy y'all are. I really wish you were here with me but you're not missing anything – there's nothing doing here, apart from some film festival coming up later this month that seems to be pretty disorganised. That actress I was telling you about, Molly? She's their guest of honour. I think she's going to try to put some wind in their sails. The cottage is real pretty, and the other guests are friendly. We're all just trying to get Charlie home – wherever home is – so, anything you can do ...'

When Ryan finished the call, he breathed a huge sigh of relief. It had gone well, better than he'd expected. And once Joni was on the case, he'd bet things with Charlie would start moving along pretty quickly. When Joni got her teeth into something, no stone was left unturned. He had played down, of course, just how lovely he found Derrybeggs and how he knew she would love it here too – but there was no point in telling her what she was missing.

He put in a call to Frank then, to tell him why it would be a good move to give the film festival committee the conference centre as an opening-night venue – but Frank didn't pick up so he left a message to call him back. He was looking forward to telling Dot and Molly the good news about Joni being willing to promote Charlie's GoFundMe page. But since the page had been Franny's idea by all accounts, he'd be passing the Seashell where she worked on his way home. He could drop in and maybe let her know first. Might even have a chance to smooth over his last encounter with Mary ...

He set out on foot, enjoying the feel of the sun on his face – he was spending way too much time on video calls or around cramped tables looking at plans. At least the clubhouse was coming along well. It was going to be spectacular when it was finished in a couple of weeks – even Frank wouldn't be able to find fault with anything, which might be a first.

Charlie and Molly were strolling along the cliff road, towards the headland. Beneath them the small cove was showing signs of activity. A few surfers were paddling out and a worried dog ran back and forth along the shore barking. In the distance, the crescent beach of Cape Clanad Island glistened in the sun.

'So, does North Carolina conjure up any memories?' Since her voice coach had confirmed that Charlie's accent was part North Carolina, Molly had been trying to jog Charlie's memory.

'Not that I can think of.' Charlie looked out to sea.

'What about the Outer Banks?' She referred to the two hundred miles of barrier islands off the coast of North Carolina that separated the Atlantic Ocean from the mainland and were famous for their shipwreck sites.

'The outer banks of what?' Charlie looked blank.

'Okay. How about the cardinal?' It was the state bird but it was worth a try.

'Like in the Vatican?'

'Um, no. Nina Simone? John Coltrane?'

'They're jazz artists, right?'

'Yes! And they're both from North Carolina.'

'You think I'm a jazz artist?' He laughed.

'Well, we can't rule anything out.'

'I'm just teasing, Molly.' Charlie smiled. 'Who knows what I am?' He stopped to take a video on his phone. 'It's kinda fun, in a strange way, thinking about who I might be. Almost like creating a fictional character. I get to reinvent myself every day.'

'I admire you – I don't think I could ever be as stoic as you are about it.'

'Even if I don't ever remember what went before, I can still create some new memories, right?'

'Of course you can!' Molly linked his arm companionably as they walked on.

They were quiet then, for a bit, and Molly found herself thinking about what Charlie had just said, about all the different characters he might be, and suddenly a light glimmered in her head. Charlie's predicament would make a wonderful starting point for a novel. One she could write with characters all of her own creation! That would be so much more fun than her memoir, which was just making her sad. This way she could make her characters and story do whatever she wanted. As some cyclists waved going past them, Molly felt a weight lift from her shoulders. She wouldn't say anything about it now to anyone. But she would start testing her idea the minute she got back.

Twenty-four

When Ryan reached the café, it was empty, apart from Franny and Merry, who were busy behind the counter. Ryan had to hand it to Franny: getting Molly to host the page had taken chutzpah. He was feeling pretty optimistic. Once he had told them he had solved the problem of finding a venue for the film festival, and got Joni to agree to sharing details about Charlie on her platform, he was hoping his reception at the Seashell might be less frosty than he had feared after his near miss on the road.

Approaching the counter, he saw his hopes were unfounded. Merry looked up from counting money in the till and, seeing who it was, scowled.

Ryan cleared his throat, and spoke to Franny, who was filling salt cellars, giving her his best smile. 'Hey,' he began. 'I hear you're the brains behind setting up the GoFundMe page for Charlie. That's a really great idea!' Franny blushed. 'Dot was telling me all about it – and I think I may be able to help you.'

Franny looked uncertain.

'Well, not me exactly,' Ryan clarified. 'But I know someone who could help you. You're in charge of it, right?'

'Yes – well, me and Molly, but I'm managing it.' Franny glanced at Merry, who was studiously ignoring Ryan.

'Cool. Well, a friend of mine back home is an influencer – quite a well-known one. She's based in New York. I figure if she shares your page and gets her followers involved – well, that could make a difference.' He didn't want to oversell the pitch. 'If that's okay with you, of course.'

'I don't really do much social media,' Franny said. 'But what's her name? I'll look her up.'

'Joni Romano – she posts as @houseofgirls. Check it out.'

Ryan waited while Franny checked out Joni's Instagram account.

'Oh, wow!' Franny's eyes grew big. 'She's got, like, over a million followers.'

'Exactly. And I'm sure she'd be happy to share your page.'

'That would be amazing!' Franny's face lit up.

'No problem. We all want to help Charlie find his people.' He turned to Merry. 'It's Mary, isn't it? I don't think we've been properly introduced despite our near collision the other day.' Merry continued to ignore him.

'It's Merry,' Franny explained. 'Like in ferry – isn't it?' She looked at Merry, who seemed to be absorbed now in searching through a drawer. 'It's short for Merope – but people are always calling her Mary, aren't they, Merry?'

'It's all right, Franny, you don't have to explain.' She didn't look up.

'Uh, great name, Merope. Well, I, uh, won't disturb you any longer. I just wanted to—'

At that moment his phone rang. Ryan looked at the screen and saw it was Frank. 'I need to take this call.' He made a rather futile hand signal to indicate he was heading to the back door of the café and immediately felt like an idiot.

Outside, he picked up the call. Frank was anxious to know if things were going to schedule.

'Hey, Frank, thanks for getting back to me.'

'What's up, Ryan?' Frank sounded antsy. 'There was something you wanted to run by me?'

'Yeah, I do. There's a film festival happening here, Frank, a local gig – it's an annual thing. They need a place for their opening night and I think we should give them the club – the conference centre.'

'I remember something about that a while back. They were looking to rent it, but I didn't want troops of people traipsing over my new club before it even opens – and I don't want it now. Why are you so keen?'

'That's just it, Frank. It would be a great trial run for our own grand opening – and there won't be that many. This is, like, a – a one-horse town, and besides, it's good to keep the locals sweet. This way we're making a nice gesture.'

'What's in it for us?'

'It might come in handy if we ever need to call in a favour in return. And, let's face it, it makes us look good.' Ryan knew Frank's obsession with people owing him favours was eclipsed only by his obsessive need to be liked.

'Okay, kid. You got it. How much you gonna charge them?'

'Uh, I was thinking *not.*'

'That's what I was afraid of.' Frank let out a sigh. 'Haven't I taught you anything at all?'

Ryan grinned. 'Everything I know, Frank. Everything I know.'

'Get outta here!' Frank chuckled. 'And this better make us look good.'

'It'll make us look *great*! Count on it!'

Ryan was putting his phone into his pocket and turning to head back into the café when he saw that Merry was just a few feet away from him, emptying some rubbish into a bin. How long had she been standing there? And how much had she heard? Impossible to tell. Damn! Heard from this end, the conversation made him sound fake and manipulative when he was only trying to help. Not that it was any of her business – but all the same, Ryan wouldn't want anyone to think he was running the place down or playing them for fools. Either way, she acted like she hadn't noticed him and went back inside.

Twenty-five

Since Dot had confirmed that Ryan had definitely arranged for the new state-of-the-art conference centre at the golf club to be at their disposal for opening night, it was all systems go for the committee. Another meeting had been called, and there was a lot of excitement.

In just under an hour, they had got through the most pressing items.

There wouldn't be very many visitors, they thought, if previous years were an indication – but Dot would contact all the other B&Bs in the area to give them a reminder just in case. They couldn't afford to hang about.

The films for the second night hadn't been ordered yet – but Molly knew a distributor who would help. She had taken the liberty of contacting them before the meeting and was anxiously waiting to hear back.

Beth had done a lovely job with artwork and graphics, which were waiting to be approved.

Peggy suggested a barbecue on the beach for the first evening. 'The weather's been so settled, and people can't stay in the conference centre all night. A barbecue on the beach would be fun for the young people. You could cater for it, Eva and Jan, couldn't you?' Peggy looked defiantly across the table at Kate Carmichael. 'Unless the other caterers someone mentioned a while back are confirmed?' Kate and Ellen mutely shook their heads.

'Well, then.' Peggy looked pleased. 'And we could have a Sunday lunch grill there the following day as well.'

'We'd be happy to organise that,' said Eva.

'The Film-on-fone competition is being very well received,' Dot said. 'We've already had thirty-four people registering for it. The in-store flyers and online word-of-mouth are working very well.'

'Splendid,' said Dot. 'Anything else?'

'There is something.' Beth sounded hesitant. 'I discussed Kate's idea of the committee erecting a memorial bench for Doug, her late husband, with Merry, and she is very definitely against the idea, although of course she appreciates the goodwill behind the gesture.' Merry had told her to leave Kate in no doubt. Eva and Jan nodded in agreement, although Eva couldn't bring herself to meet Kate Carmichael's gaze.

'I'm sure we're all very glad you discussed that with her, Beth,' said Dot. 'How one copes with bereavement is a very personal thing.'

'I agree,' said Molly. 'Merry's a young woman with her whole life ahead of her.'

'I just thought it would be nice for the committee to show we cared.' Kate looked pained. 'But of course I understand *completely*. And I agree. It's so important for

Merry to move on. I was happy to see her only last week in Zizi's having lunch with a very attractive guy – it's really good to see her embracing life again.'

'Right, I think that's everything,' said Dot, quickly. She had noticed Eva and Jan exchange a bewildered glance.

'Just one more thing,' Sheila said. 'Since we haven't appointed a secretary yet, I'm going to propose an obvious candidate. What do you say, Dot? You're a natural and you've already gone to so much trouble and put in so much hard work on our behalf.'

'Hear, hear!' said a chorus of voices around the table.

'Well, wouldn't anyone else would like to put a name forward?' Dot looked uncomfortable. 'If not, of course I'm happy to oblige.'

'Ellen, didn't you say …?' Kate looked meaningfully at her friend, who, recognising defeat when it stared her in the face, shook her head.

'That's that, then. We're in business.' And the meeting was brought to a close.

Fresh coffee was made, some wine appeared, the homemade pastries were handed around again, and a glow of quiet contentment spread across the room. Under the table Honey nudged a few legs and graciously accepted titbits. Only Kate Carmichael looked as if she had swallowed a wasp.

Merry had popped in for a chat and was sitting at Beth's kitchen table, making faces at Emma, Beth's eight-month-old daughter, who was cheerfully banging her empty bowl with a spoon.

'So, how did my ungrateful refusal of the memorial bench go down with Kate the Great?' Merry asked.

'She took it on the chin.' Beth grinned. 'But not without throwing out a well-aimed low blow in retaliation.'

'I'd expect nothing less.' Merry smiled. 'What was it?'

'Oh, it was sugar-coated to the hilt – but she said something along the lines of how she absolutely understood and how important it was for you to be moving on with your life and getting past losing Doug. Then she innocently dropped in how happy she was to see you in Zizi's last week having lunch with a very attractive guy and clearly embracing life again.' Beth looked meaningfully at Merry whose mouth was set in a thin line.

'God, she's unbelievable.'

'Is there something you're not telling me?' Beth looked hopeful. 'Because you know I'd be thrilled if you'd met some—'

'Of course I haven't met someone! You know I'd tell you if that was the case. I was having lunch last Thursday in Zizi's with a solicitor. It was about Doug's case, if you must know.'

'Oh, Merry, I'm sorry – I didn't mean—'

'It's fine, I know you didn't, and no one else *would* make anything of that except bloody nosy Kate Carmichael. So you can rest assured there is no mystery man in my life.'

'Not yet.' Beth lifted her eyebrows. 'But I live in hope.'

After a long and difficult pause in which Beth worried that she had maybe said the wrong thing, Merry blurted out, 'Five and a half million.'

'What?'

'Five and a half million dollars.'

Beth was puzzled. 'I don't understand.'

'That was the price of Doug's life, Beth. Five and a half million dollars.'

'Oh, Merry, my God.' Beth's mouth fell open. 'What are you going to do with it?'

'I'm going to take it out in dollar bills and burn it.'

'*What?* Oh, Merry.'

'Stop saying, "Oh, Merry."'

'Sorry. But, Merry, you don't have to throw it away. I mean, wouldn't Doug have wanted you to—'

'*I don't care what Doug would have wanted!*'

'You don't mean that.'

'I do! You don't understand!' Across the table, little Emma's face crumpled as she sensed the change in atmosphere.

'You're right. I don't. I really don't. You're going to have to explain it to me.'

'I can't!' Merry put her face into her hands and took a deep breath. 'Look, I'm sorry, Beth. I can't do this right now – I have to go.' She kissed Emma on the top of her head.

Merry walked quickly down the lane to the road, wiping away the tears that had unexpectedly sprung, The dilemma was eating her up. How could she tell her best friend and family that the man who had died to save her life was having an affair with his ex? It would be all they'd remember about him. Between that and the huge amount of money she was going to be awarded as a result of Doug's death, Merry just couldn't think straight.

Ryan had an appointment with a lawyer acting for the golf club. They had agreed to meet in the neighbouring town of Clonty to go over the application for the film licence that was needed. Driving through the village, he decided to swing by the Seashell and pick up a coffee to go – that way he could ask them to give him some small change: he had only a fifty in cash on him and he'd need coins for the car-parking meters. Some seemed to take card payments and others didn't. It was better to be on the safe side. He pulled over and went into the café, which was empty, the jangling rope bell sounding unusually loud in the silence. 'Hello?' he called, leaning on the counter.

There was a rustle, the sound of someone blowing their nose, and Merry appeared. 'Hi,' she said, not quite meeting his gaze. 'What can I get you?'

For a second he was taken aback. Merry was not her usual bristling self. On the contrary, she was subdued and looked as if she'd been crying.

'Espresso to go. Hey,' he said, 'are you all right?' He knew he was risking a sharp rebuff, but the girl looked genuinely upset.

'Yeah, I'm fine.' She met his eyes. 'Thanks.' A shadow of a smile.

'No offence but you don't look fine.'

She turned away to make his coffee, and while the machine gushed and hissed, Ryan risked another suggestion. He was so used to her being prickly and cold with him that he was genuinely concerned. 'Sometimes it helps to talk? It's kind of my job description to sort things out, you know. Comes in useful sometimes.' He shrugged and gave a half-smile.

She turned around then. 'Thanks for the offer, but unless you can rewind time, you won't be much use to me. Besides, this is really something I need to sort myself.' She passed him his coffee and their hands touched briefly. For an awkward second their eyes locked.

'I know what you mean. Well, I, uh, hope it works out for you. Whatever it is.' He nodded and made for the door. It was only when he was back in his car that he realised he had forgotten to ask for some small change. He wasn't going back in there now – the shock of adrenalin he'd felt when their hands touched had left him quite rattled enough.

Twenty-six

In the dream it was always the same. She and Doug were lying on a raft in the ocean under a deep blue sky with the sun beating down, and he would reach for her hand. Then the sound would begin, a slow-building rumble. The water began to bubble and roil, faster and harder until it rose up and engulfed them. She was sucked down, further and further, far beneath the noise until everything was black and deadly silent. Then she was propelled to the surface, emerging gasping for breath, the water eerily calm now, but no raft, and Doug was nowhere to be seen. And she would try to scream, but no sound came from her mouth.

She'd had it last night and she must have screamed, because Eva had woken her up, stroked her face and made her sit up to drink the water she had brought. 'It's only a dream,' she whispered. 'You're safe now, Merope.'

Merry had nodded and said she was fine, that she would go back to sleep. 'Don't fuss, please, Mum – I'm sorry I woke you up.'

But when Eva had left, Merry lay awake long into the small hours. She wasn't safe. That was the problem.

No one could harm her physically – she was home, safe and dry, literally – but emotionally she was still wide open and unprotected. And there was nothing she could do about it – no one she could talk to. Now she slipped out of bed and went to the chest of drawers by the window. Opening the top drawer quietly, she took out the envelope, turning it in her hands. It struck her as ironic that something so light held the contents of a dilemma that weighed so heavily on her heart. The written documentation had arrived last week, along with the news the solicitor had confirmed in person, that she was now a millionaire several times over. Doug's case had been settled for the amount of $5.8 million. Now he was dead and she had to decide what to do next. She had to figure this out on her own for both of them.

Dawn was breaking, rosy pink fingers of light reaching through the mauve sky, turning the ocean silver beneath. But not today, she thought. Today looked perfect just as it was. Outside this room, beyond the window from which she gazed, the perfect canvas of summer was about to unfold. She would not spoil it. Not today. The envelope was replaced in the drawer, and Merry went back to bed. But every time she closed her eyes, she saw Doug, tense and unusually pale, coming home to their small apartment.

'What is it, Doug? I know something's bothering you. What is it?' He had been quiet and withdrawn for the past few days.

The air was suddenly heavy with dreadful possibilities. Doug was usually so relentlessly upbeat and positive, even while they had been going through the awful time – when Doug had had to break it to Kristy and his family that he had met and fallen deeply in love with someone new, an Irish girl. It hadn't been the ideal way to begin their relationship but Doug had sworn to Merry his family would come around. And even when they hadn't, Doug had stood by Merry, had chosen her. Their attraction had been that strong.

For an awful moment she'd wondered if he was sick. 'Doug, what is it? Please … you're scaring me.'

'You have to believe me, Merry, I didn't know.' He put his head in his hands.

'Know what?'

He took a deep breath and looked at her, shrugging helplessly. 'I have a son. He's six months old. Kristy just discovered she was pregnant the day before I broke up with her. She was about to tell me when I told her about you. She was too shocked to tell me, then.'

'Are you sure?' Merry tried to be rational as she took in the startling news.

'The paternity test was positive. I have it here.' He pulled the piece of paper from his pocket and held it, gazing at it.

'Okay,' she said, thinking aloud as she walked to the window. 'This is a shock. A really big shock, but we'll work it out, Doug. It's – it's just an unexpected curve ball. For a minute there you had me really worried.' She went to sit beside him and take his hand. 'I thought you might be sick.' Merry was trying to lighten the mood, focus on the positive. Even though she felt as if all the air had been sucked out of her, she was determined to move past this. It was a shock, that was all. She and Doug could face anything together. But it didn't matter how positive she was about the situation: events would take a turn that even she would never have expected.

Twenty-seven

Franny had been thinking about the Film-on-fone documentary long into the night and decided on her topic. She announced it at breakfast the next morning: 'I'm going to do my film on the new golf course and the effect it will have on the environment. I'll interview Ryan Shindler for it.'

Across the table, her dad, Mike, looked up from his bacon and eggs. 'We're flat out at the golf club, Franny. Ryan Shindler is a very busy man – I can't imagine he'll have the time to be doing interviews for a phone competition.' He looked to his wife Sheila for support.

'Why don't you do your film on your canoeing?' Sheila said. 'It would be lovely seeing some nice sea-view angles.'

Franny shook her head. 'Someone's already doing that. Anyway, I've made up my mind.'

'I don't want any funny stuff up at the club – don't even think about a protest,' said Mike. 'Ryan's a nice bloke, what I've seen of him, and there's a lot of people, including me, working to a very tight schedule. We won't appreciate any unwelcome interruptions.'

'I wouldn't worry about that.' Franny's older sister,

Clare, reached into the fridge. 'What are you thinking of, Fran? I can just see you holding up a cardboard sign saying, "Save our Snails".' She grinned.

'Sneer all you like. I have a right to investigate. It's a free country, isn't it? Last time I checked.' Franny shot her sister a glance.

'If it is, there's an awful lot of us paying for it,' said Mike, getting up from the table. 'I mean it, Franny – no funny stuff.' He dropped a kiss on his daughter's head. Franny had stuck out her chin in a manner he knew all too well. 'Tell her, Sheila.'

'She's grand. Have a good day, love.' Sheila kissed her husband goodbye.

'You could do it on the animal shelter,' Clare said to Franny. Clare hoped to become a vet and was working at a local shelter. 'We're always looking for publicity.'

'It's too sad.' Franny chewed her toast. 'I can't stand watching animals who've been badly treated. Besides, it's not for publicity, this film. It's to, like, demonstrate a talent for documentary-making, condensed into five minutes. That's hard.'

'It is *not* sad.' Clare was put out. 'We rescue and rehome animals every day. If it wasn't for the shelter, we wouldn't have Muttie.' Their one-eared rescue collie-mix perked up under the table at the mention of his name.

'Anyway, loads of people will think of doing a film on the shelter.'

*

Later that morning at the Surf Shack, which was really an old shed down at the harbour for storing people's boards and canoes with a few tables and benches out front, Franny caught up with Sheena and a few of the girls, some of whom, including Sheena, were wearing wetsuits. They were sitting down, drinking coffee. 'Are you coming out?' Franny was eager to go canoeing.

'Nah, maybe later.' Sheena inclined her head towards the two lads from Donegal who were in town for a few days, and winked.

'Oh.' Franny was deflated, but accepted the coffee Sheena pushed her way and slipped into the bench table beside her friend. 'Have you decided what to do your film on?'

'Yeah. It was kind of obvious, really, once Mum pointed it out.' Sheena stirred her coffee thoughtfully. 'Like, with me going to be an actress, and everything. I'm going to do mine on Molly Cusack,' she said. 'I've a got a real celebrity to work with – and I'll learn from her as I'm doing it. It's a win-win.'

'Cool,' said Franny. 'That's a great idea. Have you asked her yet?'

'No.' Sheena was unconcerned. 'But, like, Mum's head of the committee, and all, and anyway, Molly agreed to work with you on Charlie's GoFundMe page, so what would be the problem?' She seemed bemused.

'None. I'm sure.' Franny was envious of Sheena's confidence and the obvious support her family were showing in her undertaking. Unlike some people she could think of.

'What are you doing yours on?'

'The environmental impact of the new golf-course development – with or without Ryan Shindler's input.'

'The American guy?' Sheena's eyebrows lifted. 'Good luck with that – Mum's been trying to get him for days.'

'What for?'

'I don't know – dinner or something – but he never returns her calls.'

'Well, like I said, with or without. Come on, Muttie!' Franny whistled and her dog raced up to her. 'Sure you won't come out with me?'

'Nah, you're all right.' Sheena smiled. 'There might be something going on here with the lads.' She inclined her head towards the two fit guys waxing their boards.

'Okay, catch you later.'

Out on the water, with Muttie standing at the bow sniffing the wind, his one ear twitching back and forth as gulls whirled and cried overhead, Franny wished life could be simple. The water was calm and translucent in this part of the bay – although further out a powerful rip tide lurked beneath. She kept an eagle eye out for any sightings of the giant jellyfish that sometimes appeared. Lion's manes were enormous, and only the other day thousands of them had turned up on the west coast overnight, stranded in the low tide. Biologists reckoned they had been sent off course because of climate change, losing their bearings. Franny could relate to that.

She paddled slowly, feeling the sun warm on her back, laughing as Muttie barked at a diving cormorant. Merry had taught her to canoe. They used to head out together in the early morning, sometimes even at night, when Merry showed her the different constellations and the wonder of bioluminescence lighting up the ocean. But then Merry had gone to live in America, and met Doug. And Doug had been killed – and now Merry never went into the water. Franny missed those times more than she was able to say. A tiny, horrid, mean part of Franny had been secretly glad when she'd heard Merry would be coming home to Derrybeggs, although she was as shocked and upset as anyone at the news her husband had been killed. But the fantasy she had nurtured that things would somehow be the same between her and Merry once she was back home had faltered very quickly when she realised the older girl she hero-worshipped wasn't the person Franny remembered.

'It's post-traumatic stress disorder,' her mam had tried to explain. 'She's been in a horrible, terrifying accident, love, and her husband was killed.' Sheila shook her head at the tragedy. 'And they were just starting out on married life.'

'But not to go in the water? Like, never?'

'I don't know, love. Maybe she will one day – I wouldn't blame her if she never did, poor girl. It's not something she can force, Franny. The mind has its own way of dealing with trauma. But don't be pestering her about it.'

'As if!' Franny was insulted. 'I'm not *that* thick.'

'She'll go back in the water when she's good and ready.'

In the meantime, Franny had to paddle her own canoe - literally. Sheena wasn't that keen on the water, although she liked wearing the gear and hanging out at the Surf Shack, and the girls who *had* been regulars spent more time, these days, on dry land unless the lads were going out. Everything had changed, and Franny hadn't even noticed when, or why, she thought miserably. Maybe that was why she loved nature so much, she thought, as she paddled closer to Gulls' Cliffs. At least in nature the same rules applied, year in and year out. The seasons came around no matter what else was going on and animals did what they had always done – unless, of course, humans were going to ruin all that, too, which it certainly looked as if they might. That reminded her of Ryan Shindler and the golf course remodelling. She would find him today and challenge him to let her do her video documentary on the project. Someone had to keep an eye on what was going on and it might as well be her.

Twenty-eight

Ryan slid into a booth at the Seashell and opened his laptop. He'd been out for a few drinks last night with some of the contract guys working on the clubhouse, and things had gone on a little later than he'd planned. He was feeling pretty ropy, truth be told, but it was nothing a good dose of coffee wouldn't fix. Eva came over to take his order – there was no sign of Merry, although Franny was busy polishing the countertop.

Franny looked at him every couple of minutes, surreptitiously – as if she was trying to work out something about him.

It was a few moments before Ryan realised he had been hoping to see a flash of pink hair weaving between the tables – and that it wasn't just the thought of coffee that was invigorating him. He was curious after their last interaction to talk to Merry – find out more about her, see what lay underneath that prickly exterior.

'What can I get you?' Eva smiled.

'Espresso, please – double shot.'

'Anything to eat?'

'No – wait, maybe that's an idea.'

'I'll get the breakfast menu.'

'No need. I'll have what he's having.' Ryan pointed to a guy tucking into a full Irish.

He felt a lot better after the bacon and eggs and a much-needed carb boost. He was just about to settle up and head to work when he noticed Franny approaching the table. 'That was great,' he said. 'Just what the doctor ordered.'

'I'm glad – but I'm not here to take your plate.' She looked serious.

'Is everything okay?'

'Yes, fine. I just need to ask you something.' She was determined but her eyes darted nervously.

'Shoot!' He leaned back, wondering what on earth was coming.

She took a deep breath. 'You know the film festival we're having here?'

'Uh-huh.'

'Well, there's a competition for a five-minute documentary shot on your smartphone. I thought I'd do mine on you and the golf club, on the environmental angle, if you'd, um, agree to that.' She hovered anxiously.

'Yeah, I heard something about that.' He looked at her. 'What would it involve, do you think? We're pretty busy up there.'

'I know. I thought maybe we could do a sort of interview – I could follow you around for a bit and ask you questions and stuff ...' She trailed off.

'Tell you what.' He checked his phone. 'Come up to my office tomorrow. I'll give you one day. You can follow me around, ask any questions you like, but that's it. After that you're on your own – but I'll give you clearance at the club to do your own research from there. Take it or leave it.' He grinned. It was a good offer.

'I'll take it!' Franny's face lit up. 'And thank you.'

'You're welcome.' As he left the Seashell, Ryan wondered just what he'd let himself in for.

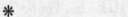

Molly yawned into her coffee. 'There I go again.' She blinked. 'I haven't stopped yawning since I got here – I can hardly keep my eyes open.' She was enjoying a quick cuppa with Dot – they were becoming good friends.

'It's the air,' Dot said. 'It'll take you a while to acclimatise.'

'I'm not sure I want to. That was the best night's sleep I've had since, well, since I can remember. I don't even have time to take my sleeping pill before I pass out.'

'You won't need sleeping pills here – a good walk along the sea front every day and you'll sleep like the just.' Dot had been about to say *sleep like the dead* – but corrected herself just in time. 'How's the book coming along?' She was rummaging in the fridge. 'Is it all set in the past? Or are you going to put any of this summer into it?'

'It's funny you should ask that.' Molly looked pleased. 'Something Charlie said the other day set me thinking and I realised what's been holding me up, and how to get around it.'

'That's good, isn't it?' Dot was learning to tread carefully around Molly's creative endeavours.

'Yes, it is. But I can't say anything yet.' She was apologetic. 'I haven't even told my agent.'

Molly's days were falling into a happy rhythm. In the morning she went for a walk on the beach, sometimes alone, which she found soothing, or she met locals, like Peggy, who sat and had a cigarette looking down at the beach from the walkway.

'I used to swim every day when I was younger,' Peggy had informed her. 'Are you not going to get in?' Molly had promised she would consider it.

Then, after a coffee and a chat with Dot, Molly would wait for Charlie to come down and they would set off together for a ramble. She had begun to look forward to these walks more and more.

'I'm just waiting for Charlie now,' said Molly. 'We're heading out shortly.'

'Where are you off to today?' Dot asked.

'No idea.' Molly laughed. 'That's part of the charm of these outings – we sort of wander wherever the spirit takes us. The scenery is stunning – Charlie's taken to videoing it. He's almost as attached to his phone now as that Sheena girl.' Molly laughed. 'Since I agreed to let her do her Film-on-fone documentary about me, she's constantly ambushing me when I least expect it and asking me silly questions. It's rather unnerving!'

'How do you think Charlie really is?' Dot asked. 'You know, in himself.'

'It's hard to tell. He's so nice and well-mannered that I can't help wondering if he's really struggling and being too much of a gentleman to be honest about it.'

'It must be so awful for him.'

'He's a wonderful listener – and very wise. I can't imagine how he's ended up on his own like this. Isn't there any news?'

Dot shook her head. 'Not that I know of. Rob has a theory he's leaning towards, fugue state …' and went on to describe it.

Molly shuddered. 'I wish you hadn't told me that – now I'll imagine it happening to me! But what's going to become of him? If …'

'If no one claims him? I don't know. Rob said it if it came to that, some kind of residential care …'

'Oh, surely not.' Molly bit her lip.

'Well, let's hope not,' said Dot. 'At least the GoFundMe page will help pay for it – or perhaps a flat with a carer to come in.' She signalled to Molly not to say any more. 'Anyhow, here comes your rambling companion.' She smiled as Charlie came into the kitchen.

'All set, Molly?' He waved a shillelagh. 'Sure you won't think of joining us, Dot?'

'Not this time, Charlie – enjoy yourselves. I'll see you later.'

*

They wandered along the winding lanes that brought them to the beach, then up the steeper climb to the cliffs above where the bay spread out beneath them, a few white sails dotted below making a haphazard pattern on the cornflower blue of the sea. Charlie was so easy to talk to that Molly found herself confiding in him easily.

'Well, you're fitter than I am! We can establish that much.' Molly laughed as Charlie waited for her to catch up. 'Let's sit down for minute – I can get my breath and we can admire the view.'

'Good idea,' he said.

'It's wonderful, you know, Charlie, being able to talk to someone like this,' Molly said. 'Much better than therapy. The trouble with therapists, I always think, is that you can never really *relax* about information you reveal to them – I mean, they're always going to be storing it up to quote back at you when you least expect it to illustrate some ghastly pattern of behaviour on your part, or similar. Talking to you is much more fun.'

'And you have the added bonus there's a good chance I won't remember any of what you've told me when my memory comes back.' He grinned. 'That reminds me.' He took out his phone. 'I just want to take some video shots of this beautiful place – you don't mind, do you?'

'Of course not, shoot away. I'm used to posing.' She sighed. 'I can't help thinking how my two dear friends would have loved it here – we used to travel a lot together.'

'Tell me about them.' Charlie sat down.

Molly shared with Charlie some of the great times she'd had with her two great friends. 'So you see,' she went on, 'it was bad enough when Nigel died suddenly, but when Julia – when Julia had that stroke' – she fought to keep her voice steady – 'well, it was sort of the last straw.'

'I can only imagine.' Charlie looked grave. 'Friends are often more important to us than family. That's a big loss to take on board. How do you feel you're handling it, so far?'

'I'm not sure I *am* handling it, to be honest,' Molly said. 'But I do feel better for getting away. Being somewhere different has definitely helped.'

'That's often the case. You know what they say, Jessie. A change is as good as a rest.' Charlie nodded.

'Who's Jessie?' Molly asked.

'What?'

'You called me Jessie just then.' Molly was on the alert. 'Is that someone you know?'

She looked at him to see if the remark had upset him, but he seemed unperturbed, gazing serenely out to sea. 'Jessie … I don't know … Maybe.' He frowned, concentrating. 'I'm thinking of cheerleaders, for whatever reason. High school, football matches …'

Molly didn't want to press him too much. She risked another question. 'How are *you* doing, Charlie?'

'I'm good, today, thank you. I'm happy here – it's a very nice place and people are being very kind to me.'

It was impossible to know whether Charlie was being truthful, or whether he was saying what he thought might be expected of him. Molly hoped very much it was the former.

'Shouldn't we be getting back now?' He looked at her expectantly.

'Yes, we probably should.' She kept up a steady stream of chatter along the way. 'I think Dot mentioned something about going for a drive to get some shopping in Clonty. We could go along with her, she said, if we felt like it.'

'That sounds like a nice thing to do,' said Charlie.

Of course Molly knew she should go back to her cottage to do some writing – but the thought of a diversion was much more appealing. She checked her phone as they came within sight of the village: there was an email and a missed call from Larry. She would attend to them later.

Twenty-nine

For a second, just one deliciously long second, Joni had allowed herself to hope. Perhaps it had been the warmth in his voice, the genuine longing she had heard when he said he was missing her. And then he'd said he had a proposition for her, something he wanted to ask her, a role she would be ideal for, that he couldn't think of anyone else ... and she had allowed herself to dream that this was it: he had come to his senses and was going to propose to her. But as she continued to listen, simultaneously deflated and annoyed, she realised that the only proposal Ryan had in mind was that she help him and his new friends in Ireland to track down who this crazy guy, Charlie, belonged to – or where he was from. I mean, what the hell was going on over there? What did Ryan think she was? A detective now? Joni pulled her robe around her tightly and walked quickly down three flights of stairs to the kitchen, where she began to pace.

Calm down, she told herself, deep breaths ... This is not as absurd as it sounds. Sure it wasn't what she'd expected or wanted to hear but, on the other hand, there was always an opportunity in any given situation if one was prepared to look hard enough for it. There would be one here, too. She put on a pot of coffee and began to think. Where was the upside in this? Where was the problem? Well, the problem was staring her right in the face. The problem was she had allowed Ryan to go to Ireland on his own (against her grandmothers' advice), and now, instead of missing her beyond all else, he seemed to have got caught up in this local mystery, which was clearly distracting him from thinking about her and reflecting on their relationship. That was the problem.

But – and it was a significant 'but' in Joni's opinion – he had asked for her help. He had sought her out immediately. That had to be an upside! So, what she had to do now was prove to Ryan that he had put his instincts and trust in absolutely the right person to handle this. She just had to do a terrific job and, come hell or high water, she had to find this guy Charlie's relatives or retirement home or asylum or whatever – she had to track them down and, more importantly, make sure he was returned to them or it. The more she thought about it, the better she felt. Not only would it put an end to this ridiculous situation that was distracting Ryan so much, but if she could pull it off – here she allowed herself briefly to imagine the glow of triumph – it would prove to him that she was more competent and caring and resourceful than anyone else, even the police!

Not only that, but she could get her followers involved – this would be a whole other ball game, away from fashion and beauty and health, her usual website subjects. It would really attract attention – it might even make the news. She might be invited on a current-affairs programme or feature in a local news clip. Her followers would love it! As if the Fates were encouraging her, another email pinged on her phone with the link to the GoFundMe page that Ryan had spoken about.

Joni grabbed her laptop and fired it up to look at it properly. Charlie had a nice face, she thought, handsome, for an old guy – and she definitely recognised the woman called Molly Cusack whose name the page was in. She was an actress, Ryan had said – Joni couldn't remember anything she had been in Stateside, but she must have seen her over the years, perhaps in magazines or on Netflix, because she definitely knew her face. This was even better than she had hoped. She called Becca to organise a catch-up over cocktails, with her and Imran. This required careful handling and she couldn't afford to put a foot wrong. Charlie's people would be found – and she had to find them before anyone else did.

'Online already?' Joni looked up to see Grandma Millie come into the kitchen bleary-eyed. 'You work too hard, just like your mother.' She shook her head as she made for the coffee on autopilot. 'It's not even seven thirty.'

'I was just checking some emails.' Joni closed her laptop. 'Top me up, would you?' She held out her cup.

'Sure, honey.'

'Can I ask you something?' Joni said, when Grandma Millie poured the coffee.

'Sure, anything.' Her grandmother's eyebrows lifted.

'If some old guy was found wandering – like, hypothetically, you know – lost, and he didn't know where he was, or who he was—'

'You mean like Alzheimer's?'

'Yeah, something like that. And suppose people were trying to find out where he lived, but no one had reported him missing.' Joni gazed at her speculatively. 'Where would you begin to try to find his people?'

'You're writing a mystery novel now?'

'No. I'm just thinking about something someone said to me.'

'Well, first of all, you're assuming he *has* people.' Millie sat down heavily and sighed.

'Well, if no care home or hospital has reported him missing, he'd have family, wouldn't he?'

'That depends,' Millie said, cradling her coffee mug in both hands.

'On what?' Joni was curious.

'Well, he could have been living alone and wandered off.'

'Someone would be looking for rent − retirement chalets would have noticed him missing.'

'True. Or …' Millie drummed her frosted-pink nails on the counter '… there's always the possibility he's been dumped.'

'Dumped?' Joni was dismissive. 'You mean, like, deliberately?'

'Happens all the time,' Milly said darkly. 'It's even got a name. They call it "Granny Dumping".' She shot Joni a look. 'And don't even think about it!'

'Seriously?'

'Yes, seriously. Romi and I know someone whose second cousin was dumped. She had a bad stroke a couple of years before – guess her mind went – and the old gal was dumped in the local ER. It took the police months to track down her family and prosecute them – they'd fled the state. Last I heard she was in a government-supervised care home. But it's a thing, all right. Modern families can't or won't cope with elderly relatives, especially with Alzheimer's or dementia, and since the poor creatures can't articulate or don't even know where they are half the time, they're easy for families – or, rather, cold-blooded relatives – to dump.'

'I can't believe that!' Joni was open-mouthed.

'Can't believe what?' Maria, her mother, came into the kitchen wearing her scrubs.

'She can't believe old people get granny-dumped. I told her not to get any ideas.' Millie grinned as she accepted a kiss from her daughter.

'Believe it, honey.' Maria turned to her daughter. 'Happens regularly in the ER – one old gal was left in a wheelchair last month and she had a Post-it note stuck to her forehead.'

'What'd it say?'

'"Please take care of her."'

'That is so unbelievably sad,' Joni said.

'Tell me about it,' said Millie. 'That's why I intend to keep this house in my name – come hell or high water.'

'Honey, you can get as crazy as a soup sandwich and we'll still love you!' Maria gave her mother a squeeze before she grabbed her purse and made for the door. 'Later, guys.'

*

Over cocktails at the Four Seasons Joni told Imran and Becca of her plan. 'So I have to find this guy's family, or people or whatever.'

'You're a detective now?' Imran lifted his eyebrows.

'I'm simply trying to help, Imran. Wouldn't you do the same, Becca?' she appealed.

'Well, sure, I'd want to help out – but it's not, like, your responsibility, Joni.'

'I never said it was. Ryan just asked me to help and since I have so many followers now someone out there is bound to know something about this Charlie guy.'

'If you say so.'

'Why are you both being so negative?'

'I'm not.' Imran held up his hands. 'I just think that maybe involving your brand in this Charlie business is a mistake – it's not like you're in the business of selling tracking devices, after all.'

Joni got up to greet an acquaintance.

'This is ridiculous,' Imran said to Becca.

'I know that – and you know that – but once Ryan Shindler is involved, any logical thinking on Joni's part goes out the window.' Becca shook her head. 'I know he's handsome and successful.' She grinned. 'But I don't know why he's suddenly the One.'

'It has nothing to do with that.' Imran scrolled through his phone. 'It's because no woman has been able to pin him down – that makes him unavailable.'

'She was never attracted to anyone unavailable before.' Becca was puzzled.

'Exactly – because none of the others could resist her.

Ryan's the first guy who's a challenge, which is triggering a subconscious pattern she doesn't even know she has with men.'

'Her dad?'

'Exactly.'

'I never thought about that.'

'Neither has Joni, unfortunately.'

'Since when have you become such a relationship expert?'

'It doesn't take a genius to work it out.'

'You really care about her, don't you?' Becca was looking at him curiously.

'Of course I do – she's one of my oldest friends.'

'So am I – but I think this is something else. OMG!' Becca said. 'How did I not see this? You're in love with her – aren't you?'

Imran shrugged.

'You have to tell her!'

'Really, Becca, for a commodities trader you can be very ignorant. Unrequited love is not a prospect I'm aspiring to – however smitten I may be.'

'But Joni adores you!'

'As a friend.' Imran was resigned.

'That's only because she's never considered you as a romantic prospect.'

'How do you think I've lasted this long?' He grinned.

Thirty

It was a lovely evening so Dot decided it would be nice to sit outside on the patio. She and Rob were catching up over a leisurely G&T. The garden was looking wonderful and a few ragged clouds drifted aimlessly through the clear blue sky.

'How's the GoFundMe page doing?'

'It's going from strength to strength,' Dot was happy to say. 'It's extraordinary how these things work and how generous people are. I'd heard of them before but I never actually knew how they worked.'

'Well, I imagine it certainly helps having a famous actress as an ambassador for the cause. How much have they raised so far?'

'Well, I can hardly believe I'm saying it but as of yesterday they were at seventy-five thousand.'

'Fantastic!' said Rob. 'And how are things going on the committee?'

'Really well, believe it or not. Things are finally sorted. It's full steam ahead.' Dot smiled. 'Ryan has been instrumental in that. He was able to persuade his boss to give us the golf club as a venue. Kate had approached them earlier but they quoted a fee we couldn't afford. Luckily, Ryan was able to turn that around for us. The café has got the catering contract back, and B&Bs are mostly all booked.'

'I could always move, out, you know.'

'What?' Dot gasped.

'Into the small room at the back, I meant, if you needed more space for guests. Just a thought,' Rob suggested.

'Oh, no, not at all, Rob, that won't be necessary. Although it's very thoughtful of you to offer.' Dot was alarmed at how dismayed she felt when she'd thought for a second that Rob meant moving out of her house, not just his room.

'I must say, I'd never have thought things could improve so quickly. Molly's been wonderful too. Apart from knowing how everything works, the fact that she is who she is means Kate Carmichael hangs on her every word and daren't contradict anything she suggests – which makes life *much* easier.'

'Sound like a win-win situation to me.' Rob clinked his glass with hers.

They sat for a few minutes in companionable silence, enjoying the feel of the sun on their skin and the flurry of activity on one of Dot's birdfeeders. Honey sat between them, ever hopeful of a treat, panting loudly.

'All the same,' Rob said, 'I think it's probably best to prepare ourselves for some difficult decisions concerning Charlie – which reminds me, are you all right to continue having him here for the time being?'

'What?' Dot was roused from her thoughts. 'Oh, yes, of course! To be honest, I love having him around. He feels like a friend – one of the family.'

Rob patted her hand. 'I'm beginning to feel that way as well – like I'm one of the family. You're a good friend to me, Dot.'

The unexpected contact of his hand brushing over hers took her by surprise, the innocent physicality of the gesture highlighting the absence of any real affection in her life of late. She was startled by how happy it made her feel. She glanced at Rob, but he was sitting back in his chair again, eyes closed, the sun on his face.

It was a nice compliment, Dot thought. That's all. Don't read anything into it. All the same, she felt a little tendril of hope unfurl inside her.

Thirty-one

The café was quiet mid-morning, apart from Charlie, who was sitting at his corner table, looking out of the window, tapping his fingers on the table to a beat that only he could hear. Franny was at Dot's place, collaborating with Molly on the ongoing GoFundMe page quest to track down any relative or acquaintance belonging to Charlie. And Eva and Jan were on their rounds delivering vegetables.

Merry was grateful to be left in peace. She was finding it hard to accept that, as a result of Doug's insurance payout, she was now a millionaire several times over. The responsibility weighed heavily on her. This was not money she had ever wanted – but she had to think carefully going forward. The solicitor had told her to take as long as she needed.

She was propping her elbows on the counter, her chin in her hands, when Charlie waved at her.

'How're you doing, Charlie?' Merry came over and leaned against the table.

'I'm good – but how are *you* doing?' He considered her. 'You're always working so hard and rushing around – we never get a chance to talk. Why don't you join me in a coffee?'

'Don't mind if I do – save me that seat.' She went to pour herself a cup and came back, sitting across from him.

'If you don't mind my saying' – he looked her in the eye – 'I was wondering why you look so sad all the time.'

The remark caught her off guard. 'I wasn't aware I *did* look sad, not all the time.'

He nodded. 'Most of the time. You're happier when the other girl, the younger girl, is around.'

'Franny.'

'Franny, that's the one.' He smiled. 'But I couldn't help noticing.' He stirred his coffee. 'I was wondering why – and if there was anything I could do to help.'

'Not unless you can rewind time.' Merry lowered her cup and bit her lip.

'I know that feeling.'

'Sorry, I didn't mean …' She dipped her head.

'It's all right.' His eyes were kind. 'Sometimes it helps to talk. Even I can remember that.'

She made a small sound, somewhere between a breath and a laugh, then looked up to meet his frank gaze. 'I thought I had my life all sorted out … and then everything was turned upside down.' She took a deep breath. 'My husband was killed. He died saving my life.'

'I'm so sorry – I heard talk to that effect. Tell me about him.'

'Doug?' She shook her head. 'He was – incredible, and I don't mean that in an "out of this world" way. He was a regular guy, I guess, it was just that he was everything I could ever have asked or hoped for. He was just perfect for *me*. That made him incredible.'

'So what happened?'

'We were on holiday, a vacation – a research project on my part. It was a chance for Doug to take some time out from his business, to come along with me and surf. He was from a family who didn't approve of aimless travel so when he was younger he never got the chance to take a gap year. We were in the Caribbean when it happened. Doug and I were in the water, snorkelling. A bunch of rich Americans had been partying and two of them thought it was a great idea to take their daddy's power boat out. They were drunk and stoned.' She stopped for a moment, transported in remembering. 'It happened so quickly … We heard the boat heading for us but it didn't seem real … didn't seem possible. Then Doug pushed me out of the way and got hit in the process. He was dead before I could get him back to shore. He saved my life.' She paused, gave a little shrug.

'And sometimes you wish he hadn't?'

Merry nodded. 'All the time. I wish it had been me.'

'How long ago did this happen?'

'Coming up to two years, this December.'

Charlie shook his head. 'Oh, sweetheart, that's a lot to be sad about. I'm so sorry for you.'

'Thank you. And thank you for not saying it will get better or that I'm young enough to meet someone new or all the other well-meaning useless stuff people feel compelled to say.'

'Have you ever talked to anyone – professionally, I mean?'

'In the beginning, yeah, but all I really knew for sure

was that I couldn't stay on in Florida, not without Doug. So I came home. When I was able to I started working in the café again. It was something I could do – I didn't have to think about it. It was the only thing I *could* do that didn't remind me of our life together …

'Doug's family' – she swallowed – 'they blamed me for it. He wouldn't have been there if it wasn't for me. He wouldn't have died if it wasn't for me.'

'That's as may be.' Charlie was serious. 'Some people believe the day you die is ordained and there's not a damn thing you can do to escape it. But blaming anyone won't bring Doug back – not for you or them. Sometimes people need to use a scapegoat while they process their own grief. It's not a noble practice, but it's not an uncommon one either. In time they'll understand how wrong and unfair they're being, but in the meantime you have to keep your own head above water, right? Sorry, that's a bad metaphor.'

Merry bit her lip. 'But it was my fault. We'd been having some problems – rowing a lot. I guess I must've made Doug feel so guilty that he thought he had to—'

Charlie cut in: 'He would have saved you whatever was going on, Merry. He would have been glad to save you. Any husband worth his salt …' He paused, frowning. 'I wish I could have saved …' He trailed off as a look of deep sadness came over his face. 'Never mind …'

Merry went on: 'So here I am, back in the café I spent my whole life working to get away from and looking like that's where I'm going to stay. Ain't life strange?'

'That's just your story so far,' Charlie said.

'Speaking of stories,' Merry changed the subject, 'I believe your own is gathering a lot of interest. Franny and Molly tell me the GoFundMe page is inundated.'

'I'm not familiar with this vehicle.' Charlie smiled. 'But I'm very grateful for everything people around here are doing to help me. I just wish I could think of a way to repay them. I feel pretty useless, just taking up everybody's time and energy – not to mention space.'

'Wouldn't you do the same for any of us if the situation were reversed?'

'I'd sure like to think so, yes.'

'Well, then.'

'I take your point,' Charlie said slowly. 'Sometimes we have to sit back and be grateful – just let things unfold.'

'Exactly.'

'I'm glad we had this little talk.'

'Me too.' Merry smiled. She hadn't told Charlie the whole truth – but even sharing what she had with him had made her feel better.

Thirty-two

The beach was filling, thanks to the settled weather forecast, and summer in Derrybeggs was in full swing. Lines of cars overflowed from the car park at Pirate's Cove and stretched back on either side of the narrow winding road – some precariously – for as far as the eye could see. Struggling parents negotiated the steep, twisting pathway to the beach, laden with folding chairs, lilos, buggies, bags of food and sun protection.

'Lucky we got here early,' Beth said. She checked on Emma, who was fast asleep in her buggy. They had escaped for a few hours to the smaller beach, around the far side of the rocks, harder to get to, but far more private, where they had set up camp. Merry and Eva had brought lunch, which included a chilled bottle of rosé, its temperature artfully maintained by hanging it off some nearby rocks where it dangled in the bracing water.

Eva sat with her latest book while Beth had been half-heartedly sketching. Merry sat on a towel, leaning back against the large slanting rocks, idly watching some paddle-boarders take to the water. At the shore, a dog barked and leaped to catch a ball some kids kicked back and forth. Merry felt her stomach rumble and glanced at her phone. 'Anyone for lunch? I'm starving.'

'Can you wait ten minutes?' Eva looked up. 'If I don't swim now I'll never go in after – and I promised myself a dip.'

'I'll join you.' Beth stretched. 'Are you okay holding the fort?' she asked Merry.

'Apart from the chance that I might run away with your daughter – yes.' She grinned, squinting up at her friend. 'Just don't drip cold water over me when you get back.'

Eva squeezed Merry's shoulder as she passed her. She and Beth were fully aware of how she was struggling with being the beneficiary of Doug's huge payout. All they could do was support her as best they could.

Merry checked on Emma, who was still fast asleep, and watched Eva and Beth get into the water – Beth with a neat dive, and Eva slowly, wading in agonising inch by inch. It was a special kind of torture. Merry smiled thinking of it. No matter how warm the temperature on land, the Atlantic stayed its own level of cool – fifteen or sixteen degrees on a day like this, dropping to as little as six in winter. But the initial shock was worth the high you felt when you came out. There was nothing like it. Merry wondered if she would ever know it again. That was the worst part, losing her natural therapy, her element, the one thing that would have helped her escape the relentless memories of the last two years.

It had taken her completely by surprise – this ambush of fear – in the most awful way. In the immediate aftermath of the accident Merry had stayed indoors, mostly because she was still in severe shock. It was later, when she came home to Derrybeggs, and drove to a nearby cove for an early-morning swim that it had happened. She'd got as far as about six feet from the water's edge and frozen, overcome by nausea, light-headedness and an inability to go any further that bordered on sheer terror. For a few moments she wondered if she was going mad. Then she turned and fled back to the car, where she sat shivering, trying to catch her breath. Her GP had sent her to a therapist who had diagnosed PTSD – post-traumatic stress disorder. She was a textbook example, apparently. 'It's hardly surprising,' the woman had said gently, 'given what you've gone through so recently.'

'How long will it take? I need to be able to get into the water.'

'You need to let yourself heal – that may take some time.'

'But that's the only thing that *will* help me heal.' Her voice sounded thin, reedy.

'Evidently your mind doesn't agree with you.'

'So how do I ...?'

'Merry, you can't plan this – you can't dictate it. It will happen when you're ready – when your psyche has recovered from the trauma you've gone through. Go as far as you feel comfortable with. The minute any panic arises, breathe through it and try to stay with it as far as you're able. Don't force it. Given time you'll be able to do more and more. In the meantime, find some other ways to relax.'

She had listened to the apps and relaxation recordings, walked on the beaches and by the harbour – but the closest she had got to getting back into the water was in her bathtub. But that was something. At least there she could shut out the world, light candles, plug in her headphones, breathe her aromatherapy oils and listen to sounds of the ocean – albeit recorded ones. One day she would swim again. One day ...

She wondered if she should just be honest about everything – if she told everyone the unvarnished truth about what had happened in her marriage, would it help? But she couldn't. If she did, she would be betraying Doug and his memory. He had made the ultimate sacrifice in saving her life. The least she could do was preserve the good memories her parents and friends had of him. It was hard, especially when Eva and Jan kept saying exactly what Beth said, that Doug had loved *her*, had chosen *her*, but she could do it. Merry could keep the truth about Kristy to herself.

Thirty-three

Franny was at the new clubhouse bang on eight a.m. as she had been told. Now that she was there, she was pretty overawed by what she saw. The new building was really cool. Better even than Sheena's house. It was made of wood the colour she sometimes saw washed up on the beach. Other parts were made of local stone and there was tons of glass, especially on the upper floor. The building sat into the backdrop of the dunes, and although she knew the gardens had been expensively landscaped, they looked wild and natural, as if they'd been there for ever, just nicer, as if Nature had been given a little nudge but not interfered with too much. She particularly liked the tall, pale, waving grasses along the boundaries that leaned gracefully in the breeze.

Franny was just going over what she had planned to say at Reception to announce herself when the huge double doors of the clubhouse slid open silently and a man in uniform came out to her. 'Franny Relish?' He ushered her through the doors. 'I'm Tom O'Rourke, general manager. Welcome to Derrybeggs Dunes! Mr Shindler is expecting you. Allow me to show you up to his office.'

Tom was very nice and chatted all the way up in the lift – but when Franny caught sight of her reflection in the mirror, she wished she'd taken Sheena's advice and worn some foundation. 'At least some mattifying BB cream?' Sheena had begged. But Franny had resisted: her heroine Orla Guerin wouldn't have stopped to beautify herself or apply blush before reporting on the political tensions in Caracas. Now, looking at her red cheeks and the burgeoning spot on her chin, her face grew even hotter.

'Here we are.' Tom opened the door for her to walk through, revealing a huge room decorated with tasteful modern furniture. At the end – which seemed very far away – Ryan Shindler sat behind a cool desk. He finished a phone call when he saw her. 'Hey, Franny.' He stood up and smiled, indicating one of the two chairs in front of the desk. 'Great to see you. Have a seat.'

'Um, thanks.' She untangled her backpack and fished out her phone.

'Have you eaten?'

She hadn't. All she'd been able for was a quick gulp of coffee before she left her house, and now she was starving.

'I took the liberty of ordering some breakfast for us. I thought we could eat while we talk.' At that minute two girls came in with trays they laid out on the table between them: tea, coffee, juices, smoothies, fruit and a selection of breads, croissants and pastries. 'If you'd like a cooked breakfast, we can arrange that.' One of the girls smiled at her.

'No, thanks – this is great.' Franny felt a bit weak.

'Dig in!' Ryan said. 'Tea or coffee?'

'Coffee, please.' He poured them each a cup.

'So, how do you want to do this?' He sat back and munched a pastry, regarding her.

'I've prepared some questions I'd like to ask you.' Franny hoped she sounded assertive.

'Well, let's get to it, then.'

Franny made herself focus. She wasn't going to be bribed by a fancy breakfast. If anything, it made her more suspicious.

'How will we know you'll really do your best to protect the snails when no one's looking?' she began.

'We've complied fully and will continue to do so with all European legislation, regarding the environment, Franny.' Ryan was definite. 'In fact, I've arranged for a Zoom call with our environmental lawyer in about fifteen minutes.' He checked his watch. 'He'll be happy to take you through it all.'

'Er, right. Are you going to expand further at any time in the future?'

'No. We do not have any plans to expand.'

'Not now, maybe, but you might in the future?'

'Franny.' Ryan looked her in the eye. 'These eighteen holes are as perfectly laid out as they ever could be.'

'But what about car parks and things – other facilities?'

'We've got everything we need here, Franny. I'll give you the guided tour afterwards.' He gestured out of the huge window. 'You're looking at the final result. There are no plans, and there is no need, to alter or extend this golf course in any way whatsoever. You have my word on that.'

More than two hours later, Franny had learned more than she'd ever anticipated about building a golf course. Ryan had shown her the many legal documents of research and environmental legalities gone through by his company in order to be in exact line with EU legislation. He had also talked to his environmental lawyer, Hank, on a Zoom call, who reassured Franny that everything was being followed to the letter – his segment was going to sound great on her documentary.

Now Ryan was walking Franny around the newly designed golf links. 'We've spent a lot of money on this, Franny,' he said. 'We can't afford to get it wrong, either. Your *Vertigo angustior*'s home will not be disturbed. Not by us at any rate.' They stood at the top of a dune looking out to sea. 'It's a beautiful place you've got here.' Ryan sounded wistful. 'I can see how you'd want to protect it.'

Franny nodded. 'It's more than that, though, I think.' She dug the heel of her trainer into the sand. 'I don't like when things change.' The words hung in the air.

'I won't lie to you.' Ryan looked down at her. 'Change is hard.'

'But it has to happen?'

'Pretty much – it's kind of inevitable. It gets easier, though, because you kind of get used to it. It's part of life, I guess.'

'I just wish there were some good changes happening.'

'There are always good things happening, Franny – you just don't always hear about them. Good stuff doesn't make for newsworthy headlines. The media prefer to bombard us with the bad stuff. But everywhere, every day, good people are doing good things, helping each other. You have to remember that,' Ryan said. 'Focus on the good stuff. You live in this beautiful part of the world and you have a family who love you, right?'

Franny nodded.

'That's huge. What do you enjoy doing?'

'Going out in my canoe with our dog, Muttie.' Franny grinned. 'I love that. What do you enjoy?'

The question caught Ryan off guard and he had to think about it. Since coming to Derrybeggs he was discovering what life was like when you weren't running at ninety miles an hour. He'd started swimming in the mornings, hanging out with Charlie when he could, and shooting the breeze with the local fishermen in the harbour. It felt good.

'What's so funny?' Franny asked, as he smiled.

'Nothing, really – just that I haven't done any of the things I enjoy for way too long.'

'Like what?'

'Well, I like fishing – used to do a lot of that back in Kentucky, when I was younger, before I moved to the city.'

'You could go fishing here. Loads of people go angling. Or you could go out further – you can charter boats.'

'And I used to enjoy playing the guitar, writing songs – some of 'em were even quite good.' He grinned.

'Why don't you do either of those things any more?'

'Good question.' Ryan turned to head back towards the clubhouse. 'I guess life got in the way and other things seemed more important.'

'Like making money?'

'That's part of it – but not all.' Ryan glanced at her. 'You have to remember, Franny, I know what it's like to be poor. I mean really poor. And I don't ever want to find myself in that situation again. Being poor sucks.'

Franny considered this. 'So it's not just cos you love making money that you do all this stuff?' She waved at the general area.

'No, it's not just because I love making money. I've worked hard to make myself a better life, Franny. Make myself a better person. Most people who get rich don't start out with that exact intention – but some people, I guess, get addicted to having a lot of money, same way others get addicted to alcohol or drugs or gambling.' Frank, Ryan's boss, came into his mind. 'Thing is, it doesn't make you happy.'

'What makes you happy, then?'

'If I had all the answers …' He smiled at her. 'I don't know – I guess having someone you love in your life is nice, having a family, or a dog, or something.' He grinned. 'Good people around you.'

'I love dogs. And my family's all right. They can be pretty annoying. I'm glad Merry's back – you met her in the café.'

'Yes. I know who Merry is.'

'She's kind of like an older friend of mine. She

taught me how to canoe. I missed her when she went to America.'

'I nearly drove into her last week.' Ryan frowned.

'I heard about that.' Franny grinned.

'I was swerving to avoid a sheep – Merry came around the bend and I almost caused a collision. We haven't gotten off to the best of starts.'

'You should talk to her – get to know her a bit. Merry's really nice.'

Ryan was thoughtful. 'Do you think she'd have a drink with me, sometime, maybe?'

'Only one way to find out,' Franny said.

'So,' Ryan checked his watch, 'how are we doing? You got enough for your film?'

'For now.' Franny put away her phone. 'But don't think because you've been nice to me it means I'll stop asking difficult questions when I need to.' She was serious again.

'I wouldn't dream of thinking that, Franny,' Ryan said. 'It's good you're passionate about what you do. Liking what you work at is important – cos you're going to have to be doing it for quite a while. You ever think of becoming an investigative reporter?'

'Sometimes.' She tilted her head. 'I think I might like it.'

'You should think about it,' Ryan encouraged. 'I think you'd be pretty good at that.'

Thirty-four

Imran was fiddling with the sleeve of the dress he had chosen for Joni. She would be sitting down for this video and in close-up so you wouldn't be able to see the figure-hugging lines, which he thought was a pity. 'I want a different look for this post – more serious,' Joni had said. 'Think Fox News anchor Megyn Kelly, *circa* 2015.'

'Are you sure about the hair?' Imran asked. He regarded Joni's tightly coiled topknot dubiously. 'It's a lot more severe than your usual style. And I think those glasses are too much. They're also too big for your face, honey.'

'They're staying, I like them. They lend credibility.' Joni was definite. 'I need people to pay attention to what I'm going to say. It's not a fashion post.'

'Let's hope for both our sakes no one thinks that,' Imran murmured.

'Imran, this is a matter of life and death. This post could make the difference between a man finding his family, or – or—'

'Roving the earth like a lost soul?'

'You shouldn't make fun of the less fortunate.'

'I'm not. I just want to know why Ryan Shindler is involved in all of this – don't you think it's a little weird?'

Joni did. But she wasn't saying. 'I think it's very caring of him. Besides, that's not the point, Imran. The point is I have to find these people.'

'Why?'

'Because it's the right thing to do.' Joni did not intend to articulate that she was not only determined to earn Ryan's undying admiration but to put an end to this ridiculous expedition that was going on in Ireland, thanks to 'Charlie'. The sooner the whole thing was over and put to bed (how hard could it be?) and Ryan was back in New York where he belonged, the better. She suspected Imran knew this already.

'Maybe, but why you, honey?' he persisted. 'It's not a good fit for your brand.'

Joni had considered this point – and thought it worth the risk. 'It's good to change things up a little, broaden out the horizons. We need to expand.'

'With a detective segment? Hmm, interesting.'

'It's not a detective segment.' Joni flashed him a look. 'It's a call to arms. Petitioning the general public to get behind this poor lost man and find his family.'

'If you say so.' Imran knew when to quit.

'Just start videoing me.'

'And … action.' Imran pressed record.

'Good morning, everybody!' Joni swung into action. 'Joni here from @houseofgirls. I hope you're all feeling super-well today! Those of you who know me will spot that this is not a regular look I'm rocking. There's a reason for that, my lovelies. Today I want to talk to you about something very serious.' Here she paused very briefly, and rearranged her features. 'It has been brought to my attention that we have lost one of our countrymen ... and I don't mean that he died. I mean in the sense of misplaced ... except it's not that either ...'

Behind the camera, Imran closed his eyes.

'This,' she held up the picture of Charlie, which Imran had enlarged, 'is Charlie. That is not his real name. The thing is, we don't *know* his real name ... and that's where you guys come in. Charlie has been found alone and wandering in a small town in Ireland, called Derrybeggs. He's suffering from memory issues. The people of Derrybeggs have called him Charlie because he was wearing a *Je suis Charlie* T-shirt when he was found – isn't that cute? Charlie didn't know his name or how he wound up in Derrybeggs ... and the good people of this town have taken him in until his people, or place of home, can be notified. The reason I'm telling *you* all this is that even though Charlie wasn't carrying any ID, he has an American accent. Which means that at some point in his life – or perhaps for all of it ... he has lived here. We're hoping that by showing you his picture, someone out there might recognise him and help us find out where Charlie calls home. To make this happen as fast as possible, the good people of Derrybeggs and a certain well-known actress have set up a GoFundMe page to help find Charlie's family.' Here Joni showed a close-up of Molly Cusack with Charlie. 'Molly Cusack, who many of you will be familiar with from various

British small-screen dramas, is in Derrybeggs as guest of honour for their annual film festival, which is taking place later this month. Molly was so moved by Charlie's plight that she decided she must get involved. We'll be putting up a link to the page on the site, of course. But in the meantime, my lovelies, please share this story as much as you can. Someone out there must recognise this man. Of course there'll be a substantial reward for any legitimate information leading to Charlie's place of home – just exactly how much, we can't be sure of, but the donations are pouring in as we speak, thanks to the good people of Ireland and the UK. We can tell you that people's generosity is humbling, so, please, share this story, America … and share Charlie's GoFundMe page. And let's bring Charlie home. Follow this link for constant updates. There will also be a link to the Derrybeggs film festival for any of my followers lucky enough to live in Ireland – or film buffs anywhere who might like to attend. And don't forget to watch out for the latest tip from @ Milliesfillies, which will be posted later today. So, lots of things are happening! Have a great day and see you next time, my lovelies!' Joni wrapped it up.

'How was that?'

'Pretty good! It always is – you're a natural. The comments are flying in. People even want to know where to get those glasses.' Imran shook his head.

'That's why I always follow my instincts,' Joni said, flashing him a look.

'Why don't you just come right out with it and say, "I told you so"?'

'Because this is only the beginning and I don't want to jinx anything.' Joni was superstitious. 'We still have to bring Charlie home – in every sense of the word.'

'Well, I'd say if anyone can, you can, girl.'

'Thank you, my friend. Then rest assured I will tell you I told you so.'

'Wait a minute.' Imran frowned as he studied the screen.

'What?'

'I never made that connection.' He was shaking his head and smiling.

'What connection?'

'Molly Cusack – the actress in Derrybeggs?'

'What about her?'

'Well, she's the star of *Hornetsville*.'

'What are you talking about?'

'You must have heard of *Hornetsville*, Joni? It's, like, the biggest crazy niche show on cable, right now.'

'Isn't it about insects, or something?'

'Think *Game of Thrones* with wings, kinda,' Imran said. 'But hipster kids have gone crazy for it. It's, like, *huge* right now. Molly Cusack plays the local sheriff and …' he scrolled down his screen '… it looks like your followers are among some of its many devoted fans.'

Joni came to look over Imran's shoulder at the live streaming comments that were pouring in. 'We've never had a response to anything like this.'

'Well, it can only be good for your brand. Shows you're super-current – down with the kids. It'll certainly be good for Molly Cusack and, I'm guessing, the Derrybeggs film festival. It's a win-win. You were right to go with your instincts.'

'Who would've thought?' Joni slipped behind her desk, and began studying the comments.

'What do the GMs think of all this?' Imran valued Joni's grandmothers' collective wisdom.

'They think I should have gone to Ireland with Ryan.'

'You still could.' Imran left the thought there.

'That's what the vote was about, Imran. You know that.' Joni sounded tetchy. 'My followers are invested in this ultimatum and they voted to let him go alone – to let him reflect properly on what I'd told him.'

'Your followers would love a trip to Ireland – and I'm guessing a few of them will be going if they know Molly Cusack is there. Maybe the GMs have a point – it's not like you're conceding anything.' He looked at her.

'I'll think about it.'

*

Joni messaged Ryan just as he was leaving the club. *So, how's it going?*

Hey, sweetheart. Good to hear you. I'm just leaving for the day. What's up?

Just letting you know I've put up the link to Charlie's page – and the weirdest thing has happened.

Oh?

Are you familiar with Hornetsville?'

Uh, I've kinda heard of it – it hit me when I met Molly here. I thought she looked familiar, then realised that's where I'd seen her, or read about her – something like that. Why?

Here's the thing. Apparently, it's, like, huge over here now – got a mega hipster following. I happened to mention in Charlie's segment that there was a film festival in Derrybeggs and that Molly was guest of honour to open it – and the comments started flying in. We've never had a response to anything like it! So I guess she knows but in case she doesn't tell her she's big in America right now! I mean, her fan base must be going through the roof. Anyway, I gotta run, just wanted you to know I was on top of things.

Thirty-five

Since Franny had made the suggestion, Ryan hadn't been able to get the idea of talking to Merry out of his head. He had no idea why – but it suddenly seemed important. Now he had a bona-fide excuse to swing by the Seashell as Dot had asked him to drop back a serving dish Eva had loaned her, if he was going that way. He was now. It was coming up to six: if he hurried, he'd make it before they closed. There was no guarantee that Merry would be there but, as Franny would say, there was only one way to find out. She was there, behind the counter, with her back to the door. It was quiet in the café – the weather meant most people were still at the beach or sitting outside. When she turned around to see who had come in, for just the briefest second pleasure crossed her face. Then, as if she had been caught out, her features instantly rearranged in neutral.

'Hi.' She pushed a lock of hair off her face. 'What can I get you?'

'Dot asked me to drop this back for Eva. I said I was going this way.'

'Thanks.' She took the dish. 'Coffee?'

'Uh, actually I was thinking of having a glass of red – cabernet sauvignon, if you have it.'

'We certainly do.'

'Care to join me in a glass? Seems unsociable, drinking alone. Besides, I really wanted to apologise for almost running into you last week.'

She hesitated for a second. 'Yeah, why not?'

'I really was avoiding a sheep,' he explained, 'when I swerved.'

'I figured. It's an occupational hazard around these parts – a regular cause of car wrecks.'

'Well, I'll know better next time. Next time the sheep gets it.'

'Be a shame to put a dent in your groovy car – quite a machine you've got yourself there.'

'It wouldn't have been my first choice – there was a mix-up of sorts with the rental company back home.'

'Where's home?'

'Right now, New York – but I'm from Kentucky, originally.'

'Bluegrass country.' She lifted an eyebrow.

'Not the part I'm from, ma'am. Nope, I grew up in a trailer park in Jackson County – one of the ten worst counties to live in in the USA. It was a long way from fancy cars or fancy horses. Trust me, I've come a long way.'

A flicker of curiosity. 'Sounds like quite a journey.'

'You could say that.'

'So how'd you get from a trailer park to fancy cars and golf clubs?'

Ryan told her about meeting Frank Levi and how it had changed his life. 'Frank was pretty drunk that night. I helped him into a cab, made sure he got back to his hotel. He gave me his card and told me to look him up if I was ever in New York. A couple months later I took him up on his offer.'

'The rest is history?'

'Pretty much. Frank taught me everything I know – he treats me like a son. I owe everything to that man.'

'What about your own father?'

'We haven't spoken in a long time. There was just my younger brother and me. Mom left and Dad hit the bottle – it wasn't pretty. My brother went to live with an aunt and I got out as soon as I could. Jimmy's at college now – I made sure of that. What about you?' Ryan asked. 'I heard you were in the States for a while?'

'Yeah.' She looked away. 'I needed to come back – there's some business I need to take care of at home.' The shutters had come down again. For a moment there he'd thought she might open up to him.

He brought the subject back to safer territory. 'I hear Charlie's page is going well – that's good.'

'Yeah, it's great. I really hope it works out for him – he's such a lovely guy.'

'A lovely guy with a price on his head,' Ryan said, frowning. 'There's a lot of money stacking up on that page – might attract some unscrupulous people. Need to watch out for that.'

'Rob and Dot won't let anything happen to Charlie – he's one of us now. Everyone loves him.'

'Well, let's hope so.' Ryan knew when to make an exit. 'I'd better get going – nice talking to you.'

Thirty-six

Dot was feeling a bit flat. The girl who came in to help her had finished Charlie's room and done both the cottages. All her shopping was up to date. Molly was holed up in the cottage at her laptop. For the past few days she really seemed to have got into her book – whatever it was about. And the others were out. It was a beautiful day, and from the sitting-room window she could see a few small boats bobbing about on the sea below. She did a last check of rooms before heading down to the kitchen.

She was being ridiculous – she knew that much. She had been waiting, hoping that Rob might suggest spending more time together yesterday evening, and when he hadn't she'd felt disproportionately let down. This had led her to the realisation that she was beginning to depend far too much on their recent friendship. If she was honest – which she tried to be, ruthlessly – she suspected Rob's more frequent presence in the house had more to do with him hoping to bump into and spend time with Molly, not her.

Dot's life had changed immeasurably in a little less than two weeks. Since Charlie had arrived, the house had become a hive of activity – a meeting place for all things to do with him and, of course, the film-festival committee. She was making new friends, finally beginning to feel she was part of the community. Sheila and Eva were great fun, and since she had been elected secretary, even Kate Carmichael had reined in her dismissive attitude. Dot was finding that, with the right support and network around her, she was possibly developing more self-confidence than she'd thought. *But –* a little voice warned her – *don't forget they'll all be going home, moving on. This won't last for much longer.* Perhaps that was the reason she was feeling low. Well, there was only one cure for that and that was to keep busy. The wash she had put on earlier should be finished now: there was laundry to be done.

She was halfway down the first flight of stairs when the strains of a familiar and beloved piece of music floated up to her, making her pause to listen – she didn't think she had left the TV or radio on. Then, to her astonishment, she realised the sound was coming from the reading room where her old piano stood, unused. It had belonged to her late father, and Dot's children had all dutifully banged out their scales on it – although none had developed his love of playing. She had never had the heart to get rid of it. Hurrying down the stairs, she stood transfixed at the doorway, as the notes from Tchaikovsky's Piano Concerto No. 1 in B flat minor filled the room, rising and swelling in exquisite crescendo. Completely oblivious to anything but the music, Charlie sat at the piano, head bent, hands running fluently along the keys, one suspended in mid-air, as gracefully as any maestro, making the old instrument sound like a Steinway. Dot sat down quietly on a chair until he finished the piece, then clapped. 'Bravo!' she said. 'That was just wonderful!'

'Oh, hello, Dot.' Charlie stood up. 'I hope I didn't disturb you?'

'Disturb me? That was exquisite! It's my favourite concerto. Come and have a cup of tea with me and a scone – you've certainly earned one!'

'I'm glad you liked it.' Charlie smiled.

A while later, over tea, with the washing-machine whirring companionably in the background, Dot couldn't resist asking, 'Where did you learn to play like that, Charlie?' then clamped her hand to her mouth. 'I'm so sorry – I don't mean to ...'

'It's all right. I've been thinking about things a lot lately ... Truth is, I don't know.' He frowned. 'But I just felt drawn to the piano – same way you'd be pleased to greet an old friend. It was a hunch, I guess. Dr Rob explained that to me and I wrote it down. He said it's possible to ...' He paused to pull out the little notebook he carried with him. 'Here we are ... It's possible to retain a procedural memory, that's knowing how to do things, while not being in full possession of my emotional memory.' He smiled and put away the notebook. 'It basically means I can be able to do things but not know *how* I know to do them – if that makes sense. Obviously I wouldn't attempt anything dangerous – you won't find me behind the wheel of a car anytime soon.'

He was thoughtful then. 'Something odd did happen when I was out walking with Molly last time. I called her "Jessie" – didn't realise I'd done it till she drew my attention to it.'

'And did the name mean anything to you?' Dot was curious.

Charlie shook his head. 'Not that I can say ... but it does give me a good kinda feeling when I think of it. It's very frustrating this *not knowing* thing. I got the feeling, too, the other day when I was in the harbour that I lived somewhere close to the water – but that could be wishful thinking.' He shrugged.

'I can't even begin to imagine,' Dot said, 'but it's good that you're beginning to feel things or say things on your walks – I mean, who knows when something will suddenly trigger a memory for you?'

'I keep hoping ... talking of walks' – Charlie finished his tea – 'I wouldn't mind a stroll now – it's such a nice day out there. Say, would like to come with me?'

'Yes! Why not? I was beginning to get cabin fever. I'm feeling a bit low, to be honest, and I've no idea why.'

'*The mind is its own place, and in itself can make a heaven of Hell, a hell of Heaven,*' said Charlie.

'Who said that?'

'Milton.'

'Smart man, he knew what he was talking about. Just let me pull my walking boots on – they're in the kitchen. We can go out the back way.'

They headed through the village and around towards the harbour, Honey close behind.

'Tell me why you're feeling low,' Charlie said.

'I'm not sure why. Do we always need a reason?' Suddenly Dot felt shy.

'No, I guess not. But usually there is one, lurking there.' He smiled. 'I just thought talking might help – but feel free to tell me to mind my own business.'

'I'm feeling rather useless. I think that's part of it.'

'You? Useless?' Charlie chuckled. 'You're about as useless as a screen door on a porch. Look at all you do around here! You run your beautiful house, you look after guests, and on top of all that you take in waifs and strays, like me.'

'You're not a waif or … Well, I suppose you are a bit of a stray.' Dot laughed.

'Dr Rob and Molly don't think you're useless – quite the contrary.'

'I think I'm a little bit lonely too,' she said. 'That's partly why I moved here. I know that sounds odd because I didn't know anyone at all when I first moved here, but after the children had left home and Martin, my late husband, had died, I was rattling around my old place in Dublin like a spare tool.'

'Nice analogy.' Charlie nodded.

'Renovating this place gave me a project for a year or so, and now I'm up and running – and I love it, I really do … but I suppose I've become very fond of having you all around, and I'm not looking forward to when everyone has to go – to move on. I suppose we've become a little family of sorts, or at least that's how I'm beginning to think of everybody.'

'I know just what you mean, Dot,' Charlie said. 'And I think your family, wherever they all are, are very lucky to have you.'

'Well, I feel very lucky to have met all you lovely people too. This is a very special time in my life, anyway, one I hope we'll all remember fondly. Oh, I'm sorry – there I go again.' She clamped her hand to her mouth.

Charlie laughed. 'I'm going to make sure I remember it – let me take a photo of you beside the water ... You know,' Charlie said, as they walked on, 'not everyone will be going home, Dot. Merry, Eva and Jan will still be here – and Dr Rob.' Charlie shook his head. 'He's been so kind to me, that man, just as you have.' He smiled. 'You make a good team, you two.' He looked at her. 'I've noticed how well you get along when you're together – you share a sense of humour.'

Dot felt her face pinking – had she been that obvious? 'Rob's a very nice man, but he's here as a locum. He'll be moving on eventually.'

Charlie nodded. 'Forgive me speaking plainly – my condition makes me seize the moment these days – but I get the feeling you and Rob like each other. Would I be right?'

'Well,' Dot blustered, 'I should hope so! I mean, there's no reason *not* to like each other.'

'That's not what I'm saying here.' Charlie was patient – as if he were explaining something to someone rather dim. 'I think you're attracted to each other.'

Dot groped for words. 'Well – I – uh—'

'It's all right, Dot.' Charlie smiled. 'I won't tell anyone. I just get the impression you'd be good together, that's all.'

'Do you?' She was being really pathetic now, seeking

reassurance like a young girl, but part of her was delighted. 'You see, I think it's Molly he likes – he's just being nice to me because he *is* so nice. Rob would be nice to everyone.'

'I wouldn't be too sure about that,' Charlie said. 'He speaks very highly of you. Why don't you ask him?'

Dot looked at him as if he were mad.

'It's one way of finding out.' He rubbed his chin. 'I think Dr Rob may be quite shy behind his professional manner. That's my impression.'

'That would make two of us.'

'I told you you'd make a good team.'

Thirty-seven

The café kitchen was piled with morning-fresh bread and plates of salads, finely sliced meats and local cheeses. 'Don't you miss doing all your old work?' Franny asked, as she and Merry raised a stack of sandwiches for the festival committee – which at lunchtime would be having what everyone hoped would be its last meeting before the big day.

'Sometimes,' Merry said.

'Joni says it's really important to be single-minded about your career ambitions – otherwise it's too easy to get side-tracked.' Franny had taken to listening to Joni's YouTube channel.

'I'm sure she's right.'

'But Sheena says you should change careers every ten years – except if you're going to be an actress, like she is, because every part you play is a change.'

'Franny, you don't have to do everything people tell you to – you don't have to follow every single suggestion,' Merry said, trying not to sound impatient. 'That's why we all have to think for ourselves. If we followed every line of advice that came our way, we'd all be locked up.'

'Sometimes I wonder if there's something wrong with me because I can never make up my mind what I should be doing – or even really *know* what I want to do. Mostly I want to be a marine biologist, like you – I mean like what you used to do – but now I'm thinking I'd like to be an investigative reporter. How come some people are so sure all the time?'

'You'll know when the time comes, and even if you don't you can find out by discovering what you *don't* like doing.'

'But that could take for ever!'

'At least you'd have an interesting life – better than wasting years in some job you hate.'

'Ryan said he thought I'd be a good investigative reporter. He said he could help put me in touch with some journalists he knows who might be able to help me break into it – you know, maybe even get me some kind of apprenticeship.' A dreamy note had entered Franny's voice, which Merry was beginning to recognise.

'I think you're a little young right now to be rushing off to America to do an apprenticeship. What's wrong with doing one here?'

'You sound like my mam!' Franny laughed. 'You don't like him – do you?' She tilted her head and looked at Merry speculatively. 'Ryan, I mean.'

'I don't have any feelings about him one way or the other.' Merry was casual. 'But I don't like what he represents – no.'

'What does he represent?'

'Greedy people, who only care about what they can

grab from any situation and turn it around to make a fast buck.'

'I think Ryan is nice.'

'He is – those sorts of people usually are. It's part of their stock-in-trade.'

'What does *that* mean?' Franny was bewildered.

'It means they always appear charming so they can lull you into a false sense of security while they go about doing whatever business it is they're after – which is usually something pretty unpleasant.'

'He was really nice to me that day when I interviewed him at the golf club.'

'I'm sure he was.'

'We were talking about you,' Franny remembered. 'He was saying about how he nearly crashed into you on the road and that he'd like to take you for a drink to apologise.'

'Did he now?'

'Dad said all the sparks working at the club like him – he said he's a good guy.'

'He has a girlfriend, Franny. Joni – remember?' Merry gave a small laugh.

'I think he just wants to be friendly.' Franny was earnest.

'I'm not sure his girlfriend would see it that way. Sounds like he's pretty shallow and untrustworthy to me. But, then, what do I know? I'd take anything he says to you on film with a pinch of salt.'

'What do you mean?'

'Don't necessarily believe everything he tells you, Franny. He may seem charming and nice, but I heard him talking on the phone one day at the café when he thought he was out of earshot. He was calling this place a one-horse town and saying it was important to look good to the locals and get them onside. Just be careful, okay?'

Franny looked crestfallen. 'Okay.'

The moment she had uttered the words, Merry regretted them. What was the matter with her? Ryan *had* been nice to her – both that day when she had been upset and again when he had dropped back Dot's dish. But, she reminded herself, she was right about one thing: Ryan had a girlfriend. Even if Merry found him attractive, which she had to admit she did, she'd experienced up close the trouble another woman could cause. No matter how nice Ryan might appear, she wasn't going anywhere near another American man who already had a girlfriend. And not just a girlfriend, an almost fiancée. Didn't he even practically ask her to help choose the damn ring? A wave of anger washed over her, and she no longer regretted her advice to Franny.

Thirty-eight

Sheena had been up in Dublin with her mother and they had taken the opportunity to visit their favourite hair salon where Sheena had been allowed to have her hair coloured for the opening-night ceremony, which was only a week away. 'As long as it's subtle,' her mum, Kate, had insisted. Sheena's hair was now a combination of honey-brown tones and highlights, graduating subtly to golden blonde at the ends, and she was keen to show it off. She arranged to meet Franny at the Seashell, where they had settled at one of the outside trestle tables with a big umbrella over it.

'It's gorgeous.' Franny was mesmerised. 'How did they do it?'

'Balayage.' Sheena inspected a waved tendril she twirled around her fingers. 'Yeah, I'm pleased with it. Took, like, for ever – but it was worth it.'

'I'd love to get mine done but Mam says I can't until I'm *at least* sixteen.'

'Bummer.' Sheena was sympathetic.

'Here you go, girls.' Eva arrived with Franny's ice cream and a smoothie for Sheena.

'Thanks, Eva,' said Franny. 'Isn't Sheena's hair gorgeous? She got it done up in Dublin.'

'It's lovely, Sheena,' Eva said. 'It reminds me of Merry's hair.' She seemed wistful.

'Merry's?' Sheena was horrified. 'But her hair is—'

'Oh, not now.' Eva laughed. 'Before she put all those awful colours in it. Merry had the most beautiful hair, didn't she, Franny?' Franny nodded. 'Merry's hair is that colour.' She pointed to the darker golden tones in Sheena's hair. 'She's a natural blonde – gets it from her Dutch grandmother. I know they say that people wear their scars on the inside. But when Merry came home with that awful hair … I knew then that my daughter was hurting in ways she couldn't even articulate.' Eva looked sad. 'Enjoy, girls!'

'Poor Eva,' Franny said. 'It's been so hard for her, Jan too.'

But Sheena's concern was focused elsewhere. 'I'm not sure what she meant by all that – like, blonde is blonde.' She frowned. 'Who cares if it's natural or not?'

'I don't think that was her point, Sheena.'

'Hey,' Sheena smirked at Franny, 'here comes your hero.'

'Who?'

'Your film-star hero – Ryan Shindler.'

'He's not my hero.' Franny scowled.

'Well, the subject of your film, then. Mum doesn't like him. She tried to talk to him about something the committee need to do, and he was, like, way dismissive to her.'

'Merry doesn't like him either,' Franny said thoughtfully. 'But he was really nice to me.'

'Why doesn't she like him?' Sheena was interested.

'She didn't say she *didn't* like him. She said he was probably shallow and untrustworthy. I told her he wanted to ask her to have a drink with him.'

'No way!' Sheena looked up from her phone. 'How'd you know that?'

'He said so when I was interviewing him. Just like in a friendly way.' Franny was feeling uncomfortable.

'Sssh. He's coming over.' Sheena studied her phone again.

'Hey, Franny!' Ryan came by their table. 'Joni tells me you've got over two hundred thousand followers on Charlie's GoFundMe page already. That's really great!'

'Um, yeah.'

'So, how's the documentary shaping up? Hope you're showing us in a fair light?'

'Any reason why she shouldn't?' Sheena looked at him and grinned. 'Franny's going to be an investigative reporter – you can't, like, *bribe* her.'

'Who said anything about bribing?' Ryan laughed.

'No one.' Sheena looked innocent. 'Only someone said that you're probably shallow and untrustworthy.'

'Excuse me?' Ryan looked at Franny.

'I did *not* say that, Sheena!' Franny was mortified.

'Sorry. I forgot.' Sheena pretended to frown. 'It was Merry who said that.'

'Sheena!' Franny looked desperately at Ryan. 'That's not—'

'Whatever!' He held up his hands and laughed. But the warmth had left his eyes. 'Sorry to disturb you girls.'

He turned to go and looked back at Franny. 'If you need anything else for your documentary, Franny, you know where to find me.' Then he walked away.

'What did you do that for?' Franny was furious.

Sheena shrugged. 'It was true. Besides, Mum says he needs taking down a peg or two. He's, like, arrogant. Who does he think he is, anyway? Don't worry about your film, Franny. You've got all the footage you need – you said so yesterday.'

'That's not the point.' Franny was miserable.

'What *is* the point?' Sheena looked at her.

'You wouldn't understand.'

Thirty-nine

Ryan wasn't a man to let things get to him, but as he walked away from Franny and Sheena, he found himself growing more and more annoyed. It was Sheena's final throwaway remark that had got his attention, when she'd smirked and said, 'Sorry, I forgot – it was Merry who said that.' Or something along those lines.

One thing was becoming abundantly clear: that Crazy Hair Girl had been pulling the strings to make him look bad. What the heck was her problem with him, anyway? What had he ever done to her? He was bringing business to this town, a lot of business. Everyone would benefit. He didn't hear any of the other townspeople complaining. It was time he found out what was eating her and he might as well do it now. He turned back to the Seashell where Franny and Sheena were still sitting outside, Franny looking sheepish. Ryan ignored them and pushed open the door. 'I'm looking for Merry.' He walked up to the counter where Eva had come out from the kitchen.

'She's not here.' The woman smiled. 'Can I help you?'

'Ah, no, thank you.' Ryan didn't want to sound abrupt, but he had worked himself up to a fighting level of righteous anger and was anxious to maintain it. 'Can you tell me where I might find her?'

Eva looked at her watch. 'It's her afternoon off so she's most likely running down on the beach. It's Ryan, isn't it?' she went on. 'I know you to see, of course. I'm Merry's mother, Eva.' She held out her hand to shake, disarming him. 'Franny can't stop talking about you and your girlfriend.' She smiled. 'You've made a big impression. It's good of you to help us out like this with poor Charlie.'

Ryan certainly hadn't been expecting that reaction. 'It's my pleasure, er, Eva. I'm sure we all want to see Charlie reunited with his people.'

'Still, not everyone would want to get involved. I mean, why should you? You have important work to be doing, yourself. I think it's very nice of you, very kind. So does everybody here.'

Not quite everybody, clearly, Ryan thought. But he was touched by Eva's kind manner and welcome. He was also struck by how unlike her daughter she seemed – she had a slight accent too, which he tried and failed to place. 'Well, it's been good to talk to you.'

'Good luck finding Merope, by the way. That's her real name, you know. We named her after a star.' She smiled. 'A very small star because she was so tiny when she was born.' Eva made a rueful face. 'But she turned into a fish, anyway!'

Now he had no idea what she was talking about. Maybe they were more alike than he imagined. Appearances could be deceptive. 'Well, so long, Eva.'

The long rope of bells and seashells jangled as the door closed behind him.

Walking back through the village, he passed Dot's place, where Charlie, Dot and Molly were setting out for a stroll. They didn't see him so he pressed on to the cliff path. He stood for a moment to take in the beautiful view as the bay spread out beneath him, cornflower blue, dotted with tiny rocky islands that stretched into the distance. Some of them, he'd heard, had been inhabited back in the Middle Ages. For a moment he remembered his other life, before things had got bad, happier times, fishing with his dad as a little kid, and he was reminded how he rarely, if ever, took the time to stop and look any more. That was something he needed to address.

In the distance, on the shore below, a couple of people were running – but it was too far to make out if one was Merry. Either way, he was going to have it out with her, before the embers of his smouldering anger deserted him completely. Ryan didn't care what Merry thought of him, although they had been getting on better recently – but he cared very much if she was trying to turn Franny against him. What kind of person would try to influence a fourteen-year-old girl just because of her own prejudiced opinions? First, though, he had to find out if what Sheena had attributed to Merry was true.

He followed the steps down to the shore and leaned against a wall of tall rocks. He wasn't as fit as he'd have liked to be – too much time spent sitting in planes, trains and automobiles lately. He wasn't totally out of condition but he sure wasn't going to run after her. If one of the joggers he'd seen from the road was Merry, she had to come back this way sooner or later.

Soon two of the joggers were heading towards him – neither of whom was Merry. But a woman was following them – a woman in very good shape. Sure enough, he could soon make out a bright pink ponytail as an identifying marker. If she saw him as she approached this end of the beach, she gave no indication, just slowed down, but didn't stop and kept looking straight ahead.

'Would you by any chance have a minute?' He stood up as she reached him.

She shook her head. 'Sorry, but no.' Her expression was closed. 'I'm very busy and I'm running late already.'

'I need to talk to you.' His tone made it clear he expected to be heard.

She stopped, pushing her hair off her face while she caught her breath and put her hands on her hips. 'What?'

'What exactly is your problem with me, lady?'

'What makes you think I have a problem with you?' Her voice was cool, but Ryan sensed her annoyance and that she was taken aback.

'Oh, I think it's pretty obvious that you do when you tell a fourteen-year-old girl that I'm shallow and untrustworthy.'

That got her attention. Although she gave little away, Ryan saw surprise flare in her eyes. 'Franny told you that?'

'Does it matter who told me? What I'd like to know is what gives you the right to say that about me?'

'It does matter, actually.'

'It was Franny's table companion – Sheena, I believe

her name is – who informed me. Now I would appreciate if you would answer *my* question. I'll refresh your memory if you like. I would like to know why you see fit to label me as you have, when I have made it my business to keep pretty much to myself, do whatever work I have to do, apart from trying to help out in whatever small way I can, finding Charlie's people, and a young girl to make a documentary film for her local festival. I would be obliged if you would explain to me how that somehow makes me the bad guy here.'

'When you put it like that,' she said, 'I couldn't possibly think of you as a bad guy.'

'I'm sensing a "but".'

'Franny shouldn't have shared those comments with anyone – but if you must know, she told me you mentioned you wanted to have a drink with me. Since you have a girlfriend, not that it's any business of mine' – she held up her hands – 'I merely mentioned that in my book that would suggest you were untrustworthy and probably shallow.'

'That's it?'

'Isn't that straightforward enough for you? Now as I said, I'm running late. I'm sorry if you don't like my opinion but it's mine and I see no reason to change it.'

Ryan laughed. 'You're pissed because I thought about asking you to have a drink with me?' He whistled. 'You really do have a problem! Maybe you should check back with Franny for the complete version before you go around bad-mouthing people. Franny suggested I ought to get to know you better. She told me you were really nice, despite what I referred to as your somewhat unfriendly manner. I simply replied and said that maybe I could buy you a drink to apologise for running you off the road that time. It's called being friendly – at least where I come from. And I can assure you I had no ulterior motives. As you correctly pointed out, I have a girlfriend, which I believe is common knowledge, one, I'm happy to report, who is entirely confident enough as regards the affection and esteem I hold her in to have no problem whatsoever if I choose to have a friendly coffee or drink with another person – even, scandalous though it would appear, if that other person is a female. If I have offended your sensibilities, Merope, by behaving in a manner so clearly inappropriate to you, I can only apologise, as I do now for interrupting your run. I'm glad we cleared that up. I feel duty bound to warn you, though, that I will in all probability continue to ask other people to join me for a drink. I sincerely hope they won't find the invitation as incomprehensible as you do. In the meantime, I suggest you keep your opinions of me to yourself. Especially the unfounded ones. If you'll excuse me, ma'am ...' He inclined his head, turned and took the steps back up two at a time.

Forty

Rob listened to the sophisticated young man sitting in front of him and wondered when life had become so complicated. He remembered him as a youngster, knew the family well, and Fergus – or Fergie, as he had been known back then – had been a regular young fella with a bright future ahead of him. No shortage of brains there, Rob remembered. Plenty of drive too. Everyone had said that Fergus would do well, make a name for himself – and he had. He was part of a new tech start-up that was making millions and predicted to double and treble its output. No problem there, but the very brains and drive responsible for setting up that wonderful new company were doing him in. Rob listened to the familiar litany – the waking at three thirty a.m., the inability to sleep, the low mood, creeping anxiety and now, horror of horrors, loss of libido. Fergus had been too worried, too ashamed, to visit a doctor in the city, where he now lived, and it had taken his mother begging him to come home for a couple of days and see Rob while he was in Derrybeggs that had resulted in this covert visit.

Rob had heard it all before, of course, too many times, and he knew Fergus would inevitably ask for the antidepressants or the tranquillisers, when what Rob really wanted to say was 'Why are you doing this to yourself? Is it really worth it?' He wanted to (and would) tell him to ease back on the alcohol or cut it out completely, get out for some exercise before he started his day glued to a screen, a swim in the sea preferably – yes, even in winter: the cold-water therapy was better than any medication. To get out and kick a football around with his kids and not worry about sending them to expensive sports camps. And not to worry what people thought of him. But he knew the trap Fergus was already ensnared in: a demanding, equally competitive wife, children in expensive schools, a busy social life, and the attendant worries and responsibilities that went with climbing the deceptively gilded ladder of success.

Not for the first time, Rob thanked God that he had had a relatively stress-free life as a younger man. He had worked hard, very hard, but it had been manageable. Life went by far too quickly even if you were taking it slowly. He was sixty-four now – he could still hardly believe it. If only April had had as long. Still, life was good. In fact the last two or three weeks had been positively uplifting. And he had to put it all down to Charlie showing up when he had. If it hadn't been for that, Rob probably wouldn't have got to know Dot as well as he had of late. He found himself looking forward to spending time with her and Charlie, and enjoyed particularly the lively dinners they shared. Dot was a fabulous cook and Rob's expanding waistline was proof of it. He'd have to do something about that. Then there was Molly: if anyone had told him he would be hobnobbing with a famous star of British sitcoms and dramas he would have said they were off their head. But Molly was just like Dot and him, a regular person (well, a very glamorous regular person), who was great fun and terribly nice and … This was where things were getting tricky. Rob had the distinct feeling that she liked him. Or was he imagining it? After all, Molly was lovely to everybody. It was rather confusing, really. He wished April were there to advise him – she'd get a good laugh out of that! He had been thinking of asking Dot out to dinner, to say thank you for all the delicious meals she had cooked for him and the others, but then he worried about offending Molly. Oh dear, it was very awkward.

'… so, you see, I really need to be on top of my game here, Dr Rob. I *need* to perform. I can't possibly scale back on my commitments, not when we're working on floating the company.' Fergus was outlining the importance of his undertakings.

'I hear you,' Rob said, looking over his glasses at him. 'I'll put you on a course of antidepressants, but it's just part of the programme I want you to follow. You need to look at your lifestyle. I mean it,' he said emphatically, seeing the relief creep over Fergus's face at the mention of a prescription. 'It might not be easy initially, but you'll feel better for it very quickly. Here's a diet sheet and an exercise programme I recommend. There are links to lots of other excellent sites. And, Fergus?'

'What?'

'I want you to knock off that beer belly before your

next appointment – and there *will* be a next appointment, won't there? Otherwise I won't sign this prescription. I want you back here and I want less of you back here. Understood?'

'Sure, Doc.' Fergus laughed.

'Now let's have a listen to your old ticker, and slip that cuff on for me.' The blood pressure cuff tightened around Fergus's arm and he winced.

'You want to know what I think?' Rob leaned back in his chair afterwards.

'You've been very clear, Dr Rob.' Fergus was itching to get out.

'How old are you?' He checked his notes. 'Hmm, forty-two. Here's a bit of advice, Fergus, from an old fella. If you have to continue with your current stressful lifestyle, try to make enough cash to get out of it by fifty. Then you might stand a chance of being around for your wife and kids – and that's *if* you drop the weight and get fit. Otherwise you're a walking heart attack or stroke – and if that doesn't get you, cancer will. Then it won't matter how much money you've made, will it?'

'I'm not that bad.' Fergus looked horrified.

'I mean it, Fergus. I've known you and your family since you were a small child. Don't throw it all away for a pipe dream. A bright young man like you shouldn't be suffering from anxiety and panic. Life's too short – trust me.'

After he saw Fergus out, Rob learned that his last patient had cancelled. It never ceased to amaze him how quickly a sunny day could clear a surgery – but he wasn't complaining. He might pop back to Dot's for a cuppa.

Ryan had mentioned something to him about fishing the other day, and it had been too long since Rob had been out on the water. Also, seeing Fergus so beautifully turned out – despite his additional weight – had reminded Rob that his own wardrobe left a great deal to be desired. He might ask Ryan for some sartorial advice … although, on second thoughts, he was unlikely to be much help: jeans and hoodies weren't really Rob's style. If only April were here, she'd know what needed updating without him ending up looking too ridiculous.

As it turned out, Rob ran into Ryan in the village. Rob had popped into the local store to pick up some tulips for Dot. He emerged with his armful of flowers and almost collided with Ryan, who, lost in thought, took a moment to register that Rob was inches from his face.

'Ryan! The very man! Don't suppose you can spare a moment?'

Ryan shrugged. 'Sure.'

'I was hoping to run into you. I wanted to continue our fishing discussion from the other night. What do you say?'

'Happy to.' Ryan was relieved by the distraction. Losing his temper with anyone was a rare event and was weighing on his mind. His skill was to smooth rough edges during interactions. Getting angry was a last resort. But after hearing Merry's comments about him, he had been left with no choice but to confront her.

'Great! Let me buy you a drink.'

Over a quiet pint in O'Hagan's, they discussed the finer points of salmon fishing, how the golf course was coming along, and the latest regarding Charlie's situation.

'There must be quite a substantial amount involved. How much is the fund now?'

'Over five hundred thousand dollars, last I heard.'

'Which makes Charlie pretty hot property,' Rob agreed. 'That was my only reservation about this approach. We'll have to proceed very carefully here – Charlie is my responsibility.'

'Well, with respect, we're kind of all in this together.'

'Yes, but in the absence of his usual medical supervisor, I feel it's my responsibility to make sure he doesn't suffer any further unnecessary trauma.'

'How do we go about that?'

'I'll work out the finer details with Dot later, which reminds me. I wanted to ask your advice about something. Do you think I look old-fashioned?'

Ryan blinked.

'What I mean is, I was thinking I should probably get some new clothes. My wife died some years ago, you see, and I really never went shopping without her. My daughter's in Australia and my two boys are in America so they won't be much use. I don't want to look ridiculous, of course, but I don't want to turn into an old dinosaur either, so I thought some new threads might be in order. Maybe some new glasses … What do you think?'

Ryan chewed his lip. 'Um, I think women are better at this sort of thing. I'm a pretty relaxed dresser and, uh, I wouldn't really know the vibe here for—'

'An old guy like me?' Rob grinned.

'You're not old, dude!' Ryan punched Rob's arm. 'It's just that I don't think I'd be much help.' Then inspiration struck. 'Why don't you ask Molly? She's pretty cool and, being an actress, she'd know how to pull a look together, wouldn't she? That's who I'd ask, if I were you.'

The suggestion didn't seem to thrill Rob as much as Ryan had hoped it would.

'Well, that might prove a little awkward,' Rob said.

'Why?'

'Well, I was planning on asking Dot out to dinner, you see, to thank her for all the meals she's cooked, and then, well, we've all become great friends, you see, and I thought Molly might feel a bit hurt if I didn't include her as well so I thought I'd ask her along too.'

'You're taking two women out to dinner?' Ryan lifted his eyebrows.

'You don't think that's good idea?'

'Depends which one of 'em you really like.' Ryan grinned.

'Surely that doesn't matter.' Rob looked uncomfortable. 'I like both of them, of course.'

'Uh-huh … Look, it's none of my business, dude, Doc, but you know how women can be.' Ryan was still fuming over Merry bad-mouthing him to Franny – what had possessed her to drag a kid into whatever was bugging her?

'Then it's not a good idea?'

'I know! Why don't you take Charlie along? Then you guys can be a foursome. Problem solved!'

'That's a great idea! Why didn't I think of that?'

'So that's why you don't want to go clothes shopping with Molly, right?'

Rob nodded. 'Yes. I don't want to offend Dot – do you think she'd be offended?'

'You're asking me?' Ryan laughed.

'Oh dear. I thought this sort of thing got easier as one got older but it's just as full of pitfalls as ever. Fancy another?'

'Sure.'

Rob returned with two more pints. 'Cheers.'

'I'm sorry to hear about your wife.'

'Thank you. April was fab. She had so much life left in her.' Rob shook his head.

'Cancer?'

'Yes, mercifully quick in the end…I don't think either of us could have stood a long, protracted illness.'

'Man, that's tough.'

'Thing is … life is very lonely on your own and it goes by terribly quickly. You're too young to appreciate that, of course, but it really does.'

'I can believe it.'

'So you have to make the most of it.'

They chatted for a while longer about golf, life, the incomprehensibility of womenfolk, while Rob's tulips sat beside him, forgotten and quietly wilting.

It was when they were leaving O'Hagan's that Ryan noticed the poster advertising the music session for Saturday night. 'Might have to check that out,' he said to Rob.

'Nothing like a good session – haven't been to one in years. If the girls are good for Saturday night, I might drag them along here afterwards.'

'I'm not familiar with local music, although my mom was Irish – but I used to be handy with a guitar, played a bit of country …' Ryan felt a twinge of regret at giving it up.

'That settles it!' said Rob, taking out his phone to put in a reminder of the event. 'We should get a few of us together for that.' He perked up at the thought.

'Well, so long, Doc. I enjoyed our conversation.'

'We must do it again soon,' said Rob. He headed for home feeling considerably better about life while his flowers languished behind him in the pub – a distant memory.

She had taken extra care with her appearance. Since her talk with Charlie the other day, Dot had given a lot of thought to what he had said. Perhaps Rob *was* shy – a professional manner could hide a lot – and while as a doctor he was used to talking to patients all day, he might be more circumspect at social or even more intimate events. Perhaps she ought to take the bull by the horns and try to navigate their friendship towards something more … But how? She had no idea how these things worked now. People met online or swiped left or right on their phones – it sounded like a minefield of horror to her. But perhaps she had been so caught up with Charlie's predicament and looking after her guests that she had neglected to present herself in a more flattering light. Maybe if she could make him see her a bit differently ...

But that posed other pitfalls: she certainly didn't want to appear to be trying too hard. On the other hand, a new look wuldn't hurt – she had been stuck in a rut of late. While she had been happy to invest thousands of pounds in renovating her house, Dot rarely, if ever, spent any money on her own appearance. She had grown accustomed to being relentlessly practical in that respect. She had been considered good-looking when she was younger – perhaps it wasn't too late to polish things up a bit. She could ask Molly, who always looked so glamorous, even when she was in jeans and wellies. She'd know all the tricks of the trade – but then Dot would have to explain *why* she wanted the advice, or even if she didn't Molly might guess, which would be even more mortifying. For all Dot knew, Rob and Molly might already have an understanding. The thought depressed her. So she had washed and blow-dried her hair carefully, put on some subtle makeup – she couldn't remember whether Rob had said he'd be there for dinner this evening but he wasn't always so it was better to be prepared. But there was no sign of Rob later, just a text to say he was meeting a medical colleague and wouldn't be back till later. When Molly and Charlie joined her for dinner, they found her unusually subdued.

Forty-one

She had had to cancel her late-night opening shift at the café, she was so angry. She knew that if she went in, she would very likely end up hurling every piece of crockery at the walls so that it smashed into smithereens. Even if she managed to refrain from that, it would be obvious to everyone there that she was in a foul mood. And what if he came in? And she had to serve him? There was every chance she'd throw the order in his stupid face. So she had called around to Beth, who was finishing off a painting outside her small home studio and said she was in such a good mood that even Merry at her worst couldn't bring her down.

Merry brought two cups of coffee with her and pulled up a stool to sit and admire the work in progress, lighting a cigarette, which she drew on heavily.

'I thought you'd given up years ago.' Beth took the coffee gratefully.

'I had. This was an emergency.'

'What happened?' Beth's palette knife paused in mid-air.

'I was accosted on the beach.'

'Really?' Beth was intrigued.

'In a manner of speaking.'

'Plain English, please – I don't have the time or energy to decipher the finer nuances of conversations these days. Baby brain.'

'The American guy, Ryan, followed me to the beach and had a go at me.'

'For what?' Beth looked at her.

'For telling Franny he was shallow and untrustworthy.'

'Did you tell her that?'

'Yes. But I didn't mean her to say it to him – obviously.'

'And Franny told him?' Beth was surprised. 'That doesn't sound like Franny.'

'Franny didn't tell him – Sheena did. So Franny must have told Sheena.'

'Ah. That would explain it.' Beth lifted her eyebrows. 'Poor Franny. That Sheena's a little witch.'

'The apple doesn't fall far from the tree. Anyway, apparently Franny and Sheena were having coffee. Clearly Franny confided in Sheena what I thought of Ryan, and Sheena, in her wisdom, decided to tell him, thereby dumping me and, worse, Franny, royally in it.'

'And what makes you think Ryan is shallow and untrustworthy?' Beth was curious.

'It was just a throwaway remark. Obviously, I didn't mean for him to actually *hear* it.'

'Yes, but why do you think that?'

Merry shifted uncomfortably. 'It was just something Franny said to me. It sounds silly now – we were just chatting.'

'Go on.'

'Well, Franny's doing her Film-on-fone thing on the environmental effects of the golf course redevelopment. She was interviewing Ryan at the club and he was taking her through it all.'

'That was nice of him.'

'We were discussing how her interview with him went and Franny mentioned that he wanted to take me for a drink.'

'And this bothered you why?' Beth was careful to keep her tone light.

'Oh, come on, Beth. The guy has a girlfriend back home. I just happened to mention that he probably wasn't a very trustworthy person, and that Franny should take whatever he told her with a pinch of salt.'

'Hmm.'

'You know what these people are like.' Merry looked at her friend as if it was obvious. 'He's just cruising through here and only interested in turning a fast buck – I heard him on the phone. He was calling Derrybeggs a one-horse town and us a bunch of yokels.' Merry felt a little exaggeration wouldn't go amiss.

Beth cut in: 'Aren't you being a little presumptuous here?'

'Look, I just don't want Franny, or anyone else for that matter, being taken advantage of by him. I was just marking her card.'

'What are you? Her mother now?'

'Beth!'

'No, really.'

'Anyway, Ryan came looking for me in the café. Mum

told him I was probably at the beach, and that was where he found me. Interrupted my run to give me a piece of his mind.'

'Really? What did he say?' Beth added some paint to her canvas with the palette knife.

'What does it matter?'

'Humour me.'

'Oh, some rant about what gave me the right to tell anyone he was shallow and untrustworthy when he's done nothing but try to help people since he got here – made himself out to be a regular saint.'

'Well, he has been pretty helpful, hasn't he?' Beth shrugged. 'That's what I've heard anyway. Dot told me he was brilliant with Charlie. He's going beyond the call of duty to make sure the conference hall is ready for the film festival, and his girlfriend – *said* girlfriend – who has gazillions of followers, has put a link up to Charlie's GoFundMe page. She's going to post the winning documentary film on her site as well. That's being pretty helpful in anyone's book.'

'What exactly are you getting at?' Merry frowned.

'I'm not getting at anything, Merry. At least I haven't, not up until now … but maybe it's time I did.' Beth sighed and put down her knife, sitting on the low stone garden wall so she was facing Merry. 'Hang on. I might need one of these.' She got up to retrieve a packet of cigarettes from behind a bottle of turpentine. 'My emergency stash.'

'You haven't smoked since before you were pregnant!' Merry was shocked.

'Now you're *my* mother?' Beth sat down again putting one into her mouth and inhaled, then blew a plume of smoke over her shoulder. 'The thing is, Merry, you've got to let go of this anger.' There, she had said it. 'It's understandable, of course it is, but in the beginning it was different. Now, it's – it's beginning to consume you. It's like it's defining you, and that's so not *you*. It just isn't, and – and Doug would *hate* that, seeing you turn into some angry, bitter woman. He'd just hate it. You know he would.' Beth paused.

Merry didn't say anything. Her face went a little white, and for a moment she seemed to Beth as if she might crumple.

'Sweetheart.' Beth forced herself to go on. 'We all know how hard it's been for you – how hard it *is* for you, and maybe it always will be – but you've got to stop letting this anger take over your entire personality. It's like – it's like you're just radiating it, all the time, and it's so unfair of you to do that to yourself. It's like it's become more important for you to hold on to that anger than it is to try to start living some sort of a life without Doug – and he'd hate that for you. He'd hate you to become that person. We all would.' Beth sighed. 'I don't know what this Ryan guy said to you, Merry, or what you said to him, or Franny, or what the hell is going on. But I'm willing to bet that just because he's here and alive you resent him for it – because Doug isn't.' Beth stopped to draw breath. 'And I wouldn't be any sort of a friend to you if I didn't say this. If you're going to get angry at anyone, get angry with me – I can take it – but your mum and dad are out of their minds with worry about you. And Franny ... Ryan ... whoever' – she waved a hand – 'you've got to let it go, Merry. It's not going to bring Doug back.'

Neither of them said anything for a few seconds that stretched unbearably, taut with dreadful possibilities.

Then Merry looked at Beth. 'I know,' she said. Her voice was small. 'I do realise that.' She gave a tight little smile.

'Then don't make it harder on yourself than it already is. You've been amazing.'

'No, I haven't!'

'You have! You've been amazingly strong, and – and I don't know how you've kept going, but if it's only anger that's fuelling your strength, you need to find another way.'

'Is that what everyone's been saying?'

'No – well, yes, in a manner of speaking. But we love you, Merry. You know that, and we miss you. This – this person who radiates anger and resentment, this isn't you. It's gone on too long, and if you don't do something about it, it'll warp your personality for good. And that would be a double tragedy.'

Merry bit her lip. 'Tell it like it is, why don't you?'

'You know you can always count on me to do that. Come here.' Beth gave Merry a long hug.

'The thing is,' Merry said, sitting down again, 'I haven't been entirely truthful about Doug and me.'

She had told Beth and her parents about Doug's baby boy, and the shock of finding out the way they had. But she hadn't told them the rest of the story.

'What do you mean?' Beth frowned.

'Doug didn't choose me.'

'What?'

'Not exactly, anyway.' It was a huge relief finally to unburden herself. 'When Doug went to visit his new son, he and Kristy discovered they had unfinished business.' Merry threw Beth a meaningful look. 'Doug felt that maybe he was still in love with Kristy – that he and I had been – a mad attraction, call it what you will. He was seriously considering going back to Kristy, being a perfect little family – you get the drift.' Merry chewed her lip. 'That holiday we – well, we were trying to save our marriage, work out what he should do, and then—'

'Oh, Merry.'

'The rest is history. So no, Doug didn't really choose me. Or love me more. He was having an affair with his ex. In fact, I'm wondering if he ever really loved me at all.'

Forty-two

'So you see, Joni' – Jenna was emotional on screen – 'this really is extraordinary, a blessing, such a coincidence. I mean, what were the chances?' She shook her head in wonder. Behind Jenna, her husband Kyle, who looked as if he'd been shoehorned into a shirt and tie for the occasion, nodded vigorously.

Joni smiled her agreement – although she would have liked to stress that coincidence or luck had had less to do with recent developments than her unshakeable and relentless determination in this matter. All the same, even she had to admit this was a stroke of fortune. Over Zoom, she was talking to a woman who claimed Charlie – or Jonathan, as they referred to him – was a cousin of her late mother. They had photos to prove it and, more importantly, military records they were going to send her – and this was the best bit: Charlie, or Jonathan, turned out to be a retired veteran of Afghanistan, who had been traumatised in action. 'He escaped physically,' Jenna said, 'but he was never the same up here, after it.' Jenna tapped the side of her head.

Joni closed down the on-screen meeting with a feeling of deep satisfaction. Things were finally turning around. She had found Charlie's people. This would be sensational for the blog. More importantly, it meant she could proceed with the next part of the project – going to Ireland and getting Charlie and Ryan back home to the US of A.

She called Imran to tell him the good news.

'That's great, Joni – I'm happy for you.' He sounded weary.

'Why don't you come on over for dinner tonight?' Joni's grandmothers adored Imran. 'I need to bring everyone up to speed, tell them I'm going to Ireland. It'll be easier if you're here with me.'

'You know me,' Imran said. 'Anything for a free dinner.'

'I knew I could rely on you.' Joni smiled into her phone. 'I'll tell them to do your favourite pasta. They'll be psyched. Later! Ciao!'

Much as she wanted to ring Ryan immediately with the exciting news, she decided to wait until she had run the idea by her grandmothers.

Ryan had decided to give himself the afternoon off. Everything was pretty much on schedule with the golf club, and the film festival next Saturday was well under control, thanks to Dot. When he returned to the Old Rectory for his swimming stuff, it was quiet – no sign of Dot or Molly or Charlie, probably because everyone was out enjoying the sunshine. He packed his trunks and a towel, yet instead of going straight to the beach, he found himself pacing the little cottage, brooding. He simply couldn't shake the confrontation he'd had with Merry. He didn't like confrontations but sometimes only plain speaking would do – and in this case he felt vindicated. But he was puzzled too. He wouldn't have put Merry down as a controlling type – someone who would have a problem if a guy so much as had a friendly drink with another woman, even if he was sort of engaged. Ryan wasn't usually wrong about people. Something didn't add up, but whatever it was, no one was paying him to figure it out.

It was late afternoon and warm, so he grabbed some water from the fridge, then picked up the guitar that lay against the wall. One of the guys in the golf club who played in O'Hagan's had found him one. The Cordoba Paco Flamenco had been worth every cent he'd paid for it. With its solid cedar top and back, its rosewood sides, the classical guitar produced a full, mellow sound. More importantly, it fitted into his arms like it belonged there – until he'd picked it up he hadn't realised how much he'd missed playing. He was about to tune it when he had a better idea. He grabbed his guitar and got into the car, heading for a beautiful beach just twenty minutes outside Derrybeggs.

He found himself some rocks to sit on, flexed his fingers, tuned it, and ran through a few old numbers, songs he'd forgotten he'd written coming back to him. He wasn't sure how long he'd been there – an hour, two maybe – but when he heard clapping and looked up. A small crowd had assembled around him. 'Can you play "American Pie"?' an old dude asked him.

'Sure.' After that he played some Garth Brooks, Neil Young, Kenny Rogers, while everyone sang along. It felt good. He wrapped up with one of his own.

'You're good!' one of the women said admiringly. 'Are you playing locally?'

Ryan shook his head and grinned. 'Just having some fun.' They seemed disappointed.

The sun was low in the sky by the time Ryan pulled himself to his feet – stiff and sore from sitting so long.

Checking his phone on his way back to the car, Ryan saw a text from Dot. *Will you be back any time soon? Franny's here, we're in the kitchen – she wants to talk to you.*

Ryan sighed. Losing himself in his music for a while had been just the therapy he needed to forget about recent events. He was looking forward to the music session in O'Hagan's later this evening and really didn't want to get into this Franny and Merry business again.

Be there in twenty, he texted back.

'Would you like something to eat?' Dot indicated some platters of leftover food on the counter. Charlie and Molly were having tea and cake and Franny was between them, looking extremely awkward. Ryan sat down across from them. 'Not for me, thanks. I'll have some water, though.'

'I'm really sorry, Ryan,' Franny blurted, 'about what Sheena said.' Her face was very red.

'It's not your fault, Franny. Forget it.'

'But it is. If I hadn't said anything, then—'

'If Sheena is anything like her mother, then she'll very likely need to learn some manners,' Dot interjected. 'What she said and did was both rude and hurtful, and she put you in an awkward position, Franny. If I were you, I'd rethink my friendship with a girl like that.' Dot was surprised to hear herself speak so forcefully – but she had strong feelings on the matter.

'I don't think that about you, Ryan – what Merry said.' Franny's voice was small. 'I told her I thought you were okay.'

'I'm glad to hear that, Franny.' Ryan sat with his arm along the chair beside him. He frowned. 'What's her deal, anyway?' He looked around the table. 'It feels like she's had it in for me ever since I got here.'

'Who, Merry?'

'Never was someone so misnamed,' Ryan said. 'I don't think I've ever seen her smile. I know I almost ran her off the road a while back when I swerved to avoid a sheep – but I've apologised for that.'

An embarrassed silence ensued, leaving only Charlie unperturbed.

'What?' asked Ryan. 'What have I said?'

'She hasn't *had* a lot to smile about, poor girl,' said Dot. 'Her husband, Doug, was killed almost two years ago.'

'I'm very sorry to hear that.' Ryan was taken aback. 'When you say killed, what happened? Was it a car wreck?'

'No, it was a terrible accident,' Franny said. 'They were on holiday in the Caribbean. One day they were out in the water snorkelling and apparently some rich kids were partying and took a power boat out and ran into them. Doug pushed Merry out of the way. He saved her life.'

'I think I remember reading about that.' Ryan was serious. 'Did it happen off St Bart's?'

'I think that's the name of the place,' Franny said.

'So' – Dot looked at him meaningfully – 'you can see why Merry wouldn't have a lot to feel cheerful about these days.'

'Poor girl,' said Molly. 'Life can be so terribly cruel.'

'Although I really don't think she has it in for anyone,' said Dot, 'grief can make you very angry.'

Ryan could relate to that. Things were beginning to make more sense, now, as regards Merry. If a bunch of spoiled, partying American kids had mown down someone he loved, he wouldn't feel too kindly towards them either.

'I think she probably likes you.' Charlie nodded as if confirming something to himself. 'I've noticed the way she looks at you in the café. You might like her too, if you gave her a chance. She's a real interesting girl.'

'That's what I was trying to say to you,' Franny said. 'Up at the golf club – before everything went wrong and got all twisted.'

Molly hid a smile, while Dot cleared her throat and busied herself clearing away plates.

*

Back in his cottage, Ryan poured himself a beer and sat down. He needed to figure this out. What the heck was going on with him? He loved Joni: she was everything he had ever looked for in a woman. So why did he suddenly want to spend time with Merry? Why did every little thing about her fascinate and infuriate him equally? Why was he so eager to ask her for a drink – even if it was just platonic? He was alarmed at his reaction to the idea that Merry might like him. When Charlie and Franny had suggested the possibility, he had almost felt elated, which was ridiculous. His responsibility was to Joni. Or was he really the awful, fickle human being Merry thought he was? In which case, how could he possibly convince her otherwise?

Forty-three

Over spaghetti all'amatriciana at the kitchen table with her grandmothers and Imran, Joni broke the news. 'So, I have something to tell you ...'

The grandmothers were immediately alert. They exchanged a hopeful glance, then looked to Imran – but he just smiled.

'I've found Charlie's relatives! And I'm going to Ireland! They made contact with me today and it was unbelievable – everything checked out. Kyle and Jenna are the names of the couple related to him and Charlie is a cousin of Jenna's late mother. His real name is Jonathan Dubois. They recognised him immediately from the video and photographs. Isn't that amazing?'

The grandmothers seemed deflated.

'That's it? You're going to Ireland? That's your news?' Grandma Romi said.

'This is huge! Aren't you happy for me?'

'If you're happy, we're happy. Aren't we, Romi?' Grandma Millie looked meaningfully at Grandma Romi.

'Does this mean the ultimatum is off?' Grandma Romi was hopeful.

'I'm not thinking about that right now.' Joni was cross.

'What's important is to reunite Charlie with his family so everyone can come home.'

'How's Ryan doing, these days?' Grandma Millie sipped her wine.

'Busy, as usual,' Joni said. 'The golf club is keeping him occupied and of course he's lending his support to Charlie's situation.'

'This Charlie sure is taking up a lot of people's attention.' Grandma Romi helped herself to more pasta.

Joni couldn't have agreed more but wisely kept her thoughts to herself. Her grandmothers were from a different generation: they didn't understand. Anyway, if things progressed as positively as they looked like doing, she wouldn't just be flying to Ireland for a belated vacation with a boyfriend she was missing. If things panned out the way she hoped they would, Joni would be flying in, with information on Charlie's family, to a reunion that would be worth every anxious moment. And when Charlie was successfully reunited with his blood relatives, Ryan would see for himself how capable she was – how indispensable she would be to him. She would secure unbuyable media coverage in the process, and gain millions more followers – possibly a new career, even. She just had to believe in herself.

'What do you think about all this, Imran?' Grandma Millie asked innocently.

'If it makes her happy, Joni has my full support.' He raised his glass to Joni.

'Some people never see what's right under their own noses.' Grandma Romi shook her head mournfully.

*

There was a general air of gaiety as Dot, Molly, Charlie and Rob took their seats at the very cool new restaurant in the nearby town. Dot was trying hard not to reveal how skittish she was feeling, like a new filly, unsteady on her legs. She was relieved to take her place at the table, and grateful for the artfully subdued lighting, which apart from being flattering, would hide any of the nervous blushes to which she was prone when she was flustered. Rob was looking very well this evening, she noticed. He'd had a haircut, was wearing different glasses and a lovely blue and white striped shirt, which brought out the blue of his eyes. But since their chat in the garden, when Dot had begun to hope her feelings might not be altogether unrequited, Rob had been his normal polite and jovial self. Perhaps tonight with a drink or two on board she might get another clue – although at the moment he seemed a bit on edge. Sitting between her and Molly, he was studying his menu with great intent.

Fortunately, Molly was animated enough for both of them – thank goodness! Heads had turned when she came into the restaurant, followed by covert glances and hushed whisperings as people realised they had a celebrity in their midst. Dot wondered how long it would be before someone approached their table and asked for a selfie. She marvelled at how Molly managed it, always behaving so unflappably and taking everything in her stride even though she was recognised almost everywhere she went. She herself would never have that kind of composure, she thought.

'This is an excellent menu.' Rob looked up. 'Which reminds me, how's the writing coming along, Molly? You haven't mentioned it lately.'

'Oh, in dribs and drabs. Speaking of which' – Molly reached for the wine list – 'I think a little liquid refreshment will definitely keep the inspiration coming.' And everyone laughed.

'Spoken like a true pro,' said Rob.

Soon the food began to arrive. Between admiring each other's appetisers, listening to some of Molly's stories of her time in television and just enjoying being out together, the evening began to slip by in a haze of fun.

Dot was grateful to Molly for holding forth at the table – it meant that no one noticed her own mood, which had deflated at the meal wore on. It was clear to her now that Rob had invited her to accompany Charlie – and to thank her for all her cooking, which was silly as it was all part of the service included in the price she was charging. Still, she told herself, at least she didn't have to be flustered any more. She could relax and enjoy the meal for what it was: just a pleasant evening with friends.

'So, Charlie,' Molly was saying, 'have you any idea where you learned to play the piano like that?' Since Dot had told them about hearing him play Tchaikovsky, Charlie had played for Molly and Rob at the house.

'I'm afraid not.' He shook his head. 'But I feel it's an important part of my life. That's all I can say.'

'I wonder if you can play any other instruments.'

'I can't tell you that.' He shrugged.

'Well, maybe you'll be drawn to some other instruments at the session afterwards,' Rob said.

'Maybe.'

When she had first heard they were going to the session in O'Hagan's after dinner, Dot had been rather disappointed. Although she loved music, she would have preferred to sit on, lingering over Irish coffees, but that was when she'd still hoped that Rob had feelings for her. Now, seeing him so engaged in talking to Molly, she couldn't get away from the table and into O'Hagan's quickly enough. The more people there would be around her, the better.

Then the main courses arrived, including Charlie's very large and delicious-looking burger, which was placed in front of him. He looked at it, frowning.

'Everything all right, Charlie?' Rob said. 'You don't look too happy with your order.'

But then Charlie looked up and raised his hands. 'I've just remembered!' he said, his face lighting with excitement. 'I know what my name is!' He looked around the table.

'What? What is it?' Dot, Molly and Rob were riveted.

'Mac,' Charlie said proudly – as if it were the most obvious thing in the world. 'My name is Mac!'

'Mac what?'

'I don't know! I just know they call me Mac.'

'Right. I guess that's a beginning,' Rob said cheerfully. 'We have to start somewhere, don't we?'

＊

By the time they got to O'Hagan's, the place was thronged, humming with anticipation and laughter as the musicians tuned up. People were gearing up for a good night. Fortunately, Rob had reserved a table earlier and, after weaving their way around several animated groups, they were able to slip into the booth relatively easily. Rob went to get the drinks in while Molly, Dot and Charlie settled themselves and looked around. From her place in the semi-circular booth, Dot could see most of the village was there. She waved at Jan and Eva, seated at a small table across from them.

First, the group played a few traditional Irish pieces, just to get the room warmed up. The crowd responded with plenty of clapping, whooping and foot tapping. Despite her earlier feelings of disappointment, Dot couldn't help but find herself caught up in the lively atmosphere with the others. Then the trad group made way for a couple of Irish country numbers from a well-known duo on the national circuit. The woman sang of lost love and heartbreak, and the man of taking the boat to Liverpool and emigration. Together they sang a few old favourites. They stopped for a break, while people went to the bar, to greet each other or to slip outside for a cigarette.

It was just as people were getting settled for the second half that Dot noticed Ryan. He was laughing at something one of the musicians was saying and shaking his head. But then the man took the mic and said. 'Ladies and gentlemen, and the rest of you! We have a visitor here, Ryan Shindler, all the way from Kentucky, USA!' An appreciative cheer went up. 'He's handy with a guitar, and

I hear he can sing pretty good too!' More whoops and whistles. 'Will you do us the honour, Ryan?'

Ryan held up his hands in a gesture of defeat. 'I can hardly refuse an introduction like that!' He took the guitar that was handed to him, ran through a few chords, positioned himself in front of the mic. 'I'm happy to play for you guys, but I'm warning y'all, it's been a while!'

He tuned up and began to play, starting with some well-known hits. The musicians followed along, taking his lead and the room responded warmly, Ryan's low, clear, perfectly pitched voice ringing out some much-loved country classics. He sang hits by Garth Brooks, John Denver, Willie Nelson and Johnny Nash, and with each number the crowd sang along or swayed in their seats. When he sang about 'friends in low places', he waved at Dot, Rob, Charlie and Molly, who all laughed and raised their glasses to him.

'I had no idea he could sing like that – did you?' Dot looked at the others.

'No,' said Molly, equally surprised.

'He did mention something about playing the guitar to me recently.' Rob scratched his head. 'But he's as good as any professional.'

'Better,' said Molly. 'That's what we call "star quality" in the business. 'He's a natural.'

Ryan was enjoying himself, but he didn't want to hog the limelight. He was about to finish up when he caught sight of Merry, standing at the back, leaning against the wall – she seemed as transfixed as everyone else in the room. He decided to play one last number. 'Okay, this is it, folks, I'll wrap up after this one.' He leaned in to the mic. 'This is one I wrote myself – a long time ago.' He didn't say it had been for his mother, after she had left their little family. He didn't need to say how her abandonment had hurt him as a boy, how he'd felt when the last flicker of hope that she'd come back was replaced by despair, leaving a gaping hole of loneliness and abandonment he'd never been able to fill. The lyrics told their own story. Everybody assumed Ryan was singing for a lost love – and in a way he was. When he lingered over the refrain 'the day I sent you away', he was looking straight at Merry, who couldn't seem to tear her gaze from him. Only Ryan saw her quickly turn and leave the pub, as the resounding applause began.

Dot was relieved that everyone was on their feet clapping and whistling. It meant she didn't have to look at Rob – who at a tender moment in the song had caught her eye and smiled. Now she was feeling confused all over again. Did he have feelings for her – or not? Perhaps he was just feeling sentimental – it was hard not to.

People were rushing to the bar again to get their orders in. Others were forming an admiring group around Ryan, clamouring to know more about him and begging him to sing again. Molly was laughing at something Rob had said, and Charlie had slipped away from the table, presumably to get some air. Dot had hardly noticed as he squeezed past her. She sipped her Irish coffee thoughtfully, hoping the traditional Irish players would start a rousing tune again to defuse the romantic yearning that Ryan's last song seemed to have left throughout room.

She was never sure exactly when it began – there was so much activity at the time. But, gradually, she became aware of people stopping what they were doing, pausing in their discussions to listen, or turning their heads from the bar. She followed their direction and saw the object of their attention. Seated at the piano, lost in a world of his own, and playing one of the most exquisite tunes Dot had ever heard, was Charlie. This wasn't a classical piece, as he had played before, rather a lilting, haunting melody that made people return to their seats and listen, spellbound. Anyone who had a phone had taken it out to record him. The pub was completely silent – you could have heard a pin drop.

'That's so beautiful,' Molly whispered.

When he finished, and stood up, acknowledging the applause, he said quietly, 'Thank you. That was "Jessie's Song" – I wrote it for her.'

Charlie made his way back to the booth, where a well-earned drink was waiting for him. Rob tried to deter the people crowding around him, although Charlie took their curiosity in good humour and did his best to respond to them. The original musicians had taken to the floor again, trying to reclaim what was left of the evening's gig, but they were very much background noise at this stage.

By closing time, when Molly, Dot, Rob and Charlie finally made their way home. 'Jessie's Song' was already well on its way to becoming a viral internet sensation.

Forty-four

By the following day, Ryan decided he couldn't go on like this any longer. He'd played his heart out for Merry last night in the pub – but then she had turned around and left. He was beginning to accept that maybe instead of confronting her on the beach that day he should have handled it differently. After that talk they'd had over a glass of red, he'd thought she was getting over whatever bad opinions of him she had formed. He'd been honest with her too, told her more about himself than he usually revealed. He wondered what Frank would say about that. 'I'd say she's gotten under your skin, kiddo!' and he'd give his famous bellow. 'When a woman makes you feel that crazy, you can be sure there's something more than feeling a little miffed going on – and, trust me, it'll be expensive, whatever it is.'

Well, Ryan wasn't Frank. He didn't have his impressive list of ex-wives for starters. Which made him think of Joni, and the four or five missed calls he'd seen from her on his phone. He wondered what that could be about. If it was important, surely she'd text him, or email. He'd call her when he got back to the cottage – obviously it was something she wanted to talk about. Right now he felt like walking. He needed to clear his head.

What was going on with him? He was supposed to be focusing on getting married to Joni, yet all he could think about was a girl he'd just met, with multicoloured hair and an attitude that drove him mad. Yet there was something about her. Something he was inexplicably drawn to. He headed for the harbour, strolled along the waterfront, and stopped to shoot the breeze with a couple of fishermen. It was only when one of the guys asked him how long he was here for that he realised with a thud he would be going back to New York in less than a week. The thought that just seven hours in a plane would take him a world away from this gentle place and back to the maelstrom of craziness that was his other life sat with him uneasily.

Then, since it was almost one o'clock, he decided to stop and have a pint, sit outside the Pullman, a popular gastropub, and watch the world go by. The weather was a lot warmer now, the breeze had lost its edge, and the sound and smell of the ocean were making him hungry. Being around water always did that to him. A couple of charter boats went out deep-sea angling, the guys had told him, and Ryan thought he might go out one day. They fished for conger, ling and cod – even blue shark off this part of the coast.

When she passed by, it took him a minute to recognise her out of her usual café uniform. And before he knew it, he was on his feet, calling her name, 'Merry!'

She turned, perplexed, a bag of messages slung over her shoulder, her hand shielding her eyes from the sunlight as she looked back to see who was calling her. In the thin summer dress and trainers, with a denim jacket over her shoulders, she looked younger and more vulnerable than he remembered. When he caught up with her he didn't waste time. 'Please, will you have a drink with me?' He gestured back to his table outside the pub. 'I want to apologise for my behaviour the other day.'

She clearly hadn't been expecting that and her eyes darted nervously left and right. 'Look,' he went on, 'I just want to talk to you for a few minutes. At least let me buy you a drink, coffee – something. What harm can it do?'

'Okay.' She didn't look thrilled. But that was all right. It was a start, and that was all he was asking for.

When the coffee she'd ordered arrived, he was already a good way into eating his humble pie and she met his eyes. 'I need to apologise too,' she said, pushing a strand of hair out of her face. 'You were right,' she said simply. 'It was wrong of me to say what I did to Franny. Obviously I didn't intend you to hear about it, but I wanted to prejudice her against you and that was wrong of me.'

'Why? Why did you want her to think of me that way?'

Merry shrugged. 'It's hard to explain. Franny's at an impressionable age and she was – is – really impressed with you and your girlfriend … the influencer.' She smiled. 'You guys are all she's been talking about lately and it was beginning to get on my nerves.'

Ryan gave a wry smile. 'I can understand that.'

'But that's not all.' She paused and looked out over the water. 'I've been angry for other reasons – far too angry – and I've been taking it out on people around me. It hasn't been pretty and it's got to stop. I have no right to do that.'

'I heard your husband was killed. I'm truly sorry.'

'Thank you.'

'I think that gives you as much right as anyone has to be angry.'

'I used to think so too – but I was kidding myself. It has its place in the early stages – but it's too easy a place to stay. It just keeps you stuck. Thankfully, my oldest friend took me aside and told me a few home truths the other day that I needed to hear.'

'I guess that's what best friends are for.'

'I wouldn't have taken it from anyone else – so it was brave of her – but she was right. I knew it, of course, on some level but I needed to hear it. That's the trouble with bereavement. It can make you very selfish. And anger – well, it's just another mask for fear.'

'What kind of fear?' Ryan was intrigued by her frankness.

'Having to go on without him,' she said. 'I don't just mean in the obvious romantic sense.' She looked away again, before turning back to face him. 'Doug made sense of me.' She searched his eyes. 'He made all the funny, irregular, annoying and maybe even weird parts of me that I didn't know what to do with make sense. Together everything made sense – it just fitted into place. And I can't tell you how much I miss that kind of …' – she paused, searching for the right word – '…*peace*.' She smiled. 'Do you know what I mean?'

Ryan didn't – but listening to her he wished he did. It sure as hell sounded like something worth holding out for.

'But then the peace was shattered.'

'I can't even begin to imagine what it's been like for you.'

'No one can.' She looked him in the eye. 'They can't imagine because they don't know the truth.' She chewed her lip. 'They think I'm heartbroken, destroyed with grief and anger, when the truth is – what I'm really afraid of – that Doug never loved me.'

'I'm not sure I understand.' Ryan frowned.

'Of course you don't.' Merry sighed. 'In reality, my marriage was a sham. At least, that was how it felt to me, last time I checked. Doug and I, we got together pretty quickly. It was a whirlwind thing, a *coup de foudre*, call it what you like. He was engaged to his long-term girlfriend, Kristy, when we met. He broke it off with her and chose me. It didn't go down well with either her or Doug's family. You can imagine.'

'I'm sure they would have respected his choice over time. People usually come around.'

'It didn't matter to us. We were happy – at least, then we were. We waited almost a year to get married. For the first three, maybe four months everything was great. Then Doug became quiet, withdrawn and eventually he told me he'd been seeing Kristy.' Merry gave a small laugh. 'She had just found out she was pregnant when Doug broke up with her and when he found out he had a child he was blown away.' Merry's voice caught. 'He was torn apart with guilt and – other things. Our Caribbean vacation was a desperate attempt to try to save our marriage. I promised Doug he could see his son, he could be part of our life – but it wasn't that simple. Doug told me he thought he might still be in love with Kristy.' Merry shrugged. 'Then, before we could talk any more about it, he was killed. How do you hate a man who makes the ultimate sacrifice and gives up his life to save yours?'

Ryan closed his eyes and shook his head.

'We were snorkelling off our boat, not even that far out. Some kids had been partying in the harbour, clowning around. I found out later that two of them jumped into Daddy's power boat and went for a ride.' Merry became very still.

'You don't have to—'

'No, I do. I remember hearing it, the boat, but it didn't seem real. It was heading straight for us ... I remember Doug yelling and waving ... and then he shoved me out of the way.'

Ryan shook his head. 'I can't even imagine ...'

'They ploughed straight into him – and just kept going. I don't think they even noticed. He was dead before we could get him back to shore.'

'I remember reading about it ... the inquest.'

'They were drunk and high. They got fifteen years ... but it won't bring Doug back. His parents blamed me for it, especially his mother.'

'I'm sure they—'

'No, they did, they do – and I can understand why. If it hadn't been for me showing up in the first place, if I hadn't persuaded him to come away, if he hadn't felt so guilty that he had to risk his own life saving mine, he'd still be here.'

They were both silent for a few minutes.

'Anyhow,' Merry changed the subject, 'what about you? Where'd you learn to play and sing like that?'

'Self-taught, mostly. I hung out with some of the guys on the country circuit for a while. What do you want to know?' Ryan played with a glass tumbler.

'How you're finding hanging out in a one-horse town like Derrybeggs.' She grinned.

'So you *were* listening ...' Ryan smiled to himself, remembering the phone call to Frank outside the Seashell, and noticing Merry as soon as he'd hung up.

'I couldn't help overhearing.'

'Would it make a difference if I told you I said that because it was part of my strategy to get him to allow the opening night of the festival to go ahead at the golf club?'

'Very thoughtful of you.'

'Actually, I think Derrybeggs is pretty special – and I haven't even had time to check out the town properly, never mind the surrounding countryside. It was supposed to be a part-work part-vacation trip.'

'What happened?'

'My girlfriend checked out. She's, uh, given me an ultimatum.' Ryan wondered why the hell he was telling this to Merry – but it was too late now.

'An ultimatum?'

'Yes. She was very precise. She has given me eight weeks exactly to reflect on our future together. During this time I may either propose marriage to her or ...' he paused '... she may propose marriage to me. She may also record whatever transpires, so to speak, for her followers.'

'Phew.' Merry gave a low whistle. 'That really is an

ultimatum, isn't it? I'm impressed. So that's why you were looking at rings that day.'

'Joni doesn't do things by halves – she's kind of all or nothing.'

'So, technically, she could turn up here at any moment and propose to you.'

'Technically.' Ryan felt extremely uncomfortable. He shifted in his chair.

'How interesting.' Merry leaned her elbow on the table resting her chin in her hand. 'And what would you say if she did? Like now. Suppose she turned up with a crew and, I dunno, got down on one knee and asked you to marry her, what would you say?'

'I don't think she'd really do that.' Ryan laughed nervously. 'She just wanted to get my attention.'

'You haven't answered my question.'

'I don't know.' He cracked his knuckles and looked away.

'Hmm. Awkward.'

'It wasn't – at least, not until now. I thought it was really good what we had between us.' Ryan knew he was sounding confused. 'And now, well …'

The waiter dropped a menu on the table. 'I don't know about you, but I'm pretty hungry. Would you join me in some lunch, if you're not in a hurry?' Ryan asked. 'I like the sound of those mussels.'

Merry checked her watch. 'Um, yeah, sure, why not? I was just picking up some stuff from the health store for my mum – there's no rush.'

'Good.'

Forty-five

Early that evening, as Ryan got out of the shower after washing off the salt of a long, leisurely swim, his phone rang.

Joni.

With a twinge of guilt – he had been reliving the lunch with Merry – he put his phone to his ear.

And twenty minutes later, he was walking up the stone steps towards the Old Rectory, his head reeling. Joni had solved the mystery! Joni had found Charlie's family. It struck him that he didn't feel as happy as he should …

Was that because he'd miss Charlie being around? Yet Ryan hadn't been planning to stay in Derrybeggs much longer, so that was absurd. Was it that he dreaded telling Dot, after all her perfectly laid plans for the festival, there were now two hundred excitable *Hornetsville* fans heading her way? That would certainly be an unexpected challenge, but if he knew Dot she'd find a way to cope …

Or was it that Joni was coming to Ireland?

But that was ridiculous. He loved Joni.

But it's Merry who's on your mind, a voice in his head reminded him.

Merry … Damn.

But Merry was just a friend.

The kitchen was empty. Dot seemed to be out. Ryan grabbed a beer from the fridge – Dot had always told him he was free to do so – went back out into the sun and settled down on the old stone garden bench looking out to the ocean that stretched all the way back home – and a niggle of insight began to register. The thought of going back to New York suddenly didn't seem appealing. It didn't feel like home any more – which was ridiculous. But usually at this stage in a project Ryan was eager to wrap things up and move on to the next challenge. But that wasn't the way he was feeling now. He was feeling like he wanted to spend more time here, discover more about the place, the people … He was just getting used to the rhythm of things here, becoming attuned to people's ways. He was childishly chuffed when the postman called him by his name. He liked shooting the breeze with the fishermen down in the harbour – and it really tickled him the way the driver of every car he passed on the road, whether he was in the Porsche or on foot, raised a finger off the steering wheel in greeting. It was as if he had become part of the place while his attention was elsewhere. And Charlie … Ryan felt kind of proprietorial about him. He had absolutely no right to, of course, he was aware of that, but he felt protective towards him, almost as if Charlie was a member of his own family … And that was the thing. It wasn't just Charlie but everyone he'd met since he'd come here, particularly Dot and Molly and the Doc, Franny even, was beginning to feel like family … the family Ryan had never really had. And Merry … Well, they'd gotten off to a very bad start, that was for sure. But once they had talked, properly talked, over lunch at the harbour, he had seen a whole other side to her. She had opened up about her husband's tragic accident and the aftermath and what it had done to her. She was interesting too, and she lit up when she talked about her work as a marine biologist, although clearly she didn't realise that just now. He wondered idly if she'd ever go back to it – it seemed so wrong to let all that study go to waste.

He sat like that for a while, staring out to sea, which was where Dot found him.

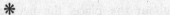

Dot was just back from the hairdresser. She'd had a busy time of it since Charlie had informed them over dinner that his name was Mac. They had all been terribly excited – but their hopes had been dashed when Mac was all he could come up with. Mac What? He had no clue – just Mac. She and Molly had been poring over Facebook pages and online directories with no discernible luck. So, Dot had decided to take a break and clear out her wardrobe. She needed to do something reasonably mindless with a guaranteed result and had duly donated her unwanted items to charity, then gone on a bit of a shopping spree with Molly. After that, she felt her hair was in need of freshening up too. She had intended going shorter, but the new girl at the salon persuaded her to keep it just touching her shoulders, but reshaped it with a fringe and a new colour, a lovely coppery shade, darker than her natural base and adding some rather (daring for her) interesting freehand-style painted-on golden highlights. When she had finished, Suzy, the stylist, seemed triumphantly pleased with her work, and after the initial shock, Dot had to admit she had lost a decade and found some much-needed confidence. She had felt a bit faded lately, washed out, and this new cut and colour certainly brought her back into sharp focus. She had been sneaking looks at herself in mirrors and windows since she had left the salon, and was just coming out to her favourite spot in the shade to put her feet up with her latest book and a nice G&T. That was where she found Ryan.

'New hair?' He grinned. 'It's real nice.'

'Thank you.' Dot sat down. 'I had to make myself decent for opening night. We have quite a weekend coming up.'

'Uh, that's what I wanted to talk to you about. I've got some news.'

'Oh?' Dot shielded her eyes from the sun and shifted in her chair.

'I just heard from Joni. She reckons she's found Charlie's family – or at least some of 'em.'

'Seriously?' Dot sat up straighter. 'Who? What? How?'

Just then Molly came out, drink in hand. 'You two looked so comfortable I had to join you.'

'You're just in time,' said Dot. 'Ryan has some extraordinary news.'

'Joni has found some of Charlie's family – they got in touch with her.'

'No!' Molly sank to a seat and took in the news. 'Who are they?'

'Some regular couple, as far as I know right now. The wife says Charlie is a first cousin of her late mother.' Ryan paused. 'And Charlie – or Jonathan Dubois, as they know him – is a retired army vet. He was in Afghanistan and apparently traumatised after his deployment.'

'An army man! I'd never have guessed that.'

'Me neither. And is she sure about these people?'

'She reckons they're the real deal. But they're providing photographs and some records, I believe. That's not all.' Ryan turned to Molly: 'Were you aware your show *Hornetsville* has developed a serious hipster following in the US?'

'That's news to me!' Molly was taken aback.

'Well, since Joni's followers saw your picture with Charlie, and recognised you from the show, two hundred of 'em have decided to come to the film festival at the weekend. Since they heard about it through Joni's website she wants to be here to make sure everything goes smoothly for them.' He sounded apologetic. 'She, ah, also intends to set up an online meeting for Charlie with these people – Jenna and Kyle are their names, I believe.'

'Two hundred people?' Dot's eyes widened. 'Seriously?'

'Uh-huh.' Ryan nodded. 'That's what she said.'

'Well, that's good – I think. It's just … where are they going to stay?' Dot was worried.

'So what happens now?' asked Ryan.

'Well, first things first.' She looked at Molly. 'We need to call an emergency committee meeting. I'll send out the email and phone around.'

Kate Carmichael didn't want to go and said as much to her daughter, Sheena. 'I don't see why I should, especially after that ungrateful girl Merry shot down my incredibly thoughtful suggestion of a memorial bench for her late husband.' Kate was still smarting at what she saw as Merry's ingratitude, and the extremely unfair and biased support shown to Merry by the committee.

'You have to go,' Sheena said. 'I heard Joni might be joining in on Zoom. I think I might consider being an influencer myself instead of acting.' Sheena had not found her interviews with Molly terribly forthcoming in the way of job prospects. She had expected more enthusiasm, more encouragement from her to help Sheena on her way – some introductions even – but none had materialised. But meeting Joni would be way more exciting anyway – not to mention all her super-cool followers who would be coming to Derrybeggs. That was something worth waiting for.

'Sheena's right,' said Don, her dad, who was hoping to get his wife out of the house for a couple of hours so he could watch the football in peace. 'You'll enjoy it when you're there. Think of all the work you've put into it, Kate.'

'You're right. I'm not letting that shower take the credit for everything I've set up. If it wasn't for me …' The rest of the sentence eluded her.

'Exactly,' said her husband. 'See you later, love.'

Everyone else was very excited. Things were finally starting to happen. After a few false starts, it was all beginning to feel real. Eva and Jan were relieved they had trusted Dot and Molly and made sure to include the extra vegetables needed – the catering was in hand now for the two days of the festival. Franny's mother Sheila was genuinely taken aback at her daughter's documentary on the golf club. From the little she had been allowed to see, she thought Franny had done a surprisingly professional job. She wanted to hear now who would be judging the Film-on-fone competition.

When everybody was finally seated, there was an air of anticipation around the table. Kate Carmichael was scrolling through her iPad, tight-lipped, so Dot opened the meeting. 'Thank you all for coming at such short notice,' she said. 'You'll see from the agenda in front of you there is a lot to be done, and done quickly – but this sudden influx of visitors to Derrybeggs, although intimidating in the short term, will be very beneficial for our festival and in the long term.'

'Will Joni be joining us on Zoom?' Kate enquired, as Sheena had asked her to.

'No.' Dot was brisk. 'I spoke to her earlier. We had

a good discussion. She's very much looking forward to meeting you all when she gets here.'

Accommodation was the most pressing problem, but already a nearby hotel had been contacted and rooms set aside, as well as all the local B&Bs. Better still, a large field had been sought from a local landowner, and was now allocated to the committee with camping facilities for the hipsters, who had expressed a desire to stay in tents. A marquee was to be procured to facilitate the extended screenings and, in case of a change in weather, the barbecue. A tour of the surrounding area was to be organised, along with an opportunity to view the dark sky reserve hot spots with a local guide. This was of particular interest to the hipsters, many of whom were keen on astronomy.

At the end, when everyone had calmed down and things were starting to look viable, Molly cleared her throat. 'Since I feel somewhat to blame for this sudden upheaval in your lovely and normally serene village' – she smiled – 'I felt it was the least I could do to make a phone call just before this meeting – and I'm thrilled to be able to tell you that David Blackthorn has agreed to come over and judge the Film-on-fone competition.'

There was a moment of stunned silence as the committee took this in. David Blackthorn was a household name for his wildlife documentaries all around the globe. Sheila spoke for all of them when she whistled and said, 'Wow.'

Everyone was allocated their respective tasks going forward and told to report to Dot on an hour-by-hour basis. 'Thank you, all.' Dot was heartfelt as she wrapped up the meeting. 'I can't tell you how much I appreciate all the hard work you've put into this. I think it's going to be a really fine festival we have to look forward to.'

*

'What do you make of it all?' Dot was putting some shallots around her roasting chicken. She and Molly were having a chat in the kitchen – Rob would be joining them in a bit.

'I don't know what to think, really.' Molly was thoughtful. She reached for the bowl of nuts beside her. 'It's the army bit that threw me.' She popped a pistachio into her mouth and chewed. 'I just don't see Charlie as an army sort. He's too gentle.'

'I know what you mean, but I suppose a brain injury or trauma would affect the personality. Perhaps that's what happened. I mean, we don't know what he witnessed if he was in Afghanistan.'

'Yes, that's true, of course. What do you think?'

'I can't really take it in yet – and all those fans of yours coming over to the festival!'

'You could have bowled me over with a feather! But I spoke to Larry, my agent, and it's all true, apparently. *Hornetsville* is having an unanticipated "moment" in America.'

'Will you make some money from it?'

'No – I was paid all I was due. But Larry said it's really raising my profile in the US, which certainly won't hurt.'

Molly had emailed him to check out the *Hornetsville* theory and asked him to call her. Fortunately, Larry had been so excited to confirm Molly's new status as a hipster icon in the US that he had been distracted from asking about her memoir – which he didn't know had turned into a novel. Molly was writing like mad, but didn't want to show it to Larry until she was confident of her first draft.

Dot listened to Molly as she took some gravy out of the freezer to defrost – but found her mind wandering. She wondered if Rob would notice her hair. Men were funny like that, she mused. He'd be bound to notice something was different about her – she just hoped it wasn't too drastic a change. All of the comments had been positive so far, and her daughter Laura had even pronounced it groovy over FaceTime, which made Dot wonder if she'd gone too far. The golden highlights still gave her a shock every time she caught sight of them in a mirror – she felt she was looking at someone else entirely. Still, no point worrying about it now: that horse had bolted. Ryan wasn't joining them this evening – and Charlie was going to eat with Merry's parents, Eva and Jan, at their place, where he had been helping Jan with his polytunnels, so it would just be the three of them, her, Molly and Rob. She had set the table, roasted a chicken with all the trimmings, and factored in enough time for a nice pre-dinner cocktail. She fancied a large G&T, with some of that nice pink gin Molly had bought the other day – or was it the tonic that had been pink? Perhaps both – she couldn't remember. Molly went to freshen up while Dot retrieved the tonic from the fridge.

Just then Rob turned up carrying a bunch of supermarket flowers. 'Hello, Dot! Something smells good.' He handed them to her with a rueful expression. 'Coals to Newcastle and all that – you have much finer specimens in your garden, I know, but these were all I could find.'

'They're lovely – and thank you. We're having roast chicken but we've plenty of time for a drink. G&T?'

'Oh, yes, please!'

'Be a dear, help yourself and make me one, while I put these in a vase.'

'What are you doing?' Rob fetched some ice from the fridge and watched Dot as she sliced the flower stems, then added sugar to their water.

'Sugar, and cutting the stems at an angle helps them to last.'

'You'd have made a good surgeon,' said Rob, impressed. 'Here's yours.' He paused with the glass midway between them. 'You look very nice.' Rob rocked on his heels and looked at her quizzically. 'Have you done something to your hair? Although that's almost always a risky question.'

'Yes, I have.' Dot kept her eyes on the flowers. 'I fancied a change. I was feeling in a bit of a rut.' She took her drink and sat down, feeling absurdly self-conscious.

Molly came back into the kitchen. She looked lovely in her crisp white shirt and jeans – and Dot immediately felt overdressed, even though she was only wearing a simple linen dress. The girl in the shop had told her it complemented her new hair.

'So, what do you think about Charlie's news?' Molly asked Rob.

'Which news? That his family has been found? Or that he's an internet sensation?' The villagers were delighted that the clip of Charlie playing 'Jessie's Song' had already got almost a million hits. They were talking about little else.

'It's extraordinary.' Molly poured herself a glass of wine. 'I can't keep up with all this internet stuff – but his family coming forward is what I meant.'

'Well, I'm very happy for him, if these people are his relatives, as Ryan's friend says – but I suppose it's too early to be definite about anything.'

'It's just that I would never have pegged him as an army chap,' said Molly.

'Well, he may have had a complete personality change – trauma can do that. But I haven't ruled out fugue state yet – the best-case scenario would be for Charlie to remember something significant. What did they say his real name is?'

'Jonathan Dubois,' said Dot.

'Hmm.' Rob was thoughtful. 'Doesn't sound like Mac fits with that – although Mac could be a nickname for anything if, indeed, it's correct.'

'I just couldn't bear Charlie to be unhappy,' Dot said, feeling suddenly emotional. 'I've become so fond of him.' She got up to take the plates.

'We all have,' Molly agreed. 'I've come to depend on our daily chats. He's helped me an awful lot – he's remarkably insightful ... which makes me even more curious about who he really is.'

'I know what you mean. I've grown used to having him about the place, too.'

'He's certainly brought us all together in a most unexpected manner,' Rob said. 'And I for one am very grateful to him.' He raised his glass to Dot and Molly.

There was a silence as they remembered that Charlie might be leaving them soon.

'Are we going to tell Charlie we might have a lead on his family?' Dot asked, looking at them both.

'My feeling is we should wait a day or two,' Rob said, 'until we know more about these people who have come forward. We don't want to upset Charlie unnecessarily.'

'Have you heard we're having an influx of visitors for the festival – including Ryan's influencer friend?' Dot wanted to lighten the mood.

'Yes.' Molly laughed. 'We're going to have some very hip hipsters descending on us, apparently.'

'Speaking of hip, I wouldn't mind getting some new gear myself – I'm beginning to feel a bit threadbare.' Rob pulled half-heartedly at a sleeve. 'April used to get me togged out. I'd live in Christmas jumpers and cords all year round, if I could.' He grinned. 'Can't abide going shopping.'

'We could go with you, couldn't we, Dot?' said Molly. 'We could make a day of it – go into town and have a nice lunch.'

'Well, you'd be doing me a real favour.'

'Oh, I don't think I could spare the time, just now.' Dot heard herself saying. 'There's just too much to do …'

'There's no rush,' Rob said amiably. 'Nothing that won't wait until after the festival.'

Dot busied herself then with carving the chicken and dishing up. Throughout dinner she found herself averting Rob's sometimes curious gaze, which was making her feel as if she had somehow offended him by declining the shopping suggestion. Truth be told, she didn't know why she hadn't just gone along with the suggestion. Sure, she was busy, but a day shopping in town and lunch with Rob and Molly would have been nice. She was quiet while they ate. Fortunately Molly was happy to keep the conversation going. They chatted for a while more, until the wine had run out, and Molly suggested a nightcap. 'Oh, go on, then.' Rob wasn't working in the morning.

'Oh dear,' said Dot, getting up and looking in the cupboard. 'I'm afraid that was the last of the gin we polished off before dinner and I'm out of anything else. I was going to do a wine run tomorrow.'

'Well, I've got a bottle of white in the cottage,' said Molly. 'I insist you both come back to mine for a nightcap.'

'I'll pass, I think,' said Dot. 'I feel one of my headaches coming on – I think it must have been all that time I spent online earlier. It's always a trigger. I'm going to call it a night, if you don't mind. Have fun, children!' She waved cheerfully and disappeared upstairs.

'That's not like Dot.' Rob was concerned. 'Do you think she's all right?'

And Molly, who knew perfectly well what was wrong with Dot, inclined her head towards the back door and lifted her eyebrows. 'Come back to mine for that nightcap and I'll put you in the picture.'

The minute she was upstairs in her room, Dot could have kicked herself. What was the matter with her? She could be sitting in Molly's cottage right now with her and Rob, having a nightcap and some much-needed fun. Instead she was behaving like a needy teenager. She had to pull herself together. But, try as she would, she couldn't forget the look that had passed between her and Rob when Ryan sang that lovely song at O'Hagan's. She was sure it had meant something – but what? She was just fanning the flames of her own silly romantic fantasy, that was what. Dot ran herself a bath, forced herself to be happy for Charlie and put all ridiculous thoughts of her and Rob out of her head. She found her phone, and clicked on the link Sheila had sent her, which had now gone viral, of Charlie playing 'Jessie's Song', then lay back in her bath to close her eyes and enjoy it. Whoever Jessie was, she was a very lucky woman to have someone compose such a beautiful tune for her …

'I hope your neighbour doesn't see us,' Rob said, as Molly unlocked her front door. 'I wouldn't want to compromise your reputation.'

'My reputation has withstood far greater assaults, I can assure you, than having the local doctor back to my place for a nightcap. Besides, I think Ryan has more pressing matters to occupy him.'

'What a pretty cottage.' Rob had a stroll around while Molly opened the wine and came back with two glasses. 'What shall we drink to?' They sat down opposite each other on the two facing couches.

'Taking life by the throat.' Molly raised her glass.

'I didn't know you had an aggressive streak. Chin-chin.' Rob sipped, and stretched his legs out, one arm along the top of the couch.

'So what's going on with Dot?' Rob was curious. 'I thought she was odd tonight – not herself, if you know what I mean. In fact, now I think of it, she hasn't really been herself for the last week. Is anything the matter? I mean, do you know? Perhaps we could help.'

'Men can be so dim sometimes.' Molly rolled her eyes. 'Didn't you notice anything that night at the restaurant?'

Rob looked worried. 'I knew I shouldn't have suggested that dinner. Ryan warned me about it.' He made a sound of exasperation.

'Ryan? What's he got to do with it?'

'Nothing – never mind. But did Dot think I was overstepping the mark asking everyone to dinner? I just thought it would make a nice change for her – you know, not having to cook.'

'I'm sure it was a nice change for her. But it would have been even nicer if you hadn't added me and Charlie into the mix.'

'You were offended too?' Rob looked mystified.

'No, you idiot!' Molly laughed. 'You were doing fine asking Dot out to dinner until you included us as well. Dot likes you. She was hoping it would be just you and her having dinner.'

There was silence as Rob digested this. 'Are you sure?'

'I'd put a considerable amount of money on it.'

'Has she told you this?'

'She doesn't need to. Not in so many words. Trust me – I know what I'm talking about. And you like her too – don't you?' Molly twirled her glass in her hand.

'Well ... yes, I do, very much, actually.' Rob sounded surprised to hear himself say it.

'There. It's easy when you admit it, isn't it?' Molly smiled.

'I've made a mess of it, haven't I? What am I going to do?' Rob was worried.

'Be honest. Tell her you panicked and asked us all out – when what you really intended and wanted to do was to ask *her* out to dinner. And don't say it's to repay her for cooking! Just say you would like to take her to dinner.'

'But what if she asks why?'

'She won't. But if she does, tell her you enjoy her company and you'd like to have a chance to get to know her better.'

'Why am I acting like an incompetent fool?'

'Because you like her. It reduces us all to foolishness. But that's part of the fun, isn't it?'

Forty-six

'Have you heard who's judging the Film-on-fone competition?' Franny was on the early shift at the café. She was watching Merry and Eva prepping food for the festival.

'Yes. It's exciting, isn't it?' It was hard not to be infected by Franny's enthusiasm. Merry didn't go out much, but she found herself caught up in the general good feeling about the festival. She was looking forward to it and to the barbecue on the beach afterwards.

'I can give you a preview of my phone film. It's finished now – I had to do a lot of editing. There was loads of footage.' Franny sounded very professional. 'Ryan thinks it's great – he said it has a real chance of winning.' She set up her laptop on the table. 'This could be a real opportunity for me. I mean, who would have thought David Blackthorn would be coming to Derrybeggs to judge a documentary competition? Even getting to meet him is like a dream.'

'Well, it certainly is exciting news, Franny,' Eva said.

'Nothing ever used to happen in Derrybeggs,' Franny said, 'and now it's all gone mad!'

'That reminds me,' Eva said, pulling on her gardening gloves. 'I said I'd help Jan with the salad leaves. We're catering for an awful lot more people than we ever expected – which is great but there's a lot to be done. I really hope the weather stays dry for all those people who want to stay in tents.'

'It'll be like having our own Electric Picnic without the music,' Franny said. 'It's brilliant that Joni's coming over too. I can't wait to meet her.'

'That makes two of us.' Merry lifted her eyebrows at Eva. She'd heard about Joni's impending visit after the impromptu committee meeting.

'Joni's going to put the winning documentary on her site as well.'

'I see,' said Merry. 'That's even more exciting.' It certainly would be, she thought, if a surprise proposal to Ryan was on Joni's itinerary in Derrybeggs. Suddenly she felt overwhelmed by misery. What on earth was the matter with her? Maybe the whole idea of marriage was bringing up uncomfortable memories. It couldn't be that she didn't want Joni to propose to Ryan – could it? No. It had to be about Doug. Which meant she had to stop being stuck in the past and angry with him about everything. She had to move on, and make her peace, not just with her own life but with Doug's son and family and everything that had happened.

*

Merry had a word with Ryan later that morning, when he came by to grab a coffee to go. 'Could you meet me in the village later? Say twelve?' She told him where.

'Sure. Everything okay?'

'Yeah, fine – just something I want to run by you.'

'Cool. I'll be there.'

Ryan pulled up five minutes early, and parked outside the holding on Harbour Row that he could see was in a pretty advanced state of disrepair, even from the car. When she heard him, Merry emerged from the doorway stepping over some wayward planks. 'Thanks for coming. I know you're busy.'

'What's going on?' Ryan followed her into the single-storey building that, judging from the collective debris left behind, seemed to have been some kind of a grocery store in a previous incarnation. 'You thinking of setting up as the competition?'

'A café? No.' Merry smiled. 'But I am thinking of taking this on – and I'd appreciate your professional opinion.'

'What you got in mind?' Ryan leaned back against the wall.

'I've been doing a lot of thinking lately, and I've decided not to go back to Florida. But I can't go on working at the Seashell – that was only ever a temporary measure – and I don't want to leave behind my marine experience.'

'That sounds positive.'

'The university are keen for me to continue with my research – but I can do that in my own time. I figured I could set up a facility right here in Derrybeggs, but not an academic centre. I was thinking more along the lines of somewhere kids, tourists – anyone, really – could come to learn about the ocean. I've always loved working with children, and God knows we need to educate the generations coming after us.'

'What are you looking for in the premises?'

'Room to set up educational displays, audio visuals, some interactive stuff – an area with seating for classes, that kind of thing.'

'Let me take a quick look around.' Ryan had a walk-through. 'Seems in fair enough shape where it matters – and it's a good size for what you want. If you're serious about it, I'll have my surveyor come check it out for you.'

'Would you? That would be really great. I'm pretty sure this is the right premises – I've had my eye on it for quite a while, and the location is perfect. I just wasn't sure if I was going to stay around, or not.'

'What made your mind up?'

'Nothing particular. It was more of a feeling. I just think it's time to move on with my life and I don't want to go back to the States, so I might as well put down some roots here.'

'What are you gonna call it?'

'What makes you think I have a name for it already?'

'Just a feeling.' Ryan grinned.

'Well, now that you mention it, I was thinking Oceanworks.'

'I like it.' He leaned against the wall. Then he mentioned the elephant in the room. 'I don't know if maybe you heard? Joni's coming over.'

'Yeah. Mum mentioned it.' Merry looked away. 'That's really great.'

'She reckons she's found relatives of Charlie's – some couple recognised him from her post, claim he's a cousin of the wife's late mother.'

'Seriously?' That's … amazing! They know who he is?'

'So they say. Claim he's a retired Afghanistan vet and that his name is Jonathan Dubois.' Ryan scrolled through his phone to find the email. 'There are photos and some kind of military record.'

'My in-laws are a military family – back in Florida. I'm sure my father-in-law would see if the details check out.'

'Hey, that'd be great. Charlie's got quite a price on his head now – and a lot of people would take advantage of his situation.'

'Sure. I'd be happy to run it by them – send me those details and I'll email them on. At least then we can be sure these people are legit.'

Forty-seven

She didn't discuss it with anyone. Eva would only have worried about her and probably insisted on hovering somewhere nearby in case she needed to pick up the pieces post conversation. Jan would have shaken his head, looked sad and retreated to his polytunnels. Beth would have counselled her about what to say – and there wasn't any script for this: she would have to work with whatever came to her. But she had promised Ryan she would check Joni's story about Charlie and she wanted some answers herself. Merry grabbed a coffee to take with her, toying momentarily with the idea of something stronger – it was after five – but she could always avail herself of that after the phone call if necessary.

The sun was warm on her back as she strolled over to the harbour where a couple of trawlers wove their way around each other while gulls cried and wheeled between them. A group of dishevelled German hikers argued, deliberating between the pub and a local craft display. Merry turned up Harbour Row and slipped in through the open doorframe to what she now privately called her office. One of the things she had noted when she was exploring the old place was that the Wi-Fi signal seemed to be strong – a big plus anywhere in rural Ireland. She made her way to the back, carefully negotiating the few ramshackle piles of loose planks and partitioning, to access the opening that led onto a sheltered yard. Then she sat down on an upturned crate, took a sip of her coffee, pulled out her phone and pressed the call button. The dial tone rang out repetitively and rhythmically across the miles until Merry's nerves felt as stretched as the distance between them.

Then, just as she was about to hang up, Betty answered, her voice uncertain. 'Hello?' She wouldn't have recognised the number, of course, since Merry was using her Irish cell phone.

'Hello, Betty,' Merry said. 'It's me, Merry. I wanted to talk to you.'

In the silence that ensued, the awkwardness and sharp intake of breath at Betty's end spoke volumes. Merry pressed on: 'I wanted to catch you before you left to go about your day, if you can spare a moment.'

Merry wondered if Betty had any idea how much it had taken for her to make this call but it was the only way. Then she could finally put the past to rest – and she owed herself that. 'Look, I know you probably don't want to hear from me, Betty, but I need to run something by you – something that might help someone vulnerable.' Merry knew her erstwhile mother-in-law was deeply attached to her goodwill work and was on the board of several non-profits.

'Hello, Merry. This is a surprise, but go ahead. What can I do for you?' Betty's tone was cautious but not chilly – if anything, she sounded tired. Merry pictured her, probably in her kitchen, looking out over the hills and valleys that swept down to the ocean. She wondered if the last two years had brought her any peace.

Merry guessed Betty probably thought she was about to berate them for keeping the news of Doug's little boy from her – but that wasn't Merry's intention. She was simply going to ask the help of a woman who had resented her from the moment she'd set eyes on her. As quickly as she could, Merry related Charlie's story, his showing up in Derrybeggs, the memory issues, how Dot had taken him in, and the local community who thought of him as one of their own now. Finally she told Betty about the couple who were purporting to be his relatives and Merry's reservations about their story.

'It's the military aspect that doesn't fit,' she said. 'We have all the details of this man Jonathan Dubois and I was wondering if you could check them out at your end. You'd be doing a vulnerable man a great kindness.' Merry held her breath.

'I'm sure we could do that for you, Merry. Why don't you send me what you've got? I'll have Jeff look into it himself for you. I'll text our email to this number, shall I?'

'That would be amazing. Thank you so much, Betty. I can't tell you how much I – we all – would appreciate it.'

There was the briefest of pauses. Then, 'How are you doing, Merry? I often think of you and – and I want to say how sorry I am for the way I spoke to you at Doug's … at his memorial service.' Betty's voice caught. 'I know it was just as hard for you, harder maybe, and – and I hope you've been able to rebuild your life.'

'Thank you, Betty. That means a lot. I know how hard it was for you guys, too,' Merry said quietly. 'I – I'm doing okay, thanks. And – and I'm glad you have your grandson, Doug and Kristy's little boy. He must be a great comfort to you.'

'He is.' Betty's voice warmed. 'Life sure throws up some curve balls when we least expect it.'

'There was something else, too, Betty.' Merry took a breath. 'Doug's case has finally been settled. I wanted you to know I'm putting half of the money in trust for your grandson – my lawyers are setting it up with Kristy's. I felt it was what Doug would want – and I want it too.'

'Well, that's – that's very, very generous of you, Merry, in more ways than one. I'm sure you can imagine how much we all appreciate that.' There was another pause. 'Send me those details of your friend Charlie and we'll do our best to help you out with this guy.'

'Thanks, Betty. I really appreciate it.'

After the phone call had finished, Merry was overwhelmed by relief. She would never have a loving relationship with Doug's family – and she was sorry they had never managed to accept her for his sake while he was alive – but at least now they could put the past to rest. Merry knew how hard it would have been for Betty to apologise to her. It was also good of her to agree to look into Charlie's supposed military record. If anyone would be able to confirm the legitimacy of military documents and history, Jefferson would. His military ancestry, he constantly told people, could be traced back at least as far as George Washington.

Forty-eight

After the whirlwind business of booking flights, and organising her unruly crew of two hundred followers onto the plane, then the fleet of coaches at Shannon that would drop them off at their various accommodations, Joni could hardly believe she was finally in Derrybeggs. She desperately needed a rest, but first she needed to unpack and settle herself into this weirdly quaint little cottage – so much like a film set, it seemed unreal. It was like being transported to another reality, she thought, walking over to the window where she looked out at the pretty garden, beyond which the ocean stretched beneath rugged cliffs.

She didn't get it: it was a nice view, with those tall cliffs, but she couldn't see what all the fuss was about, why Ryan kept going on about the place in his texts and phone calls. The weather had been good since the moment they'd landed – that was something – but apart from a lot of green fields they passed on the drive from the airport, she hadn't seen anything to make her sit up and take notice. It was hardly Big Sur. The village was cute, but, like, where did people shop? She turned to head back to the bedroom, and that was when she saw the guitar, leaning against the wall. How had she not noticed that before? She vaguely remembered Ryan mentioning once that he had played music or written songs for a while in his youth. At the time, she hadn't paid much attention. Now, though, she did. Joni didn't have a lot of time for music. It was all well and good in its place, but she certainly didn't want Ryan shifting his focus from his super-charged career and wasting time loafing about with a guitar again.

Then a thought occurred to her. Perhaps he was writing a song for her – maybe that was it. He might even be going to surprise her with a song, their song, and a proposal. How romantic would that be? Although it might be a bit too private for her liking.

She was looking forward to discussing all her plans for Charlie with Ryan. It had been impossible on the way here from the airport, because they'd had an overflow of three excitable hipsters crammed into the back of the car, and as soon as they'd arrived Ryan had had to rush off to deal with an emergency at work. But later, over a glass of wine, they could talk about it, when she would have Ryan to herself. Then she could tell him all about Charlie's relatives and show him the documents that proved his identity.

She thought she might take a look around and get some shots for the website, shoot a couple of videos, maybe. As it was, she couldn't even get a good internet signal in the cottage. She had just about been able to talk to the GMs. She remembered Ryan saying the best signal was at some café called the Seashell – with a bit of luck they'd serve a decent cup of coffee too. Maybe she'd get some work done there. She quickly unpacked and hung her clothes in the wardrobe – smiling as she remembered Imran insisting she bring her beautiful parka coat with the hood and luxurious fur collar. She had thought it ridiculous at the time.

'It's late June, Imran, summer.'

'Ireland's like Seattle, honey, trust me. It can rain any time.'

She pulled open a drawer, then realised Ryan had already appropriated it. That was when she saw it, underneath his passport, the computer printout of a selection of diamond rings. That could mean only one thing! Ryan was looking at engagement rings! Maybe he had even bought one! Although Joni hoped not. The trip to Tiffany's and choosing a ring of her own would be a whole other episode for her followers she was counting on, but even so, it was good to know that Ryan's thoughts were on track. He had listened to what she'd said to him. Encouraged by this latest discovery, Joni resolved to propose to Ryan at the barbecue on the beach after the film festival. After all, she'd been promising her followers something spectacular, and what better than a public proposal on an Irish beach – provided it didn't rain?

Feeling considerably better about things, Joni put on her dark glasses, grabbed her laptop bag and closed the door behind her, checking the directions to the Seashell café on her phone.

*

Joni was pleasantly surprised by the Seashell. She hadn't expected to be greeted by such an unusual interior. A rope of intertwined bells and seashells hung by the door and announced her arrival in a whispering jangle as it closed behind her. The space was larger than she had anticipated, and sectioned off with bleached strips of driftwood arranged at artful angles. The walls were washed in varying shades of blue from palest sky, to deepest indigo, and shells of every size and shape from near and far-flung oceans sat on shelves and in alcoves. A collection of wild, abandoned seascapes hung in artful arrangements.

Joni settled herself in a small alcove by a window that looked out over the ocean and set up her laptop. A pretty girl with crazy black, blonde and pink hair came to take her order, and when she returned with it, Joni had to admit the coffee tasted even better than her go-to brew back home. She'd have to enquire about that. Clearly this place wasn't quite the one-horse town Ryan had painted it to be, but then men never noticed the finer details.

She worked through her emails, had some more coffee, and was having a think about the piece she could maybe do to camera here for her followers – the backdrop of all those blues and bleached-out driftwood would be really cool. That was when she saw him. He hadn't been there before, she was sure of it – she would have noticed when she first sat down at her table – but an hour or more had gone by and obviously she had been so focused on her work she hadn't seen him come in. He was more handsome in real life for an older man and had a kind of genteel air about him, Joni thought. He was looking out of the window, a half-smile on his face. That was him. That was Charlie – it had to be – and, better still, he was alone. It was the perfect opportunity. The café was quiet, there was no sign of the girl who had served her, and two women deep in conversation sat at the only other occupied table she could see. She would just pop over, introduce herself, and ask if she could talk with him for a bit. Then she could maybe drop into conversation some of the things Jenna and Kyle had shared with her – see what his reaction was. That would help speed things up. Anything that moved along this bizarre situation, got Ryan's head out of his butt and focused on their relationship, as it should be, would be a decided improvement.

She slipped out from behind her table, made her way across the room and was just about twelve feet away from him when the girl with the crazy hair who had served her intercepted her out of nowhere. She stood there right in front of her, like some defending quarterback, blocking Joni's way.

'Can I help you?' She smiled but her voice was cool.

'No, thank you.' Joni was equally sweet and cool. What she really wanted to say was *You could start by getting out of my way.* 'I'm just on my way to say hello to the man at that table. He looks very familiar – I think he may be an old family acquaintance.'

'You're Joni, aren't you?'

'Yes, I am. And you are?' Joni switched to imperious mode, but this girl was her own height or taller and eyeballing her. Clearly she wasn't someone to mess with – but no one who worked in a café had the right to harass the customers.

'I'm Merry – and I'm guessing you want to talk to Charlie. Would that be right?' She was now, unbelievably, steering Joni back to her own table. Out of the corner of her eye, Joni noticed another woman come out from behind the counter and slip into the vacant seat opposite Charlie that Joni had been aiming for.

'That is correct. What's it to you?' Joni's eyes narrowed.

'We're very protective of Charlie around here.' Merry folded her arms. 'We wouldn't want him to be upset by anyone – however well-meaning.' She tilted her head. The smile was still there, but the intention behind it was steely.

'Are you seriously suggesting that I would want to *upset* him?' Joni was incredulous.

'I'm not suggesting any such thing. But you need to know Charlie is thought of as family around here. As far as we're concerned, his welfare comes first. What I suggest is that you leave him be. We don't like anyone approaching him who is unaware of his situation – not without Rob being present. It's better that way – for Charlie.'

Joni was furious. How dare this jumped-up waitress confront her and question her motives – like it was any business of hers. But she couldn't let her see she was annoyed, and she certainly didn't want any bad press circulating about her, particularly as regards Charlie. That could ruin everything – and Ryan wouldn't be pleased about it either.

'I understand.' Joni put a reassuring hand on Merry's

arm. 'Really I do – and it's wonderful to know how well Charlie's been taken care of while he's here.'

'As long as we understand one another.' The girl retreated behind the counter again.

Joni took advantage of the moment to gather her things and settle her bill.

It was such a nice afternoon that she took a little stroll around the village – which looked a lot more attractive on closer inspection. Soon Ryan would be back to meet her at the cottage. She wouldn't mention what had just transpired with Merry. Over dinner this evening she would present her case about Charlie. Then there was just the film festival to get through – although how they could be serious about having a film festival in this backwater … Then at the barbecue she would propose to Ryan in front of all her delighted, supportive followers – even if Ryan found it a little embarrassing, he'd get over it. Then they could wrap this whole crazy thing up and get back to their life in New York where they belonged.

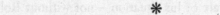

Ryan was feeling off-kilter and couldn't quite work out why. He would be going home in under a week. The golf club was finished and the festival was all set up – his work was done. But this afternoon he'd found it almost impossible to concentrate at work and that wasn't like him. The report in front of him needed scrutinising, and already he'd had to re-read the same section about three times. He wondered if it had anything to do with Joni being in town. It had been very surreal when she had walked into Arrivals at the airport earlier where he'd made sure to be in good time to meet her. It had taken her a moment to see him – a moment during which Ryan had time to observe her as a stranger might. She was stunning, no question – tall, lithe, olive-skinned and with the dark eyes and long silky hair of her Italian ancestors. She had also inherited proudly carved cheekbones and a full, sensual mouth. In her uniform of jeans, a white shirt, and dark glasses, with a glamorous parka draped over her arm, Ryan could understand why heads turned as she passed through. As he got up from his seat to greet her, he knew he was considered a lucky man.

'It's good to see you,' he said, when they drew apart and Joni looked up at him expectantly. And it was. It was just a bit *weird.* He felt as if he was watching a scene in a movie rather than reuniting with his girlfriend – who was accompanied by two hundred excited followers and might be about to propose to him at any minute. Fortunately, Joni had talked the whole way back in the car without pausing to draw breath, and what with giving a lift to three of her followers, Ryan didn't have to answer any awkward questions. Instead, he told her about the restaurant he had booked for that night, which came hugely recommended and was well worth the twenty-minute drive from Derrybeggs. It overlooked a river and a ruined castle and the food was renowned. It was also very romantic. 'Oh, let me check it out.' Joni pulled her iPad from her bag.

Ryan felt a stab of irritation as she duly googled the

place. 'It looks cute,' she said, smiling her approval. 'I can add it to my list of things to do for my followers. They'll expect decent places to eat.'

After he had dropped everyone off, Ryan had gone back to the office and left Joni to settle in. No wonder he felt antsy. With Joni, settling in could mean prowling the village relentlessly interviewing locals and making a full feature-length film about the place for her followers. He checked his watch. He might as well finish up at the club and make his way home. He wasn't going to get much more done here and by the time he'd washed off the day and grabbed a beer, heard about Joni's afternoon, it would almost be time to leave for their dinner date.

When he got back to the Old Rectory, Ryan ran into Molly, accompanied by Franny and Sheena, as they were going into her cottage – Sheena, apparently, was hoping to go over a part of her documentary about Molly, a last-minute tweak. Molly ushered the girls ahead of her into her cottage, lingering for a moment to chat to Ryan. 'They're terribly excited, the pair of them – dying to get a look at Joni.' She smiled.

'Well, I'm sure Joni will be happy to meet them – she's just settling in.'

'It's wonderful news about her finding Charlie's people – really, I can hardly believe it!'

'Well, we have to establish yet whether these people are legit – but it's looking that way. As soon as I hear the whole version from Joni, we'll bring you up to speed.'

'Oh, there's no mad rush! We wouldn't dream of disturbing either of you,' Molly said. 'You haven't had a chance to see each other in yonks. There's plenty of time for the girls to meet her. It's not as if there are many places to hide in Derrybeggs – especially not from eager teenagers.' Molly grinned. 'That's something I've learned to my cost.'

'How's Sheena's documentary going?' Ryan asked.

'Let's just say it's less about me and more about the interviewer.' Molly raised her eyebrows.

He laughed. 'I look forward to seeing it.'

'I'm not sure you ought to! See you later – and if I don't, do enjoy your dinner.' Molly waved and disappeared into her cottage after the girls.

Ryan let himself into Sundew Cottage to find Joni sitting at the kitchen table, with an array of documents spread out. 'Hey,' he said. 'I got away sooner than I expected.'

'Hey, yourself.' She smiled. 'Remember I said I had something to tell you?'

'Uh-huh.' Ryan found himself tensing. He hoped this wasn't it. Was she going to propose? He dropped his bag on the sofa, angling his head away so she wouldn't see the uncertainty in his expression, then forced himself to smile as he walked over and dropped a kiss on her head. 'What is it?'

'I've set up a Zoom meeting for Charlie's family tomorrow so he can meet them.' She shuffled the papers, sorting them into two piles. 'These'– she pointed to one set – 'are the documentary evidence I emailed you. And these' – she pointed to the other pile – 'are the photographic evidence. You, Ryan, are looking at the identity of one Jonathan Dubois, Afghanistan veteran, native of South

Carolina. Take a good look, it's all there.' She got up, went to the fridge and extracted a bottle of champagne, which she expertly popped. 'I think this calls for a celebration, don't you?'

'Back up just a minute, Joni.' Ryan was leafing through the papers, frowning. There was a birth certificate and a US Military ID card. 'This doesn't really prove anything.' He paused, remembering. 'Besides, Molly's voice coach said Charlie's accent was North Carolina – not from the South.'

'Of course it proves they're his family.' Joni ignored the comment about Molly's voice coach. She placed a flute of champagne in front of him. 'I've met these people, Ryan. I've had them in my house. They are absolutely the real deal. They saw my video about Charlie, recognised the photo and got in touch with me. Naturally I told them I needed proof – and here it is.' She inclined her head.

After a glass or two of champagne, and bringing Ryan up to date with all that had been happening in New York, Joni decided she wanted a nap. Ryan took the opportunity to shower, then sat down in the kitchen to study the papers properly. They seemed authentic, and the photographs bore an uncanny resemblance to Charlie, although the earlier ones of him as a teenager and child could have been anyone. Still, there was no denying the documentation, which did seem legit. Something about the revelation bothered Ryan, though. He just couldn't see Charlie as a military man – none of them did. He understood his personality might have undergone a change as a result of some trauma he'd suffered – the Doc had said that was a distinct possibility – but Charlie and the army just didn't square with Ryan. He'd have to run this proposed Zoom meeting by the Doc and Dot before they went any further. That was all he could be sure about right now.

He heard the shower running and realised Joni would soon be ready to leave – which reminded him that he had left his only decent jacket in the car, so he went to retrieve it. Castleview House was pretty elegant, he'd heard, not a jeans and T-shirt kind of place. When he came back to the bedroom, Joni was tying her hair up in a loose topknot – a look he loved. 'You look beautiful,' he said, truthfully.

'Thank you – and I'm not even dressed yet.'

'No need to overgild the lily.' He grinned, shrugged off his towelling robe and dressed quickly.

'Might as well have another glass of champagne before the cab gets here. Shall I pour you one?' Ryan called from the front room. He checked his phone.

'Okay.' Joni joined him. 'That reminds me – I'd love to see your documentary on the golf club if you've got a copy.' She accepted the glass and raised it to her lips.

'Sure. Why don't you watch it here on the laptop?' Ryan set up Franny's five-minute film.

Joni was quiet as she watched it, but she was looking intently at the screen.

'What do you think?' Ryan smiled.

'It's not what I expected.'

'What do you mean?'

'Well, it's not exactly professional.' She frowned.

'It's not supposed to be.' Ryan kept his tone neutral. 'It's a fourteen-year-old girl's first attempt.' He frowned. 'I thought she did a really good job.'

'Wait!' Joni seemed incredulous. 'You're telling me this is, like, a schoolgirl project? I thought it was a proper documentary you were having done for the club.'

'It is a proper documentary. The competition rules are for a five-minute film shot on your phone. Anyone can enter.'

'Well, sure – I get that – but there are some pretty sophisticated things you can do on smartphones these days, Ryan, and this isn't one of them. I mean, this is your new golf club, Ryan, it deserves suitable exposure – not some awkward schoolgirl attempt. I don't think Frank would appreciate that circulating online. Let's hope for your sake it *doesn't* win the competition because I wouldn't feel comfortable putting it up on my site. I knew this kind of place wouldn't be hosting a real professional film festival – but I didn't think it would be so amateurish. Who is she, this kid, anyway?'

The sound of a door closing made Ryan automatically look up – but it wasn't his own front door – he had left that open accidentally after getting his jacket from the car. It had been Molly's front door he had heard – and in front of his and Joni's open doorway stood Franny, frozen to the spot, within perfect earshot of Joni's casual comments. Ryan swallowed, hard. 'Franny!' He tried to sound upbeat but the horrified mortification on Franny's face tore at his heart. Worse still was that her friend Sheena was behind her – wearing a knowing smirk. Molly, busy locking her front door, turned around, unaware of what had just happened. 'Come on, girls! Stop gawking! You'll meet her tomorrow. Have a lovely dinner, Ryan.' And she shepherded the girls ahead of her.

'Who was that you were talking to?' Joni asked, looking up from the laptop.

'No one,' said Ryan. 'I just left the door open by mistake.' He closed it softly. 'My bad.'

Forty-nine

Sheila Relish had rarely – possibly never – felt so angry. Even Kate Carmichael at her worst had failed to arouse her to this level of emotion. But when someone upset her daughter, her lovely, guileless, unselfish, generous, not-a-bad-bone-in-her-body Franny, well, that was a very different kettle of fish and Sheila was on the warpath. At first she had trouble understanding what had happened. Franny had just rushed into the house – accompanied by Sheena – announcing she was withdrawing her Film-on-fone from the competition.

'Why on earth would you do that?' Sheila asked, straightening up from unloading the dishwasher. She expected perhaps an artistic disagreement between Franny and Ryan, some creative spat on Franny's part. But studying her daughter Sheila could see Franny was terribly upset. Sheena, who had been party to the episode, filled Sheila in. 'Joni said Franny's film was an awkward schoolgirl's effort and she wouldn't feel comfortable putting it up on her site if it won.'

'What?' Sheila fought to make sense of the news, which had had the double-negative effect of clearly giving Sheena a sadistic thrill to impart.

Beside her, tears ran down Franny's face, which she angrily swiped away. 'She's right – it's rubbish.'

'She said—'

Sheila cut her off: 'Thank you, Sheena – that's quite enough. You were very good to see Franny home but now I'd like some time alone with my daughter to get to the bottom of this.'

'But—'

'Later, Sheena.' Sheila pointed to the hall door. 'And if you've any sense or kindness, you'll keep this between yourself and Franny.'

Sheena chewed her lip. 'Sure. Catch you later, Franny.'

'Now.' Sheila sat Franny down at the kitchen table with a mug of hot chocolate to prise the details from her. 'Tell me from the beginning.' She listened carefully, prodding for confirmation, all the while searching for how she could frame the unfortunate situation in the most optimistic light and practise damage limitation. 'Look, love, this all sounds like a silly misunderstanding.' Sheila channelled her best schoolteacher manner. 'First of all, you shouldn't have been listening or hovering at the open doorway.'

'I wasn't listening – I couldn't help overhearing.'

'Second, Joni clearly didn't understand what the competition is about.' Sheila searched for a suitable rationale. 'She obviously got the wrong end of the stick – she must have thought Ryan had had some sort of corporate documentary made about the golf club, not an artistic one for our festival.'

'What do you mean?'

'I mean a business film – they can be very technical. Clearly it was all just a misunderstanding on Joni's part.'

'She called it an awkward schoolgirl attempt. She said you could do really sophisticated films on smartphones, these days, and this wasn't one of them. She said Frank—'

'Who's Frank?'

'Ryan's boss – she said he wouldn't be happy about it circulating online. Anyway, it doesn't matter what she said. I'm pulling it from the competition.' Franny was definite.

'After all the hard work you've put into it? And after all the access and time Ryan has let you have? I don't think he'll be very pleased if you pull it. Besides, you're overreacting, love. What Joni or anyone else thinks doesn't matter. What matters is that you've created something wonderful – Ryan thinks so, I know he does. He's told everyone how impressed he is with your work.'

'Not after this, he won't be.'

'Franny, you've got to stop putting yourself and your work down. Why don't you go up and have a nice hot bath?' This was Sheila's solution to most of life's problems. 'Tomorrow you'll have forgotten all about this.'

Unfortunately, the next day no one had forgotten about it. Least of all Franny, who was refusing to leave the house and had withdrawn to her room where Muttie was keeping faithful guard on her bed. There were murmurings in the village too, as Sheena had told her mother, Kate Carmichael, what had transpired in strictest confidence and Kate had informed her friends at the golf club, who all agreed it was most unfortunate that poor Franny had overheard her film being rubbished but, on the other hand, how was Joni to know she was putting her foot in it? Or indeed that Franny would be hovering about, eavesdropping, at the front door? Joni would be used to only the highest standards since she was a professional influencer – she couldn't be blamed for an innocent enough opinion.

A version of this narrative made its way back to Sheila, who decided she needed to nip it in the bud. She rang Dot, who on hearing of Franny's upset immediately asked Sheila round for coffee. When she arrived, Molly was seated at the kitchen table too, and over coffee, Sheila related the whole sorry state of affairs.

'Oh dear,' said Molly. 'I blame myself. I should have kept more of an eye on them, but I'd just got caught on a phone call – I told the girls to go on outside and that I'd catch them up.'

'You weren't to know Ryan's front door would be open.'

'Or that Joni would be discussing Franny's film – who would?'

'She's adamant now she's going to pull the film from the competition, and she's worked so hard on it.'

'Well, we can't have that,' said Molly. 'I might have a discreet word with Ryan about this. He's the only one who could persuade her, don't you think?'

'And you,' Sheila said. 'She thinks you're amazing. I'd be very grateful – she'll be heartbroken if she doesn't enter the competition.'

'Leave it with me,' said Molly.

After Sheila left, Dot and Molly chatted for a while. 'This was a rather unfortunate start to Joni's stay,' Dot said.

'More unfortunate for Franny overhearing – what were the chances of that?' Molly shook her head. 'It puts Ryan in an awkward position.'

'Not really,' said Dot. 'I'm sure he'll handle it sensitively – that's what he's good at after all. I think PR and damage limitation are in his job description.'

'He doesn't seem terribly sure about these people claiming to be Charlie's relatives,' Molly said.

'I don't think any of us can be absolutely certain.' Dot was grave.

'I must say I thought it rather suspicious that they contacted Joni – but not the police. Wouldn't the police generally be the first port of call?'

'That's a good point – although maybe if they only just saw the clip of Charlie ... Perhaps it was a sort of knee-jerk reaction.'

'What did you think of Joni?' Molly asked. Ryan had brought her to the house to meet Dot and Molly before heading out to dinner.

'Hard to tell.' Dot was thoughtful. 'She's very beautiful, certainly.'

'Hmm.' Molly nodded. 'Bit pushy, I thought – and I'd bet there's a ruthless streak beneath that glossy exterior.'

*

'So,' Sheena said. She blew into her coffee and checked out who was in earshot. Apart from Ray, an old surfer dude stacking boards in the back of the shed, the Surf Shack was quiet. 'Are you still pulling your film?'

'Nah.' Franny shrugged. 'They kind of made it impossible.'

'Who?'

'Ryan and Molly – they persuaded me to leave it in. They kind of put the heavy stuff on me, said it wouldn't be fair, such a waste, so I said okay just to get them off my back.'

'*Riiight*,' Sheena said casually, but her eyes narrowed. 'What did Molly say?'

'Oh, just that it was a really good piece of film and I owed it to myself – and to Ryan, of course – to enter it.'

'What about what Joni said?' Sheena didn't want the comments forgotten.

'Ryan said she didn't understand the context – she thought it was supposed to be a corporate thing or something. Anyway, they wouldn't let me pull out, basically. Like I said, it was just easier to go along with it.' Franny was too nice to say that Molly thought Franny's film on Ryan and the golf club was far better than the one Sheena had done on her – and that both she and Ryan felt Franny's film had a good chance of winning.

'Weird.' Sheena looked mystified. 'Anyway.' She lowered her voice. 'Remember that party some of the guys have organised that's going to be out on Cape Clanad, the first night of the festival?' Sheena had mentioned it to Franny before – she was very excited about it. Some really hot guys were coming down from Dublin, cousins of Ronan, and the local guys, Steve and Ro, were going to smuggle drink out in a couple of boats to the tiny uninhabited offshore island a few days before.

'Yeah.' Franny was hesitant. 'But I told you already I can't go. There's no way I'd be allowed.'

'No one's going be *allowed* …' Sheena put air commas around the word. 'Doh! We'll just sneak out. Everyone's going to be at the festival – they won't miss us. By the time they get home they'll be too drunk or tired to notice we're not in our rooms.'

'My parents would.'

'Whatever.' Sheena rolled her eyes. 'But there is something you *can* do.' She brightened.

'What?'

'A couple of the guys are into canoeing – like you. They asked me if anyone would take them out to Gull Cave, before the party. I said you would.' Sheena lifted an eyebrow. 'You can do that, can't you?'

'Maybe.'

'Cool.' Sheena smiled. 'We'll go together. I'll tell them it's sorted.' She took up her phone and began texting.

'I said *maybe*.' Franny was cross.

'Sure you will.' Sheena grinned. 'You're the only person who knows the way, and how to, like, navigate the rocks and stuff.'

'Apart from Merry.'

'Like they'd want *her* to bring them.' Sheena shook her head. 'I can't wait. This is going to be so much fun.'

*

Rob had suggested he get a takeaway for that evening, and Molly and Dot had voted for Chinese. 'This was a great idea,' Molly said, as they sat at the kitchen table munching prawn crackers. Charlie had pleaded a headache and was resting upstairs. The double doors to the garden were open to the lazy summer evening and in the distance barbecues sizzled, glasses clinked, and muted laughter drifted in on the breeze as waves broke rhythmically on the beach below.

Despite the peaceful atmosphere, Rob seemed a little on edge, which Dot put down to the implications of Joni's arrival and what would happen next in Charlie's situation, which they were discussing.

Molly knew better: she had earlier agreed with Rob that she would slip away at the appropriate time and leave him alone with Dot so he could finally get around to asking her out on a date.

'It feels wrong, somehow,' said Dot, of Charlie. 'I feel as if we're keeping a secret from him.'

'Well, we won't be able to keep it for much longer. Joni mentioned she'd organised a Skype meeting with these people, tomorrow, I think?' Molly said.

'I suppose if they are his family we'll just have to let him go. I mean, what else can we do? I just can't get my head around the army bit. I can't imagine Charlie in Afghanistan, can you? And I couldn't bear him to be unhappy.' Dot looked sad.

'Did anything more ever come of the dumping theory?' Molly asked.

'Not that I've heard.' Rob twirled the stem of his glass. 'The detectives are still working on trying to piece together Charlie's movements since he got here.'

'But what will happen to him when he goes back to America? If these people take him?' Dot wondered. 'Will they put him in some sort of residential care, do you think?'

'I have no idea, and I'm afraid that won't be up to us, will it?' Rob said. 'We're going to have to face the fact that we'll be saying goodbye to Charlie one way or another – and sooner rather than later.'

A small sound made Dot look around. 'Did you hear that?' She rose from her chair. 'Charlie must have been here – look his plate and glass are on the counter.' She went over to the sink. 'Oh, God,' she said, putting her hands to her face. 'You don't think he overheard us – do you?'

'We weren't saying anything bad, were we?' Molly was alarmed.

'Not unless you're someone who may have been deliberately dumped by your family.'

'I'll check on him.' Rob pushed his chair back quickly. 'I was going to, anyway.'

Dot knew as soon as she heard Rob's rapid footsteps coming back down from upstairs that the burgeoning dread fluttering in her solar plexus wasn't misplaced.

'He's not in his room.' Rob was brisk. 'Let's not panic,' he said. 'He may just have gone for a walk – but I should probably have a quick scout about. Will you check the house and grounds quickly? If he's not there we'll look further – he may just have gone into the village.'

Charlie wasn't on the grounds – or in either of the cottages. 'Do you think we should call the guards?' Dot said.

'Not yet. Let's have a look in the village first. Then we'll regroup and figure out what to do next. I have a feeling he won't have gone very far.'

'Let's hope you're right,' said Molly. All thoughts of playing Cupid to Dot and Rob were overtaken by far more worrying ones.

Franny was in search of some quiet time. She had spent the evening with Sheena and some of Sheena's other friends, and hadn't had much to offer in the way of the general conversation, which had mostly veered from boys to makeup and back again, except for one awful detour when the subject of sex had come up: two of the girls were discussing their opinions explicitly, which possibly suggested actual *experiences* (Franny didn't want to dwell on the implications). She had felt herself blushing then, felt the mortifying and treacherous red heat crawling up her neck and face until she wanted to die of embarrassment. They had sniggered, a few of them, from behind their glossy manes of hair, until Sheena had – for once tactfully – brought the conversation back to the latest makeup blog she was raving about.

Franny had made her excuses shortly after and left them to it. She knew they'd talk about her after she was gone – but at least she wouldn't be there to endure their covertly shared glances or, worse, their thinly disguised pity. She headed automatically to her favourite spot, her hidden sand dune. At least the dune wasn't being razed, as she had previously expected: it was to be protected and preserved, along with the others that Ryan had shown her. There was just the added hazard of being hit by a stray golf ball – but that was hardly likely to happen at this time of day and, technically, the new golf course wasn't open yet. Besides, being hit on the head with anything seemed a reasonable price to pay for some privacy and quiet thinking time.

She scrambled down the sloping sandy path, jumped off it into the cushiony sand and pushed past the irregular curtain of reeds to get to her spot. But someone was already there. Someone was sitting on the pile of driftwood she had pulled together, which served as a makeshift bench, looking out to sea. It was a minute before she recognised him. Charlie was staring straight ahead into the darkening evening. His lips were moving, but Franny couldn't tell if he was talking or maybe just singing. Whichever it was she felt she was intruding on something deeply personal.

'Hi, Charlie,' she said. 'Didn't expect to find you here!'

For a minute he didn't react, and she began to be concerned. 'Charlie? It's me, Franny!'

Then he turned, looked at her for a moment, and smiled. 'Hey, Franny.'

Something about him seemed off-kilter. 'Are you okay, Charlie?' She came over and sat beside him. 'What are you doing out here all alone?'

'Oh, I'm used to being alone. It's better this way …'

'What way?'

'Alone. I'm a problem otherwise.'

'What do you mean, Charlie? How could you possibly be a problem? You're the opposite to a problem. You're – you're a solution!' Franny wasn't sure where she was going with this but she liked the line of reasoning.

'That's sweet of you to say, Franny, but the truth is I'm not a solution for anyone. I'm – I'm better away from people.'

Now Franny didn't know what to say.

'I don't think it was always this way, though.' He looked out to sea again. 'If only Jessie was here, she'd know what to do.'

'Who's Jessie?' Franny chewed her lip.

'I was supposed to meet her somewhere.' He rubbed his face. 'Can't remember where. I wait for her in the café every day. Maybe she'll show up tomorrow.'

'Shouldn't you be at Dot's place, Charlie? It's getting late.' Franny was concerned.

He shook his head. 'I just wanted some quiet time alone – I need to think.' His mouth was working. 'It's not safe at Dot's … not any more.' He sounded genuinely upset.

Charlie wasn't making much sense, but it certainly seemed like he didn't want to go back to Dot's house, for whatever reason, and Franny wasn't going to make him. But she couldn't leave him like this. She had a better idea …

Eva picked up on the first ring. 'Stay right where you

are, Franny,' she said, after Franny had explained the situation to her. 'Jan and Merry are on their way now to get you. Don't move!'

'Merry's coming over, Charlie,' Franny told him, when she had finished the call, 'with her dad, Jan. They'll take you anywhere you want to go – but they'd really like to see you.'

'Merry and Jan, huh?'

Franny nodded. 'If that's okay?'

'Sure … sure … I'd like to see Merry and Jan. They're good people.' He sat down again.

Franny breathed a sigh of relief and took out the blanket she carried in her backpack. 'Here, put this over you. You need it more than me – you must be freezing.' She tucked it around his thin frame. Then, because she couldn't think what to say, she began talking about the constellations and stars that Merry, Jan and Eva had taught her about when she was younger. They were becoming visible now in the night sky. It seemed to do the trick, and Charlie listened to her, nodding as she pointed skywards, then added his own observations – which, as usual, were unexpected and intriguing. 'How do you know so much about stuff?' Franny asked him.

Charlie shrugged. 'I'm not sure, Franny. I think I must have read quite a bit when I was a younger man, perhaps …'

And that was how Jan and Merry found them. Two unlikely silhouettes sitting side by side in the sand dunes – chatting companionably under a sky full of stars you could almost reach up and touch.

❋

Merry immediately rang Dot to let her know that Charlie was safe. 'But, Dot, he doesn't seem to want to go back to your place.' Merry was confused.

'That's understandable,' Dot said. 'Charlie must have overheard part or all of our conversation – we had no idea he was there. We were discussing what might become of him. It was very unfortunate – it must have alarmed him.'

'He's welcome to stay at ours for tonight – Mum said so. Charlie seems happy with that.'

'That's so kind of you – but look, Merry, would you just drop in to us on your way home with Charlie? He doesn't have to stay but we're all so anxious to see him – to explain.'

'Sure,' said Merry. 'We're leaving now.'

❋

In the kitchen that, only hours before, had felt so relaxed, Charlie now paced with Franny's blanket hanging from his shoulders like a cape. 'I just feel so close,' he said, exasperated. 'This close!' He held up his index finger and thumb. 'It's like a fish swimming by on the edge of my consciousness that just keeps slipping away – like quicksilver.'

Dot had made coffee to warm everyone up and was filling mugs, while Franny had found the leftover prawn crackers.

'That's a good sign, Charlie,' Rob said. 'I'm sure you'll recover your memory any time now. I can only imagine how hard this must be for you, but please try not to let it agitate you. The more relaxed you can be, the more likely memories are to resurface.'

'When I began to play the piano that day, something shifted. I felt it. I just can't – can't seem to articulate it. But I'm so close, I know I am – I just need more time. A little bit more time.' He was panicked again. 'That's why I don't want to talk to these – these people. Not yet. I'm not ready.'

'Charlie, no one is going to make you do anything you don't want to. You have our word on that,' said Dot.

'Of course not.' Molly looked upset.

Charlie sat down on one of the kitchen chairs. 'I'm sorry. It's just so frustrating – and frightening.' He looked vulnerable. 'I don't want to end up somewhere – you know …' He gave a weak attempt at a smile.

'Charlie, we're not going to let anything horrible happen to you.' Dot walked over and put her arm around his shoulders, bending down beside him. 'Are we?' She looked at Rob and the others.

'Of course we won't.'

'That's what the money from the GoFundMe page is for – to make sure you can stay wherever you want to, wherever you're happy. We've all become so fond of you, haven't we? You mean so much to us. You're one of us now, Charlie, and we're not going to let anyone or anything take you anywhere unless you're entirely happy about it.'

*

After Merry and Jan had left to drop Franny home and take Charlie back to their house, Dot found herself alone in the kitchen with Rob, who was pouring himself a glass of wine.

Her relief on hearing that Charlie was safe had been replaced by sadness. Despite her reassuring words to Charlie, she felt tired and wrung out. The stress of the last week was taking its toll and she turned away quickly as tears spilled suddenly from her eyes, taking her completely by surprise.

'Will you join me in a glass, Dot?' Rob turned and noticed her shoulders sag as she swiped at her eyes. 'Dot? Dot!' He was aghast. 'Darling!' He took her in his arms, and tuned her to face him. 'You're crying! Why?'

'I'm sorry.' Dot sniffed, leaning against his shoulder. 'It's so silly, but I'm just so relieved and tired and – and I don't want Charlie or any of you to be going away.'

'There, there, old girl.' Rob patted her back gently. 'Charlie gave us all quite a fright. Don't you worry, everything's going to be all right – you'll see.'

'Do you really think so?' Dot looked up at him and sniffed again.

'Of course I do.' He dropped a kiss on her forehead. And when she smiled wanly, he stroked her tears away with his thumb. And then his lips were on hers, and the surprisingly tender kiss that followed made them both forget about Charlie and his predicament for at least the next couple of minutes.

Fifty

When Jan opened the front door to Joni and Ryan at eight in the morning, in his dressing-gown, he was apologetic. 'I'm sorry, but Charlie went out earlier. I'm surprised you didn't see him on your way here.'

It took all of Joni's strength of mind to muster a smile. 'Oh dear. It's just his family are anxious for Charlie to Skype them – and it's three in the morning in the States so it's really nice of them to be waiting up for him.'

'He likes to have coffee at the Seashell – that's probably where he is.'

'Thanks, Jan,' said Ryan. 'We'll catch up with him.'

'Wow, these crazy old folks really keep everyone on their toes, don't they?' Joni joked.

Jan threw a startled glance at Ryan as he closed the door behind them.

When they reached the Seashell, sure enough, Charlie was ensconced at the counter.

Something about the way he was just sitting there, content, untroubled, like nothing had ever happened, like an entire village hadn't gone out of their way to look after him – like all her work to track down his family was for nothing – ignited something in Joni's subconscious she hadn't realised she had been harbouring. It felt a lot like rage. But there Charlie was, sitting at the counter, sipping his coffee and greeting friends, like it was just another day, like he hadn't frightened the life out of people who thought he was lost – maybe for good.

Ryan steered Joni in the other direction, away from Charlie, towards a table in a cosy booth. 'Aren't you going to at least *say* something to him?' she demanded.

'What do you suggest I say to him?' Ryan sounded weary. He had waved at Charlie as normal when they had come in and Charlie had waved back.

'What the hell do you think you're doing? might be a start. He had the whole village out looking for him and all the time he was hanging out with Franny and that girl with the weird hair and her parents who, by the way, were hiding him!'

'No one was hiding him, Joni.'

'He scared the life out of us all.' Joni adopted a more moderate tone – although she didn't feel like it.

'Eva and Jan rang the Doc and Dot immediately they knew where Charlie was. It was Charlie's choice to stay the night with them at their place. Where's the problem?'

Joni didn't like his tone. 'The problem – in case it has somehow slipped your mind, Ryan – is that thanks to a whole lot of work, and a whole lot of time put into this project by me, Charlie now has some relatives he can call his own.' Joni didn't like how snippy she was sounding but she couldn't restrain herself and she was tired of faking it.

'None of that has slipped my mind, Joni. How could it? But what's important here is Charlie's welfare. That has to come first, no matter what else is going on.'

'Because God forbid anyone else's welfare could be considered. Right? What about Jenna and Kyle, who have gone to the trouble of gathering important identifying documentation to prove Charlie is who they say he is. Hmm?'

'We don't know that, Joni, for sure.'

'Oh, so now you're doubting them, too?'

'We just need to be sure, that's all.'

Joni decided in favour of applying logic. 'You do realise, don't you, Ryan, that you're implying a man who doesn't even know his own name, who he is, or where he comes from has more credibility than two completely sane people who have produced family documents to back up what they say?'

'Charlie isn't insane, Joni. He's just confused, disoriented.'

'I didn't say he was insane. And I'm not sure he's the only one who's confused and disoriented ...'

'What's that supposed to mean?'

Joni wasn't sure until she heard herself say it. 'It means that someone has to take charge here, Ryan. We can't just let things float along on some confused man's timeline. Charlie needs to come back with us right now to talk to Kyle and Jenna. And if you won't go and get him I will.'

'No, you won't.' Ryan was quiet but firm.

'Excuse me?'

'First off, Charlie feels safe here, Joni. Hanging in the Seashell is part of his daily routine. Second, Charlie doesn't know who you are – and it's actually none of your business. How would you feel if some stranger went up to one of your grandmothers and accosted them?'

'None of my business? Are you for real? This is *totally* my business! What's the matter with you, Ryan? You've been acting weird since you got to this place. And I am not going to accost anybody. I am simply acting with good sense and compassion, which is more than can be said for you.' Before he could stop her, let alone argue with her, Joni was up out of her chair and headed straight towards Charlie, with Ryan struggling to extricate himself from the table to follow her.

'Hello, Charlie.' Joni smiled at him. 'I'm Joni ...'

'Hello, Joni. It's a beautiful day today, isn't it?' Charlie appeared happy to talk.

'It certainly is. Have you any plans for the day, Charlie?'

'Plans? Hmm ... no, I don't think so.'

'Joni!' Ryan caught up with her and pasted a smile on his face.

'Charlie and me are just having a little talk, aren't we, Charlie?'

'How're you doing, Charlie?' Ryan asked amiably.

'I'm good. How are you today, Ryan?' Charlie smiled. 'I'm just having my usual.'

'Here we go, Charlie,' said Merry, putting a fresh coffee in front of him. 'Ryan.' She nodded to him. 'Can I get you guys something?' She looked pointedly at Joni.

'No, thank you.' Joni was polite but curt. 'We're not staying – we've just come to get Charlie, haven't we, Ryan?' She looked to him for confirmation. 'He needs to come with us.'

'Is that so?' Merry smiled.

'Yes, it is.' Joni was equally upbeat.

'Charlie's going nowhere with you.' Merry said, still smiling.

'We'll see about that.' Joni turned to Charlie. 'Charlie, when you've finished your coffee, Ryan and I would like if you would come back to Dot's house – where you've been staying, where Dot's been *taking care* of you. We have something we need to discuss with you.'

'Joni!' Ryan protested.

'Dot's house?' Charlie considered. 'No, I don't think I'd like to go there now. I'll get there in a little while. For the moment I'm very happy where I am.'

'Okay, that's enough.' Merry leaned on the counter and addressed Ryan. 'Take yourself and your friend back to your table or I'm going to have to ask you to leave – now.'

'I'm not going anywhere, not without Charlie,' Joni said to Ryan, ignoring Merry.

Charlie was looking at Joni, considering her. 'I don't think we've met. I'm Charlie.' He held out his hand for her to shake.

'I know who you are.' Joni was exasperated. She shook his hand, but her foot was tapping impatiently on the floor.

'Do you two know each other?' Charlie directed the question to Ryan and Joni, sounding mildly curious. 'This is Merry's boyfriend.' He gestured towards Ryan, seeming pleased to have clarified the introduction.

'No, he's not!' Merry said quickly.

Ryan rubbed his chin and looked awkward. 'Uh, Charlie …'

Joni made a small sound between a breath and a laugh. 'Am I missing something here?' She glanced from Merry to Ryan. She was joking, but suddenly her gaze sharpened. 'Well, am I?'

'No, you are not,' Merry said. 'Most definitely not.'

'For God's sakes, Joni!' Ryan threw up his hands.

'For God's sakes, what? You're not denying it!' Joni watched Ryan carefully. 'Is that why you're not backing me up here?'

'You know why I'm not backing you up here – I just told you why!'

'You need to make a choice here, Ryan. You need to decide.'

'I don't think we need to rush into any decisions,' Eva's calm voice interjected as she placed some fresh pastries on the counter. 'Charlie feels happier staying here at the moment. What's the harm in that?' She patted Charlie's hand.

'If Jessie were here, she'd know what to do,' Charlie said softly.

'Who's Jessie?' Joni snapped.

'I'm sure you'll meet her one of these days …' Charlie smiled.

'That's enough already,' Merry said to Joni. 'You need to leave – this conversation isn't happening here.' An awkward silence followed.

'Well, it would appear that I'm outnumbered,' Joni

said, glancing around her. 'This isn't over,' she whispered to Ryan, before turning on her heel and leaving. Outside the Seashell she walked quickly, head down, trying to ignore the absence of following footsteps in her wake.

'Don't you think you should go after her?' Merry said to Ryan.

Behind her, Eva busied herself behind the counter, then disappeared into the kitchen again.

'I need a minute – and a coffee, please.' Ryan sat down wearily beside Charlie, who seemed unperturbed. He was quietly humming a tune. 'I'm sorry about that, Charlie. Are you all right?'

'Yes, yes, no need to apologise, whatever it was. All good here.'

For some reason Ryan felt tears spring to his eyes – but Merry chose that moment to put his espresso in front of him, which was a welcome distraction.

'This whole thing, it's going from bad to worse. I thought …' He shook his head. 'I thought we were getting somewhere and now …'

Just then Merry's phone rang. She fished it out and looked at the number. 'Hang on a sec,' she said, retreating. 'I have to take this.'

When Merry came back from taking her call, her face was pale, but her eyes were alight. 'Can I have a word?' Merry inclined her head to indicate Ryan should follow her. She stopped and leaned her shoulder against a pillar of driftwood. 'That was my late husband's mother on the phone.'

Ryan looked blank.

'Her husband is a Major in the US military. I asked her to check out the identity of Jonathan Dubois, just to be sure. Remember?'

'And?'

'Everything they say checked out – he served in Afghanistan in the nineties. They forgot to mention one significant detail, though – Jonathan Dubois died in 2007. I have all the details on email.'

'They're using a false identity.'

'Correct. Doug's father has reported them to the US authorities so they're on it.'

'I need to let Joni know.'

'That would be wise.' Merry shrugged. 'Good luck.'

Ryan touched her shoulder. 'Thank you. I really appreciate this.'

'Any time.'

Fifty-one

Ryan opened the door to the cottage to see Joni chatting animatedly to a couple on her laptop, which was resting on the kitchen counter. He didn't have to work too hard to figure out who they were: clearly they were Charlie's so-called relatives.

'So, you can rest assured,' Joni was saying to them on-screen, 'I will be bringing Charlie back with me next week to hand him over, and—' She didn't get any further.

Ryan cut across her and addressed Jenna and Kyle. 'I'm afraid that won't be happening. What's more, if you ever attempt to contact us again I will be informing the police. We have already reported your activities to the relevant authorities.' He shut down the computer.

'What the hell do you think you're doing?' Joni was horrified.

'I need to talk to you, Joni.' Ryan was abrupt. 'They're scammers – con artists. This whole thing is a scam.'

'What are you talking about?'

'They're using a fake identity for Charlie or Jonathan – whoever they're saying he is.' Ryan looked at her. 'Jonathan Dubois was who they say he was. They just neglected to mention he's been dead for fourteen years.'

'Who told you that?' Joni was furious.

'Merry, the girl at the—'

'I know who Merry is.' Joni was sharp.

'Well, her in-laws – they're a long-time US military family. The father had Jonathan Dubois's identity checked out.'

'She's married?'

'What?' The question threw him.

'Merry? She's married?' Joni enquired eagerly.

'Widowed – her husband was killed in an accident. What's that got to do with—'

'Never mind.' Joni waved a hand, her expression closed again. 'But you believe her – you believe their story?'

'They have proof, Joni, concrete proof, and they've alerted the US authorities.'

'And you did all this behind my back.' Joni got up and walked across the room.

'I didn't even know about this until now!'

'So how did you find out, then?'

'Merry told me – she'd just found out herself. The documents are being emailed to her, but her father-in-law has confirmed it.'

'Well, hasn't she been busy?'

'That's not fair, Joni. Merry only wants what's best for Charlie – she was the first to find him. The first person to speak with him.'

'How do you know she's telling the truth? You haven't even met these people she's talking about. How do you even know they're her in-laws? How do you know she isn't trying to hang on to Charlie for the money?'

Although it was a fair question from Joni's point of

view, the suggestion was so ludicrous to Ryan that, for a moment, he was at a loss to explain to Joni. In that instant, he realised how much he had changed since coming to Derrybeggs and becoming involved in its tight-knit community. How could he expect Joni, who was used to the cut-throat hustle and dog-eat-dog world of New York, to understand? 'Joni, people here aren't like that. It's a small town, everyone knows everybody else, and why would she lie about it?'

'I can think of several reasons but clearly none of them would matter to you.' Joni was pacing now. 'You know what I think? I think this is all bullshit! Charlie or whatever his name is doesn't *have* a family ... or clearly anyone that wants him. Jenna and Kyle are prepared to take him in – to look after him, or at least see that he's placed in a good care home back in the US. Whatever happened in the past is over! This is his story now, Ryan. *This!*'

The vehemence of her argument threw him.

'Joni, these people are after the money, nothing else! Haven't you any empathy for Charlie's situation? You of all people should get how he must feel. None of us wants to be abandoned – we can't just hand him over to someone because it suits you to wrap up an instalment and move on to the next storyline for your Instalife. This is real, Joni!'

'You think I don't know it's real? Why do you think I came over here? Why do you think I went along with any of this? Why do you think I devoted my time and energy to this – this crazy stunt and had complete strangers in my house to vet them? Yet you choose to believe over me some girl you've just met with an attitude problem! You've changed, Ryan. Since you've been here you've – you've lost your edge. I don't know what's got into you – but you're the one who needs to get real. Charlie's a confused old man. What's happened to him is sad, but he's not your responsibility – and he's certainly not mine.' She paused to draw breath.

Ryan got up, ran a hand through his hair. 'I can understand how you would feel that way, Joni. And you're right, I have changed since I've been here – or maybe I've just found out who I really was all along.'

'What does that even mean?'

'I don't know right now, Joni,' Ryan said wearily. 'I don't know.'

Joni realised she needed to back off. 'Ryan, come on – this is stupid. Why are we fighting about an old man who doesn't mean anything to either of us? You know we're perfect for each other. We belong together, Ryan – in New York. Come on, honey.' She took his hand and led him to the bedroom. 'We can get past this – you know we can. We're both just tired and stressed out ...'

Afterwards Joni lay in bed to think things over while Ryan showered. Ryan hadn't been kidding when he said he'd changed. He'd been giving out mixed signals since she'd got here. And his lovemaking, which should have been passionate taking into account their separation, had been different. Something was missing. Joni wasn't good at nuances, but she knew something significant had changed between her and Ryan. She had known it was a risk, insisting that he commit to their relationship, known she might even lose him over it – but at least she wouldn't be dropped when she least expected it. This way, as her followers had pointed out, she was taking matters into her own hands, acting on her terms. She was being courageous, not foolhardy.

She knew there were women out there who would be queuing up to go out with Ryan Shindler – whether or not this local café girl was one of them remained to be seen. All throughout their relationship, back home in New York, her presence hadn't stopped women flirting openly with him, some even slipping him their phone number when they thought she wasn't looking. A good man, never mind a handsome, successful one, was fair game in New York. With or without a ring on your finger. That was just the way it was. But Joni had already been abandoned by one man – her father. She wasn't going to let another follow suit. If Ryan was about to go, then she would give the marching orders … however unwillingly.

Fifty-two

'How do I look?' Dot was fussing. She still found it hard to believe it was all actually happening – the festival was about to open and she, Dot, had a world-famous actor and documentary-maker staying in her house. He was absolutely lovely, David Blackthorn, just as Molly had assured her he would be, but Dot still felt a bit awkward around him, sort of like a bashful teenager. Thank God Rob was there to help her set things up. She had suggested they all have a glass of champagne in the garden before setting off to the festival, which Molly would open as guest of honour. David and the others were still getting ready, and Dot was setting out her favourite Waterford Crystal flutes on a silver tray.

'Absolutely gorgeous!' said Rob, taking Dot's hand and bending over it with mock gallantry to kiss it.

'Oh, stop it!' She laughed.

'I mean it! I'm a lucky man, going to a swanky gig with such an elegant date. It's years since I've worn a tux – it's making me feel very James Bond.'

'Yes, well, don't let it distract you. Just stick to opening the champagne for now, if you would.'

'Your wish is my command.' Rob twisted the bottle

expertly and smiled with satisfaction at the discreet *pffft* as he pulled the cork.

'You've done that before, I can tell.' Dot checked her canapés in the oven. 'I think we're almost ready.' She pulled out a tray of delicious-looking tiny savoury pastries and Rob promptly swiped one. 'You're living dangerously.' She warned him off with a flick of a tea-towel.

'Faint heart never won fair lady,' Rob countered, popping another cork.

Dot was overwhelmed with a rush of happiness. Who would've thought that only just over a year ago, when she was hesitantly taking on this old wreck of a house and wondering what in the world she was doing, she'd be laughing in its kitchen now, swatting tea-towels at a lovely man, who had become a cherished friend and hopefully even something more. After Rob had confessed to Dot how much he really liked her – the night Charlie had disappeared – and how attractive he thought she was, Dot had been relieved to admit she felt exactly the same way about him. They had agreed they should waste no further time in really getting to know one another. Rob had secured his position as locum for a further twelve months with an option to renew, much to the delight of old Dr Walshe and his patients. But he wouldn't be needing the smart new apartment attached to the surgery, he informed them. They were free to let it. Rob was staying right where he was in Dot's house for the foreseeable future.

*

'How do I look?' Molly asked her old friend David, who had come to help do up the back of her dress, which was quite an intricate affair of very small buttons. Molly had gone for a sort of boho look and her long floaty gown looked like something Stevie Nicks might have worn onstage.

'Quite ravishing!' he said, standing back to look at her critically. 'I can say that hand on heart, without – thank goodness – having to make good on my pronouncement at this advanced stage in my life.' He chuckled.

'You're still a handsome old devil.' Molly smiled. At eighty-three, David was still tall with a full head of silver hair. 'I don't know how you do it.'

'I owe it all to the love of a good woman.'

'You certainly do.' Molly was good friends with David's wife, Ruth, who was back in London. 'I bet Ruthie takes incredibly good care of you.'

'We've taken care of each other, I hope, over the years,' he said. 'We're lucky to have survived this long. What about you, Moll? Any lucky man in your life?'

'No, I've sort of given up on that front. I'm tired of it all, to be honest.'

'You can't think like that! You're only a youngster.' David wagged a finger at her. 'And with a burgeoning American fan club, I hear.'

'Actually I'm working on another project that's requiring my full-time attention.'

'Your memoir? I must say I'm looking forward to—'

'I ditched that idea. It's turned into something else – a novel about a central character whose name is Charlie. I'm not sure what my agent will make of it.' She made a face. 'He may very well drop me! But it's a nice story.'

'Sounds terrific! Now let's get going – you've got a leg to break.'

'Thank you,' Molly said, reaching up to kiss his cheek. 'You've no idea what this means, David, you being here to judge the documentary competition. It's really put the festival on the map. I know how busy your schedule is.'

'Don't thank me!' David was as generous as always. 'Two hundred American hipsters raving about *Hornetsville*? What an audience for an old has-been like me!'

'Oh, David, you're no has-been.'

'Compared with you, my dear, with your new American fan base and your brand-new career as a novelist, I'm certainly feeling like one.' He laughed. 'I'm only sorry I have to fly home in the morning – I'd hoped to get in a bit of fishing but Antarctica calls. Now let's go – or you'll be late.'

'How do I look?' Joni took another selfie of herself.

'Stunning.' Ryan smiled. 'You always do.' It was true: Joni always turned heads. Tonight she was wearing a long white Grecian-style dress, the neckline slashed to her waist, and high strappy sandals. She could have been going to the most glamorous of red-carpet events – he hoped she wouldn't be too overdressed for Derrybeggs – but as Joni reminded him, this was for her followers, her Instagram feed, and they expected glamour. As if on cue he heard a chorus of voices chanting for Molly –

her *Hornetsville* fans had managed to find out where she was staying. Ryan would have to ask them to leave the grounds. They were trespassing, after all.

'Let's go,' said Joni, grabbing her purse. 'You first.'

Ryan did as he was told, locking the door of the cottage while Joni posed for selfies with her followers, who were overjoyed to discover that this was where she was staying – even if Molly appeared to have escaped them. Ryan stood by patiently, but eventually stepped in. 'We really need to go, Joni. I said we'd be at Dot's for six thirty.'

'It'll wait.' Joni was cool. 'I need to interact with my followers. A few more minutes won't count.'

Ten minutes later Ryan was still waiting. 'Joni, I'm leaving now – you can come if you want or not.'

'Since when have you gotten so snippy?' She looked at him curiously. 'These people are putting this stupid festival on the map – you could at least be grateful for all my hard work.'

'I *am* grateful for all your hard work.' Ryan sighed.

'Good. That's better.'

It was going to be a long night.

'How do I look?' Sheena studied herself in the full-length mirror at Franny's house.

'Amazing,' Franny said.

'Take some shots of me, will you? Hold on, I have to get the light just right.'

The girls were getting ready in Franny's house because her mother, Sheila, thought it was the lesser of two evils. At least there would be supervision in her house whereas there would be none in Sheena's house. Sheila didn't trust Sheena not to put Franny up to wearing something awful or layering her lovely skin with stripes of contouring makeup – this way she could keep an eye on them up to almost the last minute. Sheena did look amazing, Sheila had to admit, but she looked at least twenty-five – which, when you were just fifteen, seemed a pity. Her makeup was heavy, but flawless, her dress skin-tight and her long hair waved and lacquered into submission.

Franny, on the other hand, looked as lovely as only a fourteen-year-old can. Although Sheila and Franny had chosen the dress online from the trendy chain store, she still got a shock when she saw her daughter in it. The simple white cotton dress with the long tiered skirt set off Franny's lightly tanned skin and showed off her subtly developing figure and tiny waist. Her long dark hair was loose and wildly curly. Looking at her, Sheila felt a stab of sadness for the loss of her bossy little girl but was rewarded with a glimpse of the beautiful young woman she would become. 'Are you really wearing those things on your feet, Franny?' Sheila shook her head at the chunky Doc Martin type ankle boots.

'I told you I was,' Franny said. 'It's going to get really mucky out there later and, besides, I like them.'

'They edge up the look, Sheila,' Sheena explained, eyeing Franny critically. 'Otherwise it'd be too, like, feminine ... kinda *lacy*. The Docs bring it right up to trend.'

'Right, I see,' said Sheila, who knew when to back off. 'Well, you both look gorgeous. We're leaving now – we have to be at Dot's for six thirty. Don't be late, girls – and, Franny, I know there's a lot going on tonight and I want you to have fun. Just remember we trust you to be sensible.'

'Sure. Bye, Mam. See you guys later.'

'You're really not coming to the party after?' Sheena hadn't ruled out a change of mind. She fished a flask from her satin bag, undid it and took a swig, then offered it to Franny. 'It's vodka – it won't smell. No one can tell, she'll never know.'

'No, thanks. I promised I wouldn't drink alcohol until I'm older. It smells disgusting anyway.' Franny wrinkled her nose.

'Why is your mum, like, so strict?' Sheena said wonderingly, looking out of the window as Sheila and Mike set off. 'I mean you're like, nearly fifteen. Is she always going to be this controlling?'

'I don't know.' Franny shrugged. 'I asked Dad about it once but he said it was just because he and Mam care about us so much.'

After that Sheena had nothing further to say on the subject.

The committee weren't the only ones who looked the part. Ryan and the staff had done a spectacular job with the conference room, which looked worthy of an Oscars ceremony. The committee members and their respective partners had the best seats in the house, right up front. Charlie was on the other side of Dot, looking very distinguished in his rented tux. He sat erect in his chair, relaxed and taking in the throngs of people who were coming in behind them. At six p.m. on the dot, Kate Carmichael made her way up onto the stage so as many people as possible could see her. She called for silence and introduced herself as chairperson of the committee. Her self-congratulatory speech went on longer than it should have but that hardly came as a surprise.

Then it was Molly's turn. She got the evening off to a good start. 'A very dear friend of mine,' she said, 'whom you may know from his legion of nature documentaries and many films' – she was interrupted by wild applause – 'has agreed to take time out of his incredibly busy schedule and come over this evening to judge our Film-on-fone documentaries. I can't tell you how pleased I am to welcome my dear friend and colleague David Blackthorn to Derrybeggs.'

David joined Molly onstage to more wild applause. Then, after he'd said a few words about how impressed he was with the local talent and how creative people had been with their smartphones, they showed the six films that had made it to the final. There was an interesting take on a local lady's jam-making skills, called *Sticky Business*; an amusing commentary from O'Hagan's; a film on nesting gulls, with wonderful views of Gulls' Cliffs; then Sheena's film about Molly, which showed Molly looking surprised a lot of the time as Sheena ambushed her, then grilled her for tips she could give to aspiring actresses – it raised a few laughs, which Sheena took as a positive sign; and Franny's documentary on Ryan, the golf club and the environmental challenges encountered, which was thought-provoking and interesting. Franny saw David Blackthorn nodding in agreement at some of the points she made.

The last film to be shown took everyone by surprise. Molly introduced it. 'This last Film-on-fone has been shot by a visitor – a visitor who has become a very dear friend to all of us.' She smiled down at Charlie, who looked quietly expectant. 'I think you'll find it speaks for itself,' Molly said. The title ran first – *Always On My Mind*. It opened with Charlie sitting on his usual bench, overlooking Derrybeggs Bay, spread out beneath him. Charlie spoke into his phone camera simply. 'Hello, my name is Charlie. I find myself in Derrybeggs under unusual circumstances. I have no memory of who I am, or the life I live. There may be several explanations for this, none of which we can rule out just yet. But one of them is dissociative fugue state. In a nutshell, this means my memory may return, gradually or suddenly, and when it does, I will in all likelihood no longer have any memories of *this* time, my time with you in Derrybeggs. So in case that happens, I wanted to have something to remember you dear people by, your kindness to me, and the wonderful time I have spent with you.' The remaining four and a half minutes showed various scenes Charlie had filmed: with Rob in the surgery; with Molly on the hilltop sharing a sandwich and laughing; Peggy waving as she went by on her Rollator; Dot baking in the kitchen, pouring Charlie a cup of tea; Franny in her favourite sand dune, talking earnestly; Merry in the café smiling and shaking her head at something Charlie said; a clip from the wonderful evening at O'Hagan's when Ryan got up to play – where an astute observer could see Merry watching him intently and the look he shared with her, however briefly, as he caught her eye. Finally it was back to Charlie, who said, 'Know that whatever happens to my memory, I'll always carry you dear people and Derrybeggs in my heart.' When it ended, you could have heard a pin drop – and the odd stifled sob.

Dot was particularly touched. 'How on earth did you manage it?' She turned to Charlie sitting beside her, smiling broadly. 'I'll kill Molly when I see her – she certainly kept it under wraps.'

Rob, who was beside her, nodded and blew his nose vigorously.

When the resounding applause had subsided, Molly and David said a few words about how impressed they were with the standard of entries – David emphasised what a difficult time he'd had in deciding on a winner – but everyone already knew which film had won. In reverse order, *Sticky Business*, the jam-making film, came in third place; the film on nesting gulls was runner-up; and, to no one's surprise, Charlie's entry won the competition.

Fifty-three

Franny wasn't just disappointed – she was mortified. She knew she shouldn't have let them persuade her to enter her stupid film. Joni had been right – she had come across as a stupid schoolgirl trying to sound important. Even Sheena's film had raised a few laughs – at least that was something. Now Ryan would regret letting her do the documentary or ever getting involved. She smiled and nodded as people came over to tell how good they thought it was – but she knew they were just being nice, feeling sorry for her. Now the reception was in full swing and people were thronging to greet each other and hopefully get a chance to meet David Blackthorn and Molly or at least say they had rubbed shoulders with them. Champagne was handed around and the noise level was amplifying accordingly.

To her right, Franny saw Joni looking stunning and doing a piece to her phone held on a selfie stick. Standing behind her, Ryan was scanning the crowd as if he was looking for someone. Some of Molly's *Hornetsville* fans had turned up in full costume and were attracting bemused glances from the uninitiated. Now that the festival had really begun, and looked like being a resounding success, relief mixed with anticipation was creating a real buzz. It was the perfect time to slip away.

'C'mon,' said Sheena, grabbing her arm. 'Let's get out of here.'

She hadn't known she would go – not really – until just that exact moment. But now Franny didn't hesitate. She was tired of people patting her on the head, tired of being promised things would work out, and tired of Sheena talking about how much fun she was missing out on. She and Sheena skirted a few groups, navigated the waiting tables and pushed through the large double doors until they were outside. On the horizon, the sky was shot with pink and purple. Sunset and adventure were only minutes away.

'C'mon, hurry.' Sheena had replaced her strappy sandals with trainers. They half walked and half ran through the strangely deserted village, turning left at the old church and following the road to the harbour. By the time they reached the Surf Shack Franny's breathing was heavy, but despite the warm night air, goosebumps flared on her arms. At first she thought they were alone. But as her eyes grew accustomed to the shadows, signs of movement and soft laughter came from behind the old shed. Then the ragged clouds drifted apart overhead and an almost full moon lit up the Shack, making a silvery path on the ocean towards Gulls' Cliffs.

'Hey.' Steve, one of the local lads, came out of the shadows, followed by an older boy Franny didn't know so well. 'We thought you were going to bail.'

'No way.' Sheena laughed. 'It just went on longer than we thought – where are the guys?'

'Round the side,' said Steve. 'Go and say hello.' He winked. 'You okay to go out with them, Franny?'

'I said she would – didn't I?' Sheena said. Making her way around to the side, where two of the other girls and three more lads sat at the two bench tables – everyone was already in wetsuits.

'Hey, Sheena,' said Mandy. 'Ronan was beginning to get worried.' She grinned.

'Pour me a shot.' Sheena said, indicating the bottle of vodka. 'We just need to change.' She pulled Franny into the musty-smelling shed where the kayaks and canoes stood in rows against the wall and dug out the wetsuits they had put aside earlier. 'Here.' She threw Franny's to her. Quickly Franny unlaced and pulled off her Docs, undressed and pulled on her wetsuit, but now the building excitement was tinged with something that felt an awful lot like foreboding. She pushed the feeling aside – this was going to be great, a night to remember that they would reminisce about when they were older and tied down with jobs and responsibilities. She pulled up the zip, tugged on the neoprene boots, then grabbed her life jacket and head lamp. Sheena, who had been ahead of her, was into her wetsuit too, but hadn't zipped it up: the front was open just enough to reveal her string bikini top and she was fluffing her hair in the rusted old square of mirror that sat on an shelf.

'Get a move on,' Franny said, grabbing her canoe. 'And I'm guessing you were kidding when you said to pour you a shot?' Franny hated the schoolteacher inflection that had entered her tone, but everyone knew not to think of drinking before going out on the water. Even Sheena wouldn't be that stupid. 'What are you doing?' Franny looked on, perplexed, as Sheena fished out a tube of lip gloss and smeared some on.

'Um, there's a slight change of plan.' Sheena looked impishly at her.

'What do you mean?'

'I'm not going with you.'

'What?'

'I've changed my mind, Fran. I'm going to stay here with Ronan and the others – we're going to just hang out until the others come back with the boat, maybe have a little swim. Then we'll head out to Cape Clanad together.'

'You can't leave me to go on my own!' Franny was horrified.

'You won't be on your own – Simon and Jamie will be with you.'

'But I don't even know them!'

'You just have to show them the way – not, like, *talk* to them.' Guilt was making Sheena defensive.

'You're serious, aren't you?' Franny couldn't believe it. 'I bet you never meant to come! This was all part of your plan.'

'It wasn't, really, Franny. I thought it would be great craic, but then Ro and the guys wanted to have a few drinks here before the others come back for us. They're not that keen on the water. We'll wait for you, if you like – then we can all go out to Cape Clanad together.'

'I'm not *going* to the stupid party – I never was.'

'Well, then, you won't be missing anything – so why are you getting so, like, *angry* about it?'

'Because I don't like people backing out of things.'

'Oh, shut up, Franny! You're the one who's always going on about nature and stuff – here's a chance for you to do what you like doing and meet two guys who like doing the same stuff. Lighten up!'

Just then Steve poked his head around the door. 'Everything okay here? Thought I heard raised voices.'

'Everything's fine,' Sheena said.

'Just that Si and Jamie are keen to get going,' he said.

'Franny's on it. Aren't you?'

'Are you sure everything's fine?' Steve looked concerned. 'Cos we don't need any trouble here – we really don't.' He looked at Sheena questioningly.

'It's cool. Franny's cool with everything.'

'Great. I'll let the guys know, they're really psyched about this.'

Out on the water, Franny felt her anger at Sheena subside. She wasn't going to let her and her stupid carry-on upset her. She'd rather be out on the water any day than heading to a party – however exciting. This was something she *could* do. This was where she felt at home, confident, in a way she never could on land. A little behind her, Jamie and Simon – who seemed to be nice lads – were quiet, only the sound of their paddles reminding Franny they were with her. She guessed they were being transported like she was, acclimatising to this other world, where the ocean was lighting up with bioluminescence as they paddled through a stretch of plankton, reflecting the carpet of stars above them.

'Whoa!' Jamie said, pulling up alongside her. 'This is trippy.' The end of his paddle was aglow as he gave a low whistle. Around them, the water sparkled and flickered, putting on its very own light show.

'You'll see more if you turn your head lamp off,' Franny said. 'Sometimes there's seals and otters – even basking sharks.'

'Sharks, seriously?' Simon sounded uncertain.

'Yeah.' Franny grinned to herself. Although basking sharks were the second largest fish in the world, they were completely harmless.

'Relax.' Jamie chuckled. 'They're not dangerous.'

'Yeah, maybe.' Simon laughed nervously. 'But they could, like, flip you over accidentally.'

They floated for a bit then – just because it was so beautiful.

They were headed for Gull Cave – the lads had seen a YouTube video about the cave that went right through the largest rock that you could canoe through at low tide. Franny knew it of old – but it seemed to take longer to get to than usual. She supposed it was a trick of her mind. It had been a long time since she had been out this far. The last time must have been with Merry – and she wished she were with them now.

Finally, the cliffs loomed above them – Franny

manoeuvred expertly until the mouth of the cave was before them, the moonlight coming through at the far end.

'This is it, lads,' Franny said. 'You go on ahead, I'll take up the rear.' She felt a thrill of adrenalin now they were here – and she could tell the lads were impressed. Stuff Sheena and her stupid party on the island – the others didn't know what they were missing. How could drinking and partying compare with being up close with this awesomeness?

They made their way into the mouth of the cave, no bioluminescence here – the water was inky black. Something swooped in front of them, startling Jamie – but it was only a bat. A rising tide lifted the canoes closer to the roof of the cave and in a few places they had to duck their heads, which added to the atmosphere. They were later than Franny had thought – but thankfully a strong current had developed, hurrying them along.

Suddenly Franny's canoe stopped dead. For a moment she was too startled to comprehend what had happened, until she realised it was stuck between the rock wall that reared up beside her and a hidden one underwater. 'I'm stuck!' she shouted to the disappearing shapes of Simon and Jamie, flushed along by the current – but they didn't hear her. Franny struggled stoically to push herself free with her paddle – but it was no use. *Keep calm*, she instructed herself. Think. She hauled herself out, clambering onto the large rock that jutted out from the wall of the cave, and tugged at the canoe. Nothing. It came free suddenly then – but Franny slipped, saving herself only by instinctively grabbing and clinging to the top of the rock with both hands. It was only an instant – but the canoe, free from its obstruction, was swept away by the current, taking with it Franny's dry bag and mobile phone.

Panic seized her. There was no sign of Simon or Jamie – they had been carried out by the current, which made it impossible for them to turn back for her. For a moment she thought about jumping in and swimming out, letting the current carry her, but the other side was open ocean – and the lads might or might not be there waiting for her. Also, if her personal flotation device got caught or jammed on a rock, she'd be done for – and she didn't dare take it off. Common sense dictated she stay put. She risked climbing a bit further onto a higher ledge where she half sat and half lay at an awkward angle, safe for the moment from the rising tide.

Fifty-four

Joni had just extricated herself from a group of her followers, who were anxiously trying to find out everything they could about her now that they had finally got to meet her in person. 'I'll see you guys later.' She waved. 'At the beach barbecue.' Now she just had to find Ryan, who seemed to have disappeared. She located him eventually, talking to Rob and Dot, and another couple – although his gaze seemed to be drawn over their shoulders, his eyes flicking intermittently towards something or someone beyond them. Dot and Rob, who were laughing at a mutual joke, were clearly too taken with each other to notice.

Joni followed the direction of Ryan's glances, which led to the far side of the room, and a woman in an elegant shell pink strapless dress. Then the woman turned her head – and Joni realised with a jolt that it was Merry – the café girl – who appeared tonight to have morphed into a svelte blonde. For a one-horse town, Joni figured, Derrybeggs sure had some slick operators. She made her way over to Ryan, taking his arm. 'Can I have a word with you, honey?'

Ryan excused himself from the small group. 'What is it?' He was edgy.

'Nothing.' Joni smiled. 'I just thought you looked like you needed rescuing. You had that trapped look about you – like you were trying to break away.'

'Uh, was I? I wasn't aware of that.' He ran a hand through his hair.

'Come and meet some of my followers.' Joni took his hand. 'They've been asking about you.'

'Um, can we not do this now?' Ryan seemed tense.

Joni looked at him thoughtfully, then smiled. 'Sure. Whatever. Go back to your friends. I'll catch up with you later.'

Trapped on her perch in the cave with nothing to contemplate but the rising water level, Franny's brief life flashed before her. So this was how it would end, she thought mournfully. Stuck on a ledge in a cave with an incoming tide and no one in the world knowing or caring. She tried not to succumb to self-pity. None of the heroines she so looked up to would have done that. Not Anne Frank, not Orla Guerin, not Captain Dara Fitzpatrick, and not those girls who got washed out to sea on their paddleboards and had to tie themselves to a lobster pot for the night. But those paddleboard girls were missed, and rescued – the whole country was out looking for them. Who was going to miss her? Everyone would think she was with Sheena – off having a good time somewhere – and Sheena would be on the island partying, probably with her phone turned off. The lads would know something had happened if they saw her canoe, but for all she knew it could have got stuck again and they would just think she had disappeared into thin air. Then maybe they'd get into trouble even if they did make it back to shore. That would be her fault too. Her whole life had been a failure.

A seal popped its head up, probably attracted by her head lamp, and studied her with interest. This made her think of Muttie, who really *would* miss her – Muttie adored Franny and she wouldn't even have a chance to say goodbye to him. She wondered what Mam and Dad would think and bit her lip, fresh tears hot against the chill of her skin. She was cold now, very cold. She wondered if Clare would feel bad for always making a skit of everything she did and calling her Franny Thunberg. Well, Clare wouldn't have to worry about having an eco-warrior sister any more. But Clare had been good to Franny too, she had to concede: when she was little she was always picking her up and dusting her down after her latest scrape and defended Franny hotly against the mean girls at school until Franny was big enough to look after herself. In fairness, they'd had some laughs.

She thought of earlier that evening and her lovely dress, and all the trouble Mam had taken to get it for her – and then she remembered the last thing Mam had said to her: *Just remember, we trust you* ... Look where betraying that trust had got her. And the festival, how stupid she'd been to think her film wasn't good enough. It was grand! She was only fourteen, and Molly and Ryan had thought it was good. There had been plenty of time for her to get better at filming – learn how to do it properly. Molly had wanted to introduce her to David Blackthorn after the competition – and how had Franny repaid her? She'd gone off in a huff with stupid Sheena to try to impress her and some stupid guys she didn't even know. Well, now she'd never know how her life would have turned out. Franny wasn't familiar with remorse but whatever this horrible feeling was, she wanted it to stop.

She decided it was time to invoke the big guns. 'Dear God,' she whispered. 'I'm really sorry I haven't paid you as much attention as I should have, and I'm very sorry I didn't appreciate Mam and Dad and Clare more, or be nicer to people, or take better care of your beautiful planet, but please don't let me die just yet ... Please give me another chance. At least let me get to say goodbye, to tell Mam and Dad I love them ... *please*, God.' She wasn't sure if He heard her, but the curious seal, surprised by this unusual nocturnal activity, studied her with great interest.

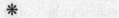

The first-night reception was in full swing and everyone was having a terrific time. But despite the euphoria of relief the committee members were enjoying, and the fun and catching up with people – even meeting David Blackthorn, whom Molly had introduced her to – Sheila Relish was having one of her 'feelings'. It had started when she was looking for Franny and couldn't see her anywhere in the room. David Blackthorn had said to

Sheila that he would very much like to meet Franny and have a word with her about her film, which had impressed him: he thought she showed great promise for someone of her age. Molly had told her that Franny's film would have come in third place – if Charlie's hadn't been submitted at the last moment and taken them all completely by surprise. As it was, she had come fourth, which was no mean feat. David had been genuinely impressed with her technique and approach.

Sheila had looked around the room, casually at first, then thoroughly, even checking the Ladies – but there was no sign of either Franny or Sheena. 'I can't find Franny anywhere,' she said to Mike, her husband. 'No sign of Sheena either. David Blackthorn wants to have a word with Franny.'

'They're probably off with a few of their pals, Sheila, having a chat outside. Don't be worrying.' Mike went back to talking broadband issues with Don Carmichael.

Sheila wasn't happy, though, and continued to duck and bob through the lively crowd until she saw Jan and Eva, wondering briefly who was the lovely blonde in the strapless dress they were talking to – until she realised it was Merry, who had obviously re-embraced her natural hair colour. 'Hi, guys,' Sheila was breathless. 'Have any of you seen Franny or Sheena? I can't find either of them anywhere. It's just that David Blackthorn wants to talk to Franny and I know she'll kick herself for missing this opportunity.' She looked at Merry. 'You know what she's been like about this film!'

'I saw her earlier.' Merry looked around. 'But that was

a good while ago, now that you mention it. I'll come with you and have another look.'

But Franny was nowhere to be found. It was Peggy O'Sullivan, who had been sitting outside on her Rollator, having a quiet cigarette, who could account for the last sighting. 'I saw the pair of them running off half an hour or so, ago,' she told Merry, who had come to look outside. 'Delighted with themselves! Probably off to some mischief or other, but sure you're only young once.' She laughed.

'Don't suppose you have any idea where they were going?'

'No. But they were heading towards the harbour, not into town.'

'It's not like Franny to leave like that without telling me,' Sheila said to Merry. 'I don't like this. Something doesn't feel right.'

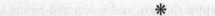

Back inside, Joni was being filmed interviewing David Blackthorn for her website, watched by an admiring circle of her followers. Professional and focused though she was on her subject, it did not escape Joni's notice that, in the periphery of her vision, she glimpsed Ryan leaning in to Merry to listen to something she was saying, then excusing himself from the group he was talking to and following her.

*

'I'm coming with you.'

'There's no need, really. There's probably some perfectly innocent excuse – maybe a party at the Surf Shack or something. If Sheena's involved, and it looks as though she is, she won't have got far in those designer heels she was sporting.'

They were heading towards Harbour Row when Merry saw Rachael, one of the part-time girls at the Seashell, wave to her. She and her friend were sharing a bag of chips. 'Are you looking for the lads?' She grinned. 'I told Ro they'd be found out.'

'Where are they?'

'At the Shack, but they'll have gone by now.'

'Gone where?'

'Out to Cape Clanad. They've been planning it for weeks to coincide with the film festival,' she explained, as if it made great sense.

'Where's Cape Clanad?' Ryan asked Merry.

'It's an island about ten minutes away by boat.' Merry sighed. 'That's what I was afraid of.'

'Don't worry about them,' said Rachael. 'They'll be fine – Ro and Steve know how to handle a boat and the water's grand and calm. Sure we all did it in our day.'

Merry tried Franny's phone again, and left yet another message. When they reached the Shack, she took off her sandals to make her way down the steep sandy path, Ryan behind her. The place seemed deserted, the rising moon casting shadows and hues, but the door to the equipment shed was open. Then, from around the back, Merry heard a movement. When she made her way to the rear, a girl was bending over on one of the benches. Merry recognised her as Keera, and her boyfriend Paul was with her, looking concerned. They seemed relieved to see Merry and Ryan. 'Keera's been really sick – I wanted to call South Doc, but she won't let me.'

'I'll be fine.' Keera gulped, looking as if she'd had her own party and was now paying the price for any overindulgence. 'I just want to go home now.' She shivered.

'Franny's not answering her phone,' Merry said. 'Her mam's worried sick about her. Are that gang planning to come back from Cape Clanad any time soon, do you know?'

Paul looked blank.

'Franny isn't with them,' Keera said, bleary-eyed. 'Remember?' She looked at her companion. 'She took the two lads out to Gull Cave – Steve's friends.'

'What?' Merry was horrified. 'On her own?'

'She didn't want to go to the party – but Sheena asked her instead to take two of the lads to Gull Cave – sorry.' Keera made a dash to the outdoor loo where she was heard retching.

'When did they leave?' Merry almost shouted.

'Dunno.' Paul shrugged. 'An hour or so ago?'

'Before or after the others left for Cape Clanad?'

'Before … Yeah, I remember it was before.'

'Then they should be back by now,' Merry said.

'Would they have joined the others on the island?' Ryan suggested.

Merry shook her head. 'Unlikely. It's in the other

direction. I don't like this. She should have been back by now, and Franny would always pick up a call from me.'

Just then Merry's phone rang. 'It's her,' she said, checking the number ID, hugely relieved. 'It's Franny. Franny!' Merry said, grasping her phone tightly. 'Where are you? Are you—'

Merry didn't get any further. She listened to the panicked voice of a Dublin lad telling her that Franny's canoe had emerged from the cave without her and that he and his friend had managed to grab it, find her phone and dial the last person who had rung her.

The two seconds Merry took to digest what had happened stretched taut with possibilities she couldn't think about right then. 'Stay where you are!' she instructed the voice. 'Don't move. I'm coming out and we're calling the Coast Guard. You have to stay there, do you understand? Can you tell me which side of the cave you're on?' Again she listened. 'Yeah, I'm pretty sure I know where you are. We're on our way.'

'What's happened?' the trio of voices demanded. Ryan was calm, but he grabbed Merry's arm. Keera was even paler than before, and she and her boyfriend looked suddenly a lot younger than their fifteen years.

'That wasn't Franny,' Merry said grimly. 'It was someone called Jamie – he was panicked. Franny was behind them, coming through Gull Cave, but she didn't make it out – her canoe came out on the current. They managed to grab it and find her drybag and phone. They pressed the last missed call.' Merry's voice shook. 'We need to call the Coast Guard.'

✳

'Listen to me.' She grabbed the startled and now shocked-sober Keera and Paul by the shoulders. 'Go back to the festival and find Sheena and Franny's parents. Tell them what's happened and everything you know about this party. Try not to panic them. I don't have time now but I'll ring ahead so they'll be waiting for you. Tell them the Coast Guard have been called and that I'm going out to Gull Cave myself. Go on – go!'

'I'm coming with you,' Ryan said quietly.

'Oh, God!' Merry put her hands to the sides of her head. 'I have to think! Where's your car?'

'Back at the house. Why?'

'Can you get it and meet me here? The fastest way to Gull Cave is by boat from Kal's place – he's a fish farmer. He'll have the gear. You can drive us. Hurry.'

While she waited for Ryan, Merry made two more phone calls – one to Sheila, which required every ounce of strength she had, telling her what had happened and that she was going out to try to reach Franny herself.

'Merry, no!' Sheila was frantic. 'I beg of you. If anything happens—' Her voice caught.

But Merry had moved on to ring Kal, whose fish farm was near the small cove where she kept her boat. She explained the situation. 'That's what I'm worried about,' she said, hearing his take on the tide. 'I'm going out, Kal. No one knows the cave like I do.'

'I'll take you, sure. I'll crank up the RIB – get here when you can. I'll be ready.'

A squeal of tyres told her Ryan was back with the car and she jumped in, telling him the way as they went. They drove in taut silence for what seemed like aeons until finally Merry directed him to pull off the road onto the boreen that led to the cove, the ominous throb of a helicopter cutting through the sky above them until it veered right over the coast.

Kal was waiting for them, the powerful engine of the RIB a reassuring rumble. A heavyset man, he was deceptively nimble, moving as gracefully as a cat as he checked the equipment. He greeted Ryan perfunctorily, giving him a hand down from the small pier, but directed his attention to Merry, who had pulled on her dry suit and was checking her weight belt and scuba set.

The ride out to Gull Cave was uneventful, but surreal, the almost full moon now high in the sky lighting a silver path ahead of them. In any other circumstances it would have been a romantic sight. Kal was behind the wheel, Merry beside him, and they were speaking in low voices as they sped through the water. It was hard to believe that, just a few miles away, the film festival was in full flight – except, of course, for the small knot of Franny's family and friends whose anxious dread might yet be allayed or confirmed.

It was the urgency that was helping her go through with this. That and the unreality of the situation. If Kal knew of her struggles about going into the water since the accident, he had either forgotten or wasn't saying. Before Keera had left to fetch Franny's parents, Merry had swapped her dress for Keera's jeans and T-shirt, which she now wore under her dry suit. Concentrating on her scuba set, she forced herself to focus, checking her buoyancy control device and the lead in her weight belt yet again. Her hands were trembling, which she put down to the surge of adrenalin rather than fear. She was Franny's only chance. There wasn't any other way. She just hoped against hope she wouldn't flake out – wouldn't let Franny down. She couldn't.

Nearer the cave, the swell became bigger. Kal navigated the near side as Merry instructed him, where the two boys waved frantically from their canoes. The empty one beside them, now tied by a rope, tore at Ryan's heart. Kal pulled up alongside them and hauled them both on board. Ryan looked at Merry, but she wasn't looking at the lads, who were breathless and grateful, tripping over each other to explain what had happened. She was looking past them, at the mouth of the cave through which the last chink of light was faltering as the tide rose and finally sealed off the entrance. As they watched, the Coast Guard boat loomed in the distance, ploughing its way towards them. 'Wait here with the lads,' Merry told Kal. 'I'm going in – it's the only way.' She hoisted the air tank expertly onto her back.

'You sure about this?' Kal asked.

'The Coast Guard won't have divers, you know that. Besides, the cave's already closed off. The drag won't be as strong further under. I can get in there, try to locate Franny, then use the current to carry us both out.'

'Good luck.'

'Merry?' Ryan opened his mouth then closed it, words deserting him when he needed them most. He shrugged helplessly.

'Say a prayer.' Merry gave a tight smile before fixing her mask and regulator. Then she tumbled backwards over the side of the boat, disappearing into the inky depths.

Kal glanced at Ryan, clearly reading his mind. 'She knows what she's doing. No one knows the cave like she does. If it were my kid in there' – he jerked a thumb towards the now sinister-looking cave – 'Merry's who I'd want to go get her.'

Ryan nodded miserably. It didn't make him feel any better. The swell had already made him queasy, but a far more nauseating dread had now replaced it. He just hoped against hope that Merry would come back out again with Franny.

Fifty-five

She had forgotten the thrill of a night dive. The minute she slipped beneath the water, Merry felt alive in a way she hadn't since the accident. Back in her element, her memories of that awful day were not revived as she had feared but, rather, submerged by the electric beauty of long-missed and achingly familiar surroundings. She pushed through plankton, lit up and sparkling, like a holiday, coming out the other side in the crystal clear water that always surprised her, shining her torch in front of her. No time now to wonder at the majestic drop-off cliff face covered with multicoloured jewel anemones – no time to notice the pair of mating bobcat squid, or the bright orange burrowing Dublin Bay prawns, a long way from home, forging their new home in the soft sediment, or to stay and watch the approaching shadow in the water, which Merry knew from experience would be a shoal of passing mackerel, possibly followed by predators. Night time was when the hunters came out and now she, Merry, was one of them.

She had to focus: the current was strong, as she had known it would be, so she dived deeper to where it was more manageable and instinctively swam alongside and against it, alternating and weaving through the water as the familiar underworld terrain came back to her. She was inside the cave now, and made for the surface, seeing the shaft of moonlight from the mouth of the far end of the cave, which was still open. She pulled out her mouthpiece and stopped to breathe, holding on to a rock to get her bearings. Something nipped at her fins, and she turned to see a playful young seal pop up beside her. 'Franny!' she called in the darkness, but heard only the lapping of water against the rock wall in reply. Dread was building in her now, like white noise. Franny had to be here. Please, God, don't let her have drowned ...

Franny was good in the water. She knew the drill – Merry had taught her. What could have happened to make her lose her canoe? Could she have lost consciousness? Had a brain haemorrhage or something awful made her fall out of it? Dreadful scenarios began to play in her mind until she forced them out. But one thing Merry couldn't ignore was that, whatever had happened to Franny, the inexorable tide had risen slowly but surely to leave the water at the most two to three feet from the roof of the cave in spots – and the rest, including the entrance she needed to get back through, completely covered.

For a while she had believed she was being silly – of course someone would come to get her. The boys would raise the alarm, wouldn't they? But as the water level rose and Franny grew more afraid and much, much colder, a primal fear began to take over. She sat upright, clutching the shelf with her two hands at her sides – but the water was now up to her mid-chest. How could she have been so stupid? She should have swum out immediately after her canoe – while the lads were still outside and within reach. What had made her wait? Now she was trapped – the entrance was sealed off and other parts of the cave too. Soon she would be under water. 'Help!' she called again, hoarsely, several more times, but her voice was as raw as her building panic. If she left her ledge now, she wouldn't even know which direction she was going – and she'd be under water anyway.

This was it: she was going to drown. God wasn't listening to her – why should He? After all, she hadn't spent any time lately communicating with Him. She wondered if her guardian angel was with her, looking at her, shaking its head, its face a mournful expression of *I told you so*. For some reason, when she tried to imagine her angel, it had her sister Clare's face, smirking at her. She wondered, weirdly, would her angel drown too? Would it go down with the sinking ship ... or would it get a free pass straight up to Heaven while Franny sank to her watery grave?

It was cold and dark and lonely and she was going mad, she realised. Grief and fear were making her deranged. She looked at her shivering limbs – the bits she could see – and couldn't believe they belonged to her. Her chattering teeth played like castanets. *Please let it be quick!* she prayed. *If I have to die – please make it quick*. Her sobs, like staccato hiccups, sounded her last gasp for help. 'I'm so sorry, Mam and Dad ...' She wept.

*

Merry was about a third of the way through, and the water was still rising. According to Kal, high tide was imminent – it was the worst possible time. That was the problem with teenagers: they tended to overlook the fact that the laws of nature weren't swayed by the lure of an exciting night-time adventure. Merry was fit – but she wasn't water fit, not in as good condition as she would have been if she had been swimming regularly. But she was trained for this – all her life she had studied the ocean and its mysteries – so she wasn't going to let it defeat her now, not without giving it her very last effort. But Merry knew better than anyone that no one could fight the sea: it was too immense, too all-powerful – it had taken too much from her already. She braced herself and pushed further into the cave, the current seemed to have lessened here, and was easier to swim against.

Something brushed beside her, and she flinched – but it turned out to be the inquisitive young seal she had seen before. He was following her. He dived again and surfaced ahead of her – seeming to beckon her on. Up ahead she saw where he was headed – two other seals had gathered, huddled together like conferring judges. Their attention focused towards the wall of the cave. It was then that she saw her, Franny, frozen, presumably clinging to a ledge, just her head and chest visible.

Never had such a short distance seemed so interminable to breach. Merry ploughed through the water, finally arriving at the group of seals, who reacted much as an admiring audience thrilled by an unexpected character appearance. 'Franny!' she yelled. But Franny seemed not to hear her. She stayed staring straight ahead, shivering. 'Franny!' she called again, diving one last time to pull up alongside her, where she was able to grab onto a rock. She surfaced then, called again – and, finally, Franny turned to squint, looking straight at her but seeming not to see her. Merry realised she was in deep shock, which wasn't going to make things easy. 'Franny.' She grabbed her leg. 'It's me, Merry.'

Surprise and disbelief dawned on Franny's face simultaneously. 'I th-thought you were a s-seal,' she said, staring at Merry in bewilderment. 'The boys … are they …?'

'They're fine – everything's fine. The Coast Guard are outside the cave.'

'B-but you're in the water … what are you doing in the w-water?'

'Listen to me, Franny.' Merry was panting. 'I'm going to get you out of here, but you have to trust me.'

'It's t-too late. L-look at the water – the c-cave's closed off – I can't. I'm so stupid – I've ruined everything.'

'We don't have time for this, Franny. Listen to me. You're going to let go and swim with me, and we're going to let the current carry us out to where they're waiting for us – just the other side, Franny, that's all it is. The Coast Guard are there, Kal is there …'

'But it's under water – I can't do it. I c-couldn't hold my breath for that long.'

'Yes, you can do it! You won't have to hold your breath. Listen to me! We're going to take off your buoyancy device. You're going put my spare regulator in.' Merry held up the 'octopus', as the spare regulator linked to her air supply was called. 'Franny, no one knows this cave like I do. You have to trust me – you've got this! I can get you out but you have to trust me!'

'I c-c-can't.'

'David Blackthorn was looking for you – he wants to talk to you about your film. Come on, Franny, everyone – everything is waiting for you, just on the other side!' Desperation had crept into Merry's tone.

'I'll only d-drag you down.'

Merry was beginning to despair. If she left it much longer the whole cave would be under water, which would make it dangerously more difficult. 'Muttie's outside in Kal's boat – he's going mental, barking. He's dying to see you – he knows you're in here. Come on, Franny, you can do this – please, for me.' The mention of Muttie's name seemed to do the trick.

'O-kay – I'll t-t-try.'

'That's it. Come on – I've got you.' Merry held on to her, giving Franny the mouthpiece of her spare regulator to put into her mouth, feeling the welcome pull of the current, eager now to get them away. As long as she could hold on to Franny – and Franny didn't panic – she had a good chance of getting her out. 'Ready? Let's go. I've got you. When I dive, just go with me. 'You can do it – you've got this. Okay?'

Franny nodded but she was clearly terrified.

'The current will get us out – you can feel it, can't you?' Merry was holding Franny tight, praying she remembered the rocks to avoid and where they were – all that mattered was holding on to a terrified fourteen-year-old who had completely lost her nerve. The roof of the cave loomed and Merry dived – pulling Franny with her. Although adrenalin was powering her, Merry was feeling her muscles give out. She checked on Franny – her small face white in the water, cheeks blown out. Just another few minutes … if she could just hold on, they'd be out. It took longer than she thought – or perhaps it just seemed that way, but suddenly the mouth of the cave was in front of them and they were out – breaking the surface, Franny gasping and spluttering.

Fifty-six

She was alive! She hadn't died! Somehow her prayers had been answered and Merry had appeared out of nowhere to save her! Merry, who hadn't been in the water since the accident. Franny could hardly make sense of anything and she didn't want to try. All that mattered was that she was sitting in Kal's RIB with Merry and Ryan's arms around her and people were shouting and laughing above the roar of the engine. On the other side of the RIB Simon and Jamie were saying something to her but she couldn't hear them as they sped through the water. But they laughed and high-fived each other so they must have been happy. The RIB was approaching the small pier now, from which Ryan and Merry had started out with Kal, and where Ryan had left his car. Kal pulled up by the steps to let Ryan clamber out. 'I'll catch up with you guys back at the harbour,' Ryan shouted, as he waved to them.

The RIB took off again, speeding into open water and around the next headland, then turning in towards Derrybeggs Harbour.

*

Ryan hardly had the strength to drive the car. Relief and elation that Franny was safe had literally made his legs weak. Once he was behind the wheel he took some deep breaths before starting the engine. As he pulled slowly off the boreen and back onto the main road, he could hardly believe he had driven this very route just over an hour ago with Merry, both of them sick with fear. The scenes that flashed through his mind now of being on Kal's RIB, finding the boys, then Merry disappearing into the water – those interminable minutes waiting for her stretching like hours – and the unspeakable joy he had felt when Kal had shouted, 'There they are!' It seemed like some tense adventure movie he had just watched. The only thing that felt real right now was just how badly he wanted to get back to Merry.

When he arrived at the Shack, the small group huddled on the beach were laughing and crying and hugging one another. Franny's parents and her sister Clare seemed afraid to let go of her, as Rob stood close by speaking on his phone. Merry, having been smothered with tearful hugs from Sheila and Mike, Jan and Eva, was clearly exhausted, as Franny's family darted back and forth between her and Franny, still thanking her profusely.

As Ryan approached them, the group began to walk towards the Surf Shack, Rob explaining to Ryan he was taking Franny to the local hospital for a thorough check – although she protested, through chattering teeth, that she was fine. No one paid him any attention as he made his way over to Merry.

'You don't have any shoes.' He grinned down at her bare feet.

'I don't, do I?' She shrugged and smiled at him. 'Who cares? The only thing I need right now is a drink. I left my sandals at the Shack – I'd like to grab a shower and change out of Keera's clothes, though.'

'I'll give you a lift back to your place – the car's right there.'

Ryan had disappeared. He had gone off almost two hours ago with the café girl and had not returned. Some kids were missing, Joni had heard. Big deal! Some illicit party had been planned and now Ryan had gone running after Merry. She didn't get it: kids snuck off the whole time to do stuff they shouldn't – that was what teenagers did! Why was it suddenly Ryan's problem? In fact, why was every little thing about this place, from a crazy guy who didn't know who he was to some kids having a party, anything *at all* that Ryan needed to concern himself about? It didn't add up. And Joni liked things to add up, because when they didn't, it meant you were off course – and then, in her experience, it wasn't long at all until wheels started falling off wagons. Then you had chaos. Joni didn't do chaos: she was all about anticipating damage limitation, and it looked like she would have to practise some right now.

The reception was thinning out and the real action, as far as she was concerned, would be the late-night barbecue on the beach organised for her followers – for which she would need to change her outfit back at the cottage. On the way there, she would ring Frank, Ryan's boss – the time difference was perfect.

Frank picked up on the first ring. 'Joni? Everything all right?' He was concerned.

'Everything's fine, Frank, don't worry – but it could be better.'

'What's going on?' Frank's antennae were up.

Joni knew she could level with Frank. 'It's Ryan. He's losing focus, Frank. This place isn't good for him. He's gotten caught up in this crazy guy's story and he's way too involved for my liking. I think you should get him back to New York as soon as you can. The project is wrapped up – the club looks amazing. I'll send you the video of the reception. But Ryan's mentioned he was thinking of staying on for a bit. I don't think that would be a good idea, Frank.' She let the implication sink in.

Frank got her drift. 'I hear you, Joni. Leave it with me. I was planning on talking to him tomorrow anyway. I'm looking forward to seeing you both again.'

'Me too – and thanks, Frank, I appreciate this.'

'No problem. I've always said Ryan is a very lucky man to have you in his life – you've been very good for him.'

'I like to think so. I'm glad you feel the same way, Frank.'

After the call, Joni felt better and stronger, more in control. Ryan needed to be back in New York for his own sake, at the very least. Look how soft he'd been getting! Even if she did decide he wasn't for her, she certainly wasn't going to leave him here in Ireland to be preyed on by the likes of that gold-digging Merry.

Half an hour later Joni had changed into ripped jeans and a white silk shirt that she tied in a knot in front, and let fall gracefully at the back. There was still no sign of Ryan. He'd better show up at the barbecue, or— Well, she wouldn't think about how that sentence might have to end right now.

When she reached the steps down to the beach, the party was already in full swing. A huge fire had been lit and three barbecues were grilling food for those who wanted it. An almost full moon was splashing its light on the water, and a blanket of stars was spread across the sky – she had never seen so many. The steady thrum of good conversation and the anticipation of a fun night to come were in the air. Joni spotted Molly talking to a group of her avid fans and was pleased to see that someone at least, besides herself, realised how important it was to connect with one's followers. Speaking of which, Ryan was nowhere to be seen. She took a deep breath and prepared to meet her fans, encouraged by the cheer that went up when her followers caught sight of her. She went to mingle with them – this was work.

When a group of girls offered her a burger and salad, Joni discovered she was very hungry. She hadn't eaten anything at the reception – in fact, not since breakfast.

She was listening to the girls' questions and advising them when she saw Ryan finally making his way down the steps to find her. Merry was just behind him, but the pink dress was gone, replaced by jeans and a hoodie.

'Excuse me,' Joni said, leaving the group. 'I need a minute.' Ryan looked distracted when she caught up with him, but relieved to see her – which was good. She kept it light. '*There* you are! Come and have some barbecue. I saved you some.'

'Joni, I need to talk to you.'

Up close, he looked shaken. Whatever was on his mind – she didn't want to hear it. 'Not now, sweetheart! I have to meet with my followers – there's something I need to do for them. Wait there – this won't take long.'

'What?' Ryan ran his hands through his hair distractedly. He was tired and, combined with the inevitable adrenalin crash in the wake of Franny's rescue he was feeling increasingly irritable. He wanted to stop this ridiculous charade that everything was fine between them, get out of here, and talk to Merry. He looked around for her, but Merry seemed to have got lost in the crowd.

Joni went over to her followers and posed for some selfies, then said something to them he couldn't hear. But they seemed to be lining up and getting their phones ready to film her. As she made her way back to Ryan, he realised with horror that she had a microphone in her hand. 'First of all,' she began, when she reached his side. 'I want to thank you all – *all* of you – my beloved followers, for being such a loyal and faithful part of my journey. I couldn't have accomplished anything without you – we're a family, right?'

Murmurings of 'aww' and 'aah' ensued and the odd tear was wiped away.

'That's why it means *so* much to me that so many of you can be here in person with me tonight, when I take this momentous next step in my relationship with Ryan, whom you have all come to know and love almost as much as I have.'

A collective intake of breath was held. Hands flew to mouths, and several OMGs escaped the onlookers.

Ryan's mouth went dry. This couldn't be happening! Even in his wildest dreams he had never really thought Joni would go through with it. She couldn't possibly think they were on solid ground as a couple after the last few days. Ryan had decided to go along with things for a day or two more – but only to spare Joni the embarrassment of explaining a break-up to her followers. Then he planned to have the proper discussion with her that they needed to have – and accept that they were over. But he never anticipated that she would carry out her threatened proposal, which he would now be compelled to decline. He swallowed hard. He really hadn't wanted it to come to this – but she was leaving him no choice. Now he'd go down in viral history as the cad who turned down the proposal of a brave, and beautiful, woman. One with over a million followers – some of whom were bound to be as angry (and possibly crazy!) as Joni would be to be cheated of their happy ending …

'Ryan.' She turned to him, a beatific smile on her lovely face. 'Our time together has been so precious to me.'

'Joni – please!'

'You have all the qualities I admire in a person … except one.' She turned briefly to her rapt audience. 'You are not *worthy* of me!' she shouted. There were a few gasps as understanding dawned on the crowd. 'For that reason, I have decided it is no longer in my interest to continue going forward with you on my life path! Our time together has been great – but not great enough!' A few catcalls and whoops went up. 'I'm sorry to have to do this to you – to us. Ryan, it's not you – it's me! I need more! I'm *worth* more! We're *over*!'

Ryan knew when to make an exit. He had to hand it to Joni – she sure knew how to work a crowd. Her followers were now chanting *Joni! Joni! Joni!* cheering her on. It was his time to bow out gracefully. He held up his hands in a sign of defeat, and said, 'Joni, it's been an honour and a privilege …' but no one was interested in what he was saying and Joni was already disappearing into the crowd that had gathered around her protectively.

*

Joni stayed on to party with her followers. She wasn't stupid – she had seen what was coming and called the situation before Ryan had told her they were over, but at least she had worked it to her advantage. Her followers were more enthralled with her than ever. She was holding her head and her viewings high. But inside she was about to crack. Even she could only fake it for so long. She was tired and emotionally spent, and the reality of what had just happened was beginning to encroach. She couldn't break down now, here – so she made her excuses and slipped away, returning to the cottage where she hoped Ryan would have the good sense to leave her alone. A tiny part of her still hoped he might be waiting for her – or that he would have followed her after her break-up speech and begged her to reconsider – but when she turned the key in the lock and went in, she realised finally she was alone. She needed to talk to someone! She couldn't call the GMs – they would say, 'We told you so.' But there was someone – someone she could rely on through thick or thin, who loved her like a – a— Well, what did it matter what he loved her like?

He picked up on the first ring.

'Imran?'

'Hey, sweetie, how's it goin'?'

'Oh, Imran.' Joni broke down and sobbed. 'I just broke up with Ryan.'

'I know. You're an internet sensation. It's gone viral.'

'Already?'

'Oh, yeah.' She could hear the smile in his voice. 'It's titled "The Only Way to Leave Your Lover"! And, Joni?'

'What?'

'This is your finest hour – trust me! You will look back on this moment as the defining, meteoric, cannonball-blast take-off in your career.'

'You think so?'

'I know so. And you looked *incredible* – the white Valentino shirt was perfect.'

Joni sniffed. 'But, Imran, I'm on my own again.'

'Ryan wasn't right for you, honey.'

'You never think anyone is right for me!'

'Yes, I do.'

'Who?'

'Me.'

Joni was so surprised she could only hiccup.

'Joni, I've been in love with you since the first moment I saw you. You're the only one who didn't see it. Now get yourself back here, and I'll meet you at the airport. We have a business to run. And if I were you I'd wear the red Armani shift, the Louboutin heels, and Chanel shades coming through Arrivals. There are bound to be paps around and you want to look empowered, *assertive*. I'll be waiting for you.'

Fifty-seven

Ryan went back to the cottage to grab a few things and get out of his tux. He called Dot to ask if it would be all right if he used a room in the main house tonight. Thankfully she didn't ask any questions when she assured him it would be fine. Now he was headed back to the barbecue to find some food – he was ravenously hungry.

The party was still going strong, the fire was blazing, music was playing and people were talking, lounging and dancing. Ryan made his way over to the grill and grabbed a burger with all the trimmings.

'Hey.' It was Merry, coming up behind him. 'Thought you could maybe use a drink.' She waved a bottle of red cheerfully. 'This is courtesy of the catering department.'

'Never has a bottle of wine looked so enticing.' Ryan grinned. 'Can we go somewhere a little more private to drink it? I think I've had enough publicity for one evening.'

'Sure. I was going to suggest the harbour. It'll be quiet there.'

They strolled in easy silence back to the road and down to the harbour – Merry occasionally helping herself to Ryan's chips. The harbour was deserted, and they sat down at the end of the small pier, the sound of lapping water at their feet. Merry filled two plastic glasses. 'So – guess you've been dumped.'

'Looks that way.' Ryan shook his head ruefully. 'Like I said, Joni doesn't do things by halves.'

'It was quite a performance. I thought she was going to propose.'

'So did I – that was the really scary part!'

'How are you feeling about it, though – really?'

'I'm okay.' Ryan shrugged. 'Joni's great – we've had some terrific times together – but we weren't working out. It took a change of perspective for me to admit that to myself – to see things properly. Coming here gave me space. I think Joni realised that too.'

'So what are you going to do now?'

'I thought I might stay here – if Dot can let me have the cottage for a while longer. I'll talk to Frank later – I'm due some time off. Might as well spend it here. I've got Irish relatives somewhere – I might try to track them down – and I'm not in any rush to get back to New York just yet.'

'Sounds like a plan.'

'What you did tonight' – Ryan was serious – 'that was phenomenal.'

Merry shrugged. 'I was Franny's only chance. I didn't have to think about it. The Coast Guard would have had to rally local divers anyway, and by then it would have been too late.'

'You saved her life.'

'I wasn't sure I could do it – but I had to try. I hadn't

been in the water since the accident. But once I was back in, I was fine.'

'How is Franny, do you know?'

'She's fine.' Merry smiled. 'Tucked up in bed with a hot-water bottle and Muttie keeping guard, last I heard.'

'She's such a great kid.' Ryan smiled. 'What about the others? The ones on the island?'

'Everyone's back in one piece and accounted for – but I'd say the party vibe was well and truly quashed.'

'You know what kids are like. Let's hope they've learned their lesson.'

'It's been quite a night – all things considered.'

'I was thinking I'd like to learn how to dive – could you teach me?'

'I know a place where you can learn, near here. You need to do the proper course.'

'That figures. Might as well learn something useful while I'm here.'

'I'll meet you for an early-morning swim, though. On the beach. Seven a.m.?'

'You got yourself a date.'

The next morning Franny awoke realising she had made it out of the cave alive but almost wishing she were back there. Never had she felt so mortified, so guilty at what she had done – the terrible anxiety she had caused. Never as long as she lived would she forget her mam and dad's faces, the way they had seemed to collapse with relief when they saw her, and how they had gripped her so fiercely to themselves when she'd tumbled out of the boat. Even Clare had been crying and hugging her. Franny would never be able to face anyone again. She had been wicked and ungrateful, and put people's lives in danger to come and rescue her.

'Franny!' Her mam's head popped around the door. She looked excited. 'Hurry up! There's someone here to see you!'

'I can't, Mam. I can't face anyone. Please don't make me – not today.'

'Don't be ridiculous! David Blackthorn is downstairs and he wants to see you before he goes back to London,' Sheila said. 'Don't keep the man waiting! Get a move on!'

Franny shot out of bed, grabbed her dressing-gown, pulled it on over her pyjamas and flew downstairs to where the great man was sitting in their kitchen.

'Hello, Franny! I'm very glad to see you in one piece after your adventures.' He was smiling. 'I wanted to drop by to tell you in person how impressed I was with your film on the golf course. If Charlie's film hadn't been a surprise late entry, yours would definitely have been in the top three. Unfortunately, I'm very pushed for time … but, look, I think you've got a great future.' He took a card from his wallet and handed it to her. 'Why don't you get in touch with me when you've finished school? If you're still interested I'll be very happy to help you. How about it?'

'Th-thank you, Mr Blackthorn. That's, like, epic!'

'Good stuff!'

'You're sure you won't stay and have a cup of tea or coffee?' Sheila said.

'Much as I'd love to, I'm already cutting it fine for the airport and my driver is waiting impatiently outside. Great meeting you all – I hope to be back one day!'

*

By Monday, the general sense of relief that Franny was safe and the film festival had been such a success meant Derrybeggs was able to return to its normally relaxed state of affairs. All around the village the hipsters were cheerfully piling onto coaches, swapping numbers and stories.

When Ryan had gone back to his cottage and quietly opened the door, Joni's suitcase and belongings were already gone. His phone, when it rang, startled him.

'What's goin' on over there?' Frank was concerned. 'I just seen this crazy video Joni sent me of her dumping you. Am I missing something here? I thought this was supposed to be a romantic break for you guys.'

'It's a long story, Frank, and I'll tell you about it sometime. Right now I need to ask you a favour.'

'That sounds ominous.'

'Not really. I just need some more time – I got some things to figure out. Thought I might hang around here for a while, look up some family ties, take some time out. A sabbatical, maybe – do a little research.'

'Might this research include a woman, by any chance?'

'Who knows, Frank? They have 'em over here too …'

'Take as long as you need, kiddo.' Ryan heard the smile in Frank's voice. 'You haven't had a vacation in all the time we've worked together. Just stay in touch.'

'Will do, and, Frank? Thanks – I appreciate this.'

Back in New York, Frank hung up and shook his head. He was in the middle of his third divorce, and no one knew better than he did what trouble women could get a guy into – but he'd never had one circulating crazy videos of him on the internet. Ryan was like a son to him. He could totally get why he'd want to lie low for a while. If a woman was involved, Frank just hoped it was one without millions of followers and a social-media obsession. Life was difficult enough …

'Do you think Charlie's upset?' Molly asked Dot, over coffee, in the kitchen. 'You know, disappointed that those people didn't turn out to be his family, after all?'

'It's hard to tell. I think he was relieved, somehow. He certainly wasn't eager to talk to them, even before we found out they were scammers. Perhaps he knew something wasn't right on a subconscious level. But I'm sure he must be terribly anxious about it all.'

'I still can't believe people would take advantage of someone as vulnerable as Charlie is right now.' Molly shook her head. 'Thank goodness Merry had them checked out. How did that come about?'

'It was a fortunate coincidence, really,' Dot said, 'and very decent of Merry to step in. She had to ring her erstwhile in-laws and speak to Doug's mother to ask her to do it. They're a military family,' Dot explained. 'Merry's father-in-law was able to verify the military records were false.'

'Ah, I was wondering.'

'It can't have been easy for her. Eva told me Merry hadn't spoken to Doug's family since he'd been killed. Apparently they – well, his mother in particular – blamed Merry for his death.'

'That's awful. Poor girl – she's been through a lot. And what about Ryan?' Molly asked. 'I couldn't believe it when I heard Joni had finished with him publicly. What was that about? Can't young people do anything in private, these days?'

'Don't ask me,' Dot said. 'Apparently, it had something to do with her followers. I don't fully understand this business and I don't particularly want to. It seems to me you become slavishly addicted to the amount of people who are your followers at the expense of the real stalwarts in your life.'

'I see what you mean.' Molly was thoughtful. 'But somehow I get the feeling Ryan isn't too upset about losing Joni. I'm guessing this gave him a welcome way out of ending the relationship. They seemed to be having problems before she got here – and have you noticed the way he is around Merry? He can't take his eyes off her.'

'Merry?' Dot was astonished.

'Oh, yes. You've probably been too caught up in your own romantic escapade to notice but there's definitely something going on with Ryan and Merry. Mark my words. When he got up to play in O'Hagan's that night, he was looking straight at her as he sang.'

'I felt terribly sorry for him when he told me they'd split up,' Dot said. 'But if Joni and he weren't right for each other …'

'Call me old-fashioned,' Molly said, 'but I think he had a lucky escape. I know what these people can be like. They have no off button. I think Ryan has changed since he's been here – and he's not the only one.'

'Well, I'm just glad it's all over,' Dot said. 'I never thought I'd say it, but getting back to a dull routine will be a relief.'

'Except it won't be dull, will it?' Molly lifted her eyebrows. 'You'll have Rob to keep you entertained.'

'We're going to take things very slowly – get to know each other.' Dot was still a bit mortified about admitting that she and Rob were a romantic item. 'But we're going to miss you. It won't be the same.'

'It's not meant to be the same. Is it? That's the whole point. Life must go on. But while we're on the subject …' – Molly paused – '… I've been thinking of looking out for a place here … you know, a place of my own.' She waited anxiously for Dot's reaction.

'Seriously?' Dot's face lit up.

'Yes. If the idea wouldn't fill you with horror.' She grinned. 'I've fallen in love with Derrybeggs – and all of you, especially since I've been writing here. And as it looks like I'm going to be spending a lot more time in the States, it makes sense to have a base here. It would be great if you'd look out for a suitable property for me.'

'I'd love to have you here! And that would be another project for me! I think that's a wonderful idea – fantastic news.'

'Oh, good.' Molly was relieved. 'I wasn't sure how you'd feel about it. Depending on how things go – I might even sell up completely in London. Then I could get a lovely dog, like you, Honey.' She bent down to ruffle Honey's head. 'How's poor Franny?'

'Absolutely fine, except for a dent in her pride. I spoke to Sheila a while ago. And David Blackthorn dropped in to see her on his way to the airport, so that made her day.'

Molly smiled. 'He said he would – he's such a nice man. All the same, I could hardly believe it when I heard what happened – just shows how your life can change in a heartbeat. Thank God Merry knew where to go and found her. What about the other kids?'

'Suitably chastened.' Dot frowned. 'Apparently it's a rite of passage, this partying out at Cape Clanad – so far there's been no harm done. But it was very wrong of Sheena to let Franny go out on her own in the canoe with those two boys.'

Molly nodded. 'I hope she's left in no doubt about that. Franny's too nice for that girl. With friends like her …'

'I think Franny sees that for herself now. Sheila has

certainly made her point about it. Is that another email? Your phone hasn't stopped beeping.'

'It's another TV offer.' Molly made a bewildered face. 'Larry, my agent, says *Hornetsville* has generated a whole slew of new offers – I'm in demand again. Who'd have thought it?'

'What about your book?'

'I sent it to him and he loves it. I can't tell you how relieved I am.'

'Well, are you going to tell me what it's about?'

'It's about Charlie – well, a fictional Charlie, someone who loses his memory, gets lost, and fetches up in a small Irish village.'

'I can't wait to read it!'

'You'll be the first to see it – once I've polished it up at bit. It still needs some work. Which reminds me, I'd better get back to my desk while I still can. I may not feel quite as inspired when I'm back in London.'

After Molly had gone back to her cottage, Dot gave the house a good going-over. Molly was leaving the next day, and while Dot knew she would be visiting again as soon as she was able, that might not be for quite a while – and it was still the end of all their time together. Charlie was out with Jan, on one of his vegetable-delivery rounds, and was eating with Jan and Eva afterwards. Dot suspected that since news had spread (as it was bound to have) of her and Rob having feelings for one another, people were being tactful and giving them as much space as they could. Which made Dot feel equal parts grateful and embarrassed.

It was raining, now, a steady drizzle running down the windowpanes, and suddenly Dot had the urge go out in it – have a good tramp along the roads with Honey. It was a step back into her normal routine, which had been pretty much hijacked in recent weeks. She put on her wax jacket and wellies, and headed out, Honey at her heels.

When she got back, she had a long hot bath and applied her makeup afterwards carefully, doing her eyes as Molly had shown her. It was amazing, Dot thought, how much difference all these little tricks of the trade made – she wondered how she had done without them for so long. Martin, her late husband, hadn't been keen on her wearing makeup, not unless they were going out to a dinner party or some such. Then she pulled on some new jeans and a lovely light cashmere sweater, and went downstairs to make dinner.

When Rob came home, he seemed pretty pleased with himself. 'You look nice!' he said. Then, seeing the table set for two, 'Is it just us?'

'I'm afraid so – you don't mind, do you?'

'Of course not! Why would I?' He looked alarmed.

'I worry you'll find it dull – you know, when it's just us and everyone's gone.'

'Will you find it dull?'

'No, of course not!'

'Well, then, why should I? Now, according to my watch, it's G&T time!'

'Oh, goody,' said Dot. 'I thought you were looking pleased about something.'

'Actually' – Rob made two G&Ts, handed Dot hers and sat down across the table from her – 'I've had some good news – very good news, hopefully. Detective Foley rang just before I finished up at the surgery.'

'Go on.'

'They think they've got a genuine lead. They've found Charlie's relatives ...'

Dot listened attentively to Rob's account.

'So in the end,' he went on, 'it was 'Jessie's Song' going viral that led this woman to get in touch with the police. And between that, and what the detectives have managed to piece together with CCTV at this end and witness sightings, it looks like this is the real deal.'

'I can hardly dare believe it!'

'The breakthrough was when a cab driver came to the station to make a statement that he had picked up a man answering Charlie's description from Shannon airport. Apparently, they'd been stopped in traffic when an office building in a nearby business park was being demolished. When it imploded, Charlie was watching – and the next thing the driver knew, he'd been flung fifty euro and his passenger had fled from the car.'

'Why on earth?' Dot was perplexed.

'It's not as absurd as it sounds.' Rob paused. 'These people, Charlie's family or relatives, have claimed that Charlie was a victim of Nine/Eleven.'

'No!'

'Yes. It's very sad. He and his late wife were in New

York to celebrate her birthday weekend. She was killed instantly, while Charlie was unscathed – on the outside anyway. I don't know the exact details. But you can imagine how traumatic it was. So it's probably best if we don't say anything to him. Detective Foley thought it best not to, but that we should be there to support Charlie while he's introduced to these people and we can see how it goes.'

'What if they're more scammers?' Dot was worried. 'After the last fiasco we don't want to put poor Charlie through that again.'

'Well, we'll find out fairly soon. These people get into Shannon first thing tomorrow morning – Detective Foley's bringing them straight here from the airport. They should be with us around ten. We'll see what they've got to say for themselves then.' He paused to take a sip of his drink. 'Oh, and by the way, apparently Charlie's a retired teacher.'

'Now that I can believe.' Dot sounded relieved. 'He's so knowledgeable, and always coming out with odd little pieces of information. Well, after that, my news doesn't seem important at all.' Dot told Rob about Molly wanting to buy a small place in Derrybeggs.

'It hardly comes as a surprise but I'm happy for her. I think she was feeling a bit lost and washed up when she arrived here. Now she's discovered a whole new lease of life. I feel the same way myself.' Rob grinned and clinked Dot's glass.

Fifty-eight

At nine o'clock the next morning, Kate Carmichael was surprised to hear someone at her front door. 'Franny!' she exclaimed, when she saw who it was. 'I'm so pleased to see you!' She gave Franny an effusive hug. 'How are you, sweetie?' She held Franny at arm's-length and gazed at her. 'I said to Sheena, you know, I said to her, let this be a lesson to you all! Honestly! Going off to parties and out on boats and the like without telling anyone.' She shook her head in mock bewilderment. 'Still, you're all home safe and sound. That's all that matters.'

'I wasn't at the party, Mrs Carmichael. I was never going to the party.'

Kate winked. 'We'll say no more about it! Sheena's in her room, in a complete huff with me and her dad for daring to show some parental concern.' She rolled her eyes. 'I'll tell her you're here – she'll be delighted.' Kate's manner was conspiratorial.

'Hey, Franny.' Sheena was pleased to see her. She wandered down the stairs, in fashionable sweatpants and T-shirt. 'We're fine, thanks, Mom.' She looked pointedly at Kate who, having followed the girls into the front lounge, took the hint to leave them alone.

'Well, I'll leave you two to catch up. If you need

anything, just shout.' She closed the door softly behind her.

Sheena rolled her eyes. 'OMG, they're so overreacting. Have you been getting it too? It's like no one ever went to a party before. I mean, talk about the third degree. Like, it was so embarrassing in front of the guys when we got back. At least Steve and Ro know me but, like, Simon and Jamie – I nearly died. At least Si and Jamie got to go back to Dublin. We'll probably never see them again—'

'They came by yesterday to see me.'

'Huh? What for?'

'Just to see if I was all right – to say they were sorry.'

Sheena looked blank. 'For what?'

Franny sat on the luxurious suede couch biting her lip and studying her hands, trying to remember what she and her mam had agreed she should say. But now that the time had come, the only thing she could hear was her heartbeat, thumping in her chest. She cleared her throat. 'There's something I need to say to you, Sheena. '

'What?'

Franny took a deep breath. 'I don't think I can be friends with you any more.'

'What?'

'That's why I came over – to tell you in person, to be straight up about it.'

'Oh, I suppose you've been grounded.' She waved a hand dismissively. 'Look, don't worry, this will, like, all blow over. Give it a week or two ...'

'No, Sheena. You're not listening to what I'm saying. We can't be friends any more. I'm not going to, like, blank you or anything if we meet, but I won't be hanging out with you.'

Sheena frowned. 'I knew your folks would be really harsh. This is your mother, isn't it?'

'No, Sheena, it's not. Although Mam agrees with me. I – I could have died in that cave.'

'That wasn't my fault! How was I to know your canoe would get stuck on a stupid rock?'

'That's not the point, Sheena. You backed out on me – you let me go out there on my own so no one knew to let anyone know where I was, or what had happened to me. It was just really fortunate that Si and Jamie were able to grab my canoe, find my drybag and phone and call Merry.' Franny paused. 'If it wasn't for that, I might not be here today.'

'Like that's my fault!' Sheena's voice rose. 'You're not, like, ten years old, Franny! You have a mind of your own! You chose to go out to Gull Cave – you didn't, like, have to!'

'You're right. I didn't have to. I made a really bad decision, one that almost cost me my life, Sheena. And it's taught me a good lesson.'

'Well, then!'

'But you didn't have my back, Sheena.' Franny's voice was small, but determined. 'You never do.'

'I don't believe this!'

'Everything all right, girls?' Kate Carmichael popped her head around the door, concerned.

'Everything's fine, Mrs Carmichael.' Franny stood up. 'I was just leaving. See you around, Sheena.'

When she got home, Sheila was waiting for her. 'Well, did you tell her?'

Franny nodded, and let out a breath as her shoulders sagged. 'It wasn't easy.'

Sheila grabbed her daughter and held her tightly. 'I am so proud of you, Franny!' she said fiercely. 'So proud!'

Back in Dot's house, nerves were also frayed. Dot had slept hardly a wink all night, thinking about the people who could be arriving any minute now. Charlie had gone to the Seashell for his usual morning coffee and was none the wiser about the current situation. They were going to play it by ear.

At ten fifteen Dot heard the crunch of gravel outside and jumped up. 'That'll be them.'

'Yes, that's Detective's Foley's car all right.' Rob peered out.

They both started as the bell rang loudly. 'I'll get it.' Rob went to the front door while Dot went back to the kitchen.

Minutes later, Rob returned, followed by Detective Foley, another nice-looking young man, and a tall, graceful woman with platinum hair and a wide, beautiful smile.

'This,' said Rob, with a flourish, 'is Jessica Rigby, Charlie's friend. She recognised him playing the piano in O'Hagan's online and contacted the police and Charlie's family immediately. This is Nick, his nephew, and this is Detective Foley, who's in charge of Charlie's case.'

'And you must be Dot.' Jessica went to take her hand, as Rob was making the introductions. 'We can't thank you enough for taking care of Mac, I mean Charlie. This has all come as such a shock to us.'

'I can imagine! Please, sit down,' Dot said, warming to the woman immediately. 'We're so eager to hear what you have to tell us.'

'First of all,' Detective Foley began, over coffee, 'I can put your mind at rest that Nick here is indeed Charlie's nephew. All the ID information has checked out.'

'My father Jerry is Mac's – I mean Charlie's – brother,' Nick said. 'Charlie's been like a second dad to me. But it was thanks to Jessica here spotting the clip of him playing the piano that led to her getting in touch with us.'

'I knew Jerry and Mac in high school.' Jessica smiled.

'Right,' said Detective Foley, fishing out an iPad. 'Let me tell you what we've pieced together. On the morning of 29th June, Charlie arrived at Shannon on a flight from Logan International – Boston.'

'That's where he lives, Boston,' Jessica said.

'He got a cab at the airport headed for the train station – but never made it. A cab driver came forward in answer to our enquiries. He made a statement that he'd picked up a passenger from Shannon, but that while they were stopped in traffic, a building in an adjacent business park was being demolished. When the explosion went off and the building collapsed, his passenger threw some money at him and fled the car. Those were his words. His description of the passenger matched Charlie's.' Detective Foley paused. 'We're figuring this was the triggering incident. Charlie, as you now know, was a victim of Nine/Eleven. He and his wife were visiting New York. She was killed in the incident. We're guessing the detonation here in the business park and seeing the office block collapse was traumatic enough on a subconscious level to cause his extreme reaction.'

'PTSD.' Jessica nodded sympathetically.

'Which triggered his dissociative fugue state,' Rob added.

'Exactly. Charlie appears to have spent the night in a local B&B. He paid his bill and left early the following morning, without saying where he was headed. The woman in charge said he was behaving oddly. From there' – Detective Foley ran some CCTV footage – 'Charlie seems to have been wandering aimlessly. Here, you see him sitting on a park bench, clearly in a confused state. We reckon it was around this time that his coat and belongings were stolen. We have retrieved his passport and case, but not the wallet. That's to be expected. From there, Charlie hitched a couple of lifts – he got lucky with this man.' He pointed to a face. 'Jack Moran runs a small delivery business and was bringing a van of furniture to Clanad. He was able to give Charlie a lift to Derrybeggs – which was where he said he was headed. He had a tourist leaflet with him of Derrybeggs. He told Jack that was where he wanted to go. The rest – well, you know how it goes from there.' Detective Foley paused. 'Our guess is that Charlie just picked up a random couple of leaflets at the tourist information stand. Once he became disoriented, we think he was probably trying to hide his condition and work things out for himself. Possibly he hoped the leaflet might provide a clue as to who he was or where he was going. By the time he reached Derrybeggs, he had either run out of options, or realised he was incapable of managing on his own any more.'

'Where is Charlie?' Jessica asked.

'He's at the Seashell, our local café, with Ryan, my guest. I'll ring Ryan, tell him to bring Charlie back. They'll just be a few minutes.'

'Well, if you don't mind' – Detective Foley stood up – 'I'll be on my way. I'm glad we got all this sorted out.'

Rob saw him to the front door. 'Thank you, Detective.' Rob shook hands with him.

'All part of the job description. Although this case was more intriguing than most! Good luck!'

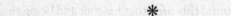

An anxious few minutes dragged by, in which Jessie and Nick told Dot and Rob as much as they could about Charlie. 'It was really extraordinary,' Jessie said. 'Mac was my first love – all those years ago! We were college sweethearts, I suppose you'd say. Then, out of the blue, we found each other on Facebook – we'd both lost our spouses and we were so delighted to come across each other. We talked on the phone, and we agreed to meet up after his vacation in Ireland – and I had a wedding in the family to get out of the way. I have the email right here that he sent me.' She patted her purse. 'As far as I knew, Mac was on vacation – then one of my daughters showed me the

YouTube clip of him playing the piano. She recognised the piece – Mac wrote that for me. That was my song.' Her eyes filled. 'I couldn't believe it when I heard he was lost and had no memory. Of course there's no guarantee that he'll recognise me – but I'm hoping he will.' Jessie bit her lip.

'Me too.' Nick patted her hand. They looked hopeful, if nervous.

They needn't have worried. Seconds later Ryan came into the kitchen, followed by Merry and Charlie. As Jessie stood up, Charlie stopped in his tracks and his face lit up. 'Jessie,' he said slowly. 'I knew you'd come!'

'Oh, Mac!' she said, swiping at tears. 'You haven't changed a bit.'

'Uncle Mac!' Nick went over to him. 'You sure gave us a fright!' And suddenly everyone was hugging Charlie and each other.

There was plenty of food fortunately, and over a hastily put-together brunch, Rob and Jessie filled in some gaps.

'It's all right here. Mac,' said Jessie, unfolding some paper from her bag. 'Here's a printout of the email you sent me right before you left.'

'Well, whaddya know?' said Charlie, and read it out.

My dear Jessie,
I can't tell you how good it was to talk with you yesterday on the phone. For all the time it's been since we've seen each other, the years fell away as soon as I heard your familiar voice and we talked and laughed like youngsters.

I still find it hard to believe we're seventy-two years old – how the heck did that happen? And twenty of those years have gone by without my beloved Linda by my side. Life without her goes by more slowly, I have found to my cost. I try to fill it as best I can. As a retired teacher, this is a relatively easy task to accomplish. I have a regular pension, I tutor from time to time – there is always something new I want to learn. For relaxation, I still play the piano. I almost took the musical route full time but my love of learning and the desire to pass that on to a younger generation won out – although I have composed a few pieces I'm quite proud of. Do you remember that song I wrote for you? I can still knock out a good tune if I put my mind to it.

Truth be told, I've been lonely since Linda died. As I mentioned on the phone, she was a victim of Nine/Eleven – we both were – but I survived unscathed, on the outside anyway. The trauma took longer. I still don't react well to loud noises. That trip to New York was to celebrate her birthday. Little did we know it would be her last. Linda and I were not blessed with a family, and we never felt the need to adopt. So now I am on my own. I have a nephew, Nick, Jerry's son – do you remember Jerry? Nick is very good to me. We meet regularly.

It was a former student of mine who suggested I look for company online. At first the idea didn't appeal. But then, I thought, why not? And that led to this happy coincidence I could never have anticipated. Who would have thought I'd come across my childhood sweetheart

*from high school? You've lost your husband, Jim, too
– I know you understand. I don't need to tell you, I'm
sure, how much I'm looking forward to meeting up in
person when I get back from my trip, a couple of weeks
in Ireland. I thought I might drive around and maybe
look up some distant cousins – I enjoy travelling solo.
There is something soul-destroying, I always feel,
about returning to an empty house full of nothing but
memories. It's a blessing to have found an old friend
to connect with – someone you don't have to introduce
yourself to. I know you have a family wedding to
organise in the meantime – but if you are still of the
same mind, I will call you when I get back and we can
arrange to meet, maybe for a good long lunch and a
walk somewhere …
Until then, take care of yourself,
Your old friend,
Mac*

'Wait a minute.' Dot was curious. 'Do you remember why
you're called Mac?'

'He's always been called Mac,' said Jessie. 'His full
name is Charles MacKenzie Elliot. He's been called Mac
since I can remember – certainly since high school.'

'So your name really *is* Charlie!' Dot was delighted.
'What a wonderful turn-up!'

'Here's your Facebook page, Uncle Mac.' Nick pulled
it up on his tablet.

'Look! There I am!' said Charlie, delighted. 'That's me!
That's my house! That's a photo of Linda, my late wife! Oh,
boy! I can't tell you how good this feels. I am so relieved.'

✱

Charlie left the following Tuesday – a day that dawned with a cloudless sky heralding the heatwave that would continue for the next ten days.

The whole village wanted to see him off, but it was deemed more appropriate that just his close familiars – as he liked to call them – would wave goodbye from outside the Old Rectory. And this indeed was the case. As Dot, Molly, Franny, Rob, Ryan and Merry gathered outside, Charlie slipped into the waiting taxi accompanied by his childhood sweetheart Jessie and his nephew Nick. Charlie bade each of his new friends goodbye with the unfailing charm and courtesy he had displayed since he had come into their lives, just three weeks previously.

'Dorothy … gift from God.' He smiled into her eyes and took her hands. 'How can I ever thank you for your kindness to me? Know that I will pray you will be blessed in return every day of my life.

'Molly, I can't wait to read this book of yours – you have a lot of wisdom to impart. I will be top of the queue to buy it when it comes out.'

To Franny, he said, 'I know you worry that the world is headed for disaster, that old people like us have ruined it for you … But you'll see, Franny, people are good and clever and kind. Everything will come right in the end. Maybe that's the job for your generation – to make sure it does.

'Dr Rob …' They shook hands, and Charlie held Rob's in his. 'I can never thank you enough for your kindness and care. Thank God I showed up in your catchment area!

Thank you for taking care of me. I owe you my life, in more ways than one.'

To Ryan and Merry, he said, 'You guys still confuse me! I think you confuse each other! But I'm going to miss our coffee and chats. I think you're good for each other. I'll probably get into trouble for saying that – but I'm old and disoriented so I don't care! Take care of yourselves.'

'Charles MacKenzie Elliot.' Jessie hustled him gently towards the open door of the car. 'If we don't get a move on we'll miss our flight. You always have been as slow as molasses. Goodbye, Dot, and the rest of you dear people.' She hugged them one by one. 'I promise I'll report as soon as we're back on home soil … and don't you worry about Charlie,' she said to Dot firmly. 'We're going to take real good care of him.'

Dot knew without a shadow of a doubt that she would. And Charlie's obvious ease and contentment in her company were welcome and much-needed reassurance as they said their final goodbyes. But that didn't make it any easier to wave him off – which they did furiously and with much good cheer, although Dot noticed she wasn't the only one to shed a tear.

The rest of the village was not to be outdone, Dot heard afterwards, and as Charlie, Jessie and Nick drove through Derrybeggs, people had gathered in small groups or outside their houses to wish him well and wave him on his way. Outside the Seashell, Eva and Jan stood with Peggy, who held Muppet and waved his paw. Between them they flourished a sign that read 'We'll miss you, Charlie!'

And they did miss Charlie for a bit in the village. It

was odd at first, Dot felt, not to see him ambling towards the Seashell, or chatting companionably at his seat in the café, his warm smile and voice greeting people, sharing his nuggets of wisdom and gentle curiosity. But there was email, and Facebook, and Charlie kept his word and stayed in touch. Watching him step back into his rightful life in Boston was reward enough for everyone who knew him.

Then life resumed, as it always did. Dot continued to let her cottages, but not the rooms in her house. Not for the moment, at any rate – she and Rob were enjoying the privacy of their own uninterrupted company, and there was a lot to learn about each other.

Molly returned to London, with promises to come back to Derrybeggs as soon as she could – and Dot was keeping an eye out for a suitable property in the village for her.

Ryan, much to Dot's surprise, had decided to stay on in the cottage for a while. He was vague about exactly how long he might be there, but seemed to think at least eight weeks, anyway. Dot was happy to have another familiar face around. Ryan had his own band of followers now, always keen to hear him play and sing country in O'Hagan's. Merry, too, seemed happy in his company – the pair appeared to have struck up an easy friendship. Dot was pleased about that and promised in her regular emails to Molly to keep her up to date with how things transpired on that front.

Merry was busy with her new marine business Oceanworks, which was attracting great interest in Derrybeggs and beyond. It was the first interactive educational marine facility of its kind in a local community, and Merry's years of experience and marine research were proving invaluable in educating children and adults alike, particularly in regard to protecting their local shorelines and islands. As Dot looked out of her window now, she saw Merry's little boat chugging out of the harbour.

Franny was going out with Merry to do a seal count on the rocky outcrop of islands offshore. As the little boat headed for open water, Derrybeggs receded behind them, the rows of colourful houses, the old castle on the hill and the church spire bathed in watery sunlight. Muttie, who was going along for the ride, stood at the stern and sniffed the air, his one ear twitching and alert to the sound of the gulls that cried and wheeled around them.

As they passed Gull Cave, Franny was thoughtful. 'You know, I don't think I ever thanked you properly, Merry – not really – for rescuing me like you did. You saved my life, and you risked your own doing it.'

Merry smiled back at her. 'You did thank me, lots of times. And you're more than welcome, Franny. I'm sure you'd have done the same for me.'

'Yeah, I would,' she said, without hesitation. 'But I'm glad I didn't have to!' She grinned. Then, as Merry seemed to be in a good mood these days, she risked another question. 'Are you and Ryan, like, boyfriend and girlfriend?' She pushed a windblown lock of hair out of her eyes. 'You seem to be hanging out a lot.'

'No, Franny. We're just friends.'

'Oh. Okay.' Franny seemed to accept the reply. 'It's just that Joni has a new boyfriend, someone she's known like, for ever, and they've just got engaged. I saw it on her YouTube channel.'

'Well, that's nice.' Merry smiled. 'I'm glad for her.' The islands were ahead of them now, and Merry held up her binoculars to scan the rockface. Just then Muttie let out a volley of excited barking.

'Look!' cried Franny, as the pod broke through the water alongside them. 'Dolphins!' Fourteen, she counted, as they gracefully surfed alongside the little boat, while Muttie ran up and down barking at them.

Merry took out her phone to film them. 'You know what this means, don't you, Franny?'

'What?'

'Well, dolphins are a sign of good luck – and protection,' Merry said.

'I've always loved them but I never knew that!' Franny trailed her hand in the water.

Such a lot had happened in the last month – and some things would never be the same again. Franny had learned some valuable lessons. But as Charlie had said on the first day she had seen him in the sand dune, most things you worried about didn't actually happen. And although things had to change, there were always good things happening and good people making sure they did. Which made Franny feel a lot better about life in general.

Epilogue: one year later

In O'Hagan's, people checked their phones repeatedly, impatient for the video clip due to land any minute. When eventually it did, they watched and shared it eagerly.

Molly Cusack's book launch seemed to be a very grand affair. Even though it was only five in the afternoon in New York, people were dressed in glamorous evening wear. In the middle of the room, underneath a huge chandelier, a round mahogany table was covered with books, stacked in rows of military precision. Sitting at the table, with her PR girl beside her, Molly graciously greeted people and signed copies, looking up to wave and blow kisses to the camera. Moving through the crowds, the camera lingered on a larger-than-life man who threw back his head and laughed at something Ryan Shindler said to him.

'Hey, Franny!' Ryan said, spotting her filming them. 'Wave to the folks in Derrybeggs, Frank!' Then Ryan pulled Merry close for a cheesy screen shot, and the camera panned down immediately afterwards to focus on them holding hands in extreme close-up. Finally it swung around to another familiar group – Dot and Rob,

Charlie and Jessie, Jan and Eva waved to the camera. 'Wish you were all here!' cried Dot.

Then Charlie leaned in to say hello to his friends in Derrybeggs. 'Hey, everybody! Greetings from the Big Apple – but I'd rather be back in Ireland with you guys!'

'Don't let Molly hear you say that.' Dot was laughing. 'I'm so exhausted from jet lag, I'm ready for bed! See you all when we get home.'

'That's all for now, folks,' said Franny, winding up her video and waving.

But at ten p.m. in Derrybeggs, where the sun was just setting on another leisurely June day, the evening was just beginning.

Acknowledgements

Writing a novel during Covid has been a strange experience. As I write, we are in our third lockdown. Describing normality – or what we formally took for granted as normality – often seemed like a journey into the realm of fantasy. Village gatherings, committee meetings, trips to the beach, and cosy evenings in the pub all acquired an aura of unreality that proved sometimes elusive to capture. Thankfully characters and stories (much like children) tend to dictate their own pace and setting – despite extraordinary circumstances.

If it takes a village to raise a child – it certainly takes one to craft a novel. *The Summer We Were Friends* owes its existence to several talented and generous individuals.

Heartfelt thanks as always to the wonderful Hachette Ireland team, in particular Editorial Director Ciara Doorley, who coaxed this often unruly manuscript (and author!) into coherence – your insights, sensitivity and patience made *The Summer We Were Friends* a far better book. Thanks also to Joanna Smyth and Hazel Orme.

Thanks to my agent Megan Carroll (@MeganACarroll) who championed *The Summer We Were Friends* from the beginning.

Thanks to Peter Carvil for inspiring the cave scene – I needed a marine drama and you didn't disappoint! Thanks also to Kate Thompson for first reading the diving sequence and for kindly putting me in touch with dive master Dan McCauley, who gave generously of his time and expertise – any inaccuracies are my own.

Thanks to everyone who said a prayer or lit a candle on my behalf (you know who you are!).

And of course thanks to you, dear reader, you make the long, lonely, often frustrating hours at the laptop worthwhile, and none of this would happen without you. I hope you enjoy *The Summer We Were Friends*, do let me know – and if you would be kind enough to post a review on Amazon or Goodreads, that would be truly appreciated.

COV
6/6/22.

THE
MIRROR
THIEF

700043592124

THE
MIRROR
THIEF

MARTIN SEAY

MELVILLE HOUSE UK
LONDON

THE MIRROR THIEF

First published in 2017 by
Melville House UK
8 Blackstock Mews
Islington
London N4 2BT

mhpbooks.com   facebook.com/mhpbooks   @melvillehouse

Copyright © 2016 by Martin Seay

First paperback edition: March 2017

The right of Martin Seay to be identified as the author of this
work has been asserted by him in accordance with the
Copyright, Design and Patents Act 1988

A CIP catalogue record for this book is available from the British Library

ISBN: 978-0-9934149-8-5

1 3 5 7 9 10 8 6 4 2

All rights reserved. No part of this publication may be reproduced,
transmitted, or stored in a retrieval system, in any form or by any means,
without permission in writing from Melville House UK.

Printed and bound in Denmark by Nørhaven, Viborg

Typeset by Roland Codd